Blind Dates

Four Stories of Hearts United with
a Little Help from Grandma

Kristin Billerbeck
Colleen Coble
Denise Hunter
Bev Huston

BARBOUR
PUBLISHING

Blind Dates

Prologue

by Denise Hunter

Prologue

H appy birthday, Gram!"

Lucille Stoddard gasped in delight at the sight of her four granddaughters in the hallway. She'd had a steady flow of visitors all day, but it had chased away the boredom and masked the lonely ticking of her wall clock.

"Girls! Come on in. Land's sake! You're going to give your old Gram a coronary."

"Gram," Callie said, "you're in better shape than I am."

Her granddaughter's words were in direct contrast to her long, muscular legs. She was a gorgeous specimen of womanhood—all six feet of her. Gram suppressed a smile. If she would just stop dressing like a spinster aunt.

They stooped to kiss her on the cheek as they entered her new apartment.

"Say, you're really settled in," Mattie said as she turned in every direction.

Chelsea set a chocolate cake in the center of her table. Gram hoped it was her double Dutch fudge recipe. Her stomach gave a hefty growl. Her jaws still hurt from that dried-up lunch that had masqueraded as pot roast. Shoe leather, Gram called it. Her mouth watered as she eyed the cake again.

"Not much to settle," Gram said. "Two tiny rooms don't hold much." Unpacking hadn't taken long. After all, what else did she have to do? Without her garden and farm to tend to, she was a woman with time on her hands. Sure, Heavenly Village Retirement Community had lots of activities for all the old folks, but she refused to count herself among them.

"What's this?" Melissa asked.

Her granddaughter was inspecting her window box on the kitchen windowsill.

"It's an herb garden. Have to keep my hands in the dirt somehow. There's a tiny plot by the patio for flowers in the spring."

Gram's gaze flittered over her granddaughters. They were all so attractive and such good, Christian girls. She didn't mind saying she was mighty proud. *They must attract men like bees to honey.*

She squeezed Melissa's hand. "What are you girls doing here anyway?"

"Gram, it's your birthday," Melissa said.

"I know that. I'm not senile yet," Gram said. "It's Saturday night. Why aren't you at the movies with some nice young men?"

"There aren't any left." Mattie lit the lone candle on the cake. Not enough room for all of them, Gram figured.

"After my last blind date I'm ready to join the monastery," Chelsea said.

One of her cousins jostled her with an elbow. "I think you have to be Catholic for that."

Gram crossed her skinny arms. "You must be looking in the wrong places. What about church? Why, there're all sorts of—"

"Where do you keep the plates, Gram?" Chelsea asked as she opened the right cabinet. "Never mind." She held up a white glass plate with blue cornflowers around the rim. "Hey, aren't these the ones we used for tea parties?"

"You go ahead and change the subject, Chelsea Stoddard," Gram said. "But there are some pretty keen perks of marriage that you're missing out on." She waggled her eyebrows.

"Gram!" Callie said.

The girls, daughters of her four children, bustled around the kitchen gathering napkins, plates, and forks. Artistic Mattie, with her mural-painting business. Career Callie, owner of an interior design company. Graceful Chelsea, who was working toward ownership of the gymnastics academy. Flighty Melissa, who was too busy trying to figure out her life to give a thought to finding a mate.

That was the problem. They were too busy. If they passed Mr. Right on the street, they wouldn't slow down long enough to know it. Gram settled into the chair in front of the cake. Across from her on the wall, a picture of her late husband stared at her from behind a glass and frame. *Ah, my Edward. If they knew what it was to have their soul mate, they'd know how empty their lives are now.* But they were so busy.

Maybe they needed a little help. Her granddaughters may be busy, but what they lacked in time she had in abundant supply.

And it wasn't as if she was inexperienced in such things. She'd played matchmaker over the years many times and could even count three couples who'd married as a result. She was *good* at matchmaking. Why, even now she could think of several prospects. . . .

Mattie, Callie, and Chelsea slipped into the red vinyl chairs, the legs squeaking across the linoleum flooring, while Melissa stood over her shoulder.

"Shall we sing 'Happy Birthday'?" Melissa asked.

"Humph," Gram said. "Better get straight to the wish. At my age, time is of the essence."

Gram closed her eyes and drew a deep breath. In her mind's eye she saw each of her granddaughters with a man at her side. As particular young men came into her thoughts, her lips curved upward. Perhaps she shouldn't be so specific. On the other hand, it was her birthday, and she could wish whatever she wanted. Besides, the prayers she added to it were what really gave the wish its power. And she was sure God wanted her to have great-grandbabies. A smile tugged at her lips.

She opened her eyes and aimed her old puckered lips at the candle flickering in the center. It didn't take much oxygen from her lungs to extinguish it in one breath. Above the candle, black smoke curled into the air like a wispy ribbon.

The girls whooped and hollered, and Gram smiled. Suddenly she felt very much like celebrating.

The Perfect Match

by Denise Hunter

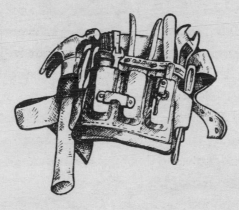

Chapter 1

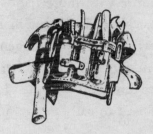

I'd better have a message," Chelsea muttered to herself as she slammed the apartment door shut. She stormed over to the answering machine, flinging the doggie bag from the restaurant on the countertop. The red light was blinking.

"Okay, maybe the man has an excuse." She jabbed the button.

"Hi, Chelsea—it's Callie. Just calling to see how the big date went. I'll call again tomorrow since you'll probably be out late. I want all the details."

The machine whirred as it rewound the tape. Her cousin's message was the only one.

"I knew it. He *is* a chump." What had Gram been thinking? For that matter, what had *she* been thinking?

Chelsea dropped her handbag on the counter. She paced back and forth in the room, the narrow skirt of her only nice dress demanding a small stride. She knew she shouldn't have agreed to another blind date. Why did she ever let Gram talk her into it?

If anyone should know better it was Chelsea. Her three experiences with blind dates had been flops. First there was Ervin. The name pretty much said it all. Then there was Jonathan, the big brute with more hands than a Swiss clock factory. And the last blind date, four months ago, was a real disappointment. Lewis was the perfect gentleman. He brought flowers, opened her door, and amused her with his wonderful sense of humor over dinner. It was the ideal date. Or so she'd thought. He'd promised to call her the next day, and she was still waiting.

No, after that, she promised herself she wouldn't agree to another blind date as long as she breathed. Then Gram got hold of her. "Kyle's perfect for you, Chelsea. Such a nice young man. He owns the company that replaced the windows on the old farmhouse. Hard-working and a true gentleman. Trust your old Gram."

Chelsea wavered. Christmas loomed ahead, and she dreaded the thought of another one spent alone. It would be nice to share it with someone special.

Despite her reservations, Chelsea finally told her grandmother she could give Kyle her phone number. Gram then fished a business card from her phone book drawer and handed it to Chelsea.

"What's this?"

"It's Kyle's business card—did I mention he owns his own business? Anyway, it has his phone number."

"I'm not going to need this." She tried to return the card, but Gram put her hands up.

"Just keep it, Dear. You never know."

Between her mom's encouragement and Gram's insistence, she hadn't had a chance. Right now she wasn't sure whom she'd like to get her hands on the most, Gram or Kyle.

❧

Chelsea rolled out of bed and pulled on her favorite gray shorts. A glance at the digital clock told her she'd slept later than usual. But that shouldn't surprise her given the way she'd tossed and turned in bed until nearly 1:30 A.M. Agitation was not conducive to a restful state. If she didn't have to teach those morning classes, she'd gladly stay in bed for another two hours.

She pulled her long brown hair into a sloppy ponytail, grabbed her keys, and shut her apartment door, sighing as the door trim slid to a cockeyed angle. "This place is falling apart."

As usual, she started with a brisk walk then worked her way up to a good jog. Two blocks into her run, she saw that the English Tudor home on the corner already sported its Christmas lights.

Chelsea quickened her pace. She knew she'd better jog an extra two miles to work off those raspberry truffle brownies she'd binged on the night before. Not to mention the veal meat loaf she'd eaten. Her face grew warm with anger as she recalled the evening.

What a picture she must have made at Les Saisons, dressed in her fancy black dress, her hair coifed in an elegant French twist. It wouldn't have been so bad if she hadn't told the host a guest would be joining her. Oh, but she had, and all evening she had to sit and look at that untouched place setting, complete

17

with eight pieces of sparkling flatware and a fan-shaped napkin.

For the first fifteen minutes or so, she thought the man was running late. She ordered a diet soda and placed the stiff napkin in her lap. After thirty minutes, then forty, she desired nothing more than to slip out the door of the restaurant. But she had to pay for her soda, and she was too humiliated to leave without ordering. The waiter knew. Everyone in the restaurant seemed to know.

She'd been stood up.

After an hour of waiting she'd decided to order. That's when she saw the prices. Veal meat loaf was the least expensive entree at $17.95. Add the soda and tip to that, and she'd be brown-bagging her lunches for the next month.

She quickened her pace, clenching her fists. "I felt so—so rejected. And I hate feeling rejected." He'd called *her* and asked her out. He'd picked the fancy restaurant. He'd even chosen the time. And then he left her waiting in a restaurant full of lovey-dovey couples, with a waiter who had nothing better to do than hover around her table saying, "Would you like to order, Miss, or continue to wait?"

As if she didn't have anything better to do than wait around for a date who didn't show. Two hours she sat there. And that didn't include the hour it took to get ready. And the humiliation. That was the worst of it.

The longer she jogged, the more upset she became. By the time she returned to her apartment, her heart was thudding with emotion. Gram had misjudged the man. In fact, she'd like to give him an earful. She tossed her keys on the table and headed for the shower.

And that's when she remembered.

Chelsea strode into her bedroom and rummaged through her hamper for the jeans she'd worn to Gram's the week before. Finally she stood, her fists clutching the denim material. She stabbed a hand into the pants pocket and was rewarded with the business card. "Aha. Thought you were going to get away with it, did you?" She reached for the bedroom extension and held the card up to read the number. " 'Morgan's Home Improvement.' Figures." Everyone knew home-improvement operations were rip-offs. "The guy's probably a con artist." Her eyes darted to the bottom of the card. "His E-mail address."

She dropped the receiver in the cradle and walked to the kitchen, where her computer occupied one end of the table. After turning it on, she grabbed a glass of water and planned what she would say. By the time the computer finished booting up, she was steaming.

Chelsea typed in his address. "Subject. . .hmm." She left it blank. *Now for the rest.*

"Dear Mr. No-Show,

"Did it give you great pleasure to stand me up last night? Was that the highlight of your week? Is this something you do every so often just for kicks? If so, let me tell you, in case you didn't know, that you are an inconsiderate, arrogant, insensitive clod."

Chelsea clicked SEND and sat back, wondering why she didn't feel as satisfied as she thought she would. Her gaze collided with the blinking red light of her answering machine across the room. "Okay—let's hear it, dear cousin." She went over and pushed the play button.

"Hi, Chelsea, this is Kyle Morgan." Chelsea stood stock-still at the haggard-sounding voice. "Listen—I apologize for last night. There was an emergency in the family. My grandfather had a heart attack."

Chelsea's gaze darted to the computer screen. She stared at it helplessly. The message had already been sent. "No, no, no."

". . .about seven A.M., and I'm just getting in from the hospital. I would like to set this up again at a later date. You seem like a nice person. I'll, uh, give you a call once things settle down here. Again, I'm really sorry." Click.

Chelsea dropped her face in her hands and groaned. "What have I done?"

The phone trilled. *What if it's him? Maybe I shouldn't answer it.* It rang again. No, he just got in; he'll be sleeping. Chelsea lifted the extension and murmured a tentative hello.

"Good morning," a chipper voice said.

"Hi, Gram."

"Hi, Dear. I'm sorry your evening was spoiled. Isn't that awful about Kyle's grandfather?"

"Yes, I just got a message from him."

"His grandfather lived here in Heavenly Village, you know. Apparently he and Kyle were very close."

Lived? Were? "Were?"

"You didn't know his grandfather passed on?"

Chelsea covered her mouth to smother a groan.

"That's what Helen Brubaker said, and apparently the woman is in the know."

Please, God, tell me this isn't happening. The only decent guy left on planet Earth, and I've—

"You'll have to set up another date with Kyle. I was so impressed with him when he did my windows. The two of you deserve each other."

I deserve something all right—

"Chelsea, are you there?"

"Uh-huh." No way was she going to tell Gram what she'd done. She hoped she wouldn't be seeing Kyle anymore—

"You sure are being awfully quiet."

"I'm thinking about poor Kyle." She had to get off. "Hey, I need to run. My classes start in an hour."

"All right—see you in church tomorrow."

After muttering good-bye, Chelsea dropped her face in her hands. "How low could I be? I sent an awful E-mail to a man who just lost his grandfather."

Everyone should be quick to listen, slow to speak, and slow to become angry—

"I know. I know."

Maybe she could e-mail him back real quick and explain the misunderstanding. If he received the two messages consecutively, he wouldn't have time to be mad. Maybe he'd even get a chuckle out of it. Chelsea clicked on "sent mail" and reread her message.

Her hopes dwindled. Who was she kidding? She'd been brutal. Even if he did forgive her, there was no way he'd ever want to go out with her now. He probably thought she was a shrew. She knew she'd sounded that way.

❧

Classes went well that afternoon. One of her students, Leslie, was a gifted gymnast. She had enough difficulty in her routines for Elite competition but needed to work on her form. Leslie's parents shelled out good money for one-on-one coaching three days a week. Chelsea's own parents had put out good money for her classes. She had fond memories of competing in high school.

As much as she enjoyed teaching, time had dragged all afternoon. She was eager to go home and check her E-mail. She hoped and prayed she would have no messages.

It was the first thing she did when she arrived back at her apartment. Her computer seemed to take forever to boot up, ancient relic that it was. Finally she was on-line and checking for messages. She had none. "Phew."

On the other hand, he was not likely to be fiddling around on his computer the day of his grandfather's death. Her spirits sank. He may not get her message for days.

❧

Sunday came and went, with no message from Kyle. At church Chelsea had avoided the subject with her cousins altogether.

On Monday Chelsea attended her accounting course in the morning then worked on her computer at home. During the school year she didn't teach until the afternoon, since her students were in school. When she'd moved out on her own three years ago, she'd taken over the payroll and accounting for the academy in order to supplement her income. Fortunately her boss had provided her a computer so she could work from her apartment. At first she was intimidated by the whole financial end of the business, but once she learned how to do it she found she had a knack for it.

Her flexible schedule also allowed her to take courses from the Heaven School of Business. Her dream of buying the gymnastics academy was becoming more possible all the time.

After finishing her work Chelsea checked her E-mail. She twiddled her thumbs while the computer scanned for new messages. There it was. She held her breath and double-clicked on his name. The computer retrieved the post—too slowly, she thought.

"Obviously you had not received my phone message."

Chelsea winced. The words themselves didn't sound particularly angry and didn't even end with an exclamation point to drive home his message. They weren't sarcastic or spiteful. She reread the message. No, it wasn't the tone that made her cringe; it was the brevity. There was no "Dear Chelsea" or even a signature. *And certainly not a request for that make-up date.*

He was angry. Not that she could blame him, but some part of her would have felt better if he'd let her have it—called her a few names or told her off. Anything but this brief, E-mail version of stony silence. The fact that he'd responded in such a calm, unspiteful manner proved the man was a decent guy. A very angry, decent guy.

"I really blew it this time, didn't I, God? When am I going to learn to think before I act?" she wondered aloud. "Now what should I do?" She could e-mail him back and apologize—she knew she owed him that.

Or she could ignore the whole thing. He probably wouldn't be seeing Gram anymore. And it wasn't as if there could ever be anything between them now.

A knock on the door interrupted her inner debate. Chelsea opened it and found her landlord, Mr. O'Donnell, standing there. He was the only man she knew who stood eye-to-eye with her own five-foot, three-inch frame.

"Mr. O'Donnell, come in."

"No, no, Lassie. No time for a visit today. I'm for having some good news." He waved an envelope in the air. "The settlement check has come in the mail. I'm telling all my tenants this place is going to be fixed up soon. No more peeling paint and drafty windows. Next week the improvements begin, and these buildings will be as pretty as a new penny."

"That's wonderful news, Mr. O'Donnell."

"Indeed, 'tis. Now it may be a wee bit troublesome for several weeks, with the noise and that, but what a fine place to live it will be. And I'll tell you another thing: I'll not be for raising the rent. That is the very least I can do after you have all been so patient with me about the repairs. Now I must go tell my news to the others. Have a wonderful day, Lassie."

Chelsea shut the door, wearing a smile. She hadn't seen Mr. O'Donnell so happy since before his wife passed away. Now that the lawsuit was settled, maybe he could begin to recover from her death.

Chapter 2

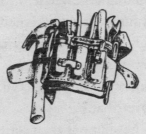

K yle shuffled through the papers on his desk, searching for a particular work order. Business was slowing down, but he could always find something to do. He liked working after hours when the phone was quiet and the show-room was dark.

A tap on the storefront glass startled him. His mom peeped through the glass with her hands cupped around her eyes. Kyle rolled his chair out from under the desk and went to let her in.

"Hi, what are you doing here?"

She smiled. "Now that's a fine greeting for your dear mom. Besides, that's what I should be asking you. Since when do you need to work till eight-thirty during the winter months?"

"Is it that late?"

"Were you here last night too? I tried to call you at home."

"You know you can call me here, Mom."

"I don't like to bother you when you're working." His mother crossed her slender arms and cocked her head. "Except that seems to be all you're doing lately."

Kyle leaned against his newest door display. "I've been working on a marketing plan to boost sales this winter."

"It's me you're talking to, Sweetie. I know how you always throw yourself into your work when something's bothering you. When you and Lori broke up, we hardly saw you for months."

"Please. Let's not talk about her."

Ellen Morgan surveyed her son. "Oh, Kyle, don't tell me you're still hurting over that."

"Of course not," he shot out then softened his tone. "That was nearly a year ago, Mom. It wasn't that big of a deal."

His mother's lips curved in a sympathetic smile. "A broken engagement is always a big deal, Kyle. And when someone uses you like that—"

Kyle held up both hands. "This has nothing to do with Lori."

"Are you upset about Grandpa? The funeral was nice. So many people. And you know he's much happier now."

"I'm doing all right, Mom. Really." Kyle wiped a smudge from a windowpane. "What were you trying to call me about?"

"Oh. Your father and I went over Grandpa's will yesterday. I wanted you to know your grandfather left you Grandma's wedding ring set."

His heart squeezed in his chest. "That was thoughtful of him. I'll treasure it, Mom."

"I know you will. Also, I called to make sure you're coming for dinner Sunday and to let you know you're welcome to bring a friend as always."

Kyle grinned. "If that's your way of asking if I'm seeing anyone, the answer is no."

"Don't be silly. I thought, with all your brothers bringing their wives and girlfriends, you might feel a little left out."

"Not at all, Mom. Anyway, it's the good food I'm after."

His mother laughed and patted him on the shoulder then stood. "Your dad's going to wonder where I disappeared to."

After Kyle let his mother out and locked the door behind her, he returned to his desk. Somehow he couldn't get motivated to work anymore and sat staring at his computer's screen saver of an impressionist painting in the works.

Funny, he hadn't even realized he'd been putting in extra hours. Sometimes he thought his mother might know him better than he knew himself. He *had* been feeling moody and bothered lately. And if he dug a little deeper, he knew what he'd find at the bottom of the hole. And it wasn't his grandfather's death.

It was a woman named Chelsea and her rude E-mail.

Although why that should bother him so much, he wasn't sure. He'd never even met the woman and shouldn't care what she thought of him. But it had rankled him, coming so soon after his grandfather's death. While he'd been sitting up all night at the hospital waiting for his grandpa to draw his last breath, she'd been stewing about being stood up. Was it too much to ask for a little latitude? At least give a guy a chance to explain.

The feisty little grandma didn't know her granddaughter as well as she thought. Chelsea was supposed to be a Christian.

Probably the same variety Lori had been: Put it on when it's convenient; take it off when it isn't. Blend in with your surroundings, just like a chameleon.

Do not judge, or you too will be judged. For in the same way you judge others, you will be judged. . . .

Kyle sighed. He could thank his mother for the prickling of guilt he felt. All those verses she'd made him memorize when he was a boy were still written on his heart.

❧

On Wednesdays Chelsea was always late to prayer meeting because of her coaching session with Leslie. This particular time she was glad because she hoped to avoid Gram, who was sure to ask her about Kyle. Lying was not an option, and it was sure to get sticky when the subject of that date came up. She had grabbed her jacket from the coat rack and started to dash out the door when Gram caught up with her. "Hold up, Chelsea. These old legs are losing their pep."

Chelsea suffered a pang of guilt. "Sorry. Was there something you wanted to talk about?"

Gram pulled her aside, away from the crowd of people filing out the doors. "I saw Kyle today," she said with a coy smile and a tilted head.

Chelsea cringed and tried for a casual tone. "Really?"

"He came to clean out his grandfather's apartment."

"Oh."

"So has he called you yet?"

"Gram, it hasn't been a week since his grandfather's death."

Gram's face fell. "I was hoping he'd make contact on his

own. Maybe I could give him a little nudge—"

"Don't you dare. He probably doesn't even want to go out with me and is trying to let the whole thing blow over." Now that was the truth if she ever heard it.

"I'm sure he wanted to go out with you. He seemed very interested when we talked before, and he was the one who called you, if you'll remember."

"Please, Gram. Don't say anything about me. If he wants to contact me, he has my phone number."

Her grandmother tucked in the corner of her mouth. "All right. You win. I just want to see my sweet granddaughter as happily married as I was."

They spoke for several more minutes; then Chelsea hurried home to watch her favorite television program. She was relieved to have that conversation over. She hadn't lied, and she'd convinced Gram not to intervene on her behalf with Kyle. As long as everyone left it alone, the whole humiliating episode would fade away.

❧

The following Monday Chelsea awoke to stomping on her ceiling. Not an unusual problem in an apartment, with neighbors living on all sides of her. She had grown used to the extraneous noises, but sounds from above were foreign to her since she lived on the top floor.

Chelsea looked at the digital clock and groaned. Seven o'clock. Whoever was up there could at least wait until a decent hour. It sounded like a buffalo stampede.

"Might as well get up now." After lingering in a hot shower

Chelsea finished dressing then started brewing a small pot of coffee. The clomping above continued, although it sounded as if it was over Lena's apartment now. While the coffee percolated, she walked to the window to read the thermometer. Her gaze shifted to the sky in the background. The sun was over the horizon, and the clouds hiding it were radiant shades of pink and periwinkle. Streaks of violet slashed across the sky.

Wow. "Good job, God," she murmured.

She started back to the kitchen when her gaze skittered over an unfamiliar blue pickup. "Wonder whose that is?" She squinted to read the white letters on the driver's side door: MORGAN'S HOME IMPROVEMENT. She remembered the rooftop noises and concluded that must be the company Mr. O'Donnell—

"Morgan's Home Improvement." The name sounded familiar, but maybe she was wrong. She dashed over to her computer and riffled through her papers. "Where is it?" Finally she found the card. Her hands flew up to her cheeks. "Oh, no. Of all the home improvement companies in Heaven, Mr. O'Donnell had to pick Kyle's!" What would she do? She couldn't stay in her apartment for the next month.

Wait a minute, she told herself. *He's never seen me before.* Chelsea released her pent-up breath. He had no idea what she looked like, just as she had no idea what he looked like. And he didn't know she lived here. Besides, he might not be here. Gram had said he owned the company. Didn't owners stay in the office and hire installers to do the renovating? Ha. She'd probably never have to see the man.

After a leisurely breakfast Chelsea gathered her accounting

textbook and folder and headed out the door. She trotted down the stairs and barreled through the main building door, nearly colliding with a man.

"Oh. Excuse me," she said.

The man's gaze traveled down her then back up. A smirk appeared between the grizzly mustache and beard. "Hey. You can bump into me anytime, Sweetheart."

Chelsea worked to keep the disgust from her face as she tried to step around him. He blocked her path

"You live here, Darlin'?"

No, I just came from a slumber party. "Uh huh." She tried again to step around him, but he shifted his weight to prevent her. She gritted her teeth. If this was Kyle, she was glad the date hadn't worked out.

"I'm still waiting for those shingles, Mark." Chelsea followed the sound of the voice to the ledge of the roof near the end of the building. A broad-shouldered figure, silhouetted by the rising sun, stood with his hands on his hips.

"Oh, right, Boss."

Chelsea seized the opportunity to slip by the man. All the way to school she reflected on the event. That man's name was Mark, not Kyle, and he'd called the other man "boss." She wondered if he was just *a* boss or *the* boss. Undoubtedly she'd soon find out.

❧

The next couple of days Chelsea found herself peeping out her window before leaving her apartment. Truth be told, she didn't want to run into either man. They'd finished the roof of her building on Monday and moved on to one of the other three buildings, so avoiding them had become easier.

Thursday she was returning from the grocery store when she entered her apartment building and saw The Boss knocking on Mr. O'Donnell's door. She tried to slip up the stairs unnoticed, but the man called out to her.

"Excuse me."

Chelsea stopped on the first stair, putting her at eye level with him when he approached her. The low brim of his cap drew her attention to his eyes. Deep-set brown eyes, with little gold flecks.

"Yes?"

"You don't happen to know where a payphone is, do you? I need to call the office." He held up a cell phone and gave a lopsided grin. "Dead battery."

"Oh. Well, I'm sure there's one at the gas station on the corner, but you can use mine if you want." *Crazy, crazy, crazy.*

"Are you sure you don't mind?"

"Not at all. My apartment's up here." She started up the stairs, but he stopped her.

"Here—let me take those." He scooped the grocery bags out of her arms before she could protest.

"Thanks."

Once they entered her apartment, she showed him to the kitchen extension and began unloading her groceries. Chelsea covertly watched him as he dialed. He wasn't especially tall, but he was at least a head taller than she. Broad shoulders, slim hips, long legs.

She couldn't help overhearing his conversation.

"Hi, Elaine. It's Kyle."

Chelsea winced. It *was* him.

"Listen—have the gutters come in yet for the apartment job?"

He paused, and Chelsea's mind stepped into gear. *What if I've left something lying around with my name on it?* She glanced around the kitchen. Nothing here.

Kyle paced a few feet to the dining room table. Chelsea sucked in her breath. Papers lay around her computer. She couldn't walk casually over there since he was blocking the way. She mentally sorted through the papers: notes from school, accounts receivable from work, bills—. Chelsea peeked over Kyle's shoulder. Her phone bill was lying right on top of a stack of mail.

Kyle continued to talk while she put away the canned goods, all the while holding her breath. Finally he walked back to the kitchen and hung up the phone.

"Thanks." He extended his hand. "I'm Kyle, by the way."

Chelsea put her hand in his and realized for the first time how attractive he was. "No problem. I'm"—her mind spun during the slightest of pauses—"Shelly." She smiled in relief. Not a lie, really. It was her childhood nickname. In fact, her dad still used it.

"Nice to meet you. You'll have a nice place here when we're finished. Mr. O'Donnell has spared no expense."

"Great, great." She bobbed her head, wishing he'd leave.

"Well, gotta get back to work."

After she let him out, she leaned against the door and

breathed a sigh of relief. "That was close." A pink slip of paper on the floor drew her attention, and she stooped to pick it up. According to the notice, the workers were going to start replacing the windows next week. Apparently they would need access to the apartments. Great. So much for avoiding Kyle.

Guilt pricked at Chelsea's conscience. She knew she needed to make things right, but she wasn't looking forward to admitting her identity to Kyle. Still, it was the right thing to do. It would be awkward at the very least. He could even get downright hostile with her, but Chelsea felt that was unlikely given what she knew of him so far. Perhaps he'd see the humor in it, now that he'd met her and knew she wasn't the shrew she'd sounded like in her E-mail message.

Chapter 3

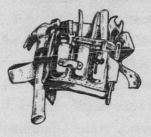

Tuesdays were laundry day, and today was no exception. The laundry room was always available then, and it worked well with her schedule. Chelsea fanned her face as she entered the laundry room, which was unusually hot. She understood why when she glanced at the window—rather, where the window used to be. She saw only a large hole in the wall. After dropping the quarters into the slots, Chelsea shoved the metal plate into the machine and waited for it to spring back. It didn't. She tugged on the end tab, trying to pull it back, but it was jammed. "Come on—I'm on my last pair of clean undies," she coaxed the machine.

Chelsea gave the coin box a couple of good whacks. Nothing. "You big yellow dinosaur—give me my money back." A few more whacks proved fruitless.

"Problems?"

She jumped and turned toward the voice, which was coming from the hole in the wall. Kyle was standing outside, his hands on his hips, looking in, his cheeks flushed from the heat.

"Do you always sneak up on people like that?" she snapped.

"Sorry." His smothered grin told her otherwise.

"Yeah, you look real sorry." She didn't know whether she was more irritated by the washing machine or his sudden presence.

"Anything I can do to help?"

"This thingy is jammed." She smacked it for good measure.

He slipped through the open hole, tucking his long legs up close to his chest to make the fit. "Well, I'm no expert on thingies, but let me see what I can do."

Chelsea moved aside while he rammed the coin tray with the heel of his hand. Finally the tray slid in the rest of the way and sprang back coinless. The washing machine whirred into action. He turned toward her with a boyish grin.

"Thanks. I was almost out of clean—clothes," she finished lamely.

Mark appeared in the window hole. "Hey, Boss, I'm back. They had everything we needed. Here's the change." He held out a wad of cash, and Kyle strode to the window to collect it. Mark turned his attention to Chelsea. "Hey, Babe."

He leered. She cringed.

"We keep bumping into each other—must be destiny," Mark said. "How about going out sometime?"

Chelsea arranged her features into an innocent expression. "You know, I was thinking the same thing." She watched as Mark stretched himself up to his full height. "How about coming to Bible study with me tomorrow night?" She heard Kyle disguise laughter with a fake cough. "My church has a nice prayer meeting on Wednesday nights."

Mark hemmed and hawed then left with some excuse about finding his tool belt.

When he was out of earshot, Kyle laughed. "That was good. Now tell me the truth. Was that an honest attempt to convert an unbeliever or a clever way of rejecting him?"

"A rejection, definitely. But if he'd accepted, I would have agreed to meet him at church."

"I knew that wasn't likely. But then a pretty lady sometimes has a way of swaying a man's decisions."

Chelsea's face heated, and Kyle shifted his weight as though suddenly uncomfortable.

"I'll let you get back to your work," she said.

"Sure."

Chelsea turned to leave the laundry room.

"Oh. Shelly?"

Chelsea was caught off guard by the unfamiliar name but recovered quickly. "Hmm?"

"We'll be doing the upstairs windows later this afternoon. Will you be home?"

"Um, yeah, at least until three or so."

He told her they would work on her windows around noon, and she returned to her apartment.

Chelsea knew this was her opportunity to set things straight. When he came up to her apartment and started working, she would explain how awful that night had been for her and how she had been fed up with blind dates. He would probably understand why she'd been so angry. He would probably even understand why she'd hidden her identity from him.

What a nice man. A real-life nice man. Possibly the last of his kind. And he was a Christian, according to Gram. Not to mention very attractive. "And I blew it before I even met him," she chided herself. When would she learn to think before she acted? Her mother had always warned her it would get her into trouble one day.

Despite her optimistic nature, dread was building up inside her. She decided to forego the fabric softener. No way was she going back in there for the final rinse.

* *

Chelsea was just finishing a tuna fish sandwich when she heard a rap at the door. She hoped Kyle, not Mark, would be doing her windows. The need to get this confrontation over with was overwhelming. Not to mention that she had no desire to fend off Mark for three hours. "The lesser of two evils," she muttered to herself.

She breathed a nervous sigh of relief when she saw it was Kyle and invited him in. While he started tearing out the window in her living room, Chelsea sat down at her computer to finish her work, waiting for the right time to bring up the subject.

She was unable to stop herself from peeking over the monitor as he worked. It took a lot of muscle to make that crowbar work effectively, and since he was wearing a sleeveless shirt she couldn't help but notice the play of his muscles. She wondered what his hair looked like beneath that ball cap.

"So are you originally from this area?" he asked suddenly.

Chelsea started and wondered if he'd sensed her scrutiny.

"Yes, I grew up in Heaven. My parents still live here."

"My folks live in Phoenix. My brothers do, too, except one."

"How many brothers do you have?"

"I'm the oldest of five." He turned and smiled, his eyes crinkling at the corners.

Chelsea's mouth dropped. "Five? My brother has two boys, and they never sit still. How did your mother ever keep up with all of you?"

"I have no idea. It was a lively household—that's for sure. Still is, when we're all there together. We eat over there most Sundays, and I sure do look forward to it. I'm afraid my culinary skills are nonexistent."

"I'm not much for cooking, either, but I'm the official dessert maker in my family. I specialize in anything chocolate. And, believe it or not, my dad is the one who cooks the meals in our family. Thanksgiving and Christmas included. Mom's expertise is limited to the microwave and toaster. She gets cleanup duty, along with me, when I'm there."

Kyle's eyebrows arched to touch the lock of hair that had fallen over his forehead. "That's different. But, hey, whoever makes the good grub is the one who should do the cooking."

Chelsea laughed. Kyle was easy to talk to, and he seemed to enjoy having a conversation as he worked. The more she saw of his good nature, the more relaxed she became about the discussion she was determined to have.

"I have to admit," Chelsea said, "I was relieved when I saw you would be doing my windows and not Mark. I didn't want him in here all afternoon."

"Well, you won't have to worry about that anymore. I had to let him go."

Chelsea sat back in the spindled chair. She hoped Kyle hadn't fired him because of his behavior toward her. "I hope it was nothing about—" She paused, uncertain how to word it without making herself seem conceited.

He seemed to read her mind. "No, it was nothing like that." He laid the crowbar down and pulled his forearm across his face to wipe off the sweat. "I sent him after supplies, and he tried to pocket some of the cash, twenty bucks and some change. I found the receipt in the truck, and when I confronted him about it he didn't deny it."

"You fired him over twenty dollars?"

Kyle shrugged. "If I can't trust him with a little money, how can I trust him to go in these apartments by himself without ripping something off? We try to work when someone's home, but that's not always possible. Besides, the one thing I can't abide is dishonesty. If you can't trust an employee—or anyone else for that matter—there's nothing left to talk about."

Gulp. Chelsea hoped her face didn't look as warm as it felt. Just then Kyle started prying on the window again.

"If he'd truly been in need of some cash, he could've asked me for an advance," he said. "I would've given it to him."

Chelsea shuffled some papers around to hide her discomfort. So much for his sense of humor. She couldn't tell him now. If it had been only the E-mail, she could've admitted to that. But she'd deceived him by hiding her name, and now she'd heard what he thought of liars. She was horribly ashamed of her behavior. Gram had surely told him she was a Christian, and she'd behaved as badly as Mark. The only difference was, *she* knew better.

Chelsea cleared her throat. "I need to get my clothes from the dryer," she mumbled. "I'll be back." *Or maybe I'll just hide out in the laundry room for the rest of my life.*

She had never taken so much time to fold laundry. When she was finished, she piled up her towels to form a perfect white tower inside the basket. Beside them she neatly stacked her academy T-shirts and topped them with under things and neatly bundled socks.

"May as well get this over with." She tucked her detergent in the basket, balanced it on her hip, and started back to her apartment. This was the problem with an upstairs apartment. She had to go up and down the stairs with laundry and groceries. Oh, well. At least she didn't have to worry about people stomping across her ceiling. She giggled to herself. Except when they were getting a new roof.

She reached her door and turned the doorknob while leaning into it with her shoulder. For all its faults the apartment did have solid doors. She pushed, and the door opened much too easily. Chelsea fell into the apartment, shoulder first, colliding with Kyle's chest.

"Ummpphh," he grunted upon impact.

Kyle stumbled backward a step then steadied her with his hands on her shoulders. She breathed in a pleasant piney scent. His shoulders were much wider than hers, and his chest was rock hard. Suddenly she realized her free hand was braced on that chest. She snatched it away and met his gaze, which was inches away. He looked as stunned as she. Then his lips curved upward into a funny smile. Nicely shaped lips, pink enough to make a woman envious. His jaw line remained angular, despite the smile, and minuscule whiskers formed a shadow over its planes. Her stomach fluttered. Some part of her brain registered the hot temperature in the room.

"Whoa, there." His hands dropped from her shoulders, and he took a step back. "You okay?"

"Um, yeah." Her voice raspy, she cleared her throat. "I'm fine." She looked down at her basket and saw it had tilted sideways, spilling some of its contents. He must have noticed, too.

"Here—let me help," he said.

They both bent down, and her head bumped the rim of his hat. Hard.

"Ow!" Chelsea raised a hand to her forehead.

"I'm sorry." The words were sincere, but his voice contained mirth.

She met his gaze. His eyes sparkled, and his lips twitched in an effort to contain his laughter.

"Yeah, you look real sorry," she said.

He laughed then, and Chelsea couldn't help laughing with him.

He lifted a hand to his ball cap and twisted it so the rim pointed off to the back. "Well, aren't we a pair?"

"A pair of klutzes, maybe." The backward cap made him look endearingly boyish and rogue-like at the same time. She noticed the way his smile transformed his whole face. *What a doll.*

The Perfect Match

Kyle had started retrieving the spilled clothing, so she reached out to help. Her hands closed around something silky. *My underclothes.* She quickly scooped them up and noticed Kyle's handful contained more of the same. Heat spread from her face to her ears. *Why, oh, why did I have to put these on top?*

She avoided his gaze as they stood then heard him clear his throat awkwardly.

"I need to get your new window. I'll be right back."

Chelsea took the basket into her bedroom and sank onto the bed. Her heart was pumping as fast as it was when she'd jogged that morning. "What is wrong with me? He's just an ordinary man, here to fix my windows." She ran her fingers through her long, brown hair. "Okay, Chelsea, he's coming back. Get it together." By the time she'd finished putting away her laundry, Kyle had returned and was setting the window in the cavity.

"Need some help?" she asked.

He slid the window into place with a grunt. "Normally this is a two-man job—no chauvinism intended—but, fortunately for me, these windows aren't that big." He turned and gave her that engaging lopsided grin. "Besides, you're awfully little to be lifting a window."

Chelsea stretched herself up to her full five feet, three inches, and crossed her arms over her chest. "I'll have you know I'm a gymnastics coach. Not only do I lift teenage girls on a daily basis, but I also catch them midair when necessary." As soon as the words were out of her mouth, she froze. Had Gram told him what she did for a living? What if he figured out who she was?

43

He bowed his upper body, tipping his head in submission as best he could while bracing the window. "My apologies, Miss. You must be a lot stronger than you look."

Chelsea relaxed and nodded her head once. "Apology accepted."

While Kyle screwed the window into place, Chelsea went back to her computer. Once the window was secured, he caulked around the edges. Chelsea watched as he slid his finger down the line of caulk, smoothing it flat as he went. He was intent on his work and seemed very particular that it was done neatly.

After he finished the first window, Chelsea helped him move the dining room table and computer so he could access the second window. As he worked, they talked casually, and Chelsea made the cake for her mother's bridge party. He told her that although he owned the company he preferred to be hands-on, especially with the larger jobs, like the apartment complex. They talked about their churches. Chelsea was careful not to mention the name of her church, in case Gram had told him, but she told him her denomination. It turned out that Kyle's church was a different branch of the same denomination.

Chelsea slid the cake batter into the oven and began melting the chocolate for the icing. She stopped periodically and watched Kyle as he worked. His shirt rode up when he lifted his arms and exposed the trim waistline of his jeans. His tool belt encircled his hips, and his jeans hung loosely on his legs. She wasn't a woman to long after a man, but she did appreciate God's handiwork when she saw it, be it in the sunrise or the human body. And she was no stranger to fit bodies, seeing trim and muscular teenage gymnasts every day. In fact, Kyle was built similar to a gymnast with his wide shoulders and narrow hips.

After he applied the caulk to the window, he wiped his hands on the towel he carried in the waistband of his jeans then began putting the trim back on. "Didn't you say you had to leave around now?" he said as he checked his watch.

Chelsea looked at the digital clock on the microwave. "Yeah, I need to leave in fifteen minutes." She drizzled the chocolate glaze over the warm cake.

"I'll tell you what—why don't I come back to do the bedroom windows tomorrow sometime?"

"Sure, that'd be fine. I have a class in the morning; but I'm back around ten-thirty, and I don't leave again until this time."

"That'll work fine for me. Mrs. Levi, downstairs, should be home by now, so I'll go do her windows." He tapped the last nail in the trim and slipped the hammer back in his tool belt. "If you have a broom, I'll sweep up for you real quick."

"That's okay. I'll do it later," she said.

Kyle gathered his tools then turned back. "I was wondering if you might like to grab a bite to eat together sometime. I've enjoyed talking to you, and I'd like to get to know you better."

Chelsea's fingers tightened around the spoon. His dark, deep-set eyes pinned her in place. He was so direct and honest. Oh, she longed to say yes. There was nothing she wanted more than to get to know him better. But what could come of it? He would eventually find out who she was, what she'd done. When he found out she'd lied—

"Oh, of course," he said. "It should've occurred to me that you might be seeing someone else—"

"No." She didn't want him thinking that. "No, it isn't that. It's just—I have some other issues I'm working out." She released the spoon and shoved her hands in her pockets, where he wouldn't see them trembling. "Can I get back to you on that? Maybe tomorrow?"

His eyebrows shot up. "Sure. Sure, no hurry." He gathered his power tools and headed out the door, turning before it closed to give her a heart-stopping grin. "See you tomorrow."

❧

Later that night, after her prayer and devotional time, Chelsea lay in bed unable to sleep. Classes had gone poorly that evening, but that wasn't on her mind.

Kyle was coming over tomorrow, and she was supposed to have an answer for him. Saying yes would be the easiest thing to do. She had been rather proud of herself for not blurting out an affirmative when he'd asked her, as she typically did. Maybe she'd learned something from this whole mess, after all.

The practical side of her warned her the relationship had no place to go. If she confessed up front, he would surely withdraw his invitation; he'd been perfectly clear how he felt about people who lied to him. And if she didn't tell him who she was and went out with him anyway, what could come of it? What if they did hit it off? He would find out eventually who she was, and when he did he wouldn't want to have anything to do with her.

Chelsea drifted off to sleep with indecision churning in her mind. She dreamed she was lost in her car and every turn led to a dead end.

Chapter 4

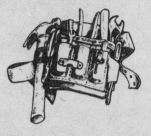

It was a hectic morning. Chelsea slept through her alarm and had to skip her jog in order to shower and make it to accounting class on time. After class, one of the other students asked for a copy of her notes from Monday so she'd had to go to the campus library to copy them. When she finally made it to her car, she saw that the tank was on "E" so she stopped for gas.

By the time she arrived home, it was 10:45, and Kyle was sitting by her door with a thermos, his back braced against the wall.

"Sorry I'm late." She dashed up the stairs and inserted the key in the door.

"No problem—I was due for a coffee break," he said.

"What a morning. It's been one thing after another."

Chelsea let him in and dropped her textbook and purse on the kitchen counter.

"How have your new windows been working for you?" he asked.

"Great. I'm getting less road noise than I used to. And I've noticed my air conditioner's not kicking on as much as it did."

"It'll be even better when we get the bedroom windows in."

"Come on back." Chelsea guided him to her bedroom, conscious of her old denims and T-shirt. Not to mention her lack of makeup and sloppy ponytail. "Here we are—we'll have to move the nightstand."

After they moved it, Chelsea left Kyle to tear out the old window and went to the living room to review her accounting notes. Cramming wasn't her style so she'd studied in small spurts all semester to be prepared for finals. She studied for half an hour, her mind wandering often to that male paragon in her bedroom; then she went to the kitchen to make the pie crusts for her Thanksgiving pies.

She was rolling out the dough when Kyle rounded the corner.

"I'll be right back with the window," he said, smiling.

He breezed out the door, leaving his piney scent behind. Chelsea inhaled a deep breath and closed her eyes. "Mmm. Smells as good as he looks."

Two pie shells later, the first window was finished and the second one started.

Chelsea sat down to work at the computer. Maybe she'd worried about going out with Kyle for nothing. He probably wasn't going to bring it up again. Most men wouldn't. Who wanted to open themselves to rejection? He'd probably wait and let her bring it up when she decided what she wanted to do. With newfound relief Chelsea went to work at the keyboard.

After awhile Chelsea heard the pounding of the hammer and knew Kyle was securing the trim. He was finished in her apartment. Moments later he appeared. He hooked the caulk gun into his tool belt and approached the table.

"All done." He brushed away the drywall dust from his shoulders. "Have you given any thought to whether you'd like to go out sometime?" No coward, this man.

"I'd love to." *Where had that come from?* "Sounds great. Anytime." *Stop babbling.* She bit her lip.

It was worth it, agreeing to go out with him, just to see the smile form on his face. She noticed a tiny cleft in his chin.

"So, tell me, what kinds of things do you like to do? Or would you prefer the dinner-and-movie routine?"

"Let's do something different."

"Like?"

"I don't know." She laughed. "I haven't thought that far yet."

He smiled. "How about if we think about it and set something up next week, after the holiday weekend?"

"All right." Chelsea followed him to the door. "Hope you have a nice Thanksgiving."

Before the door shut, he turned and winked. "You do the same."

Her legs went limp, and she leaned against the door. *Noodle-knees are for silly, lovesick teenagers, not grown, independent women.* As she pushed away from the door and walked back to the table, her wobbly knees mocked her. She didn't know what she was getting herself into, but right now she couldn't bring herself to regret it.

❧

Thanksgiving passed in a rush of food and family. Chelsea and her cousins tried to avoid their matchmaking grandmother. They agreed that Gram had too much time on her hands without the farm work she'd been accustomed to.

On Sunday Gram reminded Chelsea of her annual Christmas party scheduled for the Saturday before Christmas, and Chelsea marked it on her calendar. She always hosted a tasteful party, giving friends and family a chance to dress up, mingle, and enjoy the season for an evening. Now that Gram had only two tiny rooms, she'd reserved the large sitting room at Heavenly Village. A new dress wasn't in Chelsea's budget, but the black dress she'd worn for her almost-date with Kyle could be dressed up with some jewelry.

She'd been trying to think of what to do for her date with Kyle but hadn't come up with anything original. They could attend the theater or the ballet in Phoenix, but Chelsea didn't want to be presumptuous by suggesting an expensive date in case he was adamant about paying for it. She was in the mood to do something different. Probably because the memory of waiting in a restaurant was all too fresh.

As she popped in and out of her apartment on Monday, she looked around for Kyle but didn't see him, although his blue truck was there. When she left for work, Chelsea saw another man working on a window in one of the other buildings and figured Kyle must have found someone to replace Mark.

She was returning from her jog on Tuesday morning when she saw Kyle getting tools from his truck. She approached, conscious of her sweaty hair and unmade-up face. "Good morning."

He straightened from his rummaging, a surprised smile lighting his face. "Well, hello, there. You're out bright and early this morning."

"Just jogging."

"How was your holiday? I didn't get to see you yesterday." He shoved his hands in a pair of work gloves and adjusted the rim of his navy cap.

"Exactly as it always is, and I wouldn't want it any other way. How was yours?"

"Great, except one of my brothers' flights was delayed by the snowstorm out east. He didn't make it in time for dinner, but I spent some time with him over the weekend." He leaned against the truck door. "I'm glad I ran into you. Have you come up with any ideas for our date?"

This guy sure didn't beat around the bush. She wrinkled her nose. "Not a thing. With Phoenix so close, you'd think I'd be able to come up with something."

"Well, I have an idea to run by you."

"Shoot."

"Have you ever been to the Zoolights at the Phoenix Zoo?" His arched brows rose a notch.

"Yes, I have, but not for years. That sounds great. To be honest, I need some help getting into the Christmas spirit. I've been feeling kind of bah-humbug lately."

"Maybe this will do the trick for you. I haven't been in years myself, but I've heard it's still good."

They set their outing for Friday night and decided to grab a bite to eat at the zoo.

❦

On Friday Kyle spent the day in the office. He had some paperwork to catch up on, and since his office was close to his home he would have time to shower and change before his date. As he drove to his condo after work, he considered his feelings about this outing. There was no denying he'd anticipated it all day. All week, if he were honest.

Not that he hadn't gone out with other women since Lori. He had. Just no one he'd been excited about. He had a feeling about Shelly, almost from the first time he'd seen her, though he'd never been one to go on feelings. She was so real and natural. So unlike Lori.

He knew all women weren't users and liars. His mother was proof of that. His father was a different story altogether. In fact, with all the lying he'd grown up with, he thought he'd be used to it by now. Instead it grated on him more than anything else.

He remembered the fishing trip his dad had taken him on the summer he turned seven. A storm had advanced upon them while they were on the lake, but they returned to shore before any harm was done. Later that day he stood by his father's side and listened as his dad told the story to some friends. The embellished version bore little resemblance to the actual events. That was the first time Kyle knew his father lied.

He had many more opportunities to witness his father's exaggerations and outright lies. Some delivered to Kyle himself.

Broken promises had been his specialty. Camping trips that never happened. Baseball tournaments where he never showed up. His mom was always there, apologizing for his dad. Telling him his father loved him and didn't mean to hurt him. Kyle had become adept at hiding the hurt.

When he found out Lori had used him, he didn't think anyone guessed how it stung him. He was foolish to believe her lies.

In time the wounds healed, and he thought he was ready to move on. He couldn't deny he had feelings for Shelly. Still, it was a risk to put his heart on the line. *Say, Man. It's only a first date.* He breathed a quiet laugh. Maybe he was getting carried away. Maybe his feelings were all wrong, and the two of them wouldn't connect. *God, please lead in this relationship. Let come of it what You will. Help me be open and willing to pursue this relationship if that is what You would have happen.*

☙

The week sped by for Chelsea, and Friday arrived almost before she was ready for it. She'd seen Kyle several times since Tuesday, but she had only an opportunity to wave and say a quick hello.

Since she didn't have classes Friday afternoon, she could take her time preparing for the date. And it was a good thing. By the time she decided on an outfit that would look casual, half her clothes were on the bed, arranged in shirt-and-pants pairs as if a body were inside them. Finally she selected a green blouse that matched her eyes and a pair of casual cotton slacks. She berated herself for going to so much trouble over an outfit.

Although she liked her hair best when it was curled, she didn't want to look as if she'd gone to great lengths; so she simply curled the ends under and put the sides up in a silver barrette. There. That didn't look too bad.

Now for makeup. Chelsea applied it sparingly, going for a natural look. He'd already seen her without makeup, so it wasn't as if she would be fooling anyone. By the time she finished with wineberry lipstick, it was seven minutes until the appointed hour. Her stomach rumbled. She'd forgotten to eat lunch.

"Great," she muttered. She could grab a snack and mess up her lipstick, or she could suffer.

A knock sounded at the door. "Suffer, it is."

She stood, smoothed nonexistent wrinkles, straightened her belt, and went to answer the door. Her legs trembled over the short distance. She drew a deep breath and exhaled slowly to calm her nerves—a habit from her competition days. *Get hold of yourself, Girl.*

She pulled open the door and was rewarded with Kyle's presence. She saw immediately that he looked different. Ahh, the cap was missing.

"You have hair," she blurted out.

His dark eyebrows shot upward. "You thought I didn't?"

"Your ball cap is missing," she muttered lamely. *And so is my brain.*

His face relaxed in that adorable lopsided grin. "Oh, right." His eyes twinkled. "Were you worried about what was up there? Or rather what wasn't up there?"

55

She laughed. "Of course not. I never gave it any thought."

"You look nice," he said, gracefully changing the subject. "Are you ready to go?"

She grabbed her purse then shut the door behind her and locked it. Kyle led her to a burgundy SUV, and she suddenly realized she'd been expecting to go in his navy work truck. How little she knew about him.

※

Once they were on their way, Kyle asked Chelsea about her family. She had been born into a traditional one in which her mother stayed home, and after several minutes of talking about her upbringing Kyle realized she'd had an idyllic childhood. Although his own mother had made his childhood pleasant, his father's apathy had cast a depressing shadow over his memories.

"You said you have five brothers?" Chelsea asked.

"Four, actually. I'm the oldest. Then it's Barry, Drew, Aaron, and Shawn. We're all employed now, except for Shawn, who's working toward an engineering degree."

"Did your mother work, or did she stay home as mine did?"

"She stayed home. She's a good mother, and we've always been close." Kyle flipped the lever to turn down the air. He didn't want to spoil the conversation by talking about his dad, so he shifted the topic back to his brothers. "My brothers and I are pretty close, too. They're on the straight and narrow, except for Aaron." He turned to her with a smile and noticed she was studying him, appearing to be listening closely. "He's the one whose plane was delayed last week. We went fly-fishing over the weekend—we used to do that together a lot as kids."

"Were you raised in church?"

"My mom took us every week. We all committed our lives to the Lord before we were teenagers, but Aaron went through some bad spots during adolescence and hasn't recovered yet."

The drive to the zoo seemed to speed by, even though traffic was heavy, and before Kyle knew it he was buying their admission tickets. While he waited for change, he watched Chelsea taking in the scene. She looked cute, her bangs hanging down to her eyebrows, framing her green eyes. Her skin glowed, and her dark hair glistened under the rays of the setting sun. His mood leaped like an inner tube surfacing the water as he anticipated spending time with her this evening.

❧

Chelsea's gaze swept over the holiday decorations that embellished the entrance to the zoo. Twinkling lights beckoned her, until a delicious aroma wafted by her nose. Pizza. All thoughts of fat grams and calories fled. She felt her stomach rumble and was thankful for the cacophony that covered the noise. She saw the food stand ahead and wished she were comfortable enough to suggest they eat first.

Kyle guided her through the crowd with a hand on her elbow. "Are you hungry, or would you rather walk awhile first?"

Bless him. "To be honest, I'm famished." She smiled at him. "I forgot to eat lunch."

He squeezed her elbow lightly. "Forgot? Well, let's remedy that right now."

The wait for the pizza seemed interminable but more so

because of her hunger. After scarfing down three slices, she sat back and saw that he was watching her with an amused expression.

She gave a sheepish grin. "I'll have to jog every day this week to work all that off."

"Relax. You're just compensating for the calories you skipped at lunch. Besides, it doesn't look as if you have to worry about your figure."

She could feel her cheeks grow warm, and she tossed him a sassy grin to cover her embarrassment. "If I didn't worry about my figure, believe me, it wouldn't look like it does now."

He laughed. "Point taken."

After they ate, they strolled along the zoo's walkways. Darkness fell around them, and multicolored lights twinkled festively. A choral group had drawn a crowd, and harmony filled the cooling air, giving off holiday cheer.

They sat on a bench facing the lake and talked. Shivers of joy rippled through Chelsea when Kyle put his arm on the back of the seat. Warm heat fanned from the pit of her stomach outward.

Later they walked through the shops, trying on hats and acting silly.

When it was nearly time for the park to close, they passed a vendor and decided to wind down with a cup of hot cocoa. While Kyle paid, Chelsea went to claim the only available table several feet away. She overheard Kyle making small talk with the young man who rang up the purchase and watched as he handed over a bill.

"You gave me the wrong change," Kyle said.

The young man's eyes widened. "Sorry about that. How much did I give you?"

Chelsea watched as Kyle fanned out the bills the cashier had given him. "You gave me eight dollars in change, but I only gave you a five." Kyle handed back a bill. "Here—you only owe me three."

"Thanks," the guy said in a confused but pleased voice.

Such honesty. Most people would have pocketed that money.

Chelsea's tender feelings for Kyle deepened. The more she knew of him, the more she liked him. He couldn't be perfect, but she had yet to see a flaw. She felt almost dizzy, like when she'd been on prescription medicine after straining her ankle in high school. A happy, kind of dazed feeling. Ahh, the medicine of love. *Don't be ridiculous, Chelsea—you hardly know the guy.*

All too soon it was time to go. The drive back to her apartment seemed even shorter than the ride to the zoo. Conversation was much more natural, punctuated by short periods of relaxed silence. When they arrived at her place, Kyle followed her upstairs to her door. Her heart hammered in her chest as she speculated if he'd kiss her good night. As much as she was attracted to him, she hoped he wouldn't. Somehow she'd think less of him if he attempted to kiss her on the first date. So far he'd exhibited the highest moral standards, and she hoped he would validate her opinion by respecting their new relationship.

She unlocked her door then turned to face Kyle. He was wearing that adorable half grin and looking at her so tenderly her breath caught.

"I enjoyed being with you tonight," he said

Her stomach fluttered. "Me, too."

"Would you like to go out again?"

As if I could resist that lazy smile. "Sure."

"Maybe something indoors next time."

"Sounds great."

Kyle reached out and grasped her hands, holding her fingers lightly. She met his gaze and knew from the look in his eyes that something was going to happen. A plan was in progress behind those brown eyes. She was right.

And wrong.

"Do you mind if I say a quick prayer?"

She blinked. Her brain hiccoughed. Silence permeated the hallway. "Um, yes. I mean, no. I mean, no, I don't mind." *Spit it out.*

Kyle prayed softly, his deep voice murmuring in her ears. *A man that prays after a date. Where have you been all my life?* What a pleasant change from the doorway groping she'd been subjected to more than once. He was proving to be—

She felt him squeeze her hand lightly, and she lifted her head. Apparently the prayer was over. The prayer she hadn't even heard.

He didn't seem to notice her distraction. "Good night. I'll see you around next week."

"Good night." She stepped inside and closed the door behind her. This date had surpassed all her hopes. Suddenly Monday seemed like a lifetime away.

Chapter 5

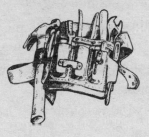

S o have you decided what you're wearing?" Mattie asked.
Chelsea wrapped the spiral phone cord around her
pinkie. "Let's see. I'm trying to decide between my
striped flannel jammies or my black velvet dress. What do you
think?"

"I guess that depends on which shoes you're wearing," her
cousin said in a mock serious voice.

"Black heels or furry bunny slippers. Haven't decided yet."
Chelsea propped her elbows on the countertop.

"Well, if you're wearing the furry bunny slippers, the flannel jammies are a sure bet. But if—"

Chelsea heard a tapping noise and turned toward the window. A face. She sucked in her breath and threw a hand to her
chest in shock.

Then she recognized the ball cap and those unsettling
brown eyes. She exhaled a breath of relief as Kyle smiled at her
through the windowpane from atop a ladder.

"Chels? You okay?" Mattie asked.

She glared at Kyle for giving her such a scare. "I'm fine. Something just. . .popped up." Kyle sent her an exaggerated glower in return.

"Listen—I've gotta go." She crossed her eyes at Kyle, sticking out her tongue for good measure.

After saying good-bye, Chelsea hung up the phone and approached the window, where Kyle was trying to best her with a distorted expression.

She opened the window. "You win," she said, referring to their ugly-face contest.

Kyle laughed. "I'm not sure that's a contest I want to win."

"Well, that's what you get for scaring me silly."

"Hey, I could have gone about my work and waited for you to turn around and see a face peeping in your window." He held up a caulk gun. "I have to finish your windows."

"You mean you didn't come up here to serenade me?"

"Well, now, if I'd known that's what you were after, I'd have dressed nicer and brought a CD player."

She could feel heat spreading through her veins, all the way to the tips of her ears.

Kyle cleared his throat and broke the moment. She left the window cracked open, and they talked as he finished sealing around the window. All the windows had been installed, so next on the agenda was putting on another layer of stucco.

When the kitchen window was finished, he moved to the living room window, and Chelsea opened that one so they could continue their conversation. He kept his gaze focused on his work most of the time, leaving her free to study his face.

His olive skin was as dark in the winter as hers was in the summer, and his long, thick lashes curled up slightly at the ends. His large brown eyes and baseball cap made him look boyishly cute, but his angular jaw line denoted a contrasting strength that was all man.

When he finished with the window, he moved on to the next apartment, telling her he'd be doing her bedroom windows later.

Chelsea packed her dinner for work, a silly grin adorning her face. Kyle was so special. She wondered why he hadn't been snapped up yet by some other woman. He must be all of twenty-seven, twenty-eight. She wondered if he'd ever been in love. She hadn't, but she realized she was getting that giddy kind of feeling everyone talked about.

The matter of the E-mail she'd sent seemed like a distant memory. As if it hadn't happened. Things were going so well between the two of them that she couldn't bring herself to feel guilty over her little fib. It wasn't even a fib; after all, Shelly was her nickname. It wasn't as if she'd given him a totally different name. Now that would have been a lie. Besides, she wouldn't have had the opportunity to know him if she'd told him who she was. He would never have asked her out if he'd known.

Eventually, if their relationship progressed, he'd find out she was the Chelsea who'd sent him that E-mail. By then he probably wouldn't care about the misunderstanding. He'd know her and, she hoped, care enough about her to recognize she'd only been angry and acted rashly.

He might even think she hadn't known he was *that* Kyle.

It wasn't an uncommon name, after all. For all he knew, she hadn't connected the Kyle she'd been set up with to the Kyle who was working on her apartment. And lots of people went by their nicknames.

Love does not rejoice in evil but rejoices with the truth.

Chelsea was startled by the words that popped into her mind. This wasn't evil. She was a Christian trying to find that special someone God had chosen for her. He was a wonderful Christian man, and she felt he might be that special one. He was even the same denomination, more or less. What could be more virtuous than pursuing a godly relationship with the man the Lord had chosen for her?

❧

"Do you have any plans for Friday night?" Kyle watched as Shelly took a bite of her sandwich and daintily wiped her mouth with her napkin.

Her mouth full, she shook her head no.

"Would you like to go someplace?"

"Sure. What did you have in mind?"

"Oh, no. I picked last time. It's your turn." He winked, and her cheeks turned pink.

Having lunch at Shelly's apartment was becoming a pleasant habit. Much better than wolfing down his meal in a fast-food restaurant or in his truck. Today he'd picked up some food and brought it back. He was getting to know her fairly well since he was seeing her every day.

"Hmm. How about the ballet?" she asked with a cocked brow.

"The ballet?" he asked, scrunching up his face.

"Sure, you know—tights, tutus, pirouettes. . . ."

"The ballet."

". . .pliés, jetés, ronde de jambes. . . ."

"Ronde de whats?"

"I take it you don't like the ballet." She winked at him. "That's okay. I'm a flexible kinda gal. How about catching an Arizona Cardinals' game?"

"As in touchdowns, sacks, interceptions?" he asked.

"Fumbles, punts, extra points. . . ."

Kyle smiled and nodded. "Now you're talking my language. The woman knows football. Well, aren't you the well-rounded individual?"

"Unlike someone else, who is clueless about ballet."

"And prefers to remain so. I'd love to catch a Cardinals' game with you, but they don't play on Fridays. What's your next choice?"

"Well, there's a movie I've been wanting to see."

"Let me guess—a romantic comedy."

She flipped her long dark hair over her shoulder. "How'd you guess?"

Kyle groaned playfully. Truth be told, he'd have gone to the ballet as long as she promised never to tell his brothers.

Kyle had never dated anyone who was such fun to be with. Sometimes his jaws hurt from laughing so much after they'd been together. And, he chuckled to himself, she wasn't half bad to look at either.

After a day at the office on Friday, Kyle rushed home to

shower and change then went to pick up Shelly. They'd decided to eat at Ming's, a wonderful Chinese restaurant, and attend the late showing of the movie.

All through dinner Kyle found himself amazed at his ability to open up to her. But he avoided telling her about his parents' restaurant chain, Family Fixin's. After getting burnt with Lori, he was reluctant to let Shelly know about his family's wealth.

Now that he reflected on it, he realized Lori had been fascinated with his family and their success in the restaurant business. He had thought her interest stemmed from her position as waitress at one of the chains, not from a desire to marry into wealth.

He and Shelly lingered over a cup of tea, content to talk until the movie started. He found some of her personality traits endearing. Like the way she talked with her hands. He'd even noticed her talking to herself on two occasions.

She asked him about starting his own business, and then he found out her goal was to buy ownership at the academy where she taught gymnastics. He encouraged her to keep working at it if that's what she dreamed of doing. His own business was finally paying off after four years of hard work.

The movie didn't turn out to be as boring as he'd feared. The writers had thrown in some action, presumably for the male viewers. Kyle took Shelly's hand halfway into the movie and was pleased when her small fingers responded by curling around his. His hand remained there for the rest of the movie.

Kyle was tempted to kiss her good night at her door, but

he didn't want to rush the relationship, which was developing more quickly than he'd anticipated. After the last disastrous one he wanted to get to know who she was before things got complicated.

After church on Sunday, Chelsea met Kyle at her apartment, and from there they drove to Phoenix for the Cardinals' game. Following a touchdown in the fourth quarter that put the Cardinals ahead by one point, Kyle bought coffee for everyone around them. After the game Chelsea invited him in to relax for a bit before he headed home. They discussed everything from sports to their churches.

Finally Kyle talked about his family, including his father. "He's a good guy—don't get me wrong. But he let us down a lot when we were kids. He told us he would come to our games, but he didn't show up; he told us he would take us fishing, but he seldom did. After awhile we stopped believing his word or expecting anything from him."

"That's sad."

Kyle leaned his head back against her sofa and continued. "I got used to it eventually, but the first few times he let me down were really hard. I still remember the first time."

Kyle had a faraway look in his eyes, and his brows pulled together in a frown. "I used to go fishing with my brothers all the time—fly-fishing. My dad fished, too, but he rarely took us. He used to make his own lures. One day he was on the back porch making some new ones, and I was sitting there with him, gawking at all those little woolly flies organized in his wooden box. I must've said how much I'd like to have some of my own, because he promised he'd make me a set for Christmas."

"It never happened?"

He shook his head. "I'd looked forward to getting those so much. Not just because I wanted some flies, but because I'd wanted something my dad had taken the time to make me, you know?"

She nodded, touched by the hurt on his face all these years later.

He scooted to the edge of the sofa and gave her a wry grin. "Sorry about going maudlin on you." He squeezed her hand. "I had a really nice time today."

"Me, too."

He glanced at his watch, and she knew it must be nearing midnight. "It's getting late." He stood and made his way to the door. "Do you have plans for Friday?" Kyle asked, placing his cap back on his head as he prepared to leave.

"No, I'm free."

"My singles' group at church is having a Christmas party. Would you like to go with me?"

"Sure—sounds like fun." *What if he asks me about Saturday?* She'd already committed to Gram's party, and she certainly couldn't bring Kyle. He'd find out for sure that she was the granddaughter Gram had tried to set him up with.

"The party starts at seven, and we eat there. Oh. I have another Christmas thing I'm invited to on Saturday night. Would you like to go with me?"

Gram's party. She had to make an excuse. Chelsea's stomach coiled. "Sorry. I, uh, have something else I'm committed to on Saturday night."

"No big deal. I'll just have to settle for Friday then."

Phew. That went better than I'd hoped.

"Friday should be my last day at your apartments. We'll be applying another coat of stucco all this week, and then we'll be finished with this job."

"Feel free to join me for lunch again this week."

Kyle touched the brim of his hat in a polite gesture. "Much obliged, Ma'am."

They said good-bye, and Chelsea closed the door behind him. He sure wasn't rushing that first kiss.

That is *what you wanted.* "I know—I know. But enough already."

❧

Chelsea's accounting final was scheduled for Friday, so she spent every available moment that week studying. She needed at least a low A on the test to achieve an A for the course, and she was determined to do that.

Kyle ate with her every day, at her invitation. Some days she threw together sandwiches and soup, and other days he picked up food to go. On one of those days he chose Ming's and brought a bag of the almond cookies she'd raved over when they'd eaten there on their date. His thoughtfulness added to the growing feelings she sheltered in her heart.

Chelsea breezed the final and was in a perky mood by the time the evening rolled around. She dressed casually in black jeans and was relieved to see that Kyle was similarly attired.

Her heart jumped in anticipation of spending the evening with him.

At the party other singles greeted them, and Kyle introduced her around. About thirty people mingled in the large fellowship hall in groups of three or four. They were a laughing, friendly bunch, and Chelsea could tell it was going to be a fun evening.

"Let's go get some punch." Kyle guided her to a table adorned with a mini Christmas tree and draped with evergreen.

Two young women at the table ladled punch into festive cups. "Hey, Kyle—glad you could make it. Who's your friend?"

Kyle shook hands with the women then bestowed a heart-stopping smile on Chelsea. "Cindy, Anna, I'd like you to meet Shelly. Shelly, this jokester's Cindy, and this is Anna"—he gestured toward the tall brunette—"who won't be in the singles' group much longer. Where is that fiancé of yours?"

"He had to work tonight. But I'm so glad you could come and bring Shelly."

Kyle handed Chelsea some punch, took a glass for himself then slipped his free hand around hers. Chelsea watched as Cindy noticed their clasped hands with raised brows then winked at Anna.

What's that all about?

"Hey, Shelly, would you mind getting us more cups?" Cindy asked. "The supply closet's around that corner on the left."

"Oh. Sure. How many do you need?"

"Just bring one package. They're all the way to the back of the closet against the wall."

Cindy immediately engaged Kyle in conversation, so Chelsea walked away, happy to be of help. But she wondered if the women had sent her on a bogus mission simply to have a private word with Kyle. They seemed friendly enough, and she was sure they weren't being unkind; she couldn't help but notice, though, that there were plenty of cups on the table.

She flipped on the supply room light and spotted the cups against the far wall tucked neatly between Styrofoam plates and a coffee urn. She reached for the cups.

"I think we've been set up."

Chelsea spun around in surprise to see Kyle standing there grinning.

"What?"

He pointed to a place above her head.

She looked up. Mistletoe. "Oh." He was close enough that she could see those golden flecks in his eyes. Her mouth went dry.

"Cindy likes to play little jokes. She'll probably do this to every couple here before the night is over."

"Oh." *Is that all you can say?*

Kyle's lips twitched.

"What's funny?"

"I was thinking about something my grandpa once told me." He stepped closer. "It seems there's a mysterious phenomenon surrounding mistletoe."

Chelsea lifted her brow. "Mysterious phenomenon?"

"Mmm. Supposedly you can kiss under mistletoe. . .without touching."

She smiled, her gaze falling on his mouth. "Really?"

"I've never verified it, mind you, but that's the way the theory goes."

His gaze met hers as he moved even closer. She froze in place as his head lowered toward her. The outward stillness of her body contrasted with the chaos that reigned inside. His lips touched hers, soft and warm. She couldn't breathe, couldn't think, didn't want to. His kiss was like a caress, feeding both body and soul, and she was drowning in the maelstrom of emotions.

He pulled back, and Chelsea stood immobile under his intense gaze. He seemed to have been as affected as she. Her hands had found their way to his shoulders, and she let them drop to her sides.

She cleared her throat. "Well, so much for the mistletoe phenomenon."

He smiled lazily. "Didn't work for my grandfather either."

Chapter 6

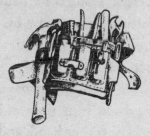

I had a great time. Your church friends were very nice."
Chelsea unlocked her door and turned to face Kyle.
"They liked you, too. I hope you didn't mind Cindy's
little prank. She didn't mean any harm."

Their gazes locked, and awareness zinged through her. "No,
it was okay."

"Just okay?" he demanded, his eyes twinkling.

She could hear her pulse thudding in her ears and smell the
woodsy scent of Kyle's cologne. Sensory overload, that's what
it was.

"Actually it was very nice," she said.

She could see desire cloud his gaze. He tilted her chin up
with a gentle touch and drew closer. His lips met hers for the
second time that night, and she knew the first had been no
fluke. She returned the kiss and found herself floating in a
delightful never-never land that seemed to promise something
better just out of reach.

Suddenly she understood what all the fuss was about. Why

people, even Christians, went further and further until they compromised themselves before marriage. It overwhelmed her, this desire, and she felt herself on the edge of losing control.

She drew back. Kyle studied her through half-shut eyes and seemed to be struggling to slow his breath, as she was. They were in this together, she realized.

Kyle smiled sheepishly. "I'm sorry."

"No, it's okay." She touched his hand reassuringly. After all, if things got too carried away, she was just as responsible as he was. He tenderly clasped her hand, and she didn't want the night to end.

She gestured toward her door. "You could come inside—"

"I don't think that's a good idea."

She sighed. "You're right. It's late."

His gaze pierced hers. "Late has nothing to do with it."

She blushed and averted her gaze. "Oh."

"Shelly, I want you to know I've come to care about you. You're easy to talk to, easy to trust. There are so many things I love about you, and I enjoy our friendship. It's obviously growing into something bigger, and I want that more than anything."

Chelsea reveled in the glow of his gaze. "The feeling is mutual."

"I'm glad." He winked, and a shiver ran through her body. "But if what happened just now is any indication, we're going to have to watch our step."

"You're right. I've never felt so—"

"Me, either."

Silence prevailed for a moment; then Kyle squeezed her

hand and led them in a short prayer, committing their friendship once again to God. Afterward Chelsea invited him for lunch following church on Sunday, and they said good night.

Chelsea had grown used to having him around every day; but now his work on the apartment was finished, and she would miss him.

❧

Kyle clasped his hands behind his head and stared up at the dark ceiling. It was funny, but a month ago he would've said women weren't worth the effort. After Lori had led him to believe she cared about him instead of his inherited wealth, he'd had no interest in pursuing another relationship.

But Shelly was different. She was a genuine Christian who lived out her convictions. But it was something more than that. She was so real. She didn't put on any pretenses. When she felt affectionate, he could read it in her eyes. When she felt nervous, she rambled. Her little quirks amused him and drew him to her.

Most of all, he was beginning to trust her. Something he hadn't thought he could ever do again. They'd met each other only a month ago, but he felt as if he'd known her much longer. He wanted to spend every moment with her. He chuckled and shook his head. He sounded like a teenager in love.

He'd become spoiled, seeing her every day. But now that his work on the apartments was over, they would be limited to evenings and weekends.

He wished he could get out of going to that party tomorrow night, but a promise was a promise. A part of him felt guilty about going, but he knew his intentions were pure. He wished his life could be fast-forwarded to Sunday. Even though he'd just left her, he couldn't wait to see her again. A smile tugged at his lips, and he shook his head. *Morgan, you really do sound like a teenager.*

Chapter 7

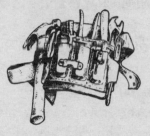

Chelsea looked over the outfits arranged on her bed and frowned. She needed a good shopping spree. The blouses and skirts draped over the bed like a colorful patchwork quilt. An *old*, colorful patchwork quilt.

She wrinkled her nose and turned back to the closet. Her black dress beckoned from the far corner. Memories of the last time she'd worn it lingered in her mind like a foul-smelling stench. It was the night she was to meet Kyle but instead was stood up for the first time ever. At least she'd thought then that she was stood up. Her actions of the next day assaulted her conscience. She would have to tell him the truth.

Chelsea shook off the sour thoughts and fingered the narrow, wispy skirt of the dress. It was her only choice. She'd known it before she pulled the first blouse out of the closet, but the dress was a reminder of something she wanted to forget.

She took the dress off the hanger. "It doesn't matter what you wear tonight anyway." It's not as if she had anyone to impress. Mostly it would be family and Gram's many friends.

The cake she'd promised to make sat on her kitchen table, decorated with festive trim and holly leaves, inside a windowed box. It was better than last year's, if she did say so herself. Mattie, Callie, and Melissa were going early to help Gram decorate the recreation room.

After she slipped on the black dress and accessorized it with a burgundy scarf, she carefully lifted the cake from the table and made her way to the car. Once the cake was safely stowed in the trunk, she drove to Heavenly Village. She would be a few minutes late, she told herself, glancing at the car's digital clock, but she couldn't drive faster and risk losing the cake she'd worked so hard on all day.

The parking lot was jammed with cars, so she slipped hers into a space in the back of the lot and removed the cake from the trunk. Moments later she entered the lobby, thankful for the handicap doors that slid open and shut on their own. The high-ceilinged lobby looked cheerful, a huge decorated Christmas tree hugging one corner of the room.

She walked through the lobby and down the hall, following the sound of music. Her arms grew heavy under the weight of the cake, and she bypassed the main entrance to the rec room, choosing instead to enter the adjoining kitchen so she wouldn't have to maneuver through the crowd.

Unable to open the door, she kicked at it with the toe of her shoe.

Just then her mother opened the door. "Chelsea! Come on in." Her gaze dropped to the massive cake. "Oh, that's beautiful!" She took the cake from her daughter.

Melissa looked up from the punch she was making. "Hey, Girl. We were wondering what happened to you."

"Look at this, Melissa." Her mother took the cake over to Chelsea's cousin. "Isn't it darling? Look at all those leaves and berries—it must've taken you all day, Dear."

Melissa sampled the punch. "Ugh!" she said, scrunching up her face. "How many quarts of grapefruit juice did you say?"

"Three *cups*, Honey—not quarts."

"Oops," Melissa said.

Her mother took the cake out of the box and carried it to the door leading to the rec room. "I'll set this on the table where everyone can see it before I cut it," she said, glancing over her shoulder.

The music and laughter drifted in as the door swung open then faded once it closed behind her.

"No Kyle tonight?" Melissa asked.

Chelsea shook her head. "I haven't told him yet."

She saw Melissa's censure in her face. "Chels, it's been weeks."

"I know—I know. I'm going to tell him tomorrow."

Melissa arched her brows.

"I am," Chelsea said sharply. "I have to."

Melissa tasted her repaired punch. "Much better." She began scooping lime sherbet into the bowl. "Things are getting serious."

"Very." Chelsea couldn't help the smile that formed on her face. "He's wonderful, Melissa. You're going to love him." Chelsea swatted Melissa on the arm. "You know, maybe Gram does have a knack for matchmaking."

"Don't start! And don't be giving Gram any ideas either."
She glared at her.

"Oh, Gram has plenty of ideas all her own—"

The door burst open, and Callie leaned through the doorway. "Hi, Chels. Gram wants everyone out here. She's ready to
give her greeting."

"Be right there," Melissa said, and Callie disappeared. "She
has a microphone this year, you know."

Chelsea laughed. "I know she's going to love that."

Melissa carried the punch bowl through the door, and
Chelsea followed. Her brother Jarod and his friend were just
finishing the last strains of "We Wish You a Merry Christmas"
on their instruments. Chelsea made her way into the throng in
time to see Gram approaching the small stage, a Santa hat
perched crookedly on her head.

"Shelly?" The familiar voice sent shivers down her spine.

She turned to meet Kyle's uncertain expression. "Kyle."

His face broke into a gorgeous smile.

A part of her was so glad to see him and wanted to hug him.
But the other part realized his presence would ruin everything.

A silence fell over the room as Gram took the microphone.

"It looks like we've been invited to the same party," Kyle
whispered.

She nodded and made a show of turning her attention to
Gram. But her attention was not on her grandmother at all. It
was on Kyle and the whole messy predicament. She realized
Gram had invited Kyle to the party—no doubt to try to set

them up again. What her grandmother didn't know was that she had already fallen for Kyle. Completely, helplessly, madly in love with him.

The audience applauded as Gram introduced her grandson and friend and thanked them for playing the music that evening.

Chelsea clapped mechanically. She had to get out of there before Gram introduced her to Kyle. She would tell him tomorrow, on her own terms. If he found out tonight, he might never forgive her. She'd have to slip out and make her excuses later. The uneasy churning in her stomach would make the perfect excuse—

"And I'd like to thank my granddaughters Melissa, Callie, and Mattie for their help in decorating the room. Didn't they do a fabulous job?"

Everyone applauded.

"Come on up here, girls."

Her cousins slowly made their way to the dais while a nervous dread rose in Chelsea's chest.

Gram slipped an arm around her nearest granddaughters. "And you must take a peek at the beautiful cake on the table before it's cut. Yet another of my talented granddaughters made it, and if you think it's beautiful on the outside, wait till you taste the inside! Chelsea, come on up here."

Chelsea's gaze swung to Kyle, and her heart quivered at the ambivalent expression on his face. He glanced around, waiting for the granddaughter to step out from among them.

The sound of applause seemed muffled, as if it originated

from deep within a cave.

"Come on, Chelsea—don't be shy," Gram said from the dais.

She took a step forward, her legs quaking under her, then cast Kyle a backward glance. She could feel her heart thud at the confusion on his face. Someone elbowed her—an uncle, she saw when she turned around. Walking to the stage, she curved her lips in a smile that felt brittle enough to crack. The several yards felt like miles as she wove between friends and family.

She stepped onto the stage, and Gram took Chelsea's hand as she faced the crowd. The bright lights heated her flesh and stung her eyes.

She was vaguely aware of Gram talking into the microphone. She squinted into the crowd, hoping for a glimpse of Kyle. Smiling faces stared back at her, but the spot where Kyle had been standing was vacant. She searched the room. Then movement in the far corner of the room caught her attention. She focused her eyes on the back of the person who was pushing his way toward the door. Even in the dimness of the room she recognized the set of shoulders, the dark head of hair. He disappeared through the doorway, while her breath jammed in her throat and her stomach clenched in a knot.

❧

Later that night Chelsea kicked off her shoes and slipped out of the black dress. She remembered again the last time she'd worn it, waiting for Kyle at Les Saisons. She remembered being stood up. Then she'd worn it tonight, and things had turned out even worse.

What is it with this dress anyway?

The dress fell in a heap at her feet, and she slipped a long T-shirt over her head before plopping down on her bed. She was tired. Exhausted. Tonight's party had gone on far too long for her. Making small talk with the guests had been wearing, especially since her gaze had continually swung around the room searching, hoping, for a glimpse of Kyle. She wanted desperately to explain. But then what could she explain? She had lied, and she had no excuse for that.

The memory of the hasty E-mail she'd sent him weeks ago caused her stomach to churn. Why had she ever sent it? Why hadn't she waited to hear from him or written it off as a bad experience instead of acting so spontaneously? Because she'd wanted revenge. She'd wanted him to know how much it had irked her to be stood up. She remembered sitting in the restaurant all alone, cringing each time the waiter checked back with her. She remembered feeling like a loser, knowing the waiter knew her date hadn't shown.

It was pride, wasn't it, God? Pride had led to her humiliation. Pride had left her so indignant. Pride had instigated that nasty E-mail. She closed her eyes and laid her forearm over her head. She remembered seeing Kyle the first time he'd come to work on the apartments. He was high up on the roof. The next time she saw him, he came into her apartment to make a phone call.

And that's when you lied.

It was true, she had lied. Giving him a false name was nothing short of a lie. She'd wanted to cover her identity. She had been embarrassed about her reaction to having been stood up, and she should have been—especially since he'd had the best of excuses. And she'd had ample opportunity to tell him the truth, but she hadn't wanted to ruin things between her and Kyle.

How selfish. How untrusting can I be? Oh, God, I'm a sinner. I acted in the flesh instead of in the Spirit, and I know better. I'm sorry, God. Sorry for the pride and the vengeance, the lies and the selfishness. I should have done what was right. I should have told him the truth and trusted You to work things out.

Chelsea rubbed her face with her hands and heaved a weary sigh. And now it was too late. She had let her lie go on for much too long, and Kyle would never accept that. Especially since she'd not been the one to set the record straight. Oh, he'd forgive her eventually. He was a good Christian man. But he'd never trust her enough to continue their relationship. She knew where he stood on honesty, and she'd violated his trust.

❧

"Hi, Dear. It's me."

Kyle shifted the phone to cradle it between his shoulder and ear. "Hi, Mom."

"I'm sorry to bother you at work, but I was calling to tell you what time to come Christmas Eve. Your brothers are arriving around four o'clock, although we probably won't eat until at least six or seven."

"No problem—I'll come early, too."

"And you're welcome to bring Shelly. Your father and I would love to meet her."

Kyle's mind snagged at the familiar name. *It isn't even her real name*, he reminded himself, but some pseudonym she'd given him to protect her identity.

"Kyle, are you there?"

"Yes, Mom, I'm here."

His office assistant, Evelyn, handed him a stack of work orders.

"So do you think she'll come?"

"Who?"

"Kyle, aren't you paying any attention? Shelly. Do you think Shelly will come?"

He sighed. He wasn't ready to talk about her. It had only been two days since he'd found out. "Things didn't work out between Shell—between us."

"Oh, I'm sorry to hear that. You seemed so happy the last time we talked. She seemed so good for you."

Kyle couldn't stop the bitter laugh that escaped. His mother remained silent, and his laughter seemed to echo across the line. He knew he should say something. At least a brief explanation, especially considering his glowing words about her the last time they'd spoken. "She lied to me, Mom."

"Oh. I'm sorry to hear that."

Despite his earlier desire not to discuss it, he closed his office door and found himself spilling out the whole story, ending with Saturday's party. By the time he was finished, he could feel the heat in his face and the angry knot in his stomach.

"Why do you think she lied about who she was?" she asked.

"Why do I—because she's a liar, that's why. Maybe a habitual one, for all I know." Maybe she lied about lots of things.

But, even though she'd been caught red-handed in a whopper of a lie, his heart denied the thought of her being a liar.

"Think, Kyle. Why would she give you a false name?"

"Because she didn't want me to know she was the one who'd sent that ridiculous E-mail."

"Because. . ."

What was she getting at? "Because. . .I don't know, Mom. I still can't figure out why Dad lies, so how am I supposed to know why Shell—Chelsea does?"

"Honey, it's as plain as the nose on your face. She was embarrassed. I'll bet she regretted sending that E-mail."

"Then why didn't she say so?"

"Maybe she cared for you and was worried about what you would think of her."

His stomach clenched at the thought, but he brushed away the feelings. He'd thought Lori cared for him, too, and she'd only been after a wealthy husband. "Whose side are you on, anyway?" The gentleness in his voice belied the harshness of the words.

Silence echoed across the lines, and Kyle wondered if he'd spoken out of turn. He was about to apologize when his mother spoke again.

"I know it's hard having a father who, well, who doesn't keep his word. And then Lori came along and shattered what little trust you had in the human race. But think about it, Kyle. Lori lied because she was greedy. She wanted a man with money, and she was willing to do anything to get it. And your dad. He means well when he makes a promise. But then the time comes to fulfill it, and, well"—she sighed—"he'd rather be doing something else. I'm thankful he enjoys running the restaurant, but when it comes to his free time. . . . The truth is, I guess he cares more about himself and his own wants than anyone else's."

Kyle felt a stab of sympathy. He may have grown up with his dad, but his mother had to deal with it for the rest of her life.

"Everyone has faults," she continued, "and I'm not saying what Chelsea did was right. But I suspect she did it because she cares about you. Maybe she was afraid of losing you."

Kyle closed his eyes and rubbed his fingers over them. He didn't want to think about Chelsea's viewpoint. He didn't want to imagine that she might have a good excuse. And he was afraid to let himself believe she might care as much as he did.

"What did Chelsea say when you told her about the restaurant chain?"

A lump of guilt formed in Kyle's throat. After the fiasco with Lori, he'd held back that little piece of information. *So you weren't exactly honest with her, either, were you?*

"Kyle." Her voice sounded a warning. "Please tell me you didn't keep that from her."

He'd love to tell his mother that. Except it wasn't true.

Kyle didn't know what to say. He hadn't thought that withholding the information was wrong. He'd only done it because he was afraid. *Maybe Chelsea was afraid, too. Afraid of losing you.*

No, I won't let myself believe that. What she did was no better than what Lori did. She probably has a whole slew of selfish reasons for lying.

"I'm not going to say anything else, Kyle. You're a grown man. You can work this out yourself."

A light blinking on the phone indicated he had another call, so he eagerly ended his conversation with his mother. For the rest of the day Chelsea's image stayed in his mind like a backdrop in a play. How could she have lied to him when he'd come to care so deeply for her? *Let's face it, Man—"care deeply" doesn't begin to describe it. You love her.*

That only made her deception sting more and made ending the friendship harder. But he had to stay away from her. As much as his heart fought the notion, she was like his father. Like Lori. She probably hadn't given him another thought since Saturday night. She was no doubt too wrapped up in her own world.

All through the day, though, his mother's words rang in his mind. *Please tell me you didn't keep that from her. Maybe she was afraid of losing you.* A deep ache and even greater denial accompanied the thought. As much as his heart wanted it to be true, he wouldn't let himself believe it or even think it.

ঌ

Chelsea walked through the shopping plaza, her spirits as low as the pavement under her feet. She'd been searching for a cute T-shirt for Gram, but so far she'd found nothing outrageous enough for a feisty woman in her seventies.

Holiday music blared through the outdoor speakers and mingled with the wreaths and pine boughs gracing the storefronts.

But even the appearance of Saint Nick himself wouldn't

cure Chelsea's holiday blues. It had been five days since the party, and still she'd had no word from Kyle. If only she hadn't been so selfish. If only she hadn't been so impulsive. The "if onlys" were about to drive her crazy. She couldn't change the past. She'd wanted to call him so many times and explain. But what was there to explain? Her deceptive behavior only added to a long list of lies Kyle had endured from his father. He would never trust her again no matter what she said. She'd not only lied from the outset, but she'd made no effort to correct the deed in all the hours they'd spent together. If only he knew how much she cared. How much her heart ached at the thought of losing him. But words were cheap. And misleading, as they both knew only too well.

She glanced at the next shop, *Hook, Line, and Sinker*. No T-shirts in there, just fishing poles and such. She started to move on, but her steps faltered. Through the glass pane her gaze connected with something that stirred a fresh memory in her heart. *My words may not convince Kyle, but perhaps I can show him I love him.* Hope stirred in her heart even as excitement flowed through her veins. She had four days until Christmas. It was not much time, but it would have to be enough.

Chapter 8

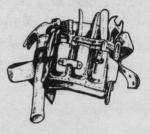

Kyle looked up from his stack of papers and stared at the bulletin board in front of him. Messages and appointments, sticky notes, and ad proofs stared back at him. The office was unnaturally quiet since the store was closed for the day. All his employees were at their homes, no doubt getting ready for Christmas Eve services and family get-togethers.

Just as you should be.

He looked at the wall clock and saw it was way past lunchtime. The thought of eating held little appeal. The thought of going home held little appeal. The fact was, nothing much held any appeal for him these days. The past week had been like going through withdrawal from Chelsea. He missed her. Missed the way she rattled on when she was nervous. Missed the way she talked to herself when she thought no one else was listening. Missed the way she—

Stop it, Morgan. This is not doing any good.

He glanced around at the neatly stacked files and papers.

And neither is staying here doing any good. Business was slow with the holidays in progress, and he was caught up on his work. Not a phone call to make or a job order to approve. "That's it. I'm going home."

He stood and grabbed his cap from the wall hook and left, locking the door behind him. The afternoon passed in a flash, as did the family Christmas dinner at his parents' house. They exchanged gifts and witty remarks, and his father read the story of Christ's birth to remind them of the real meaning of Christmas.

The night felt flat for Kyle, and all the festivities only made it seem more flat. *I'm sorry, Jesus. It's Your birthday, and I can't seem to think about anything but Chelsea.*

It was dark when he pulled into his driveway. He felt alone under the starry Christmas sky. When he stepped out of his truck, the strong fragrance of bougainvillea wafted by in the night air. He collected his bag of gifts and made his way up the sidewalk by starlight since he hadn't turned on the porch light before he left. He stepped up on the stoop and searched his key ring for the right key. Then his foot connected with something. Whatever the object was, it grated across the cement at contact.

Though darkness enshrouded the stoop, he knew nothing should be in front of the door. Curious, he unlocked the door and flipped on the porch light.

A wooden box sat at a cockeyed angle.

Kyle shuffled the bag of gifts in his arms and picked up the box. He lugged everything inside the house then set the bag on the floor of his ceramic foyer. Turning on the light, he carried the wooden box to the sofa and opened it.

He caught his breath. Fly-ties. Dozens of them. He glanced through the case, seeing yet another surface filled with fly-ties. Nymphs and woollybuggers, pheasant tails and hare's ears. Virtually every kind of fly-tie he'd ever used. But who—?

He'd just seen his father tonight, but his parents had already given him a gift. His dad was the only person he knew who made fly-ties—and these were obviously handmade. He looked at them closely. No, this was not his father's work. The knots were not as precise.

He closed the box and carefully turned it over, looking for some sign of who had given him the gift. There he saw a simple white gift tag taped to the bottom.

"Love, Chelsea."

He could feel his heart pounding in his chest. Chelsea had made all these for him?

His mind wandered back to the night he'd told her about the Christmas his father had promised him a case of fly-ties. It had been after the Cardinals' game, and he'd opened himself up to her, trusting her to understand.

He turned the box over again, opened it, and surveyed all the ties. There must be a hundred. He calculated the hours she'd spent making them.

She had understood. Understood the hurt of that Christmas so long ago. Understood the love that went into a gift like this.

He leaned back against the leather sofa, letting the case rest open on his lap. What does it mean that she'd spent all those hours making these?

She's trying to make up for the disappointment you felt all those years ago.

But why?

Because she loves you. The thought came unbidden and sent shivers of hope through him. He pulled the card off the bottom of the box. "Love, Chelsea." If the gift didn't say it, the card certainly implied it.

Maybe his mom had been right. Maybe Chelsea did love him. Yes, she'd lied to him, but perhaps she'd only been afraid of losing him. And he hadn't exactly been honest with her about his family's wealth.

"Love is patient, love is kind. It does not envy, it does not boast, it is not proud. It is not rude, it is not self-seeking, it is not easily angered, it keeps no record of wrongs."

Is this the kind of love he had for Chelsea? He'd been wronged, no doubt about that, but had he forgiven? No, he'd stewed and ignored her for over a week. *I'm sorry, God. I've been selfish and proud. That's not the kind of love we're to have for one another.*

He needed to talk to her. He wanted to tell her he was sorry. He wanted to thank her for the gift. He wanted to tell her—

His gaze fell on an object he'd left sitting on his bookshelf weeks ago. An idea formed in his mind, and excitement stirred his heart. It felt so right. So perfect. After he'd ignored Chelsea for so long, he only hoped she felt the same way.

🕊

Chelsea hugged her parents, wished them one last "Merry

Christmas," and turned to survey the mess. Melissa, Callie, and Mattie sat at the long table with Gram. They'd reserved the room at the Heavenly Retirement Village for their family Christmas dinner, though it was smaller and more intimate than the one they'd used for the big Christmas party. The fireplace, decorated tree, and dim lighting felt more like a big living room than a community room.

At the moment, though, the room looked more like the havoc at a paper factory than the scene of a family gathering.

She approached the table and noticed Gram held her hand to her temple.

"You, okay, Gram?"

"She has a headache," Melissa said, taking one last sip from her plastic cup as she rose.

Gram never had headaches, as far as Chelsea knew. Maybe this party had been too much for her. "Gram, why don't you go on back to your room? We'll clean up here."

"I think I might do that. Thanks, girls."

They hugged Gram and said good night; then Gram left the room.

"You know," Callie said, "I think I'll go with Gram. I'm sure she's fine and all, but just to be safe."

"Good idea," Mattie said.

Callie left to join her grandmother, and Mattie collected her things and started toward the door. "I hate to be a dud, guys, but I have to be at work early in the morning. See you." She waved her hand and was gone before either Chelsea or Melissa could say a word.

"Well," Chelsea said, "how do you like that?" She turned to see Melissa gathering her things.

"Uh, Chels. . ."

"Not you, too."

Melissa made a face and shrugged. "Sorry. I'm expected at a friend's house."

Chelsea looked at her watch. "At this hour?"

Melissa shrugged. "Sorry!" With a little wave she was out the door.

Chelsea surveyed the mess with dread. *Oh, well, it isn't as if I have anything better to do.*

She began tossing plastic cups and stray forks and spoons in the trash. She was glad the leftovers had already been wrapped and sent home with the families that had brought the food.

Once all the dinnerware was in the trash, she grabbed a new bag and started stuffing it with the discarded wrapping paper that littered the floor. As she worked, she thought back over the evening. It had been nice to have the family all together. She'd seen relatives she hadn't seen all year.

But nothing could squelch the sadness that hovered over her like a thunderstorm. She'd hoped to hear from Kyle after leaving her gift on his porch. Hoped to have an opportunity to apologize. Hoped to have another chance. But apparently it was too late.

All the hope she'd harbored as Melissa patiently taught her how to tie the flies crumbled at her feet. Nothing she could do would change what Kyle thought of her now. And how could she blame him?

Her eyes stung, and her throat tightened. She missed him so much. She'd give anything to go back and relive those early days.

She reached for a sheet of wrapping paper in front of the tree and crumbled it before stuffing it into the bag. Her fingertips still ached from all the winding and twisting and tying she'd done the past four days. She was about to reach for a scrap of paper when a tiny wrapped gift under the tree caught her eye. "Oh, no, we forgot one."

She knelt down and reached under the prickly branches for the gift. Its red foil paper glistened under the lights of the tree, and a white bow topped it. She turned it over, looking for a name.

"*Chelsea*."

It was hers, but who—?

She pushed the bag aside, sat back on her heels, then began unwrapping the gift. Who was it from, and how had they missed it earlier?

She tore away the paper to reveal a small box with a dark-green lid. Raising the lid, she found inside another small box, this one covered in deep-green velvet. Her heart caught as she took out the velvet box and opened it. Chelsea gasped. A diamond solitaire glittered against black satin. It was an old ring, with a silver band and intricate scrolling on both sides of the jewel. Who—Gram? Had she given Chelsea an old family heirloom?

A shuffling sound at the doorway drew her attention.

Kyle.

Her heart pounded in her chest. She was so hungry for the sight of him that she drank in his presence with her eyes. Was she only imagining him there, looking so handsome in a black turtleneck and slacks?

He moved toward her, his lips curving up on one side.

"Kyle." Did he hear the hunger in her voice?

As he drew near, she knew she should stand, but her legs wouldn't move. Like a marionette with broken strings, she sat helpless.

He knelt beside her. "I missed you," he said.

Remorse swelled in her. She was the one who'd ruined things between them. "Kyle, I—"

"Shh." He laid his fingers against her lips, and suddenly she couldn't think anymore.

"It doesn't matter." His voice was like warm honey.

"Yes, it does. I lied to you." She looked deep into his eyes. "I'm sorry, Kyle. So sorry. I was afraid you would—I was afraid I would lose you."

He smiled. "I understand. We all make mistakes. I wasn't completely honest with you, either."

She let her gaze rove over his face, enthralled by his warm eyes, his soft hair, his sweet lips.

"Oh, about that." He pointed to the velvet box that lay open and forgotten in her hands.

She looked at the diamond then back at him. It was from Kyle? Her heart pounded even faster.

"It was my grandmother's." He cradled her face in the palm of his hand. His eyes caressed her lovingly. "I love you, Chelsea. I want to spend every single day of my life with you. I want to curl up in bed beside you every night and wake up to your beautiful face every morning."

Her eyes stung anew, and love for him welled up inside her until she thought she'd burst.

Kyle's gaze burned into hers. "Will you marry me?"

Joy surged through her. All she could do was nod and whisper, "Yes." She could hardly believe it. He'd forgiven her. He wanted to marry her.

Kyle's lips touched hers in a gentle kiss.

"I love you," she said.

He kissed her again, starting a riot inside her. A moment later he moved away and gazed deep into her eyes.

Then Kyle pulled the ring from its nest in the box and slid it on her finger.

"It fits." She smiled.

"I knew it would." He kissed her hand, his eyes sparkling.

"Thank you. It's the best Christmas present I ever received."

"Funny you should say that. I found a box filled with homemade fly-ties on my stoop. Would you know anything about that?"

She fluttered her lashes. "Who, me?"

He gave her a wry look.

She leaned close and kissed him lightly on the lips. Chelsea could hardly believe this was happening. Then she remembered his earlier words and pulled back. "Kyle, what did you mean before, when you said you hadn't been completely honest with me?"

His countenance dropped and with it her spirits. She waited, afraid that what he said would change everything.

"Remember I told you about Lori?"

She nodded, remembering that his ex-fiancée had broken his heart, though he'd never said how. Was this something about Lori? What if he said he'd never be able to forget her?

"The reason I broke it off with Lori was—well, she never loved me. She wanted something I could give her. And I didn't tell you what that was because I was afraid you'd want it too."

Wanted something. . .afraid I'd want it to? "Kyle, what are you talking about?"

"Money, Chelsea. My family owns Family Fixin's."

His family owned some restaurants. So what did that have to do with her? "Kyle, what—?"

"They're rich, Chelsea. My parents are very wealthy."

"I'm happy for them, Kyle. But what does that have to do with us? I don't get it."

He chuckled. "I love you for that, Sweetheart. I guess Lori thought if she could marry me, she'd eventually get her share."

"And you were afraid I might be a golddigger too?"

He had the sense to look contrite. "Sorry."

She frowned and shook her head. Of all the silly— Then she remembered all the mistakes she'd made in their short relationship. Hadn't she blown it too? "Oh, well. Given the things I've done, I guess I'll have to cut you a little slack."

"Thank you." His lips twitched, and his eyes twinkled mischievously. "I'm glad you didn't take the bait."

She narrowed her gaze. "Oh, that's awful." She shook her head and laughed. It looked as if Gram's matchmaking had worked. "I wonder what Gram will say."

Kyle pulled her onto his lap and brushed her lips with a kiss. "Oh, I know what she'll say."

She pulled back. "What?"

He opened his eyes wide, and his tone became serious. "She'll say you caught yourself a big one."

She swatted his arm then laughed. "You're bad, Kyle Morgan."

He wiggled his eyebrows. "You don't know the half of it," he said and kissed her again.

DENISE HUNTER

Denise lives in Indiana with her husband and three active, young sons. As the only female of the household, every day is a new adventure, but Denise holds on to the belief that her most important responsibility in this life is to raise her children in such a way that they will love and fear the Lord. The message Denise wants her writing to convey is that "God needs to be the center of our lives. If He isn't, everything else is out of kilter."

A Match Made in Heaven

by Colleen Coble

Chapter 1

I'll have my wife with me. She's wanting to see something of the town before we move." Warren Miller's voice was clipped as he obviously brought the call to a close. "She was hoping your wife could give her some pointers on where to shop in Heaven."

"I'm not married," Nick Darling said. And not in any hurry to be, he added silently. Not after Michelle. He winced and waited for what he knew was coming.

"Well, bring a date then. Barbara is eager to know more about the town. See you tonight at seven."

The phone clicked, and Nick sat with the dial tone ringing in his ears. Hanging up the phone, he swivelled in his chair and stared out the window. Bougainvillea bloomed in massive banks of hot pink and red, and saguaro cacti raised thick arms against the brilliant blue sky. Another day in paradise.

As far as Nick was concerned, Heaven, Arizona, lived up to its name. In this friendly little town it was hard to believe the hustle and bustle of Phoenix was less than an hour away.

Heaven had a lot going for it: friendly people, a strong sense of community, affordable housing. But not many single women. He pursed his lips and thought about his dilemma.

There were women back in Phoenix he could call, business associates mostly. But this was late notice for most of the women he knew, and most women wouldn't relish the drive. This contract was too important to risk losing. He strummed his fingers on the desk, scattered with papers and candy bar wrappers. A sweet little old lady had sat with him the last two Sundays at church. Maybe she would have an idea of whom he could invite. What was her name? Oh, yes, Lucille Stoddard.

He grabbed the phone book and flipped through the pages. Ah, there she was. Quickly dialing the number, he prayed she would have an idea.

"Hello." Mrs. Stoddard's voice was strong and confident. She sounded more like someone in her thirties than the seventy-something she looked.

"Hi, Mrs. Stoddard, this is Nick Darling." Would she remember his name? "From church," he added hastily.

Mrs. Stoddard seemed to be as alert as her voice, for she didn't hesitate. "Nick dear, how lovely to hear from you! Are you settling into our little community all right? And call me Lucille, dear boy. We don't stand on formality here in Heaven."

It felt strange to call an older lady by her first name, but Nick made an attempt. "Ah, Lucille, I have a favor."

"I told you to call me if you needed anything. What can I do for you?"

"A client is coming into town with his wife, and I need a female companion to help entertain her."

"And you thought of me? Surely you can find someone your own age." Her voice took on a teasing quality. "I'm only joking, Nicky—don't panic. As luck would have it, I have three unattached granddaughters. Let me think—which one would be right for you?"

"I'm not interested in a relationship," he hastened to add. Maybe this hadn't been such a good idea. The last thing he wanted was someone meddling with his love life. He could manage to mess it up without any help.

"I would treat her to a fancy dinner as thanks for entertaining the client's wife, of course," he added.

Lucille seemed not to hear his protests, and she swept on with her plans. "You're an architect, aren't you, Nicky?"

He hated to be called Nicky, but how did you tell a sweet, grandmotherly type that? He swallowed. "Yes."

"My granddaughter Callie is just whom you need to meet. She's an interior designer, very successful. You two will make a darling couple." She laughed, a soft tinkle that raised Nick's alarm. "A darling, Darling couple, just as your name says."

He gritted his teeth. She was only trying to help. "It's just one date," he reminded her. And an interior designer was the last type of woman he would be interested in. If he ever married, he wanted the old-fashioned kind of woman who stayed home and raised the kids, not a businesswoman. Someone as different from Michelle as desert from ocean.

She breezed past his caution again. "I'll call Callie and

arrange it. What time?"

"We have reservations at seven at Pedro's. It's that Mexican restaurant on Thunderbird."

"I know it well, Nicky. Callie lives at 122 Cholla Lane. You need to pick her up around six-thirty to get there in time. Do you know where that is?"

He assured her he could find the house and hung up with a sense of relief. He just hoped she didn't raise her grand-daughter's hopes that something would come of the date. He was much too busy to pursue anyone, even if he was so inclined, which he wasn't. He wondered idly what this Callie was like. Of course the fact that she was available at a moment's notice to go out with a man she'd never met said it all.

※

Callie Stevens turned the lamp over in her hands and consid-ered it. The base was made from a worn cowboy boot and the lampshade from an authentic cowboy hat. The Driscolls would love it. Now if she could find a table to set it on. Maybe one of those made out of peeled logs. Though the Driscolls were from Boston, they were wild about the cowboy stuff. It was her job to incorporate it seamlessly into their five-thousand-square-foot home, but she thrived on the challenge.

The cell phone in her purse trilled, and she balanced the lamp against her hip while she dug in her purse for the phone. She managed to answer it on the fifth ring. "Design Solutions, this is Callie."

"Callie, you're free tonight, aren't you?" Her grandmother's voice was excited.

"Hi, Gram. Um, I guess." Her heart sank at the thought of giving up her quiet evening. After the flurry of New York for the past two weeks, she'd been looking forward to plopping down in front of the TV and vegging out. But it was hard to deny her grandmother. Guilt rippled through her. She should have made plans to see Gram tonight without being prodded. It had been two weeks since she'd stopped by.

"Got something tasty cooking for supper?" she asked, forcing a jovial tone into her voice.

"Nick Darling is a new architect in town. He's been sitting with me in church the past two weeks and joined the church while you were in New York. He just called, and he needs a date to help him entertain some important new clients. I told him you'd be happy to help him out." She gave a soft chuckle. "I knew you wouldn't have any other plans for tonight. You never do." Her voice held more than a trace of reproach.

Callie gritted her teeth. "Gram, I've told you I don't want you to do any more matchmaking for me, and I know Melissa and Mattie feel the same way."

Her grandmother barreled over her objections like a four-wheeler over a mud track. "I gave him your address. He's picking you up at six-thirty. Why don't you wear that soft green dress that swirls so becomingly around your legs? It looks lovely with your auburn hair."

"Gram, I am not going! I just got back from New York. An evening with strangers is not at all what I want to do with my first evening at home."

"Well, now, Callie, I don't know how to reach him. I don't

have the foggiest idea what his business is called. If you don't go, I'll have to, and my eyes aren't what they used to be for night driving."

Callie let out an exasperated sigh at the plaintive tone in her grandmother's voice. She'd been boxed into a corner, and they both knew it. "All right, Gram, but I'm giving you fair warning. Do *not* arrange any more blind dates for me. Your success with Chelsea was a fluke, and I don't want you thinking you can meddle like this all the time. I can find my own dates."

Gram snorted. "When was the last time you went out on a date, Callie? In my day we called a girl your age who was still single an old maid."

"Is that so bad?" Callie shot back. "I'm perfectly happy by myself. I have Ty, my job, my friends. A man would get in the way."

"You don't feel that way, and you know it. A dog is no substitute for a husband, a companion who shares your life." Gram's voice was firm. "And I know how you love children. You're not the tough businesswoman you seem on the outside."

Callie tried to ignore the voice inside that said her grandmother was right, but it got harder all the time. "Men take one look at me and hightail it away," she said. "It's better not to get my hopes up."

Her grandmother's voice softened. "Callie, you know I love you, so I'm saying this for your own good. You seem to do everything in your power to make yourself unappealing. You dress in those severe suits and draw your hair back in a tight way that's so unbecoming. When you talk to a man, you're all business. You need to let down that guard around your heart."

"I don't want to be hurt, Gram." Callie's eyes stung, and she blinked the tears away furiously. She didn't want to be unlovable, but she had no idea how to go about changing herself. Her grandmother was right—she longed for a family of her own. The catch was that she was never going to have it, so she kept burying those dreams under her business goals.

Unfortunately they resurrected at the least invitation.

She swallowed the congealing lump in her throat. "I'll meet this guy, but don't expect a miracle. Can you still love me if I never get married?"

"Oh, Darling. You know I love you. I just want you to be happy."

"I'm fine as I am, Gram. The other girls can have the babies. I'll make a good babysitter."

"I haven't given up hope for you, Callie. I pray every day for God to send the right man your way. I know He's going to do that. Call me when you get home and let me know how it went. Some friends are coming to look at the new quartz I found while out hiking the other day, so I'll be here."

Callie promised to call then clicked off the phone. She set the lamp down and rubbed her head. A throb was beginning to build behind her eyes. She did better when she focused on her career and turned a blind eye to her private life. Gram's meddling had stirred up her discontent again.

She didn't know this Nick Darling, but she already didn't like him. Architects were usually stuffy, precise men who thought their ideas were the only ones that mattered. And he'd taken advantage of her grandma's good intentions to intrude on Callie's life. He was probably a self-centered jerk. But it was only one evening. She could do that much for her grandmother.

She stared at the lamp in distaste. Her shopping was finished for the day. She could no more concentrate on picking out a table than she could shrink her six-foot frame down to five feet six inches. Digging out her platinum Visa card, she paid for the lamp then hurried out to her car. She stopped dead in the parking lot. Where had she parked? The rows of parked cars all looked alike, and she saw no sign of her red Chrysler minivan.

The Arizona sun beat down on her head, but she barely noticed. Why was it so hard to remember where she parked? She was twenty-eight years old, but the simple task of remembering where she parked had eluded her ever since she'd started driving. She bit her lip and castigated herself for being so bubble-headed.

There was no choice but to stroll up and down the rows in the hot sun. Sighing, she tucked the lamp under her arm and trudged down the first row. Her car wasn't in that row or the next. She went around a white Jeep and barreled into a hard chest.

Strong fingers gripped her forearms. "Ouch! You stepped on my foot," a deep voice exclaimed.

Callie looked up into eyes as blue as the Arizona sky and just as piercing. The man's head towered over hers. Those arresting eyes gazed out of a face that was too craggy to be handsome, but too strong to be forgotten. He wore a cowboy hat and jeans that looked as if they'd been made for him. The cowboy boots he wore looked as battered as the one that had been used to create the lamp in her hands.

"Excuse me," she said. "I didn't see you." Men like this one made her nervous. She knew better than to allow herself to be attracted to someone like this guy. The handsome ones always went for the petite cheerleader, not an Amazon like her.

"That was obvious." He frowned down at her. "I saw you two rows over when I was parking. You lost?"

Her face burned, but not from the sun. "I can't find my car," she mumbled.

"What was that?" His firm lips twitched.

She could tell from the amusement on his face that he'd heard her the first time. "I said I can't find my car," she snapped.

"Ah. What's it look like?" His gaze never left her face.

"I don't need your help," she said with exasperation. "It's here somewhere, and I can find it by myself." She didn't need the Lone Ranger's help to find her car.

"I can see that." His lips twitched again, and he plucked the lamp from her hands. "Let's try over here." Before she could protest any further, he led the way down the next row of cars.

Just past a big dually truck she saw the sunflower she'd put on her radio antenna. "There it is! That big truck was hiding it."

He eyed the flower on her car with obvious amusement. "You don't look like a flower child. Too starchy and proper."

She snatched the lamp from his hands. "I didn't ask for an opinion on my appearance." Fishing the remote out of her blazer pocket, she pushed the button to unlock the doors. She stashed the lamp in the back then went to the driver's door.

"You're welcome," he called as she slid into the seat, started the van, and backed out of the parking space.

"I could have found it by myself," she muttered as she pulled away with a screech of her tires. And her grandmother wanted to hook her up with a species like that. She hoped this Nick Darling wasn't so crude and obnoxious. He probably wouldn't be as cute either. She made a face at herself in the rearview mirror. Not that she was interested in the neanderthal type anyway.

She parked in the garage and went inside. Ty, her border collie, greeted her at the door. She took him for a walk then rushed back home to shower and get ready for the evening. As the water coursed through her hair, she considered what she should wear. She didn't want to send the wrong message to this guy. The last thing she wanted was for him to think she was a spinster out to attract any eligible man. A suit would be a good choice, but she rebelled at the idea after what her grandmother had said. Surely she could find something in between making a fool of herself and looking as attractive as possible.

She pulled on a robe and dried her hair. Scrunching up her face in the mirror, she rolled her dark red hair in its usual French twist. She turned her face to the side and considered it. High cheekbones, dark brown eyes, nothing that seemed so very different from any other woman. What was it about her that drove the men off? Just her height? Or maybe Gram was right, and her attire sent out the wrong signal. But she was comfortable in her business attire. She felt more in charge and focused when she wore a suit.

She went to her closet and riffled through her clothes. Nothing seemed right. The green dress Gram had mentioned was too pretty to waste on a guy she never intended to see again. Her black suit was too severe for a dinner date. Her hand hovered over an orangish-red silk pantsuit. It was too dressy, but it made her feel almost as confident as a suit but had feminine detailing. With determination she yanked it off the hanger and slipped it on. A touch of makeup, and Callie thought she looked presentable. She slipped her feet into matching pumps and went to the living room.

An overstuffed sofa in soft yellow and blue flowered chintz made for lounging was splashed with yellow pillows. A brightly patterned rug in blues and yellows covered most of the nondescript tile in the living room. Coordinating chairs juxtaposed against the other wall added balance. She'd colorwashed the walls in three tones of yellow, and the color filled the room with warmth. Too bad she spent so little time here.

Her home was the antithesis of the Callie Stevens most people thought they knew. Where she was formal and reserved, her house radiated warmth and relaxation. It was a place that invited her to kick off her shoes and eat pizza straight from the delivery box. And that was precisely the effect she had designed for it because that was the real Callie. Would her life be any different if she allowed more people to see that side of her?

The phone rang, and Callie picked it up. She wished

briefly it would be Mr. Darling calling to say she needn't bother. But it was her cousin Chelsea's voice on the other end.

"I just put some chicken enchiladas in the oven. Want to come over for a pool party? Our new pool is crying out for us to jump in," Chelsea asked.

"I wish I could. Gram's on her matchmaking kick again."

Chelsea laughed. "Kyle, Gram has turned her sights on Callie," she called to her husband of two months.

A click sounded in Callie's ear as Kyle picked up the other phone. "Don't knock it, Cal. Your grandma knows what she's doing. Chelsea and I are living proof."

Callie groaned. "Don't you two start. I want to be left alone to live my life the way I want it. I don't need Gram setting me up with some stranger. And this guy's an *architect*."

"You work with architects all the time," Chelsea said. "What's wrong with dating one?"

"He'll be self-opinionated and want to talk about buildings and codes all through dinner. Pray for me—it's going to be a long, boring evening."

"Give him a chance," Kyle urged. "Look what happened with us. You never know."

"I know—believe me," Callie said. "I know that no architect is ever going to appeal to me. Besides, there's news you don't know."

"Oh?" Chelsea's voice was breathless with anticipation.

"I'm thinking of moving to New York. I even found a building to put my business in." The silence on the other end of the phone was heavy with disapproval. "It makes sense,

Chelsea. The good fabrics and designers are out East. It's just a matter of time. Besides, there's nothing to hold me here."

"Only because you won't open yourself up to other people," Chelsea said. "Someone's going to knock down that wall you've erected in a big way. All men aren't like Bart. You can't live your life in fear that a man is only interested in your money."

"Sure I can. It's the truth. Look—just pray for me tonight. I don't want Gram's friend telling her I was unfriendly. I'll get through it somehow."

"We'll pray, but promise me you'll give him a chance," Chelsea said.

"All right, but don't hold your breath." The doorbell rang, and her heart sped up. "He's here. I gotta go. Don't forget to pray for me."

She hung up the phone and smoothed the silk over her thighs as she went to the door. When was the last time she'd gone out with anyone? Two years ago, she decided. That's why she was so nervous.

It had been a fiasco too. Bart Wilson, a lawyer who specialized in accidents, had been just as smarmy as the TV ads she'd seen for personal injury suits. This guy was probably going to be worse. She sighed and opened the door.

Chapter 2

Nick drummed his fingers on the doorjamb. He sighed and turned his wrist over to look at his watch. "Come on—come on," he muttered. He should have arrived fifteen minutes ago; but his younger sister, Erin, had called, and he'd talked longer than he realized.

The door opened, and he found himself staring into the eyes of the woman he'd helped in the parking lot. She looked good, he realized. The orangish-red pantsuit she wore made her look even taller and slimmer than she had in the suit she'd been wearing earlier. He didn't normally go for tall women, but she literally glowed with color from the top of her auburn hair to the golden hue of her skin. Her hair was still up off her neck, but the severe style failed to hide the striking color. Its hue reminded him of autumn leaves, red and gold all mixed together. He pulled himself together and realized suspicion radiated from her dark eyes.

"Did you follow me home?" she demanded.

He lifted one eyebrow. "Why would I do that? Your

grandmother gave me your address. You're Callie, aren't you? Callie Stevens?"

Callie groaned and slapped a hand to her forehead. "You must be Nick Darling. My date." She said the last word as though it were an unpleasant mess left by the border collie he saw at her feet.

"That would be me," he said. He leaned down and patted the dog. The animal practically smiled at the attention. "We should be going. I don't want to keep my clients waiting."

Callie sighed. "I'll get my purse. "

She turned to grab her purse, and Nick glanced inside the house. A country French decor, it almost made him wish this was a real date and he'd get a chance to lounge on that comfy sofa while they ate popcorn and watched a movie. Almost.

Callie joined him on the front stoop. "Where are we going?"

"Pedro's. It has the best Mexican food I've ever eaten. You like Mexican, I hope?" Somehow she looked more the type to enjoy French food with a maitre d' hovering over her shoulder.

"I love it," Callie said. "Pedro's has the best chili relleno I've ever eaten."

Okay, so he was wrong. He slid his palm under her elbow and escorted her to his vehicle, a Dodge Ram pickup 4 x 4. He opened the door, and she eyed the running board then clambered onto the seat. At least she didn't complain like his sister.

He shut the door once she was seated then strode around to his own side and climbed in. When he started the truck and pulled into the street, he became conscious of her stare. "What?" he asked.

"You don't look like an architect," she said. A blush touched her cheeks, and she looked away.

"Well, you look every inch a designer, right down to the perfectly matched shoes and purse," he said. "What's an architect look like? I thought we were all different breeds."

"For one thing, you're too—too *cowboy* to be an architect," she said.

The way she said it made Nick think of pickles, and he hid a grin. He liked a challenge, and this woman revved up his adrenaline like facing an opponent at the Cowboy Action Shoot. What would she think if he asked her to come along on the next shoot? He glanced at her from the corner of his eye.

"This *is* Arizona," he reminded her. "It's allowed out here. Besides, you have something against cowboys?"

"Of course not." The starch crept back into her voice, and the color on her cheeks heightened. "I'm surprised you get much business if you go to meetings in that getup."

"This *getup*, as you call it, is comfortable. I have all the business I can handle. People hire me for my expertise, not my attire."

"I'm sure," she said, but her tone dripped with irony.

Nick lost the battle to contain his amusement and let loose with a rumbling laugh. "Are you trying to make me mad so you don't have to come?" He grinned at the pink in her cheeks. "Too late. You're stuck with me just as I'm stuck with you. I'm not sure what your grandma was thinking to pair us up, but at least we won't be bored."

He didn't give Callie a chance to answer but stomped his

foot to the accelerator and gunned the truck down the street. She thought she was out with a cowboy, so he wouldn't disappoint her. He reached over and punched the button on the sterco to turn on the CD player. Marty Robbins's voice blared out, and Nick chimed in and sang "El Paso" along with the CD. The music reverberated through the truck cab.

He glanced over at Callie. Her color was high, and she was staring straight ahead. Then her lips twitched, and a dimple appeared in her cheek. He was sure it was against her will, but her left foot began to tap in time to the thump of the music.

She caught his gaze, and the wattage of her smile turned on full force. He nearly rocked back in the seat with the power of it. No wonder she was so successful in her business. All she had to do was smile and a man would do anything for her. Wonder why she wasn't married? She was a real looker with that wonderful hair and contrasting eyes. The way she carried herself impressed him. Most tall women slouched, but Callie walked with her head held high as if daring life to try to keep her down.

"Now *you're* staring," she shouted over the sound of the music. "Hadn't you better keep your eyes on the road?"

Nick came out of his trance to the blaring of a horn, and he jerked the wheel and guided the truck back into his own lane. "Sorry," he yelled.

Callie reached over and turned the music down a notch. "You've successfully put me in my place, so let's have a little peace."

He grinned. "I don't think I've met anyone like you, Callie

Stevens. Maybe your grandma was right after all."

Her dark eyes widened, and her jaw dropped. She recovered quickly and looked away. "Don't get any ideas, Mr. Darling. Gram doesn't know it, but I'm moving to New York. The last thing I'm looking for is a reason to stay here. For my business to grow, I need to be where the action is. And that's New York."

Nick was surprised at the disappointment that tightened his stomach. He inclined his head and kept his voice calm. "Well, we can at least be friends while you're here. Call me Nick. If I ever hear the word darling out of you, I'd rather it be in another tone of voice."

Callie surprised him with laughter. "Don't hold your breath, Nick. But we can be friends, I guess. Only don't expect anything more from me."

The disappointment deepened, but Nick nodded. It was just as well. He was too busy to go chasing after a woman, even one as intriguing as Callie Stevens.

❧

Cars and trucks filled Pedro's parking lot. Callie pointed out a space, and Nick swung the big truck around and slipped it into the space with the practiced ease of a man who had driven a vehicle this size all his life. Callie couldn't deny he was a very attractive man. The sheer presence of his size and masculinity nearly filled the truck cab, and she squeezed against her door to avoid contact with him. She wasn't used to an overpowering attraction like this, and she wasn't sure she liked it.

When she'd opened the door and found him standing

there, her first instinct had been to slam it shut. Her heart still burned with humiliation when she thought about his escorting her around the parking lot to find her car. But she'd learned to carry herself with dignity in the face of embarrassment and had met his gaze squarely. She'd seen the startled look on his face, though. He was probably regretting he'd ever asked Gram to find him a date.

She prided herself on her ability to think with her head and not her heart, but Nick sorely tried that ability. The less time spent in his company the better, although she couldn't help but wonder if he had been serious about wanting to be friends. She couldn't imagine ever being friends with him. Her attraction to him made her too uncomfortable.

What's more, she didn't understand it. That cowboy persona didn't normally appeal to her. She was more used to men who had an edge of sophistication about them. Maybe she was tired. The trip to New York had taken a lot out of her.

Lord, help me fight this. Her life had been fine up till now, and she didn't want some unreturned infatuation to derail her plans. She took a couple of deep, calming breaths and felt better. She was just hungry. She hadn't eaten since breakfast, and the flutters in her stomach were likely due to that. Once she ate a few tortilla chips with salsa, she'd be her old self.

She pushed her troubled thoughts away as Nick came around to open the door for her. She grabbed her purse and took his hand. A tingle shot up her arm, and she felt breathless. She pulled away from him as soon as her feet were on the pavement. Trotting a step ahead of him, she hurried toward the safety of the restaurant. She wanted to be with other people and get her emotional feet back on the bedrock of her common sense.

"Whoa, what's the hurry?" Nick demanded.

The click of his boots as he rushed to catch her added to Callie's haste. The sooner she escaped from this evening, the happier she would be. She forced herself to slow down.

"Sorry," she said. "I wanted to get out of this heat."

"Yeah, it's hot. But you're a born and bred Arizonian. It shouldn't bother you. You feeling okay? You look a little flushed," he said.

"I'm fine," she said curtly.

"Oh, there they are," he said, his attention snagged by a couple at a table in the corner. He threaded his way through the tables and people.

Pasting a smile on her face, Callie followed him.

Nick held out her chair, and she slid into it. He dropped into the seat beside her. "Sorry we're a bit late," he said. "I'd like you to meet Callie Stevens. Callie, this is Warren Miller and his wife, Barbara."

Callie shook hands with them across the table. "Have you been in the Valley of the Sun long?"

"Two months," Barbara said. "Is it always this hot?" She was in her fifties, and her ample figure strained the buttons of the plum suit she wore. She looked out of place among the rest of the restaurant's patrons who were dressed casually.

Her husband was equally overdressed in a severe black suit and tie. His florid face glistened with perspiration, and his balding head sported a vicious sunburn.

"If you think this is hot, wait until July," Nick said. "It's actually pretty pleasant in April. Today it was only ninety-seven."

"Ninety-seven!" Barbara shook her head. "I'm beginning to think Warren made a mistake accepting this job." Her voice was timid.

"You'll acclimate," Callie said reassuringly. "By this time next year you'll be wearing a winter coat in fifty-degree temperatures and complaining."

"I hope so." Barbara picked up the menu as the men launched into a conversation of their own. "Everything is so new and different here. Even the food. We usually eat at the Brazilian restaurant when we go out. We're overdressed, I see." She sounded near tears.

Callie leaned over and squeezed her hand. "You look lovely. I've been looking for a suit that color."

Barbara looked down with a woebegone expression. "I've gained weight since I bought it," she said. "I feel so out of place and friendless here."

Pity stirred in Callie's heart. She knew what it was like to feel like an outsider. She'd felt that way herself all through high school. She'd been taller than all the boys in her class until she was a sophomore, and she'd never managed to fit in with the girls. They were more interested in dating, and she had wanted to study.

"Would you like to come to church with me on Sunday? Have you found a place to worship?" she asked.

Barbara brightened. "We used to attend a prominent church in New York. All the best people went there. Maybe that would be a good way to meet others in our social standing."

Callie stared. This woman had no clue as to what church was all about. She'd been asking the Lord to send some people her way that she could witness to. Maybe this was His answer. She felt a sense of shame that she hadn't been looking for someone to help, and instead God had had to force her into a situation where she saw the need.

"Our church isn't huge or prominent, but we love the Lord," she said gently as the men's conversation hit a lull. "I'd love for you to come."

"I attend there as well," Nick added.

"Oh, is that how you met? You make such a darling couple," Barbara said. She giggled. "A Darling couple, get it?"

"I get it," Nick said. His tone was resigned, and Callie figured he'd heard that line before.

"We'd love to attend," Warren said.

"Worship is at ten-thirty," Nick said. "Want me to pick you up?"

"No, no, that's fine. We'll meet you there." Warren took out a pen, and Nick wrote down the directions for him.

Over dinner Callie found herself watching Nick from the corner of her eye. His cowboy hat stayed squarely on his head, and she wondered what he looked like without it. Maybe he was balding early, and that's why he wore it. But she discarded the notion when he pushed it to the back of his head, and she spied thick, black curls under it.

It was silly to speculate about him. She would keep her distance, here and at church, and go on with her life. This was one night, nothing more.

Callie listened as Barbara told her all about the Warren children, their yacht and mountain home in Colorado, and all other manner of minutiae. Barbara had yet to ask one question about Callie. It was no wonder Barbara hadn't made any friends yet.

"I need an interior designer," Barbara announced over coffee.

"Callie is an interior designer," Nick said. "She's one of the best in the country. Her houses have been written up in every magazine in the industry."

Barbara's blue eyes widened. "I thought your name sounded familiar! Now I remember—you were the one who was interviewed in *Designer's Showcase*. I saved the article and told Warren I wished I could hire you," she said. "Why didn't you say something sooner? You would be perfect! When can you start?"

"Hold on. Your house is still in the planning stages," Nick said. "This is a little premature. And I'm sure Callie has a full slate already."

"Actually I like to get in on this stage," Callie said. "I can suggest architectural elements that add more impact to my design for the interior."

He frowned. "I don't think so," Nick said. "I like to get input from the clients alone when I'm designing a house. You get too many ideas floating around, and you get no clear, cohesive plan."

"Oh, but I think it's a wonderful idea!" Barbara cried. "Do you have time to take us on?" she asked eagerly.

Though she was aware of Nick's glower, Callie nodded. She wasn't about to turn down a chance to do a house of this magnitude. It would add more kudos to her career and help her get established in New York. If she did a good job, the Millers would recommend her to their friends back East.

Excitement tingled along her stomach like a row of ants heading for the sugar bowl. "I'd love to decorate your home," she said. "I'll need to sit down with you and get an idea of what you'd like, what style you're comfortable with."

Barbara waved a hand. "I really don't care as long as everyone gasps when they see it," she said. "I want to bring a bit of city elegance to Heaven. It could certainly use it. I want it to stand out and be the talk of the valley."

That would suit Callie as well. "I have *carte blanche?*" she asked.

"Absolutely." Barbara turned to Nick. "She's in charge, Nicky. You do whatever she wants."

She could sense the tension in Nick, and she was sorry their earlier good relations had given way to this. But this was the chance of a lifetime, and she wasn't about to let Nick Darling spoil it. Her head buzzed with ideas, and her fingers itched for her pencil and drawing pad. It was all she could do to maintain civilized conversation during the rest of the evening.

They said good-bye to the Millers in the parking lot and promised to meet them at the front door to the church Sunday morning. As soon as the older couple had hurried away, Nick gripped Callie's elbow and propelled her toward the truck.

When they were both in the cab and out of range of others' hearing, he turned to her. His gaze was angry and uncompromising. "Let's get one thing straight. I am in charge of this project. I am the architect, and I will decide the final design. *You* work around the architectural design. I don't work around the interior design."

Callie hadn't wanted to offend him, but his high-handed manner infuriated her. "You heard Barbara," she said sweetly. "I'm in charge."

Nick gritted his teeth. "I think not," he said quietly. "When you think about it, you'll see this is the only way that makes sense."

In fact, that was the one thing Callie had never understood. If a person wanted a certain style and design, it needed to be planned into the house's architectural style right from the start. "I'm determined to make this house the pinnacle of my work," she said. "I think we can work together, Nick, but you've got to bend and listen to me. Don't make any hard and fast decisions on the architectural style until I have a chance to talk more with Barbara and decide what I want."

He jerked the truck into gear. She could hear him muttering under his breath, but she couldn't make out any words, though his anger was obvious. She was genuinely sorry for that, but at the same time she was filled with excitement over her big break.

"If you get too out of line, they can find another architect," Nick said through tight lips. "I told you—I work alone. I'm willing to listen to your ideas, but I make the final decision or I'm out of there."

Callie shook her head. "I can't give up final say," she said. "My design may stand or fall on some architectural details I need incorporated into the plan."

Nick's knuckles were white where he gripped the steering wheel. "This is my project, Callie. You were merely a guest tonight. Don't abuse that."

Guilt shuddered through Callie. He was right. "Okay, let's just table who is in charge and call it a joint effort. If we run into a disagreement, we can hash it out then. Let's not borrow trouble. There may be no areas of disagreement we can't live with."

Nick nodded grudgingly. "Deal."

Chapter 3

Nick bent over his drawing table and rubbed his blurry eyes. He'd been up most of the night going over his plan for the Miller home. Barbara had said she wanted something diffcrent, so he'd designed a nearly circular home with wide, curving windows to take advantage of the desert mountain views. The exterior would be concrete instead of the pale stucco usually seen in Arizona, and the roof would be concrete tile as well. It would blend into the mountainside lot as part of the landscape.

If Callie wanted him to change anything, he didn't know what he would do. Part of him wanted to chuck the project and move on to something else, but this plan was the culmination of a lifetime of work and experience. He'd worked hard and long on this design. He sighed and pressed his fingers against his throbbing eyes.

Taking her along last night had been a mistake. But who would have thought she would worm her way into Barbara's good graces and try to ruin his project? And the worst thing was that he had been so drawn to her. Well, that was over. It was just more proof that most women were greedy and grasping. Michelle had left him for someone with more money. Callie was more of the same type of woman. It was a shame when she'd been so likeable and honest at first.

The phone rang, and he stared at it in distaste. He sighed and ran a hand through his hair then reached over and grabbed it. "Nick Darling."

"I hope I'm not calling too early." Callie's crisp, businesslike voice carried clearly through the receiver. "I've been up all night working on ideas for the Miller home."

She didn't sound as if she'd been up all night. She sounded bright, alert, and way too enthusiastic.

"I'm up. I was working all night too. I had a catnap from about five to six but got back up and hit it again. The design is done." Maybe she would take a hint that he didn't want her messing with a completed project.

"We'll see. I have very good ideas that might call for some changes," she said. "Of course I'll need to talk with Barbara more and get to know her likes and dislikes before I call it finished. When may I come and see your plans?"

Nick pressed his lips together. She was going to be a pest, and he couldn't do much about it. "Obviously I'm at the office. Come on over if you like."

"I'll be there in fifteen minutes."

The phone clicked in his ear, and he hung it up slowly. Maybe her plans would fit with his as seamlessly as a plug into a light socket. He could only hope and pray that was the case.

He pushed the spread-out papers away and went to the coffeepot. He would need all the caffeine he could get to make it through the day. His eyes burned, and the thought of bed was inviting. The last thing he needed this morning was a run-in with Callie.

By the time the coffee aroma filled his office, he heard a light tap on the office door. He tucked his shirt back into the waistband of his jeans and went to the door. When the door swung open, he wanted to shut it again.

Callie looked as fresh and alert as if she'd slept twelve hours last night. Her brown eyes were alight with enthusiasm. She'd changed into crisp cotton slacks with a gold top that matched the golden glints in her eyes. Her freshness made Nick feel like used coffee grounds.

"Want some java?" he asked sourly, stepping aside to allow her to enter.

"I brought my own," she said, holding up an iced mocha. "I wasn't sure what you liked, or I would have brought you one."

"I like the homegrown, pure caffeine variety of regular coffee," he said. He went to the coffeepot and poured himself a mug of black coffee.

"These the Miller plans?" she asked, heading toward the drawing board.

"Yep." Nick couldn't help the note of pride in his voice.

He watched Callie as she studied the drawings. Her facial expression betrayed none of her feelings, though she pursed her lips and nodded several times. His heart hammered against his ribs, though he didn't know why her opinion should matter so much to him.

"These are good, really good," she said finally. "I can see why the Millers hired you. But I was hoping for something warmer. This feels cold with the ultra modern design. I had my heart set on a Sante Fe design with peeled logs as supports inside and at the porches."

"Barbara wanted something different," he reminded her. He could feel his temper teetering on the edge of explosion. "Santa Fe style is not uncommon out here."

"What I have in mind will be different," she said. "The Millers do a lot of entertaining, so I was thinking of a huge great room—and I do mean huge. The kitchen would be state-of-the-art and part of the room. Granite counters, cabinet fronts on the appliances, a brick hood over the stove for warmth and accent. The great room would have built-ins, but instead of being stuccoed they would be in wood tones that match the kitchen cabinets."

"Maybe I could merge some rooms in this house and give you a great room," he said grudgingly. He had to admit her idea sounded appealing. He cast a longing look over his drawings. This would be so dramatic. "And Barbara struck me as the kind who wants this as a showplace and would need formal areas. It's hard to have formal areas with just a great room."

"Barbara has a lost-soul quality about her—can't you sense it? She needs a real home, a haven, and doesn't even realize it." Callie took a sip of her mocha. "And just giving me a great room wouldn't give me the peeled logs and the feel I'm looking for," she said.

He let out a huff. "I told you it was a mistake to get involved now. Why don't you wait until the house is built and see what ideas you can come up with then? I know you're a good designer. You could make this house sparkle."

"I know Barbara would love my ideas," Callie said. Her gaze was unflinching. "Can't you come up with a different plan that would incorporate my ideas?"

"I've spent three months on this plan, and you're asking me to scrap the whole thing. I'm not going to do it. If I scrap it now, they can find another architect. And you won't find another architect any more willing to kowtow to the interior designer than I am!"

They glared at one another; then Callie dropped her eyes. "Maybe you're right," she said. "Is there a compromise? May I have a copy of your drawings? I'll leave my ideas here with you, and I'll look yours over. There has to be a way to work together."

If there was, Nick didn't see it. They were poles apart on the vision for the structure itself. "Why don't we talk to the Millers?" he suggested.

Callie bit her lip, and her gaze faltered. "Can't we work it out between us?"

"What's wrong? You afraid to let your design stand or fall on its own merits?" he asked.

"I'm only concerned about our witness," she said. "In case you didn't notice, the Millers may have gone to church in New York, but it's pretty plain they aren't Christians. If we bicker and fight like the rest of the business world, what will that say to them?"

A shaft of guilt skewered Nick. Maybe Callie wasn't just a hard-nosed businesswoman. At least she had a heart for what was right. And she was right about Barbara's needy attitude.

"Okay," he said slowly. He sat heavily in the leather chair behind his desk. "Let's get to know one another better and find out what our respective visions are for a home," he said.

Callie hesitated then nodded slowly. "I suppose you're right." She sat in the chair in front of his desk. "What do you want to know?"

"Not like this." He waved his hand around the office. "This is too intimidating of a setting. Let's get out of here and do something fun. Hey, how about touring some model homes?"

Callie made a face. "I do that all the time. I don't like other designers' ideas to clutter my own when I'm working on a new project."

"Well, what do you want to do then?"

She shrugged. "If we're going to get to know one another, we should do something normal and everyday. What's your favorite thing to do?"

"You'll be sorry you asked," he said. Wouldn't she feel out of place at a shoot? He hid a grin. But maybe if she was out of her element, she wouldn't be so set on her own way. He had a desire to rattle her a bit.

"I'm game for anything," she said.

She thought she was game. He hadn't planned on going today, but this was too good an opportunity to miss. "You'll need to change. You own any jeans?"

"Of course," she said loftily. "I live in Arizona, don't I?"

"Change into a comfortable pair, and I'll pick you up in an hour."

"But where are we going?" She followed him to the door.

"You'll find out. Bring a hat if you have one, too." Amusement bubbled inside him. He couldn't wait to see how she reacted to the day.

She paused at the door. "You realize it will be my turn to choose what we do next Saturday?"

"I can handle anything you throw my way," he told her.

"That's what you think." And with an impudent grin she shut the door behind her.

As Nick went to shower and change his clothes, he wondered what he'd let himself in for.

❧

Nick was going to be surprised. Callie grinned at her reflection in the full-size mirror. Her favorite jeans were almost white with washing. She wore a cowboy-style shirt with fringe Gram had bought her for Christmas last year in an attempt to get her to "lighten up." She'd pulled her curls into a ponytail and crammed it all into a misshapen cowboy hat she'd had since tenth grade. Her cowboy boots were battered and worn but oh so comfortable.

She hadn't dressed like this in ages. It felt good to be out of her polished and put-together persona. Maybe Nick had the right idea. It would be nice to be who she was and not be so concerned with selling her image. But old habits were hard to change.

She figured they were going horseback riding. That seemed

in keeping with Nick's cowboy image. Callie hadn't been on a horse in years, but it was like riding a bicycle—you never forget how. At least she hoped that was the case.

The phone rang when she got to the living room. She grabbed it as she sank onto the sofa. "Hi, Gram."

"Hello, yourself, but it's not Gram." Her cousin Mattie's cheery voice came over the receiver.

"Sorry. I figured Gram was calling to see how the date she set up for me went last night."

Mattie groaned. "You didn't go along with her match-making! We had a pact to refuse any more meddling. I suppose I'm in for it next." Her voice sounded gloomy.

"I had no choice. It was a done deal by the time she called me."

"So how did it go? Did he pick his teeth and belch when he was finished with dinner?"

Callie smiled. "Actually he was very nice. No, nice is too tame a word. Interesting. He's an architect. We had dinner with his clients, and I got a terrific offer to decorate the house out of it. I'm pretty excited about the whole thing. The only fly in the ointment is that Nick is being stubborn about changing his house plans to match my decor design. And you know—a home without a woman's touch is, well, just cold."

Mattie burst into laughter. "Callie, only you would ask someone to do that! It's supposed to be the other way around. You're supposed to come up with a design that's in keeping with the architectural style. I can imagine his reaction. Did he throw you out on your ear?"

"No, we're going to try to come up with a compromise."

"A man who compromises. Will wonders never cease? Better grab him while you can, Girlfriend. Better you than me, though. I'd better make sure my schedule is full. Gram will be calling any time now with some new specimen of manhood she's dragged out of the bushes for me."

"Maybe when she sees she's failed with me and Nick, she'll drop her meddling ways," Callie said. She knew better, though.

"Don't count on it. Gram lives to meddle." Mattie's voice was indulgent in spite of her words. "When are you seeing this guy again?"

"Any minute. He suggested we should spend some time together to get an idea for the other's vision." Callie rose and walked to the window. No sign of Nick yet. She walked back to the couch.

"Sounds promising. Maybe Gram is going to score another winner with you and this Nick."

"Don't hold your breath," Callie said. She heard a car door and whirled to the window again. "He's here. I gotta run. Say a prayer for me."

"Oh, I will. You need all the help you can get. Talk to you soon." Mattie hung up, and Callie flung the portable phone onto the couch.

The doorbell rang, and she took a deep breath. She had to appear calm though her nerves were strung tighter than a piano wire. She forced herself to walk sedately to the door and open it.

Nick looked even better than she remembered. He was in a

stylish cowboy outfit. Snakeskin boots matched the hatband on his Stetson and the belt around his waist. He wore a voluminous red shirt that looked old-fashioned, and Callie couldn't put her finger on why. Then she realized the styling was like in old cowboy movies.

"You look—nice," she said lamely.

His firm lips turned up. "You clean up pretty nice yourself," he said. "You look comfortable instead of starchy."

"Starchy?" Callie didn't like the word. She wanted to look anything but starchy. "I'm supposed to look competent." She peered past him. "Aha, I was right," she said when she spied his horse trailer. "We're going riding." Then her satisfied smile faltered. One horse nickered to her from the trailer. Surely he didn't intend her to ride behind him?

Nick smiled mysteriously. "Not exactly."

She frowned. "There's only one horse." She pulled the door shut behind her and walked to the trailer. "Hi, there, Sweetie," she crooned. "He's beautiful. You had him long?"

"He's about six. I've had him since he was a colt. His name is Ranger."

Callie turned to face him. "Okay, spill it. What are we doing today? You have the horse and the get-up. I'm in jeans. We're going riding—admit it."

Nick took her arm and guided her to the truck cab. "All in good time, Callie. I bet you've never seen anything like you're going to see today."

Callie climbed into the cab. She propped her booted feet on the dash. It felt good to leave behind the designer and let her real personality come out. It had been hidden too long.

She turned a smile on Nick as he climbed in beside her. "How long do I have to wait? Did I ever mention how much I hate being kept in the dark?"

"You have the nicest smile," he said abruptly. "It's no wonder Barbara threw the whole project in your lap."

Callie blinked. She knew her smile had turned idiotic, but the compliment pleased her immensely. "Thank you," she said.

The truck pulled slowly away from the curb as Nick watched the trailer to make sure it was tracking properly. Callie felt more content than she had in a long time. There was something special about Nick. They rode in companionable silence a few minutes; then Nick glanced at her.

"Tell me about yourself," he said.

"What do you want to know?" She hated to talk about herself.

"Your family, what made you take up designing, anything you want to talk about."

"Let's see. I have a younger sister, Lindsey. She's away at college right now. My childhood was pretty normal. I've lived in Heaven all my life except for my stint in college at Arizona State. As far as designing, I've never wanted to do anything else. When I was a little girl, Dad built a dollhouse for me. I repapered, repainted, and redecorated that place countless times. My mother loved to rearrange furniture. She was a painter, too—a house painter. She taught me how to do special paint techniques when I was only eight."

Nick nodded. "I need to know how you tick if we're going

to work out this problem."

Callie couldn't help the stab of hurt. Was that the only reason he was interested in her? She had to be honest with herself and admit it wasn't just the Miller project that intrigued her about Nick.

They continued to chat, and she found out Nick had a younger sister, that his parents lived in Phoenix, and that he'd designed his first house out of Legos at age three. The desert landscape zipped by until the truck slowed nearly an hour later.

Nick turned the steering wheel and pulled into a track strewn with potholes. "We're here," he said.

Callie stared as they passed horses and people. The men wore Western wear similar to Nick's, and many of the women were dressed in calico skirts that reached to their ankles. It looked like the set of a John Wayne Western.

"What is this?" she asked. "A movie set? I hadn't heard about any movies being made in Heaven."

"This is a SASS Cowboy Action Shoot. Single Action Shooting Society," Nick said. He pulled the truck and trailer into a vacant spot and opened the door. "You said I was a cowboy, but you didn't know how right you were. I'm about to show you."

Chapter 4

All the activity made Callie's head swim. Men were selling, cleaning, and repairing guns, grooming horses, practicing shooting, riding by with wild Indian whoops of delight, and generally making a noisy scene. The sun shone in a blue blaze of good weather and good times. A dust devil spun out its short life in the distance against a backdrop of saguaro, prickly pear, and cholla cactus.

"Here—take my guns." Nick offered her the handle of a trunk on large wheels.

She tugged on it and found it rolled easily over the rough, sandy ground. Callie pulled it out of the way and watched as Nick led his horse out of the trailer and tied him to a post. Taking a tarp and poles, he quickly erected a lean-to shelter from the sun and put the horse under it.

He knelt beside the chest at Callie's feet and opened it. Pulling out a gun and holster, he strapped them on then grabbed a rifle from the chest as well.

"I can't believe this," she said. She'd been smiling so widely as she looked around that her face ached. "Cowboy Action Shooting. You training to be in a movie?" This man was full of surprises, and to her amazement she found she liked that.

"Nope, just having a good time." Nick took the handle of his gun cart from her and started toward a white canvas tent. "I have to register."

Men and women hailed him as they passed, and Callie could tell Nick was well-liked. Men slapped him on the back and called him Ace, and women smiled flirtatiously—though to his credit he simply smiled and nodded. He stopped in the registration tent, paid his money, and signed up.

"I'll be assigned to a posse soon," he explained. "It's the group I'll shoot with all day."

"Congratulations, Ace!" an older man with a handlebar mustache called from the corner. "I heard you won the Ben Avery shoot in traditional."

Nick grinned. "Dumb luck. Deuce Derringer was having an off day."

"What was he talking about?" Callie whispered as they went on their way.

"Winter Range was two months ago. I won the traditional division. That's where we have to shoot with only weapons that would have been around in the 1800s. I'm the national champion."

"Wow." Callie glanced up at him. She could believe he would be the best at anything he did. Confidence and intelligence were as interwoven in his face and bearing as the warp and woof of a Navajo blanket.

"What's with the weird names? Ace and Deuce?" Callie was finding it hard to grasp everything.

"We all take handles. I'm Ace Derringer, an uncle is Deuce Derringer, and my grandpa is Pa Derringer. He won the senior division at Winter Range. I have another uncle who got us all started. He's known as Macon Sackett, and he won the duelist division."

"Sounds like your family swept the awards. Are they here today?" Callie craned her neck and stared at the crowd to see if she could find anyone who looked like Nick.

"You couldn't keep them away. We'll run into them sometime today."

"When do you ride the horse?"

"I don't. My sister, Erin, does. She's known as Daisy Derringer. There she is now." He nodded, and Callie turned to look.

The young woman hurrying toward them was obviously Nick's sister. She had Nick's dark curls and blue eyes. Male heads turned to follow her progress. Her face radiated the same good nature and intelligence as Nick's.

"I saw you pull in," she said breathlessly. She turned a friendly gaze toward Callie. "Hello, you must be Callie."

Callie's heart did a funny shudder in her chest. Nick must have talked about her. She didn't know if that was good or bad. Maybe he'd complained about her meddling with his design.

"I'm Nick's sister, Erin." She linked arms with Callie. "Don't believe a word he tells you about me." Her smile widened. "Though I must say he told the truth about you when he said you were beautiful."

Callie's throat grew tight. Unsure of what to say, she glanced up at Nick and saw him staring back at her with one eyebrow cocked. A smile tugged at his lips, and she smiled back at him. Suddenly the day seemed brighter and the air more refreshing. Her heart felt light and joyous. All the inner warning bells were going off, cautioning her to guard her heart, but she pushed them away. She intended to enjoy this day with Nick. They could worry about their disagreement on another day.

She and Erin chatted as they followed Nick to where the horse waited. Ranger nickered softly and nuzzled Erin's hand. She laughed and dug in her pocket for a cube of sugar.

"Do you ride?" Erin asked.

"Not in years," Callie admitted. "We had a horse when I was growing up, but we sold her when I was about sixteen. I love horses, though." She rubbed Ranger's nose.

"Maybe we'll get you in the competition one of these days," Erin said.

Callie laughed. "I'm not the competition type. Ask Nick."

"She's not telling the truth, Erin," Nick put in. "She's a shark. She'd cut my throat if it would mean she could do the design she wanted."

Callie's laughter faded. Was that how he really saw her? Maybe she had been opinionated about what she wanted, but she knew she was right. That should count for something. She glared at him.

He held up a hand. "Whoa, don't look at me like that. I was only joking. We both want the same thing—to turn out the finest home in the valley. Besides, we've called a truce for the day."

"You're the one who broke it," she pointed out.

"I apologize," he said solemnly. "Now can we get on with the fun?"

"Lead the way," she said.

"I'll see you later," Erin called. "My posse is gathering on the other side of the range."

Callie waved then followed Nick to the first staging area. Targets were set up in the field, and she watched as he fell in with his posse. When it was his turn, she was mesmerized at his lightning fast draw and accurate hits as he switched from pistol to rifle and back to pistol again. The other men were good, too, but Nick's expertise was evident.

At the end of the long, hot day she stood proudly in the pole building where the awards were handed out and watched Nick mount the stage to take his hard-earned trophy for winning his division. She saw his uncles and grandfather as well as they accepted awards in their divisions. It would be a day she wouldn't soon forget. This was a side to Nick Darling she knew few had ever seen.

Nick stepped from the stage and joined her. "I have to go wrap up a few things. You want to meet me at the truck?"

"Okay. Why don't you give me the keys, and I'll take your chest with me and get it loaded?"

"It's too heavy for you to lug across the field. But here are the keys." He shoved them in her hand. "You can at least rest in the air conditioning. You've been a good sport to indulge me today." He grinned then bent and kissed her cheek.

Her skin tingled where his lips had touched. His breath across her face did funny things to her heart. She would have to watch herself around the charming Mr. Darling.

She took the keys and headed across the field. Now where had they parked? Every row looked the same. Trucks, trailers, cars, and motor homes lined the roads around the range. Every cactus looked like the next. She was at a disadvantage today. Nick had no flower on his antenna as she had on her car.

She huffed impatiently. It was too hot, and she was too tired for this. Where was that truck? Her boots kicked up puffs of dust as she walked from truck to truck. Finally she remembered the canvas shelter Nick had erected for Ranger and began to look for that. But there were other shelters with other horses under them.

Her anxiety lifted a notch. What if he got there first and called in people to help search for her? She'd die of humiliation. Her parents had done that to her once when she'd lost her way coming home from school. When she arrived two hours late, the entire neighborhood was in an uproar.

Her mother accused her of always having her head in the clouds, and it was actually the opposite. She took time to enjoy the small things along the way, the flowers blooming by the side of the road, the glitter of sunshine on quartz. It left no time to orient herself to the bigger picture like how to find her way.

She glanced at her watch. Nearly six o'clock. Nick was surely back to the truck long ago. Would he be worried? Her stomach growled. The hot dog she'd eaten hadn't lasted long, but part of the empty feeling was the knowledge she'd done it again. Would she never learn to pay attention to where she was parked? No matter how often this happened and how often she promised to pay attention next time, she seemed incapable of this one simple task. It was the bane of her life.

Her good mood had evaporated an hour ago. Now all she wanted to do was get home and nurse her humiliation. Gritting her teeth, she stomped along through the dust. She would find that truck if it was the last thing she did. The system that always worked was to start at the first row and simply walk every one. But her feet throbbed, and her pride hurt even more.

She lifted her chin and marched toward the first row. Halfway down the row she saw a familiar set of wide shoulders. Relief coursed through her. "Nick!" She waved her hand and started forward eagerly.

He turned, and her smile faltered at the scowl on his face. What did he have to be angry about? She was the one who had been traipsing dusty lanes in the hot sun for over an hour.

His scowl turned to a smile that didn't quite reach his eyes. "Where have you been?"

"Looking for the truck," she snapped. "And don't look so skeptical. Surely you recall from our first meeting how easily I get lost among a bunch of vehicles."

The skepticism on his face changed to chagrin. "I forgot," he admitted. "I figured you found someone more to your liking and had gone off with him."

Her mouth dropped. "What kind of woman do you take me for? If that's been your experience, you've been hanging around with the wrong kind."

His gaze grew warmer, and Callie was drawn into the blue depths of his eyes. The fading sunshine felt warmer, but her anger hadn't cooled. She turned her back on him and went to the passenger side of the truck. Yanking open the door, she climbed inside and slammed the door shut behind her.

She wanted to be home. After a hot bath she'd slip into her pajamas, turn on some Beethoven, and start on that new novel she'd bought. All she wanted was to forget the past hour and its accompanying humiliation.

Nick opened his door and slid behind the wheel. "Would it help if I apologized?" he asked.

"Not a bit," she said. "I'm sorry my stupidity had to ruin the day."

"It's easy to get turned around out here. There are so many trucks that look alike. It wasn't your fault. I should have realized that and gone looking for you. Can you forgive me?"

He spoke in such a contrite tone that Callie felt her embarrassment and anger melting like tar in the Arizona summer sun. "It's not your fault," she mumbled. "Can we just forget about it?"

"Done," he said. "How about some supper? I'm ravenous. We can leave Ranger here. Erin is camping here overnight, and she'll keep an eye on him."

Suddenly the thought of a bath, book, and music wasn't nearly so appealing. Her stomach growled again.

"Is that a yes?" Nick's eyes twinkled, and his grin widened.

"As long as you don't expect me to eat beans from a tin plate," she said.

He threw back his head and laughed. Callie admired the

long line of strong throat and jaw. He drew her in ways she couldn't explain to herself. She'd seen more handsome men, but Nick's strong, craggy face made her long to probe beneath the surface and really know and understand him. She didn't know why that was so, but she couldn't deny the truth of it.

"Nothing ever dampens that wit of yours for long, does it?" he said, shaking his head. "I'll have to stay on my toes to keep ahead of you."

"Just what I've always wanted to see—a ballerina cowboy. I think I have a tutu that might fit."

"Don't push it," he warned, starting the truck. "I don't look good in pink."

Callie laughed and settled back against the seat. "So where are we eating? Or is it a surprise too?"

"There's a great café on the edge of town. Family Fixin's. You know it?"

She nodded. "Quite well. My cousin married into the family."

The quirk of his mouth drew her gaze; then she turned her head and stared through the windshield. She needed to keep her mind on business.

"We can talk about the plans for the Miller house over dinner," she said.

"Do we have to?" Nick said in a plaintive tone. "You're just now recovering your good spirits. I'd rather not rile you."

"I promise to stay perfectly calm as long as you do what I want," she said primly.

He gave a bark of a laugh. "That's what I was afraid of."

A few minutes later they pulled into the paved lot of the

restaurant. The low-slung building radiated country charm with its green shutters and brick facade. Nick slid out then came around and opened Callie's door and helped her down. She wanted to cling to the warm press of his fingers, but that was all the more reason to snatch her hand away as soon as she could.

They were seated at a booth near the back. A window overlooked a desert garden area. The cool blast of air conditioning felt good on Callie's heated skin.

A perky girl with strawberry blond curls approached the table. Her smile was all for Nick. "Hi, Nick," she purred. "What can I get for you today?" Her tone intimated there was nothing she wouldn't do for him.

Callie's hackles raised, and she gave a mental shake of her head. Nick could flirt with every waitress in town, and it was nothing to her. In spite of her self-chastisement, though, she couldn't help but check his response to the pretty waitress.

He smiled politely, but there was no hint of flirtation in his manner. "Hi, Andrea. I'll have some iced tea," he said. "What do you want to drink, Callie? Boiled coffee?" His grin was all for her, and the smile on Andrea's face faded.

Callie felt ashamed of her jealousy and flashed a bright smile on Andrea in atonement. The other woman blinked at its brilliance. "I'll have water with lemon, please," Callie said.

Andrea took a pad from the pocket of her apron and jotted it down. "I'll be right back with your drinks and take the rest of your order," she said stiffly. She flounced away.

Callie watched her go. "I think she likes you," she said.

Nick raised one eyebrow. "Andrea? I don't think so. She's just a gal I've seen in here a few times."

Callie knew it was more than that, but she didn't argue. "You want to talk about those plans now?"

He groaned. "If we have to." He raised beseeching eyes to the ceiling. "Why, Lord? We were having such a nice time."

She grinned. "Don't expect God to get you out of this. You're the one being pig-headed. My way makes sense. I want to give Barbara a home that satisfies her need to impress her friends, plus something more. I want her to feel relaxed and comfortable in it. If it's just a showplace, it will never be home. She won't be able to kick off her shoes and be herself, and she is a woman who needs that."

Nick snorted. "I can't imagine anyone less likely to let her hair down than Barbara Miller."

"All the more reason why she needs that," Callie said. "She doesn't realize it either. But she's like a spring that's wound too tightly. She needs her home to be a haven. I have some ideas to make it that. But not in the house you've designed. Your design would be a showplace only, never a home."

"So you expect me to go back to the drawing board and start all over." Nick leaned back and gave an exasperated sigh. "I can't do that, Callie. I can't afford to do that. There are other projects clamoring for my time. I've already allotted the Miller house more time than I should have. I'm ready to move on to the next project. Starting over would ruin my schedule for the whole year. We have to come up with another way."

"There is no other way," Callie said stubbornly. "Let me

show you what I have in mind."

"I don't think I really want to know," Nick said. "Look—can't you at least look at the design and see what you can do with it? I could make minor changes, but you're asking the impossible."

"I know I'm asking a lot, but it's necessary," Callie said. "Here—take a look at this list of things I want to do with the interior." She fished in her purse and pulled out the paper she'd jotted down ideas on.

Nick took the paper with an obvious show of reluctance. "I don't know why I'm bothering even to look at it, Callie. You don't seem to understand. I can't start over on this house. That's impossible. If you're determined to have a different house, you'll have to convince the Millers to hire another architect. This one is about to go AWOL."

"Just think about it, Nick," she pleaded.

He opened his briefcase. "Here are the plans I've drawn up. Take them home and look at them. We'll talk again later in the week. But I don't see where we can compromise right now."

"Neither do I," she admitted. "But we have to find a way."

"You're tenacious, Callie. I'll say that for you," Nick said with a sigh. He picked up his menu. "Can we forget it for now and enjoy the rest of the evening?"

Callie nodded, but a lump formed in her throat. She really liked Nick, but she knew this project would likely end in disaster.

Chapter 5

Nick scanned the parking lot for Callie's car then realized what he was doing. He gave a rueful shake of his head. She'd haunted his dreams last night. He'd never felt this intrigued about a woman in his life.

Yesterday she'd been game to play along with him at the Cowboy Shoot. He'd expected her to turn up her patrician nose at such shenanigans, but instead she'd acted as if she enjoyed it. She was full of surprises, and he intended to see her again. The thought amazed him. He was falling for her and fast.

He'd been up half the night going over her ideas for the interior design, and he had to admit she was good. And he could see the Millers loving what she planned. The trick was to figure out a way to meld her vision with his. Maybe he was just too tired, but so far he couldn't see how he could merge the two. They were poles apart.

He parked his truck and eased out. Glancing at his watch, he quickened his step. His stomach was in a state of rebellion. Today he was supposed to sing for the first time in his new church home, and nerves had left him unable to eat any break-fast. He realized it was because Callie would be in the audience.

Several people greeted him at the front door. His heart lifted when he spied Callie's radiant hair. A smile tugged at the corners of her mouth, and she chattered to another young woman. On the other side of Callie, he saw her grandmother, Lucille. Seeing them side by side, he realized how much Callie resembled her grandmother. The same determined chin graced both beautiful faces. Their eyes were shaped the same too. Callie would probably age as well as her grandmother. But even more than her beauty, that spirit would age well. Her husband would be a lucky man.

Nick pulled himself up short. He'd only known the woman for three days, and here he was speculating about her in ways that cast himself in the role of husband. He needed to know her a lot better before he should even be thinking that way. Marriage was for a lifetime and not something to be deter-mined by a passing flirtation.

"Nick!"

He turned at the sound of someone calling his name. The Millers waved to him from the church entrance. He smiled and waved back then threaded his way through the throng to join them.

"I'm so glad you could make it," he told them.

"Where's Callie?" Barbara put in eagerly. "Has she had a chance to come up with a design yet?"

"Barbara, be patient. It's the weekend," Warren admonished.

"She's here. Let's find a seat, and I'll get her." He led the way through the church and found a pew about halfway back. Lucille was already seated. The young woman she and Callie had been talking to was in the pew as well.

"Nicky, there you are," Lucille said. "I was just talking to Callie about you. She said she had a wonderful time. I knew the two of you would suit."

Nick's ears grew hot. "I enjoyed it too," he said lamely. "Um, Lucille, I'd like you to meet Warren and Barbara Miller. Callie and I are working on a house for them."

Lucille shook hands with them and insisted they all sit with her. "Callie will be right back," she told them. "She went to watch for these folks at the door. She hoped you'd come," she told Barbara in a confiding whisper that carried three pews away.

Nick helped them get seated then made his way back to the door to find Callie. She stood alone watching the entry. He was touched by the hope on her face as each new arrival came through the door.

"They're already here," he whispered into her ear.

She jumped then turned to face him. "You startled me. I didn't see you come in."

"Oh, were you watching for me? I thought you were looking for the Millers."

Delicate color blossomed on her cheeks, and she glanced away. She *had* been looking for him, Nick realized with a stab of exultation. Maybe he was having the same effect on her as she was having on him.

Her red hair was up in its customary place at the back of her head in that sedate roll. Nick itched to take it loose from its prison, and he had to suppress a grin at the thought. She'd likely wallop him with that suitcase she called a purse. Her emerald green suit fitted her as though it had been custom made for her, and he supposed it might have been.

One of these days he was going to get her to shed that fake persona for good. Yesterday she'd seemed so much more free and happy in her worn jeans with her hair stuffed into that old cowboy hat. He had yet to see her hair down, and it was taking on the proportions of a quest to see it on her shoulders. He'd have to think of what he could try next.

Her husky voice interrupted his thoughts. "Where are they?"

"With your grandmother and another young woman."

"That would be Mel. She'll be Gram's next project—you wait and see. Gram won't be content until she has us all hitched." Her voice was gloomy. "Her success with my cousin Chelsea went to her head."

"I'm not complaining," Nick said. "At least I have a friend in Heaven now." He clasped her hand and was gratified when her fingers curled around his.

"Unless we're enemies by the time this is all over."

"Whoa, you sure woke up on the wrong side of the bed! What's wrong this morning?"

Callie shrugged. "I don't see how we're going to make this project work."

"You sound downright despondent. We'll figure it out." Seeing her resignation, he felt a new surge of optimism. Maybe she would bend more than he had thought she would. They might find a way to fix this yet.

"You want to take the Millers out for lunch with me?"

"I wish I could, but I already promised Gram I'd come for lunch," she said.

The strength of his disappointment surprised him. He'd been counting on spending time with her today. "When do you want to get together and discuss the plans again?" he asked.

She shrugged. "I don't have anything new to say. I need to study your plans some more."

"How about next weekend? We'll both have a week to come up with some compromises."

"All right. When?"

"Friday night. And Saturday you get to pick what we do for the day."

Her eyes widened. "Are you asking me out on a regular date that has nothing to do with the Miller project?"

"Yep, any objections?" He held his breath.

The corners of her mouth turned up, and that delightful dimple appeared. "You're game for *anything?*"

"Uh-oh, what have I opened myself up to?"

"Nope, you've done it now. You said I could choose what we do. I'll have to come up with some fiendishly unpleasant plan." The dimple in her cheek flashed again, and her dark eyes sparkled with good humor.

"Come along and repent of those intentions." He tugged at her hand and drew her down to the pew where the Millers waited. "And I thought all this time you were a good Christian girl I could take home to Mother."

"Oh, I am," she said primly. "But even good Christian girls

159

have depths you never dreamed of."

"I'm beginning to find that out," he said with a grin.

Barbara Miller greeted Callie with a cry of delight. Nick sat on the end of the pew so he could get out to sing. Callie chatted softly to Barbara until the pianist began to play the opening hymn.

"Pray for the Millers," Callie murmured to Nick. "They really need the Lord."

"I've already started," he whispered back. He rubbed his slick hands against his pants leg. His special was the first one and would be right after the opening hymn. He hoped the words would touch hearts more than his poor voice could. As nervous as he was, he would be lucky if he could croak it out.

The music minister cleared his throat. "Nick Darling is new to our area, but he has a great heart for God. He's going to sing for us this morning. I heard him practicing, and you are in for a real treat."

Callie's eyes widened as Nick rose. Approaching the platform, he prayed he wouldn't forget the words and that the Millers especially might be touched by them.

The accompaniment music started, and his butterflies were swept away with his passion for the song. He'd chosen a Twila Paris number called "Could You Believe?" It talked about living a Christian life instead of mouthing the words. Nick was convicted the first time he'd heard it. That's what he wanted in his life—for others to see Christ, not Nick Darling. He sang with all the desire in his heart to walk true to God.

Callie had tears in her eyes as he made his way back to the pew. He slid in beside her, and she squeezed his hand.

"It appears there are hidden depths to you as well," she said softly.

⁑

A real date. Through church Callie mulled it over in her mind. Did she dare expose herself to the danger of heartache? Nick didn't seem the playboy type, but she'd been fooled before. And even if he wasn't the kind to break her heart deliberately, if he quit the Miller project in a huff, his pride would cause him to turn away from her. This project was one he'd worked for long and hard. And she had been thrust into the middle of it. She could back off and tell the Millers to choose another interior designer, but it would mean giving up the project that might really launch her into the stratosphere of the New York design world. She wasn't sure she was that unselfish.

She glanced at him from the corner of her eye. He was full of surprises. First the cowboy stuff and now the singing. His rich baritone had filled the church and made her think of her own walk. She had invited the Millers to church with a sincere desire to win them. Was she now thinking of them only as a means to her own ends? The truth cut like a spine from a teddy bear cholla. She resolved to put her own ambition and striving behind her. God had put these folks in her path for His purposes, not her own.

After church her grandmother stood and smiled in a way Callie had grown to distrust. Full of innocence, she smiled up at Nick. "Nicky dear, would you like to come to lunch? I've invited the Millers as well, but they say they are meeting with their builder. You don't have any other plans, do you?"

Nick smiled with what seemed like genuine pleasure. "I'd love to come, Lucille. I had thought to take Warren and Barbara to lunch, but since they already have previous plans, I'm free."

"Maybe we could join you next Sunday," Barbara put in.

Was that longing on her face? Callie's heart clenched with sympathy. Barbara seemed to be a lonely woman. She needed Jesus.

Impulsively Callie leaned over and took her hand. "Would you like to have lunch one day this week, Barbara? I know several great restaurants downtown. We could eat; then you could see my shop."

Too late she realized how it must look to Nick. His brows drew together, and she knew he assumed she was trying to sway Barbara to her side of any argument that was looming over the design for the house. She bit her lip and looked away.

"What day?" Barbara leaned forward eagerly.

"How about Wednesday? I have a light day, and maybe we could even do a little shopping. My favorite dress shop is having a sale this week."

"Sounds great." Barbara beamed at her.

Callie's heart lifted. It had been the right thing to do. Whether or not Barbara commissioned her to do the design work, she needed a friend. Callie knew a lot of people in town. She could take her around and make her feel Heaven could be her home. And maybe the Lord would speak to Barbara, and the real heaven would be her ultimate home.

As they made their plans, Callie could feel Nick pulling away from her. She felt bad, but she couldn't explain it to him. He wouldn't believe her anyway.

"Do you need a ride?" Nick asked after a strained silence.

"No, I came with Gram," Callie said.

"Oh, you go on with Nicky," her grandmother said. "Mel can come with me. You two have a lot to talk about with this new house project and all. Barbara was asking me about your work, Callie. I told her about all the awards you've won. She seemed quite impressed."

It was getting worse and worse. Nick's expression was thunderous. Callie followed him to the truck. He opened the door, but he didn't look at her. His lips were pressed together so hard they looked bloodless. His touch on her arm as he helped her into the truck was light and impersonal. He shut the door behind her then climbed in on his side and started the truck.

"It's not what you're thinking," she said in a low voice.

Nick didn't reply for a moment as he backed out of the parking space and turned onto the street. "Isn't it?" he said slowly. "Then how is it? You come to dinner with me then worm your way into a deal with my clients. You push yourself forward at every opportunity. Your grandmother sings your praises until Barbara thinks you're some kind of design diva sent to Heaven just for her."

Callie's eyes burned, and she stared straight ahead through the windshield. "Stop the car. I'll walk to Gram's. You shouldn't be in the same room with me if that's what you think of me." It was hard to swallow past the huge lump in her throat. She knew it looked bad, but she hadn't realized it would appear that heartless to Nick.

Nick sighed. "I'm sorry," he said quietly. "I'll take you to your grandmother's."

"I'll take myself. Stop the truck!" All she wanted was to get away from him. She'd thought she was falling in love with him, but she had to be mistaken. What did she know of love?

"I'm not dropping you by the side of the road."

She jerked at the handle, but the door was locked. "Let me out of here!"

He pulled the truck to the side of the road. "Look—I said I was sorry." He took off his cowboy hat and ran a hand through his dark curls. "Can we start over? You explain, and I'll listen."

Callie's vision blurred with tears. "You don't want to know the truth. You just want to blame someone else for the extra work you see looming ahead of you."

"Ouch. Okay, maybe you're right. Before I met you, things were going great. But even so I'm glad I met you," he said softly.

The words penetrated the wall Callie was busy constructing around her heart. She jerked her head up and stared into his earnest blue eyes. "Really?"

He nodded.

Callie blinked furiously. She hated to cry in front of anyone. "Okay, then I accept your apology. And I really wasn't thinking of the design when I invited Barbara to lunch. She's just so lonely. I could sense it. Women need good female friends. God made us that way. Barbara needs me as a friend and as someone who will share Jesus with her. I was just trying to do what your song said."

Nick rocked back as though she'd slapped him. He pressed two fingers between his eyes. "I should have known," he said. "Now I really feel like a heel."

"You should," Callie said. "Now let's go eat. I'm starved."

He grinned and put the truck in drive. "Is it beans on a tin plate?" he teased.

"You never know with Gram. One Sunday it might be roast and potatoes, and the next we might be lucky to get cold cuts."

"I like your grandma. She was my first friend here, you know. I saw my shooting buddies every month since we all travel around to the different shoots, but she's my first bona fide Heaven friend. And now I have even more reason to like her since she introduced us."

"Don't tell her that," Callie warned. "You'll have her homing in on matchmaking for my other two cousins."

"My lips are sealed."

As they parked in front of the pink stucco complex of the Heavenly Village Retirement Community, Callie marveled at the easy relationship between her and Nick. If they could just find a way to resolve the Miller design, this budding romance might go somewhere. She led the way to Gram's apartment.

Lunch was a pleasant affair with Gram hovering as she always did and waiting on them hand and foot. When she said good-bye to Nick, Callie couldn't wait for Saturday to come. She had a big plan in store for him.

The week flew by. Wednesday's lunch with Barbara went well, but Callie was careful to keep the discussion away from her design. She didn't want Barbara to lock her into anything yet. Not until she and Nick came to a compromise. They had lunch at Family Fixin's. Chelsea and Kyle were there, so she was able to introduce Barbara to her cousin. Chelsea looked radiantly happy, and Callie longed for the peace and contentment she saw in her cousin's face. Callie's career was fulfilling, but something was missing from her life.

Their meeting Friday was postponed when Nick had an emergency meeting with another client. Callie couldn't help feeling relieved that they wouldn't be locking horns again. Next week she intended to ask to tour some of his other homes and see if she could find some compromise in another design. Until they resolved this, she was afraid to let her heart get involved. She couldn't take another heartbreak.

Chapter 6

Nick's hair glistened from his recent shower. He grinned at his image in the mirror. Whistling, he quickly shaved and splashed on his favorite cologne. He couldn't help but wonder what Callie had up her sleeve for the day. She'd told him he could wear jeans, so she must not be planning to drag him to some high-class art show or something like that. Though he'd go if she asked.

He finished getting ready then headed for Callie's with a sense of anticipation. She kept him on his toes. He never knew what to expect from her. In her presence he felt alive and energized.

She was dressed in her old jeans and a cotton T-shirt with her hair stuffed up in her hat. Her smile went straight to his heart. His spirits lifted even higher when he saw her suppressed excitement.

"Follow me," she told him.

He followed her through the house, admiring the warm, inviting decor as he went. Maybe she was right, and Barbara needed more than elegance and a showy floor plan. This home made him want to stay.

She led him through the kitchen and into the garage. "Think you can hook that trailer up to your truck?"

His eyes widened. The trailer held two Fat Cats, a kind of three-wheeled motorcycle with wide tires. He'd always wanted to play around in the desert on one of them, but none of his friends owned the vehicles.

A grin stretched its way across his face. "You know how to drive these?"

She held out her slim arm and flexed her muscle. "I can wrestle a Fat Cat through the worst cactus in the state of Arizona."

He pressed against her rounded arm and winced. "You'll put me to shame." He slipped his arm around her and pulled her to him. "You are remarkable. I'll bring the truck around. Let's get to the desert while the getting is good."

Callie pressed a button and opened the garage door. Nick jogged down the driveway. The scent of jasmine and eucalyptus filled his lungs and gave him another boost of well-being. What a great day this was turning out to be.

He backed the truck up to the trailer, and within minutes they were on their way. "Where're we headed?" he asked.

"Bloody Basin Road, where else?"

"I couldn't have picked a better place myself." He turned the truck out of town and headed to the play area of movie stars and car mechanics alike. It was about an hour away, so they chatted about inconsequential things. Nick loved to hear Callie's laughter. It enveloped him in a cocoon of warmth and joy.

It seemed only minutes later that they turned into the rutted track that was Bloody Basin Road. He found a parking spot and stopped the truck. The sun was high overhead, a roadrunner scrabbled in the dirt several yards away, and cactus dotted the landscape as far as he could see. A perfect day for off-roading.

He unloaded the Fat Cats. Their chrome sparkled in the sun, and he yearned to climb onto the wide seat of one and head out across the stark hills and valleys. "Which one is mine?" he asked eagerly.

"They're identical," Callie pointed out.

Nick rubbed his hands together. "Let's go!"

They climbed onto their vehicles. The sound of the engines whined through the thin air. "I'll beat you to the top of the mesa!" Callie shouted. She didn't wait for his response but revved up her engine and tore between two clumps of prickly pear cactus.

Nick followed her, the tires of his Fat Cat kicking up the dust. They raced over mesas and ravines, through eery landscapes of cactus and sage. Hours later they stopped back at the truck for lunch.

Nick had insisted on bringing the food. He loved to cook and had whipped up his favorite potato salad and made turkey sandwiches. There was a picnic table near the truck, and he spread a tablecloth over the weathered tabletop then laid out the food.

Callie's smile was reward enough for his preparation. Her face was flushed from the sun, and her brown eyes sparkled.

"You let me win," she said.

He held up a hand. "You beat me fair and square. You've had more practice than I have with those things. How long you had them?"

"About three years. They belonged to my brother. When he moved to New York, he sold them to me. They wouldn't be much use in the high-rise buildings." She sat at the picnic table.

"What are you going to do with them when you go to New York?"

Her face clouded. "I hadn't considered it."

"You belong out here, Callie. I can't imagine you in New York, never feeling the Arizona sun on your face, never smelling the sage and creosote. That perfectly turned-out image you portray isn't the real Callie Stevens. This jean-clad sprite is the real Callie. You should let her run free."

Twin lines appeared between her eyes. "People expect a designer to look a certain way," she said.

"Kind of like an architect, huh?" He jerked his thumb at himself. "Look at me. I don't look like the typical architect, but I'm not hurting for business. God made you like you are. When you pretend to be something you're not, you throw His gift back in His face. You're special just as you are. You don't have to put on any fancy facade. Just be yourself. And you can do that right here. I think you'd be miserable in New York."

Callie didn't answer for so long that he was beginning to think she wasn't going to answer at all. She slowly spooned potato salad onto her paper plate and took a sandwich from the plastic container. "Maybe you're right," she said. "But New

York has been a dream for such a long time that I'm not sure I can give it up. And what's wrong with striving to be better?"

"Nothing as long as you're striving to be a better *you* and not something you're not. I think you're pretty perfect the way you are." He said the words softly and realized as he did how much he meant them. He leaned closer until he could smell the scent of her hair. "I've never met anyone like you, Callie. You're so caring of other people, so spontaneous when you let your guard down. I'd like to be more than friends."

The soft brown of her eyes melted his heart. He reached out and touched her cheek. "I'm giving you fair warning, Callie Stevens. I intend to court you. I don't care about the Miller house as much as I'm beginning to care about you."

He cupped her cheek in his hand and leaned forward until his lips touched hers. The sweet scent of her breath touched his face. Warmth flooded him when she returned his kiss. When he pulled away, her lashes still lay on her cheeks. She finally opened her eyes, and their gazes locked.

"You're so beautiful," he whispered. "Inside and out.

She blushed and touched his cheek. "So are you, Nick."

❧

The next two weeks sped by. Callie knew she went around like some teenager with stars in her eyes. The first time Nick kissed her she knew she would never feel about another man the way she felt about him. It wasn't infatuation because it wasn't his physical appearance that drew her so much as his inner qualities. Integrity, compassion, and, most important, a love for God that showed in everything he did.

He wooed her in earnest, calling every night and taking her out at least three times a week. It was hard to keep her mind on her work.

But the deadline for the Miller house loomed closer. Callie knew she could never move to New York now, so she decided to give Barbara the design Nick's house demanded. But every time she sat down to see what she could come up with, her mind was blank. Creativity hid its face from her like a child playing peek-a-boo.

She was going to have to withdraw from the project. Barbara would be crushed since they'd become friends, but interior designers were as plentiful as cactus. Someone else would find the inspiration she had lost for the project.

Stopping by Nick's office, she paused outside the door when she realized he was on the phone. She sat on a chair in the waiting room and idly flipped through a magazine. His deep voice carried through the door, and her hand hesitated of its own accord as she started to turn the page.

"I know you promised she could do it, but things have changed. We don't share the same vision. You'll have to trust my judgment on this one. Another designer will work just as well. Better really. The new one has twice the experience she has. I promise you'll be pleased with the end result."

He could only be talking about her. Callie's throat tightened. All the time he was professing he cared about her, he was making plans to replace her on the Miller project. She jumped to her feet and rushed toward the door. Dimly aware of Nick coming to the doorway and calling after her, she stumbled blindly down the steps and out to her car.

She jumped into her car and drove around town. Nick would find her at home, and she wasn't ready to face him. Tears blurred her vision. Though he hadn't said the words yet, she had thought he loved her. He'd acted it in everything he did. To find out he was like all the rest, that he was only out for what was best for himself, left her bereft.

"I thought this was Your leading, Lord," she whispered as she drove to Gram's. "I thought You had brought me and Nick together. What am I supposed to do?" Her lips trembled, and she fought the tears. She parked in the lot outside the retirement home and leaned her forehead against the steering wheel. "What now, God?" She stayed like that for what seemed like forever then began to feel a sense of peace and purpose.

Nick may have let her down, but God was still there and in control. She would do the best job she could. If Nick wanted a design that matched his own vision, she'd give him one he'd never forget. She grabbed her drawing pad and supplies from the trunk and hurried inside.

Her grandmother met her at the door. "Why, Callie, whatever is wrong? Have you and Nick had a fight?"

"Not exactly," she said shortly. "But I don't want to talk about it. Can I use your spare room tonight? I have work to do, and I'll be interrupted at home."

"Of course, Darling. I'll fix you a cup of tea. That will calm you, and maybe you'll be ready to talk about it."

"It would take more than tea to calm me, Gram," she said with a sigh. Carrying her supplies, she went down the hall to the spare room and shut the door. Through the long evening she drew feverishly and prayed just as fervently for inspiration. Using her laptop, she downloaded pictures of furnishings from the Internet. She pasted swatches of material on her presentation board along with the sketches and pictures. By dawn she had a new design that would wow the Millers. It wasn't what Barbara needed, but at least it would match Nick's design.

A fresh wave of despair flooded her at the thought of Nick. His perfidy had knocked the even keel out of her world and left her disoriented. If Nick could be that self-seeking, no man could be trusted. And that's what she would remember from now on. No more blind dates for her.

She slipped out of Gram's apartment and locked the door behind her. Driving through the empty streets of Heaven, she felt invigorated. Nick wouldn't be able to replace her when she showed up at that meeting with a perfect proposal. Barbara wouldn't desert her. Of course, working with him under the circumstances would be excruciating, but it couldn't be helped. Maybe it would be a reminder not to be so gullible again.

She went to her apartment to shower and get ready for the meeting. There were ten messages from Nick, each one more frantic than the last. Too bad she couldn't believe the tenderness in his voice. She blinked away the tears with determination. She had no time for weakness. There was a battle to be won, and she intended to be the victor.

She dressed in a lime green suit with a cream blouse. Twisting her hair into its familiar bun, she gazed at her reflection and shook her head. If there was one thing she'd learned from this, it was to be her own woman. With a flourish she pulled the pins from her hair and let her red locks cascade to her shoulders. She caught the sides back with a clasp then changed into a pair of khaki slacks with a blazer.

Slipping her feet into loafers, she turned and marched to the door. It was time the world met the real Callie Stevens. Including Mr. Nick Darling.

Nick sprang to his feet when she walked in the door to his office. Dark circles rimmed his eyes. "Callie, I've been worried sick. Where have you been?" His gaze traveled over her face, and a tender smile tilted his lips. "You finally have your hair down. It's so beautiful."

Heat flooded her face, and she ignored his comment about her hair. "I was at Gram's," she said shortly. "Are you ready for our presentation?"

"Yes, but I have your presentation board on the table with my drawings. You don't need another copy."

Barbara and Warren were already perusing the plans, Callie noted with a sinking heart. She was too late.

Barbara looked up with a radiant smile. "Callie, these are wonderful! I didn't know what I wanted, but you've captured the essence of Nick's design perfectly. I can't wait to get started."

The essence of Nick's design? How could that be? Her original plans were poles apart from that cold, sterile building he planned.

Warren slapped Nick on the back. "Great job, Nick. Can we take these drawings to the builder? He's eager to see them."

"They're all yours," Nick said.

Callie frowned and started to object; then her gaze was drawn to the display board where Nick's design was posted. Her heart sped up when she saw the changes he'd made. "Oh, my," she said softly.

Nick came up behind her and slipped his hands around her waist. "Like it?"

"I *love* it," she breathed. "But I thought you didn't have time for a whole new design."

"It's not. Look closer. I stuccoed the exterior with dark stucco instead of leaving it concrete. Changing the roof line helped a lot. Then I added a back portico with those peeled logs you wanted and added inside details in keeping with what you'd asked. I had a mental block for a long time and couldn't see past what I had already done. All I can do is blame it on love."

Love. He'd finally said the word. Callie's breath caught in her throat. She wanted to cry at the way she hadn't trusted him. But she'd *heard* him.

"You were talking on the phone at the office last night," she whispered. "I thought you were telling the Millers you were pulling me from the job."

His eyes widened. "I would never do something like that. I was covering for another designer who had decided not to do a small house for another client when a bigger plum of a job came her way. I didn't want to trash her reputation, even though she deserved it." He stepped closer. "You can trust me, Callie. I would never hurt you."

Callie felt as though she couldn't breathe. She pulled away as the Millers stepped up to them.

Barbara hugged her. "Thank you, Callie, and for more than just the design. Thank you for being a friend to me. And thank you most of all for sharing Jesus with us. The pastor came to visit last night, and Warren and I both have realized we lack something in our lives. The pastor has a seeker's class we're going to attend. For the first time, I've seen what being a Christian is really about. Now we have to find out more."

"Oh, Barbara, I'm so glad!" Callie threw her arms around Barbara and squeezed her tight. Joy bubbled within her. Maybe God had used her in spite of her shortcomings.

Barbara sniffled then drew away. "We'd stay longer, but I think Nick has something he wants to say to you." She stepped back then followed her husband out the door.

Nick placed his hands on her shoulders and turned her to face him. "I realized what you thought when you raced out of here last night. Trust is something that's hard for both of us, but we're going to have to learn it if we want a future together. And I want a future with you, Callie. I love you."

The tears began to flow in earnest down Callie's cheeks. "I love you, too, Nick. More than I can say."

"I've been waiting to hear those words. Tell me again," he whispered as his lips came down on hers.

"Oh, Nick," she gulped when she could catch her breath again.

"You can call me darling," he said.

So she did.

COLLEEN COBLE

Colleen and her husband, David, have been married over thirty years. They have two great kids, David Jr. and Kara. Though Colleen is still waiting for grandchildren, she makes do with the nursery inhabitants at New Life Baptist Church. She is very active at her church, where she sings and helps her husband with a young adult Sunday school class. She enjoys the various activities with the class, including horseback riding (she needs a stool to mount) and canoeing (she tips the canoe every time). A voracious reader herself, Colleen began pursuing her lifelong dream when a younger brother, Randy Rhoads, was killed by lightning when she was thirty-eight. Since that time, Colleen has published nine novels and five novellas.

Mix and Match

by Bev Huston

Chapter 1

I t's for your own good."

Melissa stared blankly at her mother. This was not the first time, and probably wouldn't be the last, that they would lock horns over an issue. "I'm not interested in dating. Every one of them has been a disaster."

"Because you set out to make them that way." Katherine Stoddard's anger reflected in her hazel eyes and her flushed cheeks. "Please do this for Gram. It's too late to back out now. She only wants to see you happy, Darling." Melissa could hear the concern in her mother's voice.

"I'm happy the way I am. All those goofy guys wanted to change me." Melissa got up from the kitchen stool. She'd never had much success with dating, and tonight wouldn't be any different. It wasn't for lack of trying, either. But it hurt too much when she wasn't accepted for the way she was. "Honestly, Mom, I don't want someone in my life whose mission is to transform and reform me."

"Gram knows that. I'm sure this guy will be different. Now

go put on a pretty dress and fix your hair."

Melissa tossed the mail she'd been holding onto the kitchen counter and fought the urge to scream. "That's what I'm saying. You know I don't wear dresses. Why can't I just be me?"

"Please. Gram doesn't ask for much, now does she? She's concerned since. . .since. . ."

"I know. And I'm doing okay." Melissa bit her lip, not daring to look at her mother. She hated how she had to struggle to keep her emotions in check. Still. After all this time. "I'll go get ready." She turned and thumped down the hall to her bedroom, slamming the door for effect. Leaning against it, arms crossed, she tried to think this through. A long-suffering sigh escaped before she seated herself in front of the vanity mirror. She raked a brush forcefully through her curls as she stared at a photograph on her wall. Though she loved this final remembrance of her dad, she hated how it showed all of her flaws.

Defeat weighed heavily on her as she scowled at the picture. She looked like a boy, with flaming red hair, too many freckles, and a pixie nose. She felt short-changed in every department, not just in height. Plus she lacked backbone, at least when it came to family.

Well, she would go out on this date, but that didn't mean she had to like it. And then an idea began to brew. "I guess I'll just have to be my charming self," she said, unable to hold back a grin. Gram wouldn't try to fix her up again after tonight, despite her prior success with Melissa's cousins Chelsea and Callie.

Jumping up, she yanked open the closet and began searching through her wardrobe. She threw a simple green cotton dress onto the bed then dove onto the floor to seek out footwear. "Ah, these will do nicely!"

Moving back to the vanity, she plopped herself down and began to do her hair. When she finished, she dug through the drawers and pulled out an assortment of makeup. After applying a thick layer of foundation, blush, lipstick, eyeshadow, and eyeliner, she decided to wash it off. "This date calls for the natural look." She giggled to herself.

A tap on her bedroom door diverted her amusement. "Yes?"

"Lissa, Honey," her mother said, "I have to run to the store. Are you almost ready?"

"Yes, Mom," she answered sweetly, feeling a little giddy about what she had planned.

"Good. I should be back before your date arrives, but listen for the doorbell just in case."

"Will do."

She heard her mother's footsteps fade down the hallway. A small pang of regret rose in her stomach, but she quickly banished it. Melissa knew she had to do this or forever deal with her family's meddling.

Using a cleansing pad, she rubbed off the makeup and stared into the mirror, lost in thought. Yes, she understood their concern. At twenty-two she still lived at home, wondering what she wanted to do with her life. But ever since that day ten months ago, she'd buried her heart. Melissa knew somewhere, deep inside her, a longing for someone to love existed, but she couldn't get past her grief. God had already taken the most important man in her life—her father—and there were no guarantees it wouldn't happen again. She knew, without a doubt, her heart couldn't bear another such hurt.

The door chime brought her back to the present day. After a last quick glance at her reflection, Melissa headed to meet her date. "Please forgive me, Gram," she whispered.

Bounding down the hall to the front entrance, her pigtails flopped like the large ears she'd worn when she had a part in the school play *Lady and the Tramp*. The capricious feeling somehow gave her courage. She flung open the door.

"Hi. I'm so glad you dropped by," she said brightly.

"You are?" He appeared surprised by her comment. Obviously he didn't think too much about this blind date, either.

"I'm Melissa. What's your name?" She twirled some of her hair around her finger as she spoke.

"Ah, my name's Greg, and I—"

"Nice to meet you!" She reached out and cranked his hand. Inwardly she cringed for making such a fool of herself, but it had to be done. Anyway, it was kind of fun.

"I wanted to invite you—"

"How sweet of you. But I have a better idea."

"I'm afraid there's been some sort of mix-up—"

"No. You're right on time." Her smile faded. Apparently the getup had worked even quicker than she'd thought. Men. They were so predictable. "Oh, I see. You're no longer interested now that you've seen me—is that right?" She hiked her chin and gave an indignant sniff. "You men are all alike. I don't fit your idea of the perfect date." She put on an exaggerated pout. "And now you've had a change of heart." She hoped he'd bought the act.

"No. I haven't had a change of heart. It's just that—"

Rats. He might be harder to lose than she'd thought. She forced her lips into a smile. "Good. Let's get going then." She closed the door and linked her arm with his. "So. I thought we could go rollerblading."

She watched as Greg did a quick visual intake of her looks. If he thought the black, five-buckle-storm-commando boots didn't quite match her feminine dress, he never said a word.

"I've never done—"

"There's always a first time for everything," she interrupted him again. "Where's your car?"

"At home."

"You walked here? No problem. We can take mine."

"Actually I live in the neighborhood—"

"Oh, did you move into the old Hanson house down the block?" She refused to let the poor man finish a sentence.

"Yes. But how did—?"

"It's been up for sale forever." She opened the car door for him and waited until he was seated before she slammed it. She walked around to the driver's side, took a deep breath, yanked open the door, and dropped onto the bucket seat. Before starting the ignition, she fiddled with the air-conditioning dials and, when Greg wasn't looking, turned up the radio volume. When the engine turned over, the music blared. She laughed inwardly as Greg's hands flew to his ears.

"You like your music loud?" he asked.

"Doesn't everybody?"

"What?"

She put the transmission in reverse and peeled out of the driveway. Greg gripped the armrest and closed his eyes. She repeated herself loudly, "Doesn't everybody?" He nodded then visibly stiffened as she cornered on two wheels. Melissa's heart pounded in her chest. She hoped she knew what she was doing.

The brief drive to the park felt like it took forever since neither could talk over the music. Still, the radio provided a nice barrier while Melissa thought up ideas to make her date hate her. It seemed a shame, too, because he had such caring eyes. His dark hair with its natural wave and a winning smile could cause a girl to swoon. She needed to stop thinking this way, or she'd lose her nerve. Besides, on closer inspection, it appeared to be more like a grimace. No thanks to her driving.

"I've never rollerbladed before," he said quietly when she turned off the engine.

Her ears rang. "You'll love it!" She hoped she hadn't just shouted at him.

They nattered about the Wildcats and their last game as Melissa pulled her brightly colored skating equipment from the trunk of the car, where she always kept it. When they reached the rental shop, Greg pointed to a simple black pair of rollerblades.

Melissa placed her hand over the skates the clerk held and shook her head. "He'll have the neon green and yellow ones, with the matching helmet." Turning to Greg she continued, "This is a fun sport, so you gotta look the part."

Greg smiled at her then took the wild skates now being offered. Together they proceeded to sit on a nearby bench.

Melissa dropped beside him and pulled out a package of gum. "Want some?"

"No, thanks."

"I find it helps me keep my rhythm and balance." She popped a piece into her mouth and pocketed the wrapper. In silence they removed their shoes and put on their skates. Melissa fought the urge to giggle when she glanced at Greg.

"I'm not sure I can even stand up in these," he said with a shaky voice as he pushed up and attempted to balance.

She stood, blew a bubble with her gum until it popped, then gathered it all back into her mouth. "You'll do fine," she said as she slapped him on the back.

The force sent him forward down a slight incline, while he waved his arms as he tried to stay upright. He headed straight for a nearby tree. Melissa raised her hand to her mouth and coughed, hoping to hide the smile spreading across her lips. "Hey, you forgot your helmet and knee pads. Wait for me!" Scooping up the accessories, she effortlessly glided to Greg's side.

"I–I wasn't trying to leave you behind."

"Oh, you were just in a mad rush to hug this pine?"

"Very funny." He pulled back from the bark. "I don't know if I can do this, Melissa."

The way he said her name caused a yearning in her heart and made her knees feel like marshmallows. But there wasn't time for that now. "Nonsense," she replied, handing him his helmet and knee pads. "It's fun and safe and anyone can do it."

"So there's no reason I need this equipment?"

"None."

"I'd watch out for a big bolt of lightning if I were you." He gave her a silly grin. Again Melissa felt shame at her deception. But she couldn't back out now.

"Well, it's like walking. You know. Everyone can do it once they learn how."

"Thought so. Did I tell you I didn't walk until I was almost three?"

"Maybe you should have taken up hockey. My dad always said I could skate before I could walk." Pain seared through her at the mention of her father. She looked away from Greg before he could see the hurt in her eyes.

"Maybe it's too late for me." He wobbled again.

"It's never too late," she said, her light tone masking her anguish. "Try leaning on me." What was she doing? She didn't want any contact with this man. She wanted him to dislike her. But as she held him close, for balance, she inhaled his woodsy aftershave. Their cheeks brushed as his muscular arm clung to her waist. "Take a step and glide."

"Okay." His voice seemed as unstable as his equilibrium.

Melissa watched as he jerked ahead. Somehow his presence was almost comforting. Maybe Greg wasn't so bad.

"Hey, I'm still standing!" he yelled back to her.

Melissa floated to his side, trying to ignore her unexpected attraction to this handsome man. "You're doing grea—" She started to respond, but he twisted and plowed into her. "Ow!"

"Sorry. I knew I wouldn't be very good at this. Are you all right?"

Rubbing her ribs and nodding her head, Melissa eyed him

for a moment. "Anyone ever tell you you're a pessimist?"

"Is that so bad?" His gaze met hers as he flashed a disarming smile.

"Well, they say opposites attract," she replied softly before she realized what she had said.

❧

Greg fought the urge to limp as they walked from the car to the coffee shop. The last two hours had been rough trying to keep up with Melissa, but he had enjoyed it. He hoped he could stay awake while they relaxed over espressos.

Normally he wouldn't have been this weary. But as the new youth pastor of his church he'd spent most of the day canvassing the neighborhood teens, inviting them to attend a fun night. The hours had felt incredibly long in the scorching Arizona sun. He'd been heading home when he felt led to Melissa's door and trusted God's direction. Maybe a troubled teenager needed to know someone cared.

Her house, no different from any of the others on the block with the red tile roof and beige stucco, drew him. He believed the Holy Spirit had directed his path.

When she opened the door, he felt a thud in his gut as if he'd been punched. He knew instantly she had been the reason God had nudged him to her home. She reminded him of Amy. With eyes that held a depth of sadness that made his heart ache. He wanted to run but couldn't. He should have tried harder to tell her she had mistaken him for someone else, but he couldn't do that, either. He wondered if some poor guy still waited on her door stoop.

And now they were sipping their drinks, enjoying a pause in conversation since he'd told her he was a pastor. She hadn't run. "So do you come here often?"

Melissa put her cup down. "I used to."

He noted the hesitation in her answer and tried to ignore the sorrow in her emerald green eyes. "I guess it's been a little too warm for coffee these days—even if it is only March."

She kept her gaze focused on the table as she rubbed her mug between her palms. "This is where my dad and I would come after a day of hiking or some other adventure."

Nope. He couldn't ignore anything she might be feeling, no matter how much it pulled at his own anguish. Greg reached out and brushed the back of her hand with his fingertips. "Grief takes awhile, Melissa."

She released her cup as if it were on fire, raised her head, and sent him a penetrating gaze that seemed to ask, "What do you know about it?"

"It's a road I'm familiar with," he told her softly in answer to her unspoken question. "It will get easier, but you need to talk about your feelings."

"I'm not so sure."

"You think people are afraid to be around you. Afraid you might start to cry or something, right?"

She nodded.

Greg continued to hold her gaze until she looked away. "If you ever want to talk, Melissa, as a friend or as a pastor, I promise I'll listen."

She visibly stiffened then rose. "We should head home.

You're going to be sore tomorrow, and it's Sunday. It wouldn't be good if you missed church." A slight smile softened her.

"I'm not sure I can stand."

Melissa stepped forward to help him as he attempted to rise, and their heads collided.

Pain shot through his temple, but he worried she was hurt. "Oh, Mel, I'm so sorry!" He reached to steady her.

"I have to leave," she whispered with trembling lips.

He sensed a deep struggle within her and felt the need to back off. "Will you be okay?"

She nodded.

"Want me to come?" he asked, already knowing the answer.

She shook her head and quietly slipped away. Greg took a few steps after her then stopped. He stood helpless as he watched her leave the parking lot at a dangerous speed.

"Father, keep her safe," Greg prayed. Then he turned, picked up the sunglasses from the table, and began walking the few blocks home.

The night was beautiful, as usual. He'd only lived in Heaven a few weeks, but already he felt like he belonged. The streets were clean, the people friendly, and he looked forward to learning all about the local history. Of course, he missed the Seattle rain. And he missed Amy.

"Just what are You doing, God?" Greg asked. "Am I to be Melissa's friend or something more?"

Chapter 2

As tears streamed down Melissa's cheeks, she carefully steered the car into the driveway then cut the ignition. Leaning back against the headrest, she closed her swollen, sore eyes.

"How could he do that? How dare he call me Mel?" she spoke aloud and slammed her fist on the steering wheel, ignoring the discomfort. Melissa took a deep breath. After all, how would Greg know that no one but her dad called her Mel? He'd always wanted a son, and she'd tried so hard to be one for him. She had learned to love hiking, fishing, baseball, and anything else he wanted to do. And now he was gone.

Melissa jumped at the sound of tapping on the glass then rolled down the window to speak to the man in uniform.

"Hi, Melissa, everything all right?"

"Yes, Charlie. Just fine. Were you following me?"

He removed his sunglasses and nodded. "You were speeding. Again."

"I don't think so." She avoided his gaze. She needed another ticket like she needed another blind date. And she didn't want Officer O'Neil to see she'd been crying.

"Must be them heavy boots."

She smiled.

"Still making those flies?" Charlie asked as he leaned down and rested his arm on the car.

"Not as much," she said, remembering the last time she'd made them. Chelsea had needed to learn, or she never would have done it. "I've been kind of busy taking care of the Marshall twins until they can find someone."

"Are you gonna put your dad's Web page back on-line? Carry on the business?" Charlie cleared his throat. "We miss your dad."

When would this hurt go away? She wanted to lash out at Charlie but knew better. His concern helped. "Me, too." Her words were barely audible.

Charlie stood up. "I'm sorry, Melissa. I shouldn't have said anything."

"It's okay. I need to be over this."

"You've got to let it run its course. You can't just decide you should be through grieving and wake up totally different." He put his sunglasses back on. "You and your daddy were close— more so than most. Give yourself a break, Melissa."

Charlie's radio squawked, giving her a reprieve. He meant well, but she couldn't bear to hear what he had to say. All the gang down at the tackle shop wanted her to stop by, listen to their reminiscing, but it would never happen. She had a stack of flies she could give Bill to sell, but she didn't want to part with them. As for the Web page, after she'd read the messages in the guest book following her dad's death, she wondered if she'd ever go back to the site again.

"I've got to run, Melissa. You watch your speed like a good girl. Remember—a day of fishing can sure help a person sort out stuff. Take care now."

" 'Bye," she managed to choke out. After a few minutes she rolled up the window, gathered her stuff, and went inside the house.

"Hi, Mom—it's me!" Melissa hollered as she closed the front door, relieved to be indoors with the air conditioner.

Her mother appeared in the foyer, her sandals clicking on the peach-colored santillo tiles. "Where have you been?" she asked, her gaze lingering on Melissa's outfit. She frowned.

"On that silly old blind date Gram fixed for me," Melissa answered, annoyed that her mother had already forgotten the torture she'd had to endure.

"I beg your pardon? Your blind date has been here, waiting for you for over an hour."

Melissa leaned against the door. A wave of unease washed over her, and she steadied herself. If he's here, who had she been out with for the last three hours? And why had this guy only been waiting an hour? She stumbled forward.

Her mother moved to assist her.

"Is he in the house or out in the back?" Melissa whispered.

She pointed beyond the large potted plants to the living room, and Melissa groaned.

"Let me help you, Dear," her mother said loudly for her blind date's ears.

"I guess I have some explaining to do," she raised her voice as well.

The young man stood when Melissa and her mother approached.

"Melissa, this is Jeff."

She mumbled a greeting then reached out and shook his hand, resisting the urge to stare at him. This was what Gram thought she should date? Despite his height and broad shoulders, the guy looked like an IBM computer salesman. Intellectuals were certainly not her type.

"So," her mother began as Melissa sat down on the corner of the coffee table close to where her date had been sitting, "Jeff was delayed with a very serious computer problem at work."

"Ah, yes, I was," he agreed, pushing his thick-framed glasses up the bridge of his nose and lowering himself back into his seat. He seemed nervous or perhaps excited. "We had a bug in an accounting formula that could have been disastrous."

"I gather you were able to fix it?" she asked, relaxing a little when her mother slipped from the room. While her efforts with Greg hadn't worked out as planned, Melissa had the distinct feeling she'd be much more successful with Jeff. And this time she didn't feel the least bit remorseful.

"Eventually." He seemed to be studying her, and she wondered how bad she looked.

"Well, I'm going to play war games tomorrow. Would you like to join me?" She managed to keep a straight face as Jeff's smile faltered.

"Oh, I never play on Sunday."

What a choirboy. "We could go bungee-jumping next weekend?" Melissa offered. Getting him to dislike her seemed like a done deal. Why, he was already eyeing his escape route.

Jeff adjusted his glasses again. "I'm not too interested in the outdoors. Perhaps we could catch a movie?"

"Oh, that would be great. We could go see that one about the serial killer. They say it's gruesome." She hoped he wouldn't agree. Gory shows did not appeal to her at all.

"To be honest, M—M—Melissa, I have a weak stomach for violence." He leaned forward, causing his glasses to slip once more. "Wouldn't you like to see something milder? Perhaps a romance?"

"Don't you want to live dangerously? Sitting at a computer all day must be tiresome." Melissa worried her last comment might have been too mean. Jeff seemed like a nice guy, but she needed to put him off. For good.

"I find computer work rather interesting and rejuvenating," he said in a mellow voice then smiled.

Yikes. How dare he be charming? "I know! What about sky diving?"

Jeff jumped up, startling Melissa. She struggled to keep from falling off the coffee table. "Is everything all right?"

Inching away, Jeff's voice sounded compassionate yet firm. "I don't mean to be rude, but I think it would be best if I just left."

"Now? But I haven't even apologized for not being here."

"Under the circumstances I think it may have been best."

"But I—"

"I'll make my apologies to your grandmother."

Now she felt like a heel. He'd seen through her and taken it like a man. She followed him toward the door. "By the way, Jeff, do you rollerblade?"

With a boyish grin he replied, "Oh, no, that's far too risky. If I were to ruin my hands, my career would be over."

She was speechless, and then Jeff laughed. A deep roar that caught her by surprise, and she joined him.

"Nice meeting you," she said and sincerely meant it. In another place or time Jeff might have been worth pursuing.

He took her hand. "Thanks for not being too hard on me for my tardiness. You're a delight."

Again she found she couldn't speak as she watched him walk away and step into a beat-up old car.

Melissa dropped to the top step and began to laugh. Could anything else go wrong? She stopped short when she turned and saw her mother in the doorway behind her.

"I'm sorry, Mom."

"I don't know what went on just now, but I'm so glad to see you laughing."

"Oh, this is not good. I was just awful to that poor man. And the other guy!" Melissa put her head in her hands.

"Want to tell me about it?" her mother asked as she seated herself beside Melissa.

What could she say? That she'd just run off someone who reminded her of Clark Kent? If she'd been honest with herself, she felt certain that had she taken those doofy glasses off Jeff, Superman would have emerged. And then she remembered

Greg. She sighed. How could things have turned out so poorly? She wanted to crawl into a hole and die.

"Okay, if you won't tell me about Jeff, can you at least tell me where you've been? And what on earth you're wearing?"

Melissa started at the beginning, choking back a sob when she finished.

"Honey, I know you. You have a good heart, and you'd never hurt anyone intentionally."

"Not unless I'm being forced on a blind date, at least," Melissa teased.

They laughed in unison.

"And two in one night is plenty, I gather?"

Melissa felt a smile spread across her lips. "After what I put Greg through, you'd think he'd have left. Yet he stayed with me."

"Can I assume your skates probably went better with your dress than those?" She pointed to Melissa's storm boots.

"I'm making a fashion statement," she said with a chuckle. "I never want to see a dress again. And I've done my duty to Gram. That's my last blind date. I don't care if I never marry."

Her mother leaned close to Melissa and whispered, "And who's the handsome man heading this way?"

Melissa swallowed and fought the excitement she felt at seeing Greg crossing the street toward her. She reminded herself she was finished with men, dating, and finding love. But her heartbeat drowned out her thoughts. Leaving her mother behind on the step, she rushed to meet Greg at the edge of the lawn.

"You left your sunglasses in the coffee shop, and I thought you might need them," Greg said as she approached.

Their hands touched as Melissa took the frames from him and slipped them into her pocket. An instant feeling of warmth flooded her. She felt drawn to him, like being pulled into a whirlpool. "Thank you," was all she could mutter.

"You're welcome."

"Hey, why didn't you tell me who you were?" Melissa asked when she found her voice a few seconds later.

Greg blinked. "Well, I don't—"

Melissa placed her hands on her hips. "It wasn't very nice letting me think you were my blind date. Was it so difficult to tell me who you were?"

"As a matter of fact, it was."

Melissa opened her mouth then slammed it shut. They stared at each other until he started to laugh. She followed suit, amazed at how good it felt. How right everything seemed simply standing there, together.

"Look, Melissa—I should have insisted you let me tell you I wasn't your date. And I'm sorry for that. But I'm not sorry about the evening." He paused. "Are you?"

"I—I—" She sighed. Why fight it? "I had a nice time. I wish I hadn't been so terrible to you." She felt self-conscious and glanced back to see if her mother had gone indoors. She remained on the stoop. *Rats.*

"I'd like to see you again." He paused. "On one condition, that is."

Melissa lowered her gaze to the ground. She knew he was going to be like all the others. He wanted to change something about her, and then all the wonderful things she was feeling would vanish. "And that contingency would be?" she asked in a steady voice belying her trepidation.

With a light touch he brushed his knuckles down her cheek. She held her breath.

"I pick the radio station we listen to in the car." Then he turned and sauntered away.

❧

Melissa dropped to the couch, exhausted. The Marshall twins were still asleep, and she'd managed to do the dishes and tidy her house. Maybe she could relax for a bit before the next feeding. She closed her eyes, enjoying the silence.

Ding-dong.

Bonnie awoke howling, thanks to the loud chime. Melissa picked up the crying baby and went to answer the door. When she looked in the peephole and saw Greg, her heartbeat quickened.

"Hello," she said, stepping back, allowing him to enter. He looked like a GQ man in his blue suit with a deep burgundy-colored silk tie. He raised an eyebrow when he glanced at the now-quiet bundle in her arms.

"Hello, back."

"Come on in. I'll make us some iced tea."

"I can't stay. I have a meeting. I just wanted to see how you were and ask you a favor."

Before she could reply, Bobbie began to cry. "Could you hold this one while I get the other one?"

"I don't know—"

"Here—just hold her like this," Melissa said as she placed

Bonnie in Greg's arms. "Don't look so scared. She won't bite."

"She's so small. I'm afraid I might crush her or something."

Melissa raced to grab Bobbie. Too late. Now both were exercising their lungs.

"How good are you at changing diapers?" Melissa asked as Greg followed her into the kitchen.

"Better at changing tires."

"Okay, how about if you warm the formula and I'll do diaper duty?"

"Ah, sure. I think."

She grabbed the bottles from the fridge and explained how to use the warmer. "I'll take Bobbie and change him then come back for Bonnie."

"Okay." Greg sounded as sure of himself as he did trying to balance on rollerblades. She left him and took Bobbie to the bathroom where she had set up a changing station. A short time later as Melissa headed back toward the kitchen, she became aware that not only had Bobbie stopped crying, but so had Bonnie. She stepped quietly into the room and watched. Greg, seated on a stool, cradled the babe tenderly in his arms as he sang. Bonnie gripped his index finger and cooed in response to Greg's soft baritone.

Melissa's heart warmed at the sight. "Well, for someone who doesn't know a thing about babies, you seem to be doing fine."

Greg didn't take his eyes off Bonnie. "Is she yours? I mean, are they yours?"

"Would it matter?" she asked, wondering why she felt so defensive.

"I could get used to them," he said, looking up with a grin.

Melissa expelled the air trapped in her lungs, not realizing she'd held her breath. "I'm the babysitter. They go back to their parents in a few hours."

"Must be a lot of work. I could hardly get the bottles in the warmer and hold her at the same time."

"I know who to call when I need help."

"I just don't know if you can afford me."

"Excuse me?" Melissa asked, aware he was teasing her.

"I wouldn't want any monetary return for my services."

She gave him one of her stern looks. "You wouldn't?"

Greg shifted on the stool. "I'd want a date."

"Oh, no," she said as she raised her hand, palm out. "I'm finished with dating. They're always disasters."

"Okay, then. I'd want a disaster."

Melissa checked the temperature of the bottles. "These are ready, I think."

"Don't go changing the subject," Greg said as he moved to her side. "I think you owe me two disasters."

"Two? You're only helping with one baby."

"You agreed to another one on Saturday night—remember, on the front lawn? And now one for services rendered today."

"Don't you have a meeting you need to attend?"

"I did. I called my boss and told him a friend needed some help. We're meeting later."

"Your boss?" she asked. "Isn't God your boss?

Greg laughed. "Still changing the subject, aren't you?"

"How late can you be?" She handed one bottle to Greg

and took the other. "Let's sit in the family room where it's comfortable."

"Pastor Jamison has another appointment this morning," Greg said, following her. "I'll meet with him this afternoon."

"Well, I'll tell you what. Once Bonnie and Bobbie are fed, I'll make some lunch. Since I'm not much better in the kitchen than I am on a date, that should count for another disaster."

"See—that's what I like about you. No pretense. A guy knows what he's getting right from the start."

"I have no idea what you're getting. I may be able to find some peanut butter, but that's about the extent of my repertoire."

"You knew what I meant." He winked, and Melissa felt weak all the way down to her toes.

"I'll get you a cloth," Melissa said as she stood, still feeding Bobbie.

Greg looked confused.

"Bonnie's leaking some formula."

"Oh."

"You don't want to smell like sour milk when you get back to work—and you use it when you burp her."

"A dainty little thing like this?"

"Just you wait. She's louder than Bobbie. She makes me proud to be a woman." Melissa giggled and hoped Greg knew her words were in jest.

Chapter 3

G reg's favor wasn't really a big deal. The church youth were having a volleyball game that evening, and he wanted her to come. She'd said yes without even thinking. Usually she thought things through first. Of course, nothing was usual about Greg.

After the long day with the twins, Melissa decided to rest for half an hour before getting ready to go out. She stretched across the bed, ignoring the smell of baby spit-up on her shoulder, and closed her eyes.

A tapping noise awoke her. "Melissa, Honey. You have company."

She rubbed her eyes and glanced at the clock. "Oh, no!" She raced to the mirror then groaned.

Her mother slipped into the tidy bedroom and patted Melissa's shoulder. "It's okay. It's the nice blind date."

"I'm late. I need a shower and don't have time. And I smell like baby formula." She felt miserable. This time she wanted to look nice for him. After last night's fiasco it seemed the least she could do. But not puffy-eyed and rumpled, with a messy ponytail. "I look horrible!"

"You're beautiful."

"This is not the time for flattery, Mom. What am I going to do?"

"I'll keep him busy. You wash up and change."

Melissa raced into the bathroom, throwing off her clothes as she went. She jumped into the shower and within a few minutes felt better—and clean. Whipping a towel from the linen shelf, she flung it around her back, knocking the bottle of baby powder over. White talc flew everywhere, covering her from the waist down. Once again she smelled like a newborn.

Leaving the mess in the bathroom—or, in this case, the powder room—Melissa rushed back to her bedroom and dressed in jeans and a T-shirt.

Greg's eyes noticeably brightened when she stepped into the living room.

"Sorry to keep you waiting."

"No problem. With the way you drive, we still have an hour before we have to leave."

"Very funny," she said as they headed for the door.

He placed his hand in the middle of her back and ushered her past him. His touch sent a tingle down her spine. As she went by, he leaned forward, inhaling. "Mmm, love your perfume. It reminds me of something."

"It's very expensive. From France. Eau des Enfants."

He laughed and gave her ponytail a gentle tug.

Melissa pulled her sunglasses from her purse and put them

on while walking with Greg to his car. She tipped the frames back down to look over the sporty red convertible.

"This is yours? On a pastor's salary?"

Greg nodded. "It was a gift." He didn't seem overly impressed with the vehicle. In fact, he sounded almost sad.

"Some friend," she replied.

"She's more than a friend." He opened the door for Melissa.

His words caused a sharp pain in Melissa's heart. She? Did Greg have an ex-fiancée? Or an ex-wife?

"I'm not as good a driver as you," he said, getting in the car and starting the engine. "So buckle up."

She grabbed the seatbelt, still pondering his earlier comment. Then she remembered. He'd spoken of grief and had said it was a familiar road. Whether he'd lost a wife or girlfriend didn't matter since it was someone he'd cared deeply about. Someone she could never compete with. Someone very feminine, no doubt. Someone unlike Melissa.

"Do you play volleyball as well as you rollerblade?" Greg's question interrupted her thoughts.

"Best on the team in school."

"No surprise there," he said with a smile.

Yeah, no surprise. She was a tomboy. She needed to stop thinking like this, or the evening would be ruined. After all, hadn't he dropped by this morning to see her? Wasn't she having a date with him on a Saturday night? *Get with the program, Girl!*

"How 'bout you?"

"Me? Would you believe captain of the men's team in seminary and MVP?"

She chuckled. "Are you familiar with the story *Pinocchio?*"

"What?" He took his eyes off the road and glanced at her. "I could have been, if we'd had a team."

"Well, I hope you play better than you drive. I don't think we can go any slower."

"I'm just prolonging our time together. Got a problem with that?"

Trouble was, she didn't. No problem at all. "Rats," she muttered.

"Star."

"Where? It isn't dark enough to see the stars, or were you talking about a celebrity?" She knew she verged on rambling.

"It's this annoying habit I have."

Melissa brushed a few stray strands of hair back from her face. "I don't get it."

"I like playing with words. Sometimes when you spell something backward, it forms a new word. Like rats is star."

"Oh. So pot is top."

"Right. It drives my family nuts."

"Stun."

"Hey, you catch on fast." He seemed pleased. "Do you like palindromes, anagrams, or auto-antonyms?"

"Auto what?"

"Antonyms. Like the word *rock*. It means solid, firm, immovable; yet it can also mean to move back and forth, sway."

"I've never heard of that," she said as she tried to think of another auto-antonym. "Left."

Greg put on his turn signal and slowed. "You know a

short-cut to the church?"

"No," she replied with a giggle. "I wasn't giving you directions. I thought of another word."

He responded with a chuckle, turned off the blinker, and resumed his speed. "That's a good one. Either you left a place or you were left behind. You're pretty smart for a girl."

And you're pretty handsome for a man, she thought, thankful he had noticed she was indeed female.

❧

What are you, ten?

Greg chided himself as he sought out Melissa on the sidelines before he served. He wanted to make sure she was watching. After looking so bad at rollerblading, he needed to do something to redeem his poor image.

"Grass is gonna grow on you, Greg. Serve," one of the teens on the other team hollered to him.

He pulled his arm back then swung forward, punching the ball over the net. The other side scrambled to volley it back but was unsuccessful. They returned the ball, and he repeated his performance. After his third serve he turned away, seeking out Melissa. He turned back to the play at hand, and the ball bounced off his head. Another player swiped it back over the net. *So much for redeeming my image.*

He caught a glimpse of Melissa on the sidelines laughing. She looked lovely.

"Keep your eyes on the ball," another teen ordered.

With his serve over, Greg took a seat near Melissa, and the next player bounded out to the floor.

"What a great turn-out," Melissa said.

"Yeah. I'm surprised."

"Rotating is a good idea. Everyone gets a chance."

"And this old man gets a break."

"Good thing. You had me worried you'd get hurt out there with that head move. Is that an old trick?"

"Ha, ha," he said, pretending to be annoyed. "I'm actually a pretty good player. I think it's in the genes."

"You know what they say about that." She smiled, and he felt a tug at his heart. "The problem with the gene pool is that there's no lifeguard." She slapped him on the shoulder. "So sit back and watch a pro." She left and took her position on the court.

Yep, he was more than prepared to watch her. But he caught sight of a young girl sitting off by herself, near the door. She seemed timid, almost afraid to come all the way into the gym. He sauntered over.

"I'm Greg, the youth pastor."

"Selina," she replied, still looking at the floor.

"Which team do you want to play on?"

She twisted her foot, causing her shoe to squeak. "I'm not very good."

"It's just for fun. We'd love to have you join us."

"Really?"

"Really!" he said. "You can take my place. I need to get some refreshments ready."

"I could help."

"Wouldn't you rather play?"

209

She didn't respond.

"You're up next. I'll stick around to make sure you're not competition for me. How's that?"

A little pip of a giggle escaped Selina's mouth. He took that as a yes and ushered the girl over to her place on the court.

Sitting back at the sidelines, he struck up a conversation with two other teenagers. The kids were bright and funny. This had been a great idea. He sure liked being the pastor here.

With Selina settled into the game, Greg headed off to the kitchen for the goodies. A couple of youths followed to help. They set up the food in the small fireside room then went back to the gym.

"Once you left, Greg, our team really got on a roll," Willy said as they walked off the court.

"Thanks," Greg replied.

Willy blushed. "I didn't mean it that way."

Greg tousled the kid's hair. "Okay, gang. Let's head into the other room for refreshments and a time of fellowship."

❧

Melissa felt like an outsider. It had been a long time since she'd talked to God; besides, she wasn't a teen. She didn't have much in common with most of the kids, and they kept Greg busy. In fact, except for a brief exchange on the sidelines, he'd practically ignored her. When he hadn't picked her to be on his team, she'd been hurt. Then his attention hadn't appeared to be on the game. He always seemed to be looking around the gym. As if he were looking for someone. Who was he expecting? Had he forgotten they had come together?

Now, after talking with the kids in the fireside room, they surrounded him. Laughing and joking. Why couldn't she join in? Being on the sidelines distressed her, but fear held her back. Gazing about the room, she noticed Greg motioning to her to come over.

She stood near him, but he didn't speak to her. He continued to talk with the teens, and eventually Melissa drifted away.

She was being silly, she knew, but she felt as if she'd been in Greg's way. He had a job to do, and she needed to learn to take second place to that. But could she? Was she being selfish to want time alone with Greg? Time to get to know him? With his being a youth pastor, would she ever get that chance? It seemed as if everyone wanted a piece of him.

What troubled her more than her unwanted feelings for Greg were her feelings about God. She felt He'd let her down. Where had He been when her father took ill? She couldn't think about that right now. Nor could she think about her overwhelming desire to have Greg comfort her.

Melissa grabbed her purse and asked Willy to let Greg know she had left. Stars twinkled in the clear sky as she walked home. She needed to sort out all the feelings and emotions that were assaulting her. Was she being a spoiled brat, wanting Greg all to herself? Just like with her dad? Her heart ached at the thought.

How could she go from not needing someone to regretting that things weren't working out with Greg? She didn't want to be like her mom. Her dad had done everything for her mom. When he died she didn't even know how to reconcile the checkbook. He had always made everything right. Yet he'd taught Melissa to stand on her own two feet. No, she didn't need a man to fix everything in her life.

But maybe she needed a man to share everything that was right. Now where did that thought come from? If that were true, she knew Greg Kelly wouldn't be that man. For two brief days, though, Melissa had felt like her old self—only to discover there'd be no time to enjoy anything with Greg. The thought made her sad.

She kicked a few stones and muttered to herself then wished she could talk to her dad about her feelings. They'd never really talked about boys. Guess maybe he'd never realized Mel was a girl. That had been fine with her. She loved the same things he did. They fished, hiked, and golfed. And she sat with him for every sports game on TV. Melissa loved being the son her dad always wanted.

"What would you tell me to do, Dad?" she asked aloud.

A gentle breeze came out of nowhere, and the sway of the bougainvillea lining the street sounded like words. As if her dad had whispered the answer to her. *Seize the day.*

It had been one of his favorite songs. She loved it, too. With a slight Celtic flair, both the words and music had spoken to them. Melissa could hear his smooth voice as clear as if he were beside her. But the beauty of the words were simply a memory now.

Melissa pulled a few strands of hair between her lips, an annoying trait she thought she'd broken. Yet, whenever she felt unsure, the hair ended up in her mouth, reminding her she hadn't grown up. She tucked the red wisps behind her ear. Well, she was all grown up, and she didn't need anyone. If that were true, why wasn't she convinced? And why did she suddenly ache for someone to understand her?

Angry with herself, she unlocked the iron grate door and jerked it open. Unshed tears blurred her vision as she struggled with the key in the lock of the front door. Once it unlocked, she marched inside and slammed it shut. The bang hurt her ears, and she cringed at being so childish.

She waited for her mother to appear, but the house remained quiet. Melissa dropped her bag on the bench in the foyer, kicked off her sneakers, and headed to the kitchen. A note on the fridge advised her she had gone to visit Gram.

"Just great. They'll probably set up another blind date for me to look like a loser," she muttered as she got a glass of water and took a few sips. "What's wrong with me?" she said as she padded down the hall to her bedroom. The mess in the bathroom from earlier caught her attention.

Setting her glass down on the counter, she went to grab the vacuum from the closet. She'd have no time to clean in the morning before the twins arrived.

When she finished, she prepared for bed. Though tired, she couldn't sleep. Turning on the lamp, she glanced at her Bible on the nightstand. Exactly where she'd left it the day of the funeral. She picked up the book and flipped through a few pages then set it back down. She knew the answers she needed were not there.

Melissa turned off the light and squeezed her eyes closed,

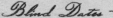

ordering herself to sleep. In the stillness of the house she thought she could still hear the song "Seize the Day" playing softly. She covered her head with a pillow. But the music echoed in her ears. *Seize the day.*

Chapter 4

You're an idiot, Kelly!

Greg hadn't noticed when Melissa left. He wanted to find her, but the equipment had to be put away and the kitchen tidied first; then he had to lock up the church. He drove straight to Melissa's when he finished, but no one answered. He felt a tightness in his stomach. Where could she be?

He dropped down on the front step to wait. He'd stay all night if he had to. With his hands braced on his knees, he rested his head in his palms. An occasional breeze helped in the warm night. Crickets chirped, oblivious to him, while some sort of whirring noise, like an air conditioner, emanated from the house.

Moments later he noticed the sound had stopped. He knocked again. Still no answer. Greg settled back into position, wondering if he should drive back toward the church in search of Melissa.

Soon a car pulled into the driveway, and Mrs. Stoddard greeted him. "You're the wrong blind date guy. Greg, isn't it?"

"That'd be me." He stood and reached out to shake hands.

"Are you coming or going?"

"I sort of lost your daughter this evening. I'm hoping she's home."

Mrs. Stoddard raised an eyebrow and stepped forward to unlock the iron grate door.

Greg felt like a student caught in school for cheating and wanted to explain. "I got kind of tied up with the kids, and I guess Mel grew tired of waiting."

Mrs. Stoddard turned back to him quickly. "What did you say?"

"I got tied up—"

"No. What did you call Melissa?"

Greg shrugged, not sure what he'd just said. "Mel, I guess."

"Oh, dear. That's not good."

He waited while she bit her lip as if trying to think.

"I see her purse and shoes, so she's home. I'll tell her you stopped by."

"I'd like to talk with her."

"It might be best if you wait until the morning." He couldn't help but notice Mrs. Stoddard's pleasantness had slipped to something almost verging on irritation.

"Is something wrong?"

She sighed. "Only Martin, my husband, called her Mel. She's still easily upset since his passing. I'm sure she'll be fine in the morning. Good night."

"Yeah, good night."

Greg stood on the step and stared at the night sky. He wouldn't hurt Melissa for anything; yet that appeared to be just what he'd done. How could he have been such a jerk?

He reminded himself that she'd made it home safe and decided he'd better leave before Mrs. Stoddard called the police. That wouldn't look good. Though he and his boss got along well, the church had already been through a scandal, thanks to some untrue gossip. As a result, Pastor Jamison had become image-conscious. Though he'd never said anything, Greg felt certain his boss would have preferred he drive a more sedate car and be married. Yes, staying on Melissa's doorstep would cause a problem.

Since it would be several hours before he could see Melissa, he decided to go home and pray. What did the Lord want him to do about the pretty redhead who'd invaded his life so easily? He knew the importance of staying in God's will. He hoped that will included Melissa.

❧

"Lissa," her mother called as she rapped on the bedroom door.

"I'm awake." She yawned and stretched.

"No need to get up. Mrs. Marshall called. The twins kept her up most of the night so she is staying home from work. She won't be dropping them off this morning."

Yes! "Thanks, Mom."

"Did you want some breakfast?"

Melissa climbed out of bed and opened the door. "I'm not hungry. I think I'll shower and head to the park."

"You're missing the most important meal of the day, Sweetie."

"It's not the first time."

Her mother reached out and touched Melissa's forehead.

"You look tired. Why don't you go back to bed?"

"I just need a shower."

"By the way, Greg came by last night. Why didn't you answer the door?"

She swallowed. "I didn't hear anything."

"Seemed as if he'd been here a long time when I came home."

"I went straight to bed after I cleaned up the bathroom. I must have been asleep."

Her mother nodded. "I'll make some banana hotcakes."

She laughed. Her mother always made her favorite pancakes whenever she believed Melissa needed some TLC. Maybe she'd feel more like eating after her shower.

An hour later, feeling like the fatted calf, Melissa headed to the park. Her body needed a lengthy workout, thanks to the pile of food she'd managed to down. She also found this to be the best place to think. Greg had laughed when she told him that.

The park appeared almost empty. Melissa donned her skates and headed off along the rollerblade route. She'd picked up quite a bit of speed when she glanced up, nearly colliding with a rather awkward skater.

"Oops. Sorry," she said as she spun around the man. Coming to an abrupt stop, she leaned down to catch her breath. "You should stay to the right."

"It seems I'm always in the wrong these days," a familiar voice replied.

Melissa's head shot up. "What are you doing here?"

Greg wobbled, and she steadied him. "Do you want the truth?"

"Will I be disappointed?" she asked, wanting to remain angry with him but unable to do so.

"I'm not sure." He pointed to a bench. "Can we sit for a minute?" Once they were seated, Greg continued. "I wanted to surprise you. I figured I'd try to get the hang of this, and then maybe we could start over."

She looked away from his earnest gaze and stared out at the small lagoon. What could she say? *Sorry, Greg—I'm too afraid of losing you?* What a dumb thing to think. And here he was learning to skate—for her. She wrestled with her thoughts.

"You don't have to give me an answer right now," he said, taking her hand. "I want you to know I'm sorry about last night. Your mom explained everything to me. Forgive me?"

Melissa couldn't hear a word Greg said. All she could focus on was that he held her hand. Little electrical shocks of excitement worked their way up her arm to her heart. If she wasn't careful, the ice wall she'd carefully built would start to melt, and then where would she be?

Greg reached up and with a gentle tug turned her face toward him. "Is this the silent treatment, or are you considering my request?"

"I'm not sure," she replied, unable to formulate a coherent thought.

"Okay." He eased up off the bench and turned cautiously to leave. "See you."

"Huh? Are you just giving up? Whatever happened to that old saying, 'If at first you don't succeed, try, try again'?"

He looked back at her and grinned. "That may be the way things are here in Heaven, Arizona. But not where I come from. My grandpappy always said, 'If at first you don't succeed, hide the evidence you even tried.' " He nodded his head. "Good thing I didn't buy these skates."

Melissa stood up, hands on her hips, and watched him struggle to maintain his balance. A light breeze rustled the trees.

Seize the day.

"I think I liked you better when I hated you."

He tossed back his head and laughed then landed on the ground.

Melissa skated to his side. "Are you okay?"

"It takes more than a fall to bruise my ego."

She stared into his eyes and felt her thoughts swimming in circles. She reached out and helped him up. "I'll race you to the rental shop. Loser buys the coffee."

"What I wouldn't give for a miracle right about now."

Melissa took off then hollered over her shoulder. "It'll take more than a miracle to beat me." She wobbled on her skates; then to her astonishment her feet separated, and she sprawled on the ground. A throb from her wrist quickly built to huge proportions, and she fought a wave of dizziness. She'd never fainted in her life, and she wasn't about to start now.

"You don't have to let me win," Greg said when he caught up to her.

His words sounded like an echo in a tunnel. "I feel like the hare," she replied then slumped forward, only vaguely aware that he'd caught her in his arms.

52

"If you two don't stop hovering over me like a couple of mother hens I'm going to scream!" Melissa said as she narrowed her eyes and glared at Greg and her mother.

Greg looked at Melissa's mother and nudged her with his elbow. "Hmm. Grumpy. Either that means the painkillers have worn off or she's really mad that she has to pay for coffee."

"Technically you didn't win. And I'm not grumpy."

"Of course not, Dear," her mother said as she sat in the lawn chair next to Melissa.

"You're right." Greg nodded in agreement. "You're too tall to be Grumpy."

"And you're no Doc," she replied, understanding the reference to Snow White. But she wasn't in a joking mood. She felt stupid that she'd fallen, broken her wrist, and even fainted. How could she possibly care for the twins in this condition?

"Do you need anything?"

"No, thanks, Mom."

"I'm going to head home." Greg stood. "I have to finish planning our fundraiser for next weekend for our upcoming missions trip. Here's my number if you need anything." He handed Melissa's mother a slip of paper.

Melissa forced a smile and nodded cautiously. A rush of warmth flooded her cheeks when she gazed into Greg's dark cinnamon eyes. And the whirlpool feeling she'd experienced once before returned.

"Thanks for taking care of Lissa."

"It's the least I could do since it was my fault." His smile faded, and she detected a note of sorrow in his voice.

Melissa sensed something deeper than just remorse for her accident. She knew her fall wasn't the reason for the pained look on his face. "Don't be silly, Greg. It was my own fault. Now get going. I need some rest." She leaned back on the chaise lounge and closed her eyes. Her mother walked Greg to the back gate.

"Lissa, Charlie's here. He had your car towed home," her mother said when she returned.

Charlie stepped closer to Melissa and looked her over like a concerned parent. "I heard you fell for someone."

Her mother stifled an obvious chuckle.

"Despite my mother's and grandmother's attempts at matchmaking, I'm still single and available. Slightly damaged now." She raised her right arm and winced.

"Well, at least you still have your humor."

"And apparently my car. Thanks, Charlie. How much do I owe you?"

"Nothing. Rob from the department did me a favor." He took a step back. "I'll let you get some rest. And remember— even damaged, you're pretty special."

Melissa didn't dare speak. Her emotions were raw, and Charlie's kindness caused a lump in her throat.

She nodded and watched him leave.

I'm blessed to have such caring friends.

The thought surprised her. But would she go so far as to think God still cared for her, after all? She drifted off to sleep wondering.

✹

Guilt was a heavy burden, and Greg knew where to place that load. Yet he had difficulty with it some days. Every time he gave it over to God, he'd snatch it back. Sometimes he wondered if he should even be a pastor with all his failings. Then he'd be gently reminded of the people in the Bible who weren't so perfect either; but God had used them.

Today, however, his guilt seemed doubled. Melissa. He felt responsible for her injury and something more. He forced the niggling thought from the back of his mind. Amy. Were the two different or somehow the same? He recognized the loss that sometimes dulled Melissa's green eyes. Everything about her drew him closer to her. Did he think he could rescue her? Did he think he could protect her when he hadn't been able to do either for Amy?

He stood and stretched his back, staring out the window at the shiny red car in the driveway. He hated that vehicle for its constant reminder of his failure, of his loss.

Help me, Lord.

Chapter 5

I'm learning the Internet!" Gram slapped her jean-clad knees in delight. "Jeff is teaching us at the community."

Melissa stiffened in her chair. Suddenly her comfortable kitchen seemed anything but. *You haven't been here for ten minutes, and already you're talking about Jeff.* She knew Gram meant well, but today wasn't a good day to be discussing her most recent disaster.

"I warned Jeff you were a free spirit. Apparently you were freer than usual."

She opened her mouth to reply then caught Gram's grin and clamped her lips together.

"Lord knows that boy could use some loosening up." She shook her head. "He's very nice, you know."

"I'm sure he is. And I'm sorry I went a little overboard. But I'm like you. From the stories Dad told me, I know you weren't a cookie-cutter mother. Then there're my own experiences with you as a grandmother."

"Don't try to butter me up."

"I'm not. Just look at you. Seventy-something and you're wearing sneakers, jeans, and a T-shirt that says, 'Old Age Ain't for the Weak.' "

"I wouldn't throw stones if I were you. I seem to recall that while my other granddaughters dressed up their Barbies in glamour gowns, you had yours doing search and rescue and examining crime scenes. Most of the time I think she even wore Ken's clothes."

Melissa feigned innocence. "I did that?"

The doorbell interrupted their conversation.

Gram stood. "I'll get it."

Melissa heard the front door open and Gram's voice registering surprise. She put down her glass and went to see what the commotion was about.

"Lissa, I mistook your young man for a delivery boy," Gram said as she pointed to the flowers in Greg's hand.

"Hi." He handed her a bouquet of pink carnations. He looked handsome in black dress pants and a crisp white button shirt. She figured he'd come straight from work to see her. The thought pleased her. Unless it was a pastoral call.

"Thanks." She reached out to take them, but Gram intervened.

"I'll put these in water. You two sit out in the back where it's quiet. Would you like something to drink, Greg?"

"Iced tea if you have it."

"Coming right up." Gram seemed to disappear. Melissa knew that wouldn't last long. All too soon she'd be out there pushing her and Greg together.

"Thank you for the flowers. That's very sweet of you,"

Melissa said as they walked out of the house. She took a seat on the lounge, and Greg sat on the chair beside her.

"How's your arm?"

"Not bad," she lied. It appeared as if he felt responsible for her fall, so she didn't tell him the pain had kept her awake most of the night.

He pulled a black marker from his shirt pocket and motioned to her cast. "May I?"

She nodded.

As he drew on the plaster he continued. "I think this is very appropriate."

A small lightning bolt and his signature were now prominently on display. "What's that for?"

"Don't you remember? When you said I didn't need protective wear to skate?"

She felt herself coloring from the warm feeling infusing her heart. Even if her words did sort of come back to haunt her, it delighted her that he'd remembered their conversation.

"I thought if you weren't up to it, we'd just stay here on Saturday."

"Saturday?" she asked.

"Our real date," he said with a half-grin. "I'll bring over some videos and pizza."

"Should I dress for the occasion?"

Greg's smile broadened.

"I'll fix her up pretty," Gram offered as she brought out a tray with iced tea, chocolate brownies, and a crystal vase filled with the pink carnations. "Though I did hear she needed new shoes."

Melissa groaned at the reference to her boots.

"I rather liked her footwear," Greg said to Gram as amusement filled his features. "Of course, I'm still trying to decide about the hair style."

Melissa swatted Greg's arm. "C'mon—give me a break."

"I think I already did."

They laughed in unison.

❧

When Melissa's alarm buzzed, she felt as if she'd never slept. She'd tossed and turned all night trying to get comfortable with the heavy cast on her arm. In the early morning hours she finally took a painkiller, but it didn't last long. Why she resisted the medication, she didn't know. But if she didn't start getting some rest soon, she'd have to give in and take them as prescribed.

She slipped out of bed and padded to the shower. Placing a plastic bag carefully around her arm, she turned the water on full force and stood under the spray for what seemed like forever. She had difficulty motivating herself this morning. And she knew why.

Last night, as Greg left, he had asked her to go to church with him. She should have said no. But it had been a wonderful night. They'd watched two movies, eaten pizza, and talked. Melissa had never felt so relaxed in someone's company. She didn't have to pretend to be something she wasn't. And, despite his affliction with word puzzles, she found Greg funny and witty.

She giggled remembering some of the games they had played. It took her awhile, but eventually she caught on. Puns, palindromes, and more auto-antonyms.

But it wouldn't be fun this morning. She felt like a fake going to church when God had drifted so far from her. She wondered if He'd even recognize her.

Melissa did her best with her hair and clothes, rushing to be ready by the time Greg arrived. Her stomach did some kind of little flip when she opened the door and saw him. He looked amazingly good in his blue suit. Not a hair out of place, and a hint of aftershave still lingered.

"Morning, Gorgeous."

She ignored his comment even though it made her heart race. "It's too early to be cheery."

"I guess I should have left earlier last night so you could have had more sleep," he said as they walked to the car. His hand touched her back lightly, guiding the way.

Melissa held her breath and resisted her feelings. She mentally argued with herself. What if she came to care for Greg and then lost him? Or maybe he only wanted a friend, since it was clear he still had feelings for someone else. Besides, Greg would probably tire of her tomboy ways. He'd look better with a feminine woman on his arm. Someone like Mattie. What could she possibly offer him? It all added up to the fact that she couldn't risk her heart right now. She felt too vulnerable.

They chatted briefly on the way, and when they reached the parking lot Greg took her hands in his. "I know this is hard for you. Thank you for coming." She thought he might kiss her, but he pulled back. "Wait, and I'll get the door for you."

He placed his warm hand under her elbow, and together they walked into the church. Music played, and she recognized the tune. People greeted one another with joyfulness, and Melissa found herself feeling like a foreigner, no longer a part of God's family.

Throughout the service she observed more than she joined in. Greg had such a pleasing voice that she found herself listening to him sing. Pastor Jamison's sermon didn't bore her, and she was thankful the time passed quickly. A sense of relief flooded her when they left the sanctuary.

As they gathered in the front foyer, many youth and young adults surrounded Greg. He greeted each of them with enthusiasm and listened to their jokes and teasing. Feelings of jealousy threatened Melissa once again.

When Greg took her arm, they moved outside and stood beside the car as another teenager hollered at him. Greg walked to meet the young man halfway across the lawn, and Melissa watched from a distance as they talked. Others stopped and chatted briefly with Greg.

A well-dressed, pretty, young woman came up to Melissa. "Hi. I'm Ursula Jamison."

"Melissa."

"Are you new to Heaven?"

"I've been here all my life. And you?"

"Almost as long." She giggled and glanced over toward Greg. Her smile faded. "Greg's just moved here, and I've been given the job of looking out for him. Since I'm a PK, Daddy thinks I'd make an excellent pastor's wife. So does Greg."

"Well, you know how Greg can pick up strays and drag them in. That's all I am to him. Just another lost sheep." She fought to keep the quiver out of her voice.

Ursula laughed and waved her hand in the air. "I didn't mean to imply that he wouldn't be interested in you. But you're definitely not his type."

Before Melissa could answer, Ursula rushed off to meet Greg, who had started toward them. Melissa couldn't hear Ursula, but Greg's face lit up as they talked. He threw his head back, with dark waves of hair bouncing like in a slow-motion commercial, and placed his hands on Ursula's shoulders. She leaned into his face, sharing more than a friendly greeting. Melissa tried to tell herself it didn't matter since she didn't know what her feelings for Greg were. But if the searing pain in her stomach indicated anything, she needed to sort things out.

"Several of the group are going for lunch and want us to join them," he said when he returned to her. "I hope you don't mind, but I declined."

She didn't reply. Did he not want to be seen with her? Or maybe Ursula had been right about her and Greg having an understanding. She bit her lip and turned to stare out the window as they left the parking lot.

"Did you want to go?"

"Nope."

"I thought maybe you and I could go someplace. . . ."

Something akin to joy fluttered through her until he continued.

"But I figured you'd need to rest, and I have things to do."

How could she even try to compete with Ursula or Amy or whomever? Her heart sank. It would be a whole lot easier on her if she could find something wrong with Greg. Or something she didn't like. Currently he had no faults, or her eyes were covered in scales.

"Is your arm bothering you?" he asked, interrupting her thoughts.

"It's okay."

"You seem rather quiet. I'll bet it hurts more than you let on. I'll take you home, and we can have lunch another time. How does that sound?"

"Sure."

"I've heard about a place called Ming's Chinese restaurant. We'll go there sometime. I don't know where it is, so when we go, it will be up to you to lead."

"Deal," she replied then waited a moment. "You didn't get that one." Suddenly their relationship seemed to be taking a downward spiral. Was it her fears? Her jealousy? Or was Greg just being a friend and she'd read too much into everything?

He slapped his forehead and groaned. "I can't believe I missed that. I think I've met my match."

I hope so, she thought before she could stop herself.

❧

A week had passed since he first met Melissa, and in every way but one she differed from Amy. He felt relieved. Today, however, the pain in her eyes seemed more pronounced than ever before.

"Melissa, we've practically spent the week together. I feel as if I know everything about you, yet nothing at all." *How corny is that?*

"My life is an open book."

"So what's on page 56?"

"That's just yesterday's stuff."

They were seated side by side on the living room sofa. With Mrs. Stoddard in the kitchen, Greg resisted the urge to reach out and take Melissa's hand or brush a strand of hair behind her ear. He wanted to touch her to make some sort of connection. Her warmth filled so many pockets of his life already. He knew he should run the other way, but Melissa's pull was greater. And then he thought about Amy.

"Are you in there, Greg?" Melissa asked, waving a hand in front of his face.

"Sorry."

"I just said how boring my life was, and you proved it." She gave him a slight smile.

"Well, maybe I can help liven it up. After all, I bet you've never had a broken wrist until now."

"You're right about that."

"And we can't forget about the blind date mix-up."

"Yes, that's right up there at the top."

"Pot."

She giggled. "Oh, stop."

"Pots." He leaned back on the sofa, placing his hands behind his head.

"Want a pillow?" she asked.

He closed his eyes. "Better not. I think I could fall asleep in this nice cool room."

"Moor."

"Yes. I'll say it again. I've met my match." He opened one eye and looked at her. "Melissa, tell me why you and God don't talk anymore?"

He watched her stiffen and the smile slip from her pink lips. "You listen to people's problems all week. You don't want to hear mine."

"I wouldn't have asked if I didn't want to know."

She picked up her glass of iced tea and took a sip. "I guess we stopped talking when He stopped listening."

His heart ached when he studied the pained look in her glistening eyes, but he remained quiet, waiting for her to continue.

"I don't think I've ever asked God for much. Just that He would heal Daddy. At first it seemed He had answered my prayers when we found out about the remission. But it didn't last long."

"And because God didn't answer your prayers the way you wanted Him to, you think He deserted you?" Though his words were harsh, he spoke them as softly as he could, understanding more than she could know. He prayed silently while she spoke.

"Didn't He?" she whispered, her bottom lip quivering slightly.

"Melissa, God is like your shadow. He's always there even if you can't see Him. He's never left you. Wherever you go. Even if you don't want Him there." He paused and sat up, leaning closer to her. "We don't know why things happen. But we have to trust that God knows what He's doing. We can't see the master plan, and sometimes the here-and-now seems painfully overwhelming, but you just have to trust Him."

She nodded, and he could tell she struggled to keep from crying.

"He's been with you through all of your struggles and pain. He yearns to hold you and comfort you. Won't you let Him?"

"I can't."

He couldn't stand it any longer and reached out to pull her gently toward him. He stroked her hair and brushed the single tear that escaped down her cheek. "He won't ever leave. You just call when you need Him. Okay?"

She tipped her head and sighed.

"Humans will let you down, Melissa. Me included. We don't want to, but we're not perfect. The only one you can count on is God." He probably sounded more like a preacher than a friend, but these were truths he'd had to relearn after Amy's accident. He shared from his own heartache, not from a seminary textbook, and he prayed that God would use his words to reach Melissa.

She pulled back from his embrace but remained silent.

" 'Trust in the Lord with all your heart and lean not on your own understanding,' " he quoted from Proverbs. "We don't know why God called your father home, but we're not told to try to understand it. We're told to trust Him."

With his final words Melissa broke down and sobbed in his arms while he struggled with his own emotions. He held her until she grew quiet and then kissed the top of her head.

"You need some rest. Let me help you up."

They walked to the front door in silence. Once outside on the step he turned to her. "You're the best mistake that's ever happened to me. I don't know what God has planned for our relationship, but I'm trying to trust Him to show me. Will you at least think about what I said?"

She nodded, still looking sad and doe-eyed.

He found it difficult leaving her like that, but he knew he couldn't stay. "Take care." He walked away, fighting the urge to run back, gather her in his arms, and make everything better. But only God could do that, no matter how much he wanted to.

Chapter 6

Y ou're in love!"

Melissa laughed. "Nowhere near it." *But maybe a little serious,* she admitted to herself. "I'm not ready for a relationship. I'm still trying to figure out who I am."

Gram gave her a warm hug as she entered the house. She moved to the living room and sat down on the sofa, patting the couch for Melissa to join her. "Tell me more about him." She kicked off her sneakers and settled in. Her jeans had tiny flecks of glitter, and her red T-shirt said, "If things improve with age, I must be near magnificent."

Once comfortably seated, Melissa started to tell Gram all about the last four weeks. "He visits almost every day, even went with me when I had the cast removed. When we came home, he cooked dinner and then later massaged my hand and wrist with moisturizer." She held up her pale arm and looked at it. A ripple of excitement shuddered through her as she remembered his caring touch.

"Is that all you've done so far—hold hands?" Gram asked,

impatience resonating in her voice.

Melissa could feel the warmth rising in her cheeks. "There's nothing between us."

Gram smiled. "He's the one."

A tingle zapped through her. How she wished this were true. "It's not that simple. He's a pastor with a great many demands on his time. And I think—I think he has or had a wife already." There. She'd said it. She'd voiced her fears.

"Oh."

Melissa wanted to laugh. It seemed Gram was finally speechless. "It's been a long time since I cared for someone." A moment of trepidation threatened so Melissa blurted out her concern. "And I'm afraid I'll get hurt."

"Lissa, you can't trust anyone but God."

"You sound like Greg."

Gram smiled and patted Melissa's hand. "He seems very wise. Maybe you should listen to him."

She'd been doing just that. "I think I need more time." Though her relationship with God still felt somewhat precarious, she now enjoyed reading her Bible and attending church and home groups. Yet, if she were honest with herself, she knew God still waited with open arms for her full surrender. When would she have the courage to step into His embrace?

"Honey, the pain of your loss will eventually fade. You may never know why, but it doesn't matter."

"I think I know that, but it just hasn't reached my heart yet. How do you deal with it? After all, he was your son."

"It wasn't easy at first. And I still have my days. A mother never expects to outlive her children. But I see our lives as though we are on a large chessboard. I'm a small piece, and my vision is restricted to the square I'm on. But there are other players and other squares. God is the only one who can see the whole board and all the moves."

Melissa liked the analogy.

"I also see how you're starting to blossom now that you are out of the shadow of your dad."

Ouch. "What do you mean?"

"I'm not trying to hurt you, but I know the Bible says all things work for good. Yes, it was difficult to lose Martin, but I think you lived for him. If any good came out of his being called home, it's that you're searching to find yourself. It may be that you still love all the things you did together, or it may be that you did most of them because he loved them. I don't know what you'll find. But I know God will be with you when you do."

Melissa fought the desire to fall into Gram's arms and weep. "Do you think that's why Dad died?"

"I would never suggest such a thing. And don't you hold yourself responsible, young lady." Gram stroked her hair and sighed.

"I took the last batch of flies I'd made down to the shop. The guys seemed really glad to see me, but I felt as if I didn't belong anymore. Charlie and I talked for awhile, but it's not the same without Dad."

"And that's what I'm saying, Sweetie. It's time to find out who you are and what you want to do with your life. It's scary, but your mother and I support you totally. So do your cousins, and I'm sure your new young man does as well. But, more important, God is with you all the way."

"Greg said God was like my shadow. Even on days I couldn't see or feel Him, He's still with me."

"If you don't snap up that man, I just might!" Then Gram jumped off the sofa and began to sing "Me and My Shadow."

Melissa watched with misty eyes, blinking often to keep the tears in check. She felt blessed. So very blessed. *Thank You, Lord!*

❧

They arrived at Heaven Stables on time. Greg, Melissa, and the teens poured out of three vehicles and walked to the stalls.

Melissa couldn't help but notice how great Greg looked in his jeans, T-shirt, and cowboy boots. She watched as he interacted with the kids. Her heart swelled with affection. She'd fought her feelings long enough and finally found herself willing to see where God would take this relationship. If the opportunity presented itself for her to discuss her growing attraction for Greg, she'd seize the day.

Unless of course her nerves got the better of her. Horseback riding was not a new experience for her, but it had been awhile. She hoped they'd give her a docile pony.

"Wow! Look at the size of that horse," one of the teens said as he pointed to a massive white stallion. "That's the one I want."

Greg chuckled. "It would figure. The smallest kid wants the biggest horse."

"And he can have him," Melissa replied. "I want this little

mare here." She moved to a small brown horse with a thick cream-colored mane.

"Need a hand up?" Greg offered with a twinkle in his eye.

"Maybe I'll let the instructor help me."

"Okay." He stepped closer to her. "Did I tell you how beautiful you look this morning?"

"A few times," she answered, not daring to meet his gaze. Her heartbeat raged, and she wished he'd move back in case he could hear it thumping wildly.

Greg caressed her cheek and then tipped her chin upward. He gazed into her eyes, and she felt the world fade away. She couldn't stop the undertow. He had pulled her in, and now her feelings were spiraling out of control. "You grow more beautiful to me with each passing day," he whispered.

"Oww, yuk!" Willy said. "No PDA, or I'm going home."

Melissa turned to the lad. "PDA?"

Greg laughed and pulled back from her. "He means public displays of affection."

"Yeah, and you two are here to keep an eye on us. We don't want to be your chaperones," Willy quipped.

Melissa and Greg laughed.

Soon everyone mounted a horse and prepared to head out on the trail. Melissa loved the early morning smells and inhaled deeply the pungent odor of the creosote bush.

They traveled in silence at first, becoming familiar with their horses. Greg was up ahead, just behind the instructor. Melissa brought up the rear. She'd grown to care for the youth group and enjoyed helping Greg whenever she could. As their relationship grew stronger, it seemed easier for her to share him. The thought brought a smile to her lips.

They rode to the abandoned mining town and dismounted for lunch. The sun beat down on the dusty old place as they seated themselves in the shade of a dilapidated building.

"I think I'll belly up to the bar," Willy said as he pointed to the saloon sign dangling precariously.

Greg nodded at the boy. "The drinks in there might give new meaning to the word *dry*."

"We have some cold pop over here, Willy." Melissa held out a can of cola for the teen.

In no time the food was eaten. With the many jokes and digs the kids had given Greg, she wondered when they'd had time to fill their mouths. She'd laughed so hard her stomach ached.

Everyone helped with the cleanup then climbed back on their horses. Melissa had been pleased that her pick, Dolly, turned out to be the quietest one of the bunch. Dolly obviously knew the route, allowing Melissa the opportunity to sit back and enjoy the journey.

They stopped when they were about halfway back to the stables. Everyone pulled out water bottles and guzzled down large gulps.

As they started to move out, the instructor's horse pranced off the trail, and she struggled to get the pinto back on course. She hollered back to the group, "Keep a tight hold! It might be a snake or something."

Melissa gripped the leather reins and prayed she wouldn't fall. She couldn't take being in a cast again. Her arm was finally starting to look normal. She glanced up ahead. None of the other horses seemed to be upset. Whatever it was had probably been as scared as they were and left. She relaxed a little.

Before she'd finished her thoughts, Dolly spooked and roared to life like a mechanical bull. Melissa held tight, her fingers white from the pressure. The horse raced past a few in the group then veered off the trail. She bounced hard in the saddle and forced herself to try to gain control of the horse. Cacti whipped against her legs, and everything blurred. She could hear a loud thundering in her ears, and then Greg appeared at her side. With muscular arms she'd never noticed before, he pulled Dolly to a stop then lowered Melissa to the ground. In one quick motion he dismounted and held her.

"Are you okay?"

She nodded and stared into his fear-filled eyes.

"I—I—" He couldn't finish his sentence and simply clutched her to him. When their gazes met again, the fear had been replaced. She knew that look. Love. He loved her. She began to tremble.

"You're shaking. Are you sure you're okay?"

"Fine," she whispered.

And then he lowered his mouth to hers. It seemed as if she'd been waiting for this forever. Her stomach did a loop-de-loop as if she were on a roller coaster. When their lips touched, she forgot her queasiness and responded. His kiss was gentle but full of emotion, and she felt light-headed. She didn't want it to end.

Someone cleared his throat.

"How many times do I have to tell you?" Willy asked.

"No PDA," everyone said then burst into laughter.

Melissa knew her face had flushed worse than a ripe tomato. But she didn't care. In fact, she didn't care if Dolly never came back and she had to walk home. She felt as if she had sprouted wings and nothing could shake her light feeling. Not even an embarrassing comment from a teenager.

Chapter 7

I love this place, don't you?" Melissa asked as she walked through the fairgrounds, holding Greg's hand. Cotton candy and caramel apple smells tickled her senses. Bells and laughter rang out around them.

Two weeks had passed since the horseback-riding incident. Or, more important to Melissa, since *the kiss*. Others had followed, but none like that first one that had sent shooting stars throughout her. Yet, despite her joy, she was still uncertain. Ursula always seemed to be hovering nearby, and Greg accepted numerous dinner invitations at Pastor Jamison's house.

"I always wanted to run away with this sort of traveling amusement company." Greg's words brought her back to the present. "I knew I wasn't good enough for the circus."

"Good enough?"

He looked embarrassed. "Yes. I have some talent."

"Am I supposed to guess what it is, or are you going to tell me?" They stopped walking, and she turned to face him.

"If you ever tell anyone, I'll have to kill you."

"Scout's honor. My lips are sealed."

"Maybe I should check?"

She laughed and shook her head. "Don't try to get around this can of worms you've opened."

Greg sighed. "I used to place three hula hoops on the floor in our playroom, grab a pair of rolled up socks, and emcee an entire three-ring show. Then I'd pick up a chair, and I'd become The Great Kelly, the world's best lion tamer."

Melissa struggled not to laugh. "And the lions?"

"The neighbor's cats. And, trust me, they could be vicious. I still have scars." He pulled up his sleeve and showed her a faint, white line on his wrist.

"Ahh, you poor thing. Let me kiss it all better," she said with a pout as she pulled his arm up to her lips.

For a moment the world stood still or simply vanished for Melissa. She was only aware of Greg. His dark eyes held her gaze. She slipped her fingers through his hair and basked in the contentment that seemed to fill her life these days.

She became aware of someone else's presence only when Greg pulled away quickly. "Hey, are you guys still at it?" the boy asked.

"Give it a few more years, Willy, and you'll understand."

"I bumped into Marcus, and he told me you were cleaning up the place. Winning everything." Willy pointed to the stuffed animals Melissa carried.

"You know how rumors go," she answered, worried that Greg might be upset with her skill.

"Don't listen to her modesty. She's incredible."

Willy's eyes lit up. "Wanna help me win something for my mom?"

"Sure."

A short time later Willy left, a large panda bear tucked under his arm.

"That was nice of you."

"I enjoyed it." She laid her head on his shoulder as they wandered through the fairgrounds. They'd been working their way toward the food area when Melissa asked if they could sit down somewhere.

"I thought you'd never ask."

"We could go, if you like."

"I'm waiting until it gets a little darker, and then I'm taking my favorite girl on the Ferris wheel. No one will catch me kissing her there."

"Do I know this woman?"

He chucked her chin. "Oh, yes."

The loop-de-loop feeling had returned. Were her feet still on the ground?

Greg left to buy food while Melissa waited. When Ursula sat down beside her, she wanted to get up and leave.

"Hey. Did Greg win all those for you?"

Melissa hesitated. "Ah, no."

"Where is he anyway? I want him to take me on the Ferris wheel."

"He's over there getting some food."

Ursula stood and headed toward him. Melissa watched as fear boiled in her stomach. Why did it feel as if their perfect evening had been ruined? No matter how much she cared for Greg, there would always be something—or someone—coming between them. *Why, Lord? What am I to learn?*

Greg spoke briefly with Ursula then carried hot dogs and cherry lemonade to their table. They ate in companionable silence, watching the crowd.

"Is my girl ready for the ride of her life?"

"I don't know. Where did Ursula go?"

"Is that what's been bothering you?"

Melissa couldn't answer.

"It's just a little crush. Give her time, and she'll get over it." He pulled her closer. "Now are you ready for the ride of your life?"

"A little sure of yourself, eh?" she teased, knowing that being with him was already the ride of her life. He accepted everything about her and didn't ask for more than he willingly gave. He respected her and appreciated her talents, never trying to compete. She'd never known a man like him, and just thinking about him gave her goose bumps.

"I'll give you your money back if it isn't," he said with a wide grin.

"Deal."

He replied in an instant, "Lead."

"You got it this time."

"Emit."

Even this silly game between them somehow caused her to feel warm and tender toward him. "If this is the experience you claim it will be, what's your reward?"

"Drawer."

"You're a nut."

"Takes one to know one." He pulled her into his embrace while they waited for their turn on the ride. "Besides, I have all the reward I need right here in my arms."

On the wheel Greg held her hand as they went around and around. She loved the view, with a crimson sunset off in the distance. When they were stopped at the top, he turned to her. "You've brought so much joy into my life, Mel." He kissed her forehead, nuzzled her neck then found her lips with his.

Melissa realized that for the first time since her dad's death it didn't hurt being called Mel. In fact, it felt right hearing Greg say it. Everything felt right, and she thanked God that she'd finally trusted Him. It seemed as if her life was now on track. And she'd finally had a date that didn't constitute a disaster.

When she looked down on the ground, she could see Ursula watching, and a feeling of foreboding surrounded her. She shivered.

❧

Melissa checked her watch. Not quite noon. Maybe she'd wait inside the church for Greg. Perhaps he could even leave early for their lunch date.

She entered the building and made her way to the office. The church secretary waved as she left her desk.

"Your timing is perfect. I have to get more paper, and we store it in the basement. Can you answer the phone if it rings? Greg's in with Pastor Jamison."

"Sure." She sat down at the desk and waited.

Daniel Jamison raised his voice. "I'm telling you, Greg— Melissa Stoddard is not pastor's wife material."

"You're right. She's not pastor's wife—"

The phone rang, and Melissa attempted a pleasant greeting, while her stomach churned and she felt like dying. Why hadn't Greg defended her? How could he have agreed? Maybe she embarrassed him.

A panicked voice drew her back to the phone conversation. "Please—I need to speak to Greg Kelly right away. Tell him it's about Amy."

"Yes," she replied, her world spinning out of control. As she turned to knock on the study door, it flew open. Greg stopped.

Melissa stammered. "Phone. It's for you. It's Amy." She turned and fled. He called after her, but she couldn't stop. What could he say? Nothing would take away this hurt, this pain. Nothing. Amy had returned, and she wasn't pastor's wife material. Anguish, like a sharp razor, twisted in her stomach.

Oh, God, why? Did You bring me this far only to abandon me? Help me. Don't let me fall apart.

Once safely in the car she put her fingertips to her lips. The memory of his first kiss, *the kiss,* burned. She'd been a fool.

She peeled out of the parking lot. A horn blared. She didn't care. She wove between the cars, attempting to put as much distance between her and Greg as she could. She checked the rearview mirror for the flashy red car. It was nowhere to be seen. She fought the disappointment. If only he'd come after her. Tell her some lie, anything.

She kept driving. A few blocks later she glanced in the

mirror again and then drove onto the shoulder. A car pulled in behind her. She waited for the driver.

"Afternoon, Melissa." He tipped his hat. "Are you wearing them big boots again or something?"

"Just give me a ticket, Charlie," she snapped, wishing she'd never noticed his flashing lights. Wishing she'd never stayed in Heaven. Wishing she'd never gone out with the wrong guy, who turned out to be the right guy. What a mess.

Charlie leaned his large frame in the window toward her. "I get off in five. You look like you could use a friend, rather than a ticket."

"I've had enough of my friends. Give me the ticket."

He pulled out his book and started writing. She stared ahead. Surely Greg would have had time to catch her by now. Why hadn't he followed her and made everything right? Amy. It always came back to her. He loved Amy, not her. Amy was probably pastor's wife material. While Melissa would only ruin his reputation. His perfect pastor image with his perfect pastor wardrobe.

Charlie handed her a slip of paper. "Melissa, go see your grandmother."

She slipped the car in gear and tore away from the side of the road. At a stoplight she looked at the ticket. Bless his heart—he'd only given her a warning. She headed toward Heavenly Village Retirement Community. Charlie had been right. She needed her Gram.

❧

"Daniel, I have to leave town. It's an urgent family matter,"

Greg said to his boss after taking the phone call Melissa had given him.

Pastor Jamison stood up behind his desk, compassion etched in his fatherly features. "Can I help in any way, Son?"

"Pray for Amy."

"I do, and I will." He stepped around the desk and laid a hand on Greg's shoulder. "And I'll be praying for you as well."

Greg felt a lump in his throat. He thanked God for the great relationship he and Daniel had established right from the start. "I'll make sure I'm back in time for the youth mission trip."

"You take whatever time you need. I'll go on the trip, if I have to. Besides, now might be a good time to get away for awhile."

He knew Daniel was referring to Melissa, but he ignored his pastor's concern. "If you see Melissa, tell her I had to leave unexpectedly."

"Let me pray for you before you go."

A short time later Greg headed to the airport. He tried to call Melissa but reached only the answering machine. He hung up without leaving a message. Something was wrong. He hadn't missed the distressed look on her face when he'd opened the door. Was it worry about the phone call? Or had she heard what Daniel had said about her?

With slow and heavy steps he wandered the airport until his flight back to Seattle. Sweat beaded on his brow, and he raked his hand through his hair in frustration. Back and forth he paced, wondering where Melissa had gone. He needed to talk to her. He needed to see her smile. And kiss her good-bye in case he didn't come back.

He called her again, and this time he left a message. "Melissa, I'm going to be out of town. I'll call you as soon as I can." It probably wasn't what she wanted to hear, but in the crowded airport he didn't want to tell her how he felt.

They announced his flight, and he picked up his bags. He marched to the gate like a solider off to war. Where were his loved ones seeing him off, praying for his safe return? Only one person here in Heaven loved him. And now he worried that might no longer be the case.

If he didn't return, would it matter anyway? Yes, it would. No matter what happened, or where he went, Melissa would always have a piece of his heart. But Amy needed him. May need him for the rest of her life.

That meant he had nothing to offer Melissa. He wished he hadn't left the phone message. Unless he was coming back to Heaven, he'd never call her again. It would only hurt her—and him. He'd rather have her hate him than to think he'd made a choice—when he'd had no choice at all.

❧

"You must be mistaken, Honey. No one would ever question your character." Gram still held her close, and Melissa didn't reply. "You sit down, and I'll get us some tea." She filled the kettle and set it on the stove.

Melissa sat in Gram's kitchen nook and pulled a tissue from her purse. She dabbed at her red, swollen eyes then sighed. "I think Greg has a wife or fiancée."

Gram sat next to Melissa. Her hair, neatly styled, belied her age, as did the jeans and top she had donned. "There's no place like Heaven" was emblazoned on the front of the bright yellow T-shirt. "Why do you believe there's someone else?"

"Her name's Amy."

"I don't think you're giving Greg enough credit. I'm certain he would have told you if he were taken."

"He gets a faraway look on his face when her name is mentioned. And then he appears to be in pain." Melissa stared out the window.

Gram poured the tea and busied herself with the sugar and cream. "You love him, don't you?"

She shook her head no then nodded. She couldn't fool her Gram. She loved Greg. She'd loved him the moment he'd hugged that silly old pine tree the first night they'd met.

"Are you going to walk away from him?"

"I have no choice, Gram. First of all, he's gone. And, second, Pastor Jamison is telling him whom he can and cannot see. And it's not me."

"I think you may be jumping to conclusions here, Sweetie."

Melissa turned and eyed her Gram. "I was there."

"I'm sure it's not what you're thinking." Gram patted Melissa's hand. "You need to talk to him."

She'd had enough pain. Did she have to face Greg and have him spell it out, too? No, this time Gram didn't understand, and Melissa couldn't take her advice. She couldn't let her heart be ripped any further. She never wanted to see Greg again. Even if it meant she had to leave Heaven and everything she loved—including him.

Chapter 8

"Greg, good to have you back," Daniel Jamison greeted him when he entered the church office.

He reached out and shook his boss's hand. "It's great to be here. I thought I missed the Seattle rain. Guess I didn't." The dreary weather didn't help with the gloom that had settled over him and his family, either.

"You're cutting it awful close, I'd say. What time does the mission trip leave tomorrow?"

He perched on the edge of the secretary's desk. "We'll be meeting here at four-thirty A.M."

"You'll forgive me if I'm not here to see you off?"

"No problem. We have a bon voyage crew. Many of our senior citizens in the church have each prayed daily for one of our youth. They'll be here tomorrow morning to pray for them and see us off. Just before I left, some strong friendships were beginning to form. I hope it's continued."

"That's great," Daniel said as he strolled toward his office. "I think this would look good in the denominational newsletter."

Greg shook his head. Some things never change. He slid off the desk and went into his own office, closing the door behind him. He picked up the phone and dialed Melissa's number. The line was busy.

He shuffled some papers then tried the number again. This time he got through, but the answering machine picked up. He left a message asking her to call him.

At the end of the day when he hadn't heard from her, he headed home to do some laundry and finish packing. He prayed she would call, but by eleven P.M. his phone had remained silent. Maybe he should go over there. He knew he should get some sleep since four A.M. came early, but he needed to talk to Melissa. He'd thought of her continually in Seattle. He had no doubts about how he felt. God had granted him a peace about it too.

He jumped into his car and drove over to her place. All the lights were out. Should he wake her up? It would be another week before he saw her if he didn't. He knocked on the door but received no answer. He assumed she must be out and went home, feeling as if he'd lost his best friend.

He had a message on his answering machine when he returned. He hit the play button and listened.

"Greg, it's Melissa."

She didn't sound right. Like maybe she'd been crying. He turned up the volume.

"I'm sorry I'm not telling you this in person." She paused. "I think it would be best if we don't see each other anymore. It's hard for me to say this, but I think God brought you into my life when I needed someone, but it's time I stopped depending on you and moved on. Thanks for everything, *Friend*."

She'd made it very clear he had only been a temporary thing. She considered him a friend by the way she'd pointedly said the word.

He slammed his fist on the bookcase, and the picture frames rattled. Not only did his hand hurt, but so did his heart.

But he would not give up. He'd pray and think of something by the time he arrived back in town. He believed God had indeed brought them together as Melissa had said, and he felt certain God didn't want them apart. He loved Melissa, and he'd prove it to her.

❦

Melissa hung up the phone and bowed her head. *Forgive me, Lord, for not telling the truth. And for trusting Greg, rather than You.*

It wouldn't be easy trying to forget him, but she appreciated what they'd shared.

"Lissa, what's the catalog for?" her mother called out from the kitchen.

She walked into the room and sat at the table. "It's for Heaven Community College."

Her mother stared wide-eyed at her.

"What? You never heard of college?"

"Okay, what's going on?"

"Since I'm no longer babysitting the twins and I've decided to give up my lucrative fly-fish business, I decided it was time to figure out what I want to be when I grow up."

"And?" Her mother sat down and waited for her to continue.

"I'm still thinking."

"Are you going to tell me what happened between you and Greg? Or are you going to run away?"

"Going to college is not running away."

Her mother shook her head. "I'm not saying that at all. I know you're hurting. I want to help."

"Let's just say I'm not pastor's wife material and leave it at that."

"Oh, Honey." Her mother stood and embraced her. "Anyone would be a fool if they thought that."

"Thanks, Mom." She pulled away from the hug. "I think I'll be okay. I'm trusting God, and I won't analyze this to death. I don't know why He brought Greg into my life, but I'm thankful He did."

"My little girl's grown up."

"Don't go getting sentimental on me now!" They laughed, and Melissa padded off to bed.

She flipped through her Bible and stopped at Proverbs 3. It was the verse Greg had shared with her. "I'm trusting You, God. Help me get past this. Help me to move on with my life."

But as she spoke the words aloud, she had the distinct feeling they merely bounced off the walls and shattered when they landed on the floor. Broken into a million pieces, like her heart. But she couldn't hold Greg back from his job, and she didn't want to take him from Amy. Why did doing the right thing have to hurt so much?

❧

"Lissa, what perfect timing. Jeff just finished our Internet class, and we're going to take some refreshments in the dining room."

Melissa felt herself freeze on the spot. She didn't want to spend time with Jeff. Especially now with Greg gone. Gram always believed in getting back in the saddle once you've been thrown. Dating, in her eyes, would be the same. Falling off a horse seemed less painful to Melissa.

Gram made certain Jeff sat beside her once they reached the busy dining hall. He seemed nervous and pushed up his glasses several times before he finally spoke. "It's nice to see you again, Melissa."

"Thanks. I hear you're doing a great job teaching."

"I enjoy it."

"Melissa loves technology," Gram said, leaning between them. "She has one of those little music players that sounds like the band is in the room when she plays it."

"MP3?" Jeff asked.

Melissa shook her head. "Mini-disc."

"And don't forget your little electronic black thingy. Jeff has one, too."

"Visor?"

"Palm IIIc," Melissa said.

"See—you two even talk the same language. Look at how well you're communicating. I knew what I was doing. . . ." Gram's voice trailed off, and a smile played across her lips. Melissa couldn't miss the gleam in her eyes. Then she read Gram's new T-shirt: *Matchmaker*.

Dread filled her. Stopping Gram would be like trying to calm a tornado.

"Jeff, why don't you show Lissa your Web page?"

He cleared his throat and stood. "Ah. Yeah. Sure."

Melissa looked around the room. No way out. She followed him to the library in silence, his shiny shoes squeaking with every step.

"Your Gram is such a great lady." He sat down at the computer and reached for the mouse. After a few clicks a video bounced onto the screen.

"Yeah, we love her." Melissa moved closer to get a better view. As the screen flashed before her, Jeff provided a brief narration.

"This is like a public service announcement site. It provides awareness for the dangers of drunk drivers. Several major medical facilities, police agencies, and fire halls help support the site."

"I like the colors you've used. The flash looks good, but can you slow down the image montage?"

Jeff clicked a few keys faster than Melissa could say Internet, and the flash ran again. Pictures of tragic crash scenes transitioned onto the monitor one after the other. Some of them were horrific.

"Wait. Can you stop that graphic?"

"I can do better than that," he replied. More fast *tick-tick-tick* as he typed in commands. The image popped up, and Melissa scrutinized it carefully.

"Someone you know?"

She blinked back tears and squeaked out, "Yes."

"Doesn't look like anyone could have survived. My stuff is

at home, but if I'm not mistaken this accident was in Portland or maybe Seattle. The driver walked away while the passenger sustained massive burns."

Melissa gazed at the screen. Greg's tortured face leaned over someone—a woman—on the stretcher. She figured it was Amy. Had Greg been driving?

". . .check my notes and find the story."

"I'm sorry. I missed what you said."

"I can probably find the article since I had to get permission for the photographs."

Did she want to know? No, she didn't. These last two weeks God had constantly reminded her to trust Him, and she had. Greg would stay devoted to Amy, even if she had been badly burned. Thus, she would never try to force Greg to choose. The time had come to let him go for good. "No. Thanks for the offer, though."

"If you change your mind, let me know."

"Your site's impressive. Is that what you do for a living?"

"No. This is just fun stuff. Like your fly-fish Web page."

"Well, don't hold that against me. I'm still learning."

"Your HTML code looked good. Use scripts much?"

"Nah. I don't have time to learn the difficult stuff. The mouse rollover is my masterpiece."

Jeff laughed, and Melissa realized he was actually a nice guy. Too bad things had worked out the way they had. She wondered what would have happened had Greg not shown up. She shook her head, hoping to rid herself of such thoughts.

"I have to get going. Thanks, Jeff."

"Yeah, it's been fun. If you ever need help with your Web page, give me a call."

"You'll be the first one I turn to if I need someone." And she meant it.

After saying good-bye to Jeff and then Gram, Melissa left the community residence. She could tell it would be only a matter of time before Gram hatched another scheme. Maybe Melissa could be in Timbuktu by then. She had to find a way to stop the blind-date disasters.

Chapter 9

Melissa gave up. She couldn't fight Gram. She missed Greg, but she knew she needed to get over him. Whether he had a wife or girlfriend or whatever didn't matter. What mattered was that he would not be hers. He'd warned her that people would let her down. She figured everyone else might, but not him. She'd figured wrong.

She figured she'd never go out on another blind date, either. Again she'd figured wrong. But this time she held her ground. This time she had terms. She'd agree to this folly, but then no more. No matter what happened, she'd never have to be set up again. What troubled her right now was how easily Gram had accepted her conditions. Perhaps her worries were for nothing. Or maybe she'd be forced to spend her evening with Jeff. Maybe she'd get a headache—fast.

"Honey, you'd better get ready. Your date's due soon."

"Can't I go like this?"

Her mother sighed.

"Fine. I'll change."

"And, Lissa?"

"I know. No storm commando boots," she said as she stood up from the table and placed her dirty dishes in the sink.

"I wasn't going to say that."

"Sorry, Mom. But you know how I hate this matchmaking stuff."

"We want to see you happy. Like you were with—" She stopped. "I mean—"

"I know what you mean." Melissa gave her mother a hug and headed off to her room to get ready for her date. Or, as Greg had called it, her disaster.

If she ever did find the man God had planned for her, she'd have lots of silly stories to share. At this point, though, it was difficult for Melissa to laugh about any of them.

She'd realized that what she'd had with Greg had not been about being dependent or having someone to fix everything. It had been about sharing. About carrying one another's burdens. It had been about loving someone and being loved in return.

Stop it. Don't think about that now.

She showered and put on a nice pair of white slacks with an emerald green shell. Pulling out the set of pearls her Gram had given her, she slipped them around her neck. Gram had told her they were for her wedding. Maybe she should take them off.

Her mother knocked. "I'm going next door to check on Mrs. Wilson. Listen for the doorbell, will you?"

It felt a little like *déjà vu* for Melissa as she opened the door and stepped out of her bedroom. Hadn't her mother conveniently left the house on her last blind date? "Okay, Mom."

"You look lovely, Darling."

"Thanks. Should I take the pearls off?"

"Gram gave them to you to wear, not keep in a box. You know how she feels about that."

Melissa knew. Gram didn't save things for special occasions; every day was a special occasion for her. "Okay."

Melissa paced the kitchen waiting for her date. She felt nervous.

The door chime brought her out of her thoughts. Her heart quickened, and she tried to calm herself. As she approached the front door, she resisted peering through the peephole and simply opened it wide.

Her mouth dropped in surprise.

"Hi," he said with a smile that threatened to stop her heart.

Melissa seemed paralyzed.

"I hope I'm not late. I wouldn't want someone else to whisk you away."

"You're my date?"

"Your real date." He held up jazzy rollerblades. "And you're not dressed right."

She snatched a lock of hair and clamped it between her lips.

"I've been practicing. I'll beat you this time for sure."

Finally she found her tongue. "Greg, I can't go out with you. We've been through this. I'm sorry."

"Mel, please. I need to explain about Amy."

She winced. He called her Mel, and it still felt so right. But it was all wrong. She needed to close the door and leave Greg behind. She couldn't bear to be hurt again.

"Please."

She let him in the house and prayed she wouldn't regret it. Once they were seated in the kitchen, she poured two glasses of iced tea and sat as far away from him as she could.

"I don't know what you heard that day at the church; but I can assure you, it's not what you think."

He was reopening her wounds. Would she be able to stand it?

"I don't know where to start."

Melissa gave him a hint. "Amy." She watched as his eyes clouded and pain etched his features.

"Amy. One of my greatest failures in life," he said with a sigh. "I should have been there for her. Protected her. Kept her safe."

"Greg, only God could do all those things. Sometimes we only see what we should have done later, after the catastrophe."

"I knew. I just didn't do anything." He raked a hand through his wavy hair.

"Why don't you start at the beginning? Were you married already?"

"Married?" He looked up, his eyes wide open. "No," he said, shaking his head. "Is that what you think? She's my little sister."

Melissa struggled with her feelings. She felt relieved that Greg wasn't married; but it pained her to think of all Amy had gone through.

"She was engaged to a guy I couldn't stand. I did everything to try to break them up. When it finally happened—after I'd stopped trying—Amy was devastated. Though I had not been responsible for the parting, I still felt like a heel. So I kept to myself. We didn't talk about what had happened, and Amy slipped away from us, becoming despondent."

Melissa moved to Greg's side and took his hand. It was simply an act of friendship, she told herself.

"She began going out drinking and trying drugs, but I never noticed. I didn't want to notice. One night she nearly died in a terrible accident."

She'd seen the pictures, and it wrenched her heart.

"Her date had been drinking, and they crashed into a guard rail. The car caught fire. Burns covered most of her body, and she's been in and out of a coma ever since."

"I'm so sorry, Greg."

"It's all my fault. I didn't want her to marry a jerk. Who was I to determine what was best for her?"

"You did it because you loved her."

"Obviously not enough. I never saw her problems. I'm the reason she spends her days in a hospital. She took a turn for the worse and nearly died. That's why I went back. She's stable again. But what type of life does she have in a bed connected to tubes?" Melissa recognized the bitterness in his voice.

"Greg, you could no more save your sister than I could my father. And, in the words of a dear friend of mine, we have to trust God and lean not on our own understanding. Forgive yourself."

"I drive her car as a constant reminder of what I did to her."

"Maybe she gave it to you as a constant reminder of the love she has for her big brother."

For the first time since they'd started talking, he smiled at her. "I told Pastor Jamison he was wrong about you."

She inhaled deeply, remembering the painful words he'd spoken. "That's not what I heard."

"Did you hear everything?"

"Just the part about your agreeing with him that I'm not suitable for you."

"Oh." He looked into her eyes with longing. "I should tell you that Ursula had a hand in her father's distrust of you. Us. Guess she wanted to pay us back for the night we went to the fair."

"That doesn't surprise me." She felt a pang of sorrow for the girl and prayed God would bless Ursula.

"And, yes, I said you were not pastor's wife material—on the outside. But that on the inside there was no one better for the job."

Had he said what she hoped he'd said?

"I know God is still doing a great work in us. We have lots of things to sort out. But that's the best part of growing old together. Sharing the joys as well as the pains. If we were perfect, what type of life would that be?"

Melissa's eyes pooled with unshed tears. "No, we're not perfect—"

"But I think we're perfect for each other," he interrupted her and looked into her eyes.

"A tomboy like me? With Mr. Immaculately Dressed and Pressed?"

"A beautiful woman, inside and out, with a heart bigger

than the state of Arizona. A heart I love. In fact, I love every-thing about you, Mel. Can you forgive me? Can you love me?"

She flung her arms around his neck. "Yes. Yes."

"Want to be married at the park on rollerblades?"

"No. I think I actually want to wear the white dress." She giggled and pulled back to seek out his eyes. Their gazes locked, and she forced herself to breathe.

"Okay, but there's one thing."

She stiffened. As she felt the panic rise in her, she closed her eyes and forced herself to listen.

Trust Me.

She relaxed. "I know—you get to pick the radio station."

"That too," he said with a grin then dropped his hands from her shoulders to her waist, encircling her. He raised an eyebrow as if he were about to lecture her. "Don't ever change. I love you just the way you are."

Joy burst forth along with a multitude of tears. "And I love you."

A sweet sensation of belonging enveloped her as they kissed. Then he leaned forward and whispered in her ear, "So will you be wearing boots under the dress?"

BEV HUSTON

Bev Huston lives in British Columbia—where residents don't tan, they rust—with her husband, two children, sister, and two cats who give new meaning to the word aloof. Bev began her writing career in 1994 when, out of frustration, she wrote a humorous column about call waiting, which sold right away. She is a contributing editor for *The Christian Communicator* and spent the last four years as the inspirational reviewer for Romantic Times Bookclub. *Mix and Match* is her first novella, and she knows it couldn't have been written without the love of support of family and friends. Bev's E-mail address is: bev@bevhuston.com.

Mattie Meets Her Match

by Kristin Billerbeck

Chapter 1

"Jeff Weatherly is back in town." Gram's voice was the epitome of casual, but Mattie knew what the simple sentence conveyed. *The man you let slip away, the one you were meant to marry—he's back in town. Let the church bells ring!*

"Gram, if Jeff is back in town, he's probably brought his new wife with him." Mattie took out a glass vase from its cardboard home, unwrapped the newspaper, and placed it on the mantel. She smiled to herself, knowing Jeff wasn't married and that her grandmother harbored the same information. But Gram, being the social butterfly she was, undoubtedly knew something more. Against Mattie's better judgment she longed to hear the latest. Her stomach twisted waiting for the story.

Luckily Gram practically burst out, "Jeff's *not* married! Had his grandmother tell me so herself." Gram winked, while Mattie's eyes narrowed. "He says he'd love to see you again."

Mattie wagged a finger at her grandmother. "Aha! I knew it, Gram. That innocent act doesn't play here anymore." Mattie smoothed the emotion from her voice. "Jeff is a very nice man, but he's not the man for me." The infamous "they" always said you never got over your first love. Sadly it was true for Mattie. She'd nursed her broken heart for ten years now, waiting for a new Mr. Right to steal the memories away. She was still waiting.

"If you'll remember correctly, Gram, Jeff dumped me for more time with the chess club. If I wasn't more important than a pawn then, why would you think ten years would make any difference?"

"Oh, that was ages ago. Have you no forgiveness in your heart? He was just a boy then, interested in boyish things. Who says he's not the man for you?"

"Perhaps it's the fact that he packed up and left town after high school, and I haven't heard from him since. Could be me, but I think that pretty much sends a message. Besides, I heard Mel had a date with him first." She heard the accusatory note in her tone that she'd meant to keep to herself. "Did you really think you could set him up with Mel and I wouldn't hear about it?"

Gram went about unpacking the boxes from the attic, humming as she did so.

"Mel said he was a geek, Gram."

More humming.

"If you're so certain he's the man for me, why did you set Mel up with him first?" Mattie crossed her arms before picking up another knickknack to display. The very idea of booted Mel with choir boy Jeff Weatherly made Mattie giggle. What could Gram have been thinking?

"Oh, you girls, you're always scheming against your poor old

Gram. I should have had grandsons. If you must know, I didn't think you'd be interested unless someone else was."

Mattie grimaced. "But someone else wasn't interested." She forced a laugh. "Someone else thinks he's a nerd!" *A nerd who would regret the day he said good-bye to Mattie Stevens.* She tossed her hair subconsciously. Hadn't she become a successful artist? Renowned among Scottsdale's elite? Her ego gave way to real emotion. The truth was she longed to see Jeff again. Just to prove to herself she was over him.

"Mel was just more interested in another young man, Mattie. There's no crime in that. Jeff Weatherly will find someone to marry. You might as well see if anything's there, you know, any of that spark left before it's too late."

"Gram, Jeff dumped me for chess. What on earth do you think has changed?" Mattie swallowed hard, hoping for an answer. If Gram knew something Jeff had said, Mattie longed to hear about it.

"Pshaw!" her grandmother said, complete with the Victorian hand motion. "He's all grown up now. You can't hold his childishness against the man. He probably wasn't ready to get married after high school. Men mature slower than women, and he's twenty-eight now. It's time. I only thought of Mel first because I thought it might pique your interest. You can be such a stubborn thing."

"Should I pick out the ring now? Or after I set the date?" Mattie raised her eyebrows, but her sarcasm belied the lift she felt inside.

She watched her grandmother closely. Although Gram was

seventy-five now, that fact hadn't slowed her in the least. She'd moved into the equivalent of a senior Club Med and had a social calendar that made Mattie's look pathetic. Gram's complexion had grayed with her hair, but her blue eyes never lost their sparkle. Her personality never lost its magnetism.

"Now you're just being a smart aleck. Hand me that vase. I'm tired of looking at that old thing. I'm going to put it in the box with the other ancient artifacts. Maybe they'll get something for it at the sale." With a spry motion she put the vase out of sight. "Forget about Jeff. I suppose if he wasn't right for Melissa, he's probably wrong for you, too. On another subject, I need help at the church flea market. Will you work in a booth on Saturday morning?"

Mattie's pulse slowed. That was it? That was all her grandmother had on Jeff? Even Melissa shared more than that! Mattie's mood lilted as she realized the day wouldn't be spent thwarting Gram's matchmaking tendencies. She'd been looking forward to feigning lack of interest and hearing more about what Jeff had been up to since returning to town. "Sure, Gram—I can help at the sale, whatever you need."

"Be in the church parking lot at 8:00 A.M. Josephine will set you to work."

The doorbell rang. "I'll get it." Mattie surveyed the new, cleaned-out apartment. "It looks great, Gram—don't you think? We should have done this before you moved."

Her grandmother smiled. Opening the door, Mattie lost her breath. Jeff Weatherly stood much taller than she remembered him, at least six foot and bigger. Much broader in the shoulders.

Gone was the lanky teen with feathered bangs, replaced by a self-assured and traditional gentleman.

Jeff's hand laced the doorway, and Mattie found herself without words. She swallowed, multiple times, but still a simple sentence wouldn't form. Suddenly his shoulders bent toward her, and he embraced her. She felt her heart pounding, and she prayed he wouldn't hear the persistent drumming that filled her own eardrums. His arms around her made her silence more pervasive. *Geek? Where was the geek, Mel?*

He pulled away, planting a simple kiss on her cheek. "Well, if it isn't little Mattie Stevens. What a surprise! All grown up and prettier than ever."

Mattie simply nodded, her limbs unable to listen to the message her mind sent them. Feeling the complete idiot, she nodded and forced a smile.

"Hi, Mrs. Stoddard." Jeff waved. "That furniture ready to go to the sale?"

"All set. Right there by the door. Mattie can help you get it to the car." Gram winked at Mattie.

"Where are your glasses?" Mattie finally said.

"Glasses?"

"Mel said you wore glasses." *Big, ugly, doofy glasses were her exact words.*

"No, I wear contacts." He paused for a moment, putting an end table down. "Oh." He chuckled. "The night with Mel. Well, I guess I should say *almost the night* with your cousin. She stood me up. I'd lost a contact, and my good glasses were at work, so I had my old pair." He laughed again. "I made an impression on Melissa, huh?"

"Not one you'd want to brag about." Mattie's heart stirred in confusion. She loved the way he looked: tall, handsome, conservative, and yet she was so angry that he seemed so put together, not the helpless nerd Mel described at all.

"Do you really think the president of the Sequoia High School chess club is worried about impressions?" Jeff smiled at her and raised his eyebrows.

The mention of her former rival for attention infuriated Mattie. "You still wear that title like the badge of honor it is." Mattie rolled her eyes. "Gram, I'll take these things out."

"Be my guest," Gram said.

Mattie took a box full of trinkets toward Jeff's waiting Cherokee. The dark blue color sparkled in the hot Arizona sun, and she waited for Jeff to open the door rather than sizzle her own hand against the dark paint. Jeff lifted the hatchback, and all the anger Mattie had felt for ten years flooded into her. With her whole being she wanted to kick the smug Jeff in the shins just to make him feel something. She swallowed the bitter pill of resentment.

"Thank you for helping my grandmother. It was nice to see you again."

He reached for her hand. "That's it? That's all you have to say to me?"

She searched his presence, letting her eyes drink in his serious good looks. Although he still made her heart pound, there was so much pain built around it. Scar tissue that hadn't ceased since the day he'd called her on the phone and put an end to their innocent, blossoming romance.

She pulled her hand away. "What is it you expect me to say?"

"Come on, Mattie—you can't possibly be angry with me." His innocence enraged her.

"I had to take my prom dress back to the store. The only more humiliating thing would be returning a wedding gown. All my friends went, and I missed out on one of the highlights of high school because *you* had a chess match. I know it sounds childish to you now, but it was important to me. I thought I was important to you. Important enough to forego a chess game."

"It was the state championship, Mattie! I couldn't help it if we had to travel to Phoenix."

Mattie laughed aloud. "I cannot believe I am standing here at twenty-eight years old, debating the importance of a high-school chess match. As I said, it was nice to see you again, Jeff. I hope life treats you well." She turned to walk away and heard his deep voice follow her.

"I didn't know what to do with a girlfriend, Mattie. You probably expected me to kiss you. I didn't know how to kiss you."

Mattie turned and saw the blue of his eyes masked under his downcast eyebrows. Her pulse quickened, and she saw briefly that hidden place in Jeff. The corner of his secret world that called out to her, beckoning her.

Her eyes teared up. "Why didn't you tell me that then? You might have saved me a lot of heartache."

His hands became animated. "Mattie, I was a nerd. You were a cheerleader. All the boys wanted you to be their girlfriend. I was the president of the chess club. All the girls wanted me to set up the AV equipment. I used to hear what the guys said about how fine you were."

They both laughed at the dated expression before resuming their conversation. "I wasn't a cheerleader in my heart, Jeff. I was a geek, and I thought the sun rose and set on one boy, and one boy only. I'm sad if you thought I cared about appearances. I thought you knew me better than that." She hesitated. "The boy I was attracted to was the smartest kid in school. He was quietly handsome and studying calculus while the rest of the class did simple math. But there was a catch. That boy just wanted to play chess. He didn't want to have a girlfriend." She smiled and started for the door, but again his voice stopped her.

"I don't just want to play chess now." His voice was deep and full of a strength she wouldn't have known he possessed. "Have dinner with me."

Her eyes closed. She'd waited for this moment for ten years: the chance to hurt him as she'd been hurt; but the barbed words she'd planned, the ones she'd rehearsed in the mirror, didn't come. Looking into the depths of his blue eyes and into the soul that had just opened to her, she couldn't do it. She had to fight saying yes with all her being.

"No. . . ." Her voice trailed off. "No, thank you. I appreciate the offer, though." She smiled faintly. "More than you'll ever know." But she wasn't about to let him hurt her again. Jeff took everything seriously except romance, and she'd do well to remember that.

She walked into her grandmother's apartment and wiped the moisture from her forehead. "I'm going to head down to the pool for a break, Gram. Do you need anything?"

Her grandmother glanced toward her; then, in Gram's knowing way, she kept quiet about Jeff. "You go ahead. You look as if you could use the break."

Mattie spoke her thoughts aloud. "I thought there would be magic. Fireworks. There's only reserved politeness, and my heart is breaking all over again."

Gram smiled gently and nodded.

Chapter 2

Even in her air-conditioned condominium, the heat of the blossoming day swelled around Mattie. Had she really volunteered for an outside yard sale? In Heaven, Arizona? In the summer? She groaned at the thought. Gram could talk the saguaro out of water. Mattie dressed in a modest pair of cuffed shorts with a T-shirt and slipped into a light pair of flip-flops. She crinkled her nose at her freshly washed face in the mirror. *Good enough.*

After loading the last few items from Gram's things into her compact car, Mattie drove the familiar road to church. The hustle and bustle of preparation filled the entire parking lot, and Mattie found Josephine Wessex ordering everyone about and maintaining calm amidst chaos. Mattie grinned. Maybe someday she would be organized like that with age, too, but somehow she doubted it. The artist in her was never far away.

"Hi, Mrs. Wessex!" Mattie called with a wave.

Josephine turned and broke into a wide grin. "Well, Mattie, what a treasure you are. Always here to help when you can." She pinched Mattie's cheek so firmly a rosy blush must have appeared. "You are so much like your grandmother, unselfishly giving your free time. Did you see all the beautiful Depression glass your grandmother donated? That will bring a pretty penny for the church."

"Gram never did care much about trinkets, Mrs. Wessex."

"No, she's what they call a people-person." Suddenly the shattering of glass broke their conversation. "I had better get over there. You're with Jeff Weatherly in booth seventeen." Josephine pointed to a booth.

Seeing Jeff's tall frame bent over a folding table full of junk, Mattie suddenly wished she'd taken more care with her appearance. She hadn't even bothered with lip gloss. She drew in a deep breath and walked forward with the last box. She cleared her throat, and Jeff looked up.

"Mattie!"

"Hi, I guess my grandmother arranged for you to help here, huh?" Her toe twisted inward, as though she were a small girl in a calico dress. *Gram's magic touch has run dry*, Mattie reminded herself. Mel had found her own husband, and Chelsea and Callie were just dumb luck.

Jeff's sapphire gaze disappeared behind a wink. "Actually I offered to help with the sale, and your grandmother said she'd find me a partner. I think she did well by me, wouldn't you say?"

Mattie nearly laughed aloud. *And will she ever find you a partner, if you let her.* "I guess she figured we're old friends. It would be nice to reconnect."

"Really? I thought she might be trying to set us up." He

raised his eyebrows, and Mattie thought she'd faint from humiliation. At the same time, she wished she understood what was behind his emotion. Was the idea ridiculous to him, or was he just nervous?

"She has been known for her set-ups, but I'll be sure to let her know we're just friends." She tried to giggle, but it came out most unnaturally. Jeff's warmth unnerved her to no end. "You're safe with me. I promise you Gram's matchmaking days are over."

"Really? That's too bad. I was hoping we could do lunch afterward." He leaned over and whispered. "Too forward, huh?"

"No!" she blurted out louder than she intended. "No, not at all." She shook her head. Hadn't she promised herself willpower? Mattie groaned inwardly. She was useless to her quickening heart. "Lunch between old friends is just that. A simple meal to reacquaint. There's certainly no harm in that."

She smiled, and when he returned it, the steeled blue of his eyes forced her to think about breathing. After all these years she was still a hopeless schoolgirl beside Jeff's weathered intelligence. In high school, the attraction had been his maturity beyond his years. She supposed it still was. Jeff always remained a step ahead of the average. Something about the way he knew so much made Mattie feel safe, as though her flaky artist's mind could wander in creativity while he stayed grounded.

"I hear you're an artist now. A pretty popular one." He placed a price sticker on a dish. "Just like in high school, as sought after as ever."

"I paint murals in children's rooms or in dining rooms usually. I don't know if I'm an *arteest*, as I imagined I'd be. Especially if you consider my work eventually gets covered over by boy band posters and bubble gum."

"My grandmother told me about your success as soon as I got back into town. I'd love you to paint one of your works in my new house. The walls are so plain."

"What?" Perhaps the hot sun was making her hear things. Jeff Weatherly wasn't interested in art on his walls—it couldn't be. "What did you have in mind? A chess board in your kitchen?"

"No, nothing like that. My sister's going through an ugly time right now. Her son has been staying with me on and off for the last year. I thought it would be nice to personalize his room a bit. Kenny's the reason I moved back to Heaven. The traveling would be too hard on him now that he's going to school next year."

Mattie's stomach lurched. Of course she'd heard the rumors about Jeff's sister and the continuous battle with drug addiction. She hadn't paid them any mind other than as idle gossip. Judging by the clouded gray in Jeff's eyes, there must have been a spark of truth to them. Mattie mentally calculated her six-month waiting list and wondered how she could push them all back without harming her carefully built reputation.

"What did you have in mind for a mural?" she asked.

"He's four, and he really likes trains." Jeff's expression softened. "He'll build tracks all day long, and he sits in there and names them all. They're his friends." All hint of a smile faded.

"With as many struggles as he's had, they're his only friends sometimes."

Mattie felt her own eyes tearing. She was ready to drop the flea market altogether and go to buy the supplies. "I can paint at night for you. I have a full schedule with a new house in Scottsdale during the day right now, and with the commute. . . . The woman wants a Roman theme in her bathroom—which is bigger than my condo, I might add—and her daughter wants pink ponies on her ceiling. I'm almost finished with that job, but it's been a bear working for this woman; so I don't want to do anything to ruin my shot at getting out of there as soon as possible."

"No, I don't want you to go through any trouble, Mattie. I'm sorry I brought it up. I just thought—"

"Jeff, I want to do this. I want your nephew to have a place that feels like it was made especially for him. A place where he can know God loves him and so do you."

Jeff still shook his head, and Mattie grasped his hand. "I want to do this. It's important to me because it's important to you." Had she really said that? Her fingertips flew to her lips. As hard as she was trying to keep her emotions at bay, she still cared about Jeff. More than she wanted to admit to him or to herself.

Jeff turned and faced her, his intense gaze meeting hers until she thought she'd melt from the heat. "Mattie, would you paint the spare bedroom for my nephew? I wouldn't normally ask. I want you to charge me whatever the going rate is for your work." His chin tilted toward the radiating cement. "I can't put it into words, but I need to do more for this little boy. To give him some semblance of a home, even if it's a place he just visits. I feel as if he's my own. Who knows? If things keep going the same way, he may be at some point."

Mattie smiled at their first customer of the day before turning again toward Jeff. "I'll sketch my ideas, and we'll buy the paint early next week, okay?" She inhaled dreamily. To think such a softhearted person lurked behind that stoic façade unnerved her. To see a man love a child the way Jeff loved Kenny was everything Mattie wished for in a lifetime. If only she knew what to do to grasp such a love for herself.

After helping a few customers, one approached looking familiar. Mattie couldn't place the face, but she knew it had an unpleasant memory associated with it. Once the woman spoke in her gravelly, straightforward way without thought to standard conversational practices, Mattie instantly remembered. Jeff's sister, Joan.

"If it isn't the high school princess." Joan laughed, a low throaty cackle that brought an underlying fear bubbling to Mattie's surface. "Still wearing your cheerleading skirt for kicks? Still leading my brother on?"

"Joan!" Jeff chastised before grabbing his sister by the arm and walking her away a bit. His loud, angry whisper wasn't hard to overhear. "Do you mind? This is my friend. Do I ask your friends about their freaky tattoos? Or why they feel the need to pierce every orifice?"

Mattie looked away but suddenly felt her hand grabbed, and a tiny hand curled into her own. She looked down to see a little boy with sandy brown hair, styled easily into a well-coifed bowl cut. His large blue eyes were unmistakably Jeff's. This had to be the nephew, and Mattie kneeled to speak.

"Hi, there, little guy. What's your name?"

"Kenny." The big blue eyes blinked, and little pudgy lips spoke with a lisp. "I get to go with Uncle Jeff today. Mommy says she has stuff to do, and little kids can't come."

"Well, we need lots of help selling all these good things today. Do you think you could help us?"

His head bobbed excitedly. "Uncle Jeff says I'm a great helper."

Jeff's voice increased in volume. "Did you even feed him today, Joan?" As Jeff saw Mattie's widened eyes, he lowered his voice.

"Are you hungry, Kenny?" Mattie asked.

He rubbed his tummy. "I'm weally ungry. Mommy said all the cereal was gone, and I ate it too fast. She's got no money for more and has to get some, but if I keep eating it too fast, I'm outta luck."

"Come on, then. Let's get a donut over here. Krispy Kremes."

"Ooh, those are my favorite! Mommy likes them, too."

"Let go of my kid! You got that, Princess?" Joan's wild black tresses fell over her face as she yelled.

Kenny's blue eyes widened, and he looked first to his mother then to the stranger holding his hand. Mattie only clung tighter to Kenny's hand and took him to the refreshment table. "It's all right, Kenny. Your uncle Jeff is right there, and so is Mommy. We'll be able to see them the whole time, okay?"

Kenny nodded. Jeff looked adept at handling his sister, and

Mattie would gladly let him. With all these church folk gathered around, Joan wasn't likely to get away with too much.

"Mrs. Wessex." Mattie smiled at the older woman. "This is Kenny, and he is so famished, he says. He simply must have a donut."

Josephine pinched the little one's cheeks, and Mattie noticed it was with less force than she'd endured. "I think he might need two. He looks like a big boy."

After downing three donuts and two glasses of milk, Kenny had more than a bit of energy to run off. Josephine noticed and eagerly offered to take him to the church playground for a time. Mattie agreed and went to find Jeff, to see if there was anything she could do to help.

Jeff's face was drained of color, as Mattie found him sitting in a folding chair behind table seventeen. He looked up and blinked slowly then stood frantically. "Where's Kenny?"

"Relax—he's with Josephine Wessex. They went to play off some of the sugar high from the donuts. They're right over there." Mattie pointed, and Jeff exhaled.

"I guess you remember my sister now, huh?" Jeff's defeated expression gave way to a resolve. His shoulders straightened. "I have to get that boy, Mattie. I can't let him grow up like this. Look—I hope you don't mind, but I'm going to have to cancel lunch. As long as I have Kenny, I don't want to do anything to destroy that or cause my sister not to trust me." He looked away for a moment. "Joan thinks our goody-two-shoes ways will harm her son, that we'll fill his head with religious notions if we take him out together." He held his forefinger and thumb up. "She's this close to signing over custody."

Mattie swallowed hard. Joan had always hated what Mattie represented, and it was no different ten years later. Jeff wasn't willing to sacrifice his nephew for the chance at a relationship that had already failed once. That made perfect sense to her, but logic wasn't on her mind.

"Of course, I understand," Mattie said over the lump in her throat.

"I'll make it up to you. I promise." Jeff's head shook back and forth. "Don't give up on me, just yet. Your Gram has a lot of wisdom, and I think there's something here we have yet to discover."

"Can I still help you with the mural? No strings attached. We'll do it when Kenny isn't around so Joan will have no qualms."

He paused momentarily. "I'll see you Monday night." He took out a business card and wrote his home address and phone number on the back. His eyes were filled with sadness, and Mattie fought the urge to touch his face and try to take some of his stress away. But she would pray, oh, how she would pray.

Chapter 3

W hat did you think of your sale partner yesterday?"
Gram lifted the corner of her mouth. "Pretty
handsome?"

"I thought it looked quite obvious, as if I were using my
grandmother to get a date. It was a little humiliating actually."
Although they'd enjoyed a nice, homemade meal her grandmother had prepared, the subject of Jeff was saved until now.
All part of her grandmother's well-executed plan, she supposed.

Gram shrugged. "All that matters is that he didn't mind
you as his partner. He enjoyed seeing you, so I see no harm
done. We tested the waters, and we're ready to move forward."
Gram rubbed her hands together.

"No harm done? He probably thinks I'm an old maid. That
no one wants to date me, and my grandmother has to force
innocent single men into working flea markets with me."
Mattie's eyebrows rose. "Your plan might be dead in those
waters, Gram. Jeff has far more important things on his mind
right now."

A giggle rumbled from her grandmother. "Mattie, you always were the dramatic one. You see so much that isn't there."

"I'm an artist. Being colorful is part of my charm."

"It is," Gram agreed. She put a Corelle dish into the cabinet, ignoring the new dishwasher like an abandoned shopping cart.

"Gram, are you ever going to use that dishwasher? Your kitchen looks like a showroom."

"A dishwasher. Whatever for? I can wash a dish without wasting electricity. You young people are wasteful. If you had to go through the Depression, you'd be more careful with resources. Especially with water in Arizona. This may be Heaven, but I don't take that name literally."

Mattie sighed. "Time is valuable today, Gram. That's why we have modern-day conveniences, so that we can do more important things than wash dishes."

"What's more valuable than spending time with the ones you love while cleaning the kitchen? A dishwasher doesn't enable you to do that." Gram dried the last dish and changed the subject back to her matchmaking ideas. "When you were young, we called you the princess, Mattie. Whenever anyone came to dinner you would dance in wearing some wild sparkly outfit you'd taken from my closet. Back from my younger days when your grandfather and I would cut a rug."

"What does this have to do with the price of rice in China?" Mattie said, quoting one of her grandmother's famous sayings.

"I'm saying you're a princess in your mind. The reason you haven't married is because you're waiting for Prince Charming to return, and no one else will do. I can't imagine you settling for a man who doesn't make your heart whirl like that smoothie blender you bought me. My opinion is that no one else will ever take Jeff's place in your heart, so what choice do you have?"

Mattie's chest deflated in defeat. What choice did she have indeed? Seeing Jeff look after his nephew would send the normal, rational woman running for cover. A situation that involved addiction, custody hearings, and ugly court battles did not exactly inspire romance. The idea sent a shiver up Mattie's spine, and yet the red flag wasn't hoisted. Mattie only thought more of Jeff for his endearing care of little Kenny.

"Jeff's sister doesn't appear to be doing well, Gram. I think little Kenny will be his priority."

"As it should be, Mattie. That little boy hasn't had an easy time of it. I know his great-grandmother tries to do what she can, but she's getting older. Preschoolers have a lot of energy."

"It would never be just Jeff and I. Even if he were interested in me that way."

"Can you ever settle for coming in third? Behind God? Behind Kenny? You dreamed of being a princess. That life doesn't sound like the one you've dreamed of."

"Gram, you're baiting me. You don't really think I'm still a princess in my mind."

"The only thing that's missing is the tiara, Sweetheart."

"You're trying to get me to admit I like Jeff, that his issues are not big enough to squelch my love. But I don't love Jeff, Gram. I don't even know him anymore. It was a childhood crush that lives on for the moment after seeing he's grown more handsome with age. It's just physical attraction. Certainly not something to build a commitment on." Mattie straightened her shoulders, trying to convince herself she felt nothing. "I don't need a man to complete me, Gram. I am a big girl, a successful artist. How many people make their living doing exactly what they dreamed of? Jeff would be lucky to have me."

"Mattie, who are you trying to convince? I'm convinced, or I wouldn't have set the two of you up."

"Aha! So you admit you set me up."

Gram smiled her secret smile.

"Don't they have shuffleboard or something here to do so you can give up these matchmaking dreams?"

Gram laughed. "If they do, you won't find me there. I have too much interest in great-grandchildren. I figure I'm well on the way with Callie, but my prayer is to leave for heaven with a good number of little hearts for Jesus. I've prayed for their salvation, and I want to meet them before I leave."

"Gram, please. You're going to outlive us all."

"I doubt that, but I am going to live to see my great-grandchildren. I know you think your Gram is just a funny old lady, but I have three successful matches under my belt, Sweetheart, and I don't plan to stop until I'm finished. Do you remember *Pride and Prejudice*? Mary and Kitty were left with no marriage prospects. I might have rewritten that book had I been around." Gram shook her head. "To me, matchmaking is like the quilting Lorraine Henke does. She cuts all those special shapes and patches them together until the pattern is such that it will be cherished for an heirloom. I think of marriage that way. Those two separate shapes must come together by some careful sewing."

Mattie sighed loudly. "Gram, enough with the romantic analogies. I'm painting Jeff's wall. Let's not read too much into that. He has enough to think about, so leave him be, all right? And I'll try to do the same."

"I hear your tone, Mattie. You're worried I'll scare him off. I'm much more subtle than you give me credit for. Ask your cousins."

Mattie bubbled over with laughter. "Gram, you're about as subtle as a city bus in a backyard!"

"Watch your tongue, little lady." Gram settled into her favorite easy chair and clicked on the television news. "Don't you have a date, Mattie?"

"Don't you?"

"No, I've kept my entire weekend free. I'm having a prayer-a-thon for myself."

"I don't even want to know what you're praying for, so don't tell me. You'll be fasting for the love potion number nine if I'm not careful."

"Mattie, sarcasm is your problem. Sarcasm shows a prideful heart. You can go home and use some prayer yourself."

"You're probably right, Gram." Mattie bent over the easy chair and kissed her grandmother. "Thanks for dinner, Gram. That's something else you might pray for, a man who can cook for me." Mattie made her way toward the door and puckered up to blow her grandmother a good-bye kiss. "Love you, Gram."

"Love you, too, Sweetheart. Call me and let me know how Monday goes. I'll be praying."

Mattie knelt in prayer and climbed into bed exhausted and uneasy. Jeff's furrowed brow kept coming to mind. Mattie wondered how much of his high school years had been spent pulling Joan from dangerous situations. Visions of Joan taunting Mattie in the hallway came flooding back.

"Little cheerleader wants to slum with my geek brother. Little cheerleader wants to be worshipped."

The raspy manly voice would never leave Mattie, not for as long as she lived. Guilt rose within her. She'd never shared Christ with Joan, not in all their horrible encounters. Mattie thought about Jeff's abandoning her on prom night and wondered how she'd left him alone to deal with his sister's issues. Mattie had been so oblivious to the burden and instead focused on a lace dress. No wonder he'd lost interest. Mattie's faith had been shallow and merely words.

Nightmares besieged her, and she tossed and turned all night. The memories woke Mattie with a start. It was then she realized the phone was ringing.

"Hello?" she croaked, her morning voice raw and dry.

"Mattie, it's Jeff. Listen—I'm sorry to call so early, but I'm at the hospital with Joan. She got some bad stuff yesterday and was rushed here. My grandmother has Kenny. She's pretty energetic, but I don't know how long she can keep up with a four year old. Can you go by and check on them after church? She's staying home this morning in case anything else happens. I'm sorry. I didn't know of anyone else to call."

Mattie sprang from bed. "Of course. Of course I'll be right over there."

"No need to hurry, Mattie. You know my grandmother—she and yours could outrun any cart on the golf course, if they had to." Jeff forced a laugh, but Mattie could hear the strained nature of his tone. "She lives on Agave Circle, 448."

"Jeff, take down my cell phone in case you need anything. Do you need anything in the hospital?"

"No, thank you. I have my Bible, and I think that's all I'll need for awhile."

The melancholy in Jeff's voice seemed familiar, and Mattie wondered how long he'd been dealing with these issues. Perhaps he wasn't as interested in chess or secondary things in high school as she'd thought. Maybe there was a reason Jeff seemed like an old man, wise beyond his years, in school. Her own obliviousness to the matter and her callousness in chastising him for a high school dance ten years later struck her as the height of selfishness.

"I'm sorry you're dealing with all this, Jeff."

"It's nothing new," he said, his voice absent of feeling. "Joan's been leading this family on a path to the depths since I can remember. The only difference is now she's involving Kenny, and I'm not willing to support that. I've paid for Joan's sins since I can remember; I'm not letting Kenny do the same thing." He paused for a moment. "The doctor's here. Tell my grandmother I'll call her as soon as I have word."

"Jeff!" she rushed before he hung up.

"Yeah?"

"My cell phone number is 555-4488."

"Mattie, look—I appreciate what you're trying to do, but

we can handle this. We've been dealing with this longer than you and I have even known each other."

"I know, but something tells me you're tired of dealing with it alone."

He grew quiet, and they both hung up without another word.

Chapter 4

Church was uplifting, but Mattie's mind was elsewhere. She wondered about Jeff and how he was at the hospital and worried about the little ball of energy wearing out his great-grandmother. After the service Mattie quickly drove to Jeff's grandmother's house. She maneuvered through the labyrinth of pink adobes, taking a few wrong turns until she found Agave Circle. She parked alongside the house and ran toward the door.

Helen Weatherly's home looked as if a flash flood had rushed through a toy store and left a wake of toys strewn in chaotic disarray. Helen's face was drawn and anxious, her gray hair still in curlers. "I must look a fright, but I'm so glad to see you, Mattie."

"Where's our little bolt of lightning?" Mattie asked, as she instinctively picked up the maze of toys that led to the boy asleep in a ball on the couch.

"He finally fell asleep watching his train video. He's been up since five A.M., but that didn't seem to deter him. I'm sorry the house looks so bad, but after chasing him I didn't have the strength to bend over and pick all that up. I wanted to."

Mattie smiled and patted Helen's shoulder. "Helen, I don't think I could keep up with his energy. I can't imagine how you did it this long. Why don't you sit down and take a rest? I'll look after him now."

"You always did have the heart of an angel, Mattie. It's too bad Jeff had too much on his plate when it was time to gather you up."

I'm still gatherable, Mattie thought.

As though reading her mind, Helen kept speaking. "I hope there's a chance for Jeff to settle down. He's always taken on too much responsibility, always been an adult. I wish the man would have some fun. I always thought you were the one to bring it to him, Mattie. Maybe I still do."

Mattie laughed. "That's something you have in common with my grandmother."

"Well, you know us old goats. We have too much time on our hands, and we hate to see our loved ones unhappy. Your grandmother and I married too well not to want the same things for you kids."

The door opened, and Jeff filled the doorway. His blue eyes looked tired but animated. When he saw Mattie she thought she saw excitement in those worn eyes. "Mattie, you're still here."

"I just got here, Jeff. It's only noon."

Jeff looked at the sleeping Kenny on the couch. The little boy's knees were tucked under him, and his backside pointed toward the ceiling. "That doesn't look too comfortable, but

I might settle for that myself."

"How's Joan?" Helen asked.

Jeff shrugged. "She's fine. That woman is a cat, and she's well past her nine lives." He collapsed into an easy chair. "So, Miss Mattie, what do you say to that lunch I promised you? I missed out on cafeteria food especially for the chance."

Mattie looked toward Kenny. "I was about to give your grandmother a break. She hasn't had one yet."

"Oh, go ahead," Helen insisted. "He'll sleep until at least three now. When Kenny crashes, he crashes but good. Besides, it will do my heart good to see Jeff enjoy himself for a change." Helen crossed her arms, tapping her foot. "He's been an old man too long." She nudged Jeff in the stomach.

Jeff grasped Mattie's hand. He stopped for a moment, staring into her eyes, and she fell silent. What did he hide in that look? What did he possess that hypnotized her so?

"I intend to forget all about my sister for the afternoon. I intend to focus on the beauty of life, of God's gifts for the day." Jeff pulled Mattie forward a bit and led her to his Cherokee with its fancy leather seats and electronic dashboard. She'd seen only the back when they loaded her grandmother's items for the sale.

"Nice car."

"It's my daddy-mobile. I needed something practical for Kenny. I traded in my jeep with the ragtop for something safer."

"You've done a lot for that boy." Mattie slipped into the front seat, and Jeff shut the door behind her and came around to the driver's side.

"That boy has done a lot for me, but I don't want to talk about him. I want to know what you've been doing, Mattie. Are you dating anyone?"

Mattie's ear suddenly itched. "No, I've been a bit consumed with painting. My business is going gangbusters." She saw Jeff look at her questioningly. "And there's no one that's interested me enough to take me away from the palette."

"Do I interest you enough?"

Mattie swallowed over the lump that rose in her throat. Jeff hadn't started the car yet; he still looked at her. His forwardness was completely out of character for the Jeff she remembered. The intensity of his gaze caused confusion, and she didn't know how to answer; but for some reason the truth bubbled out of her.

"Yes," she said. *You interest me enough to make me forget the color wheel altogether,* she added silently.

Jeff started up the car. "Good. That's all I needed to hear. You still like Mexican?"

Mattie grinned. "I love Mexican. What kind of self-respecting Arizonan doesn't?"

"Still like it as hot as it comes?"

"You bet."

"Muy caliente. Very hot. I'm glad to know some things never change."

"Me, too," Mattie said, the intent in her voice clear. "Too many things have changed."

"Not the important things, Mattie. You are still beautiful and full of life. God is still sovereign."

"Amen to that last."

"You know, I plan to be there for Kenny as long as I'm able; but if I weren't there, God would raise up somebody else. God doesn't need me. I have to remember that when I'm in such turmoil. He can fix things without Jeff Weatherly."

"What are you saying, Jeff?"

"I'm saying that I have put off courting you for ten years. I'm sorry if that expression sounds dated, but that's exactly what my plans are, Mattie Stevens. To court you until you can't resist me."

"Well, if that includes caliente Mexican food, I fear I'm putty in your hands."

The sound of their laughter mingled together brought tears of joy to Mattie's eyes. She was the princess, and this was her Prince Charming, just as Gram said. Nothing else mattered at the moment.

Once at Pedro's, Mattie felt the lightheartedness she'd felt in high school. She felt proud to be on the arm of Jeff Weatherly and wished he'd understood her fascination with him had been more than a high school crush. His spiritual maturity magnetized her, and she felt his pull stronger than ever. It wasn't her imagination the restaurant patrons stopped eating to watch them walk to their table, and she knew that whatever it was between them other people felt it, too.

Jeff pulled out her chair for her and placed the napkin in her lap. "Mademoiselle."

Mattie giggled. "I believe the word you're looking for is *señorita*."

Jeff cleared his throat. "I'm trying to be classy here—do you mind?" His eyebrows rose in mock annoyance, and the blue of his eyes gleamed, like the brilliant turquoise of the local Indian jewelry.

"I fear it's going to be futile to put on airs while eating chile relleno served muy caliente."

"You remember my order. Well, get a load of this." He lifted his hand for the waitress to come. "Watch the gringo at work." He winked toward Mattie. "*Yo quiero un chile relleno, muy caliente, y un pollo enchilada, muy caliente tambien, y dos Pepsi.*"

Mattie couldn't hold back her smile. "You remembered."

"You know, I never have been able to take another woman out for Mexican food. To watch a woman pick at her meal daintily, eat the tame stuff, and complain. It was more than I could bear." He shook his head in apparent disgust. "I lost respect for them. I like a woman who can handle her jalapeños and serranos. Is that too much to ask?"

"Not in Arizona." Mattie winked. "It was all those fancy girls you probably dated back East during college. Fancy girls can't appreciate good Mexican."

"Well, there is no good Mexican food back East." He mumbled under his breath. "I won't comment on the women. I dated very little in college. I don't think I was cut out for the casual relationship. I'm too intense by nature. I've seen too much to make light of dating."

"Is dating something you want? Or something you think our grandmothers want?"

"Both." The waitress brought their sodas and a basket of chips and salsa. "I almost forgot. Can you bring us an extra cup of salsa?" Jeff asked the waitress, picking up a water glass to insinuate size. "My girlfriend here, she kinda hogs it," Jeff whispered aloud. He turned to Mattie and laughed uproariously. The sound was like a pleasant jingle in her ear.

"So now I'm your girlfriend?"

"Hey, it wasn't nice to call my date a piggy. I made myself look good there—don't you think?"

"You are terrible."

"And you love me anyway." Jeff grinned from the side of his mouth, and Mattie had to agree. Who wouldn't love Jeff's easy candor and selfless style? If the woman was out there who could resist him, she'd like to meet her. It was then that Mattie started to giggle aloud. The woman was out there, and she came in the form of her cousin Melissa. The thought struck her as overwhelmingly humorous.

"What's so funny?"

"The idea of you and Mel on a date."

"We never got that far, but I knew I'd get the information I wanted through that date. I'd hear what Mattie Stevens was up to through Mel. That's the only reason I agreed in the first place."

Mattie's eyes thinned. "You're a convincing liar."

Jeff slapped his chest. "I do not lie, Mattie. I would think my AV classes from high school might convince you I never took the date seriously."

"You *are* terrible."

"I'm simply a man who knows what he wants."

Jeff's cell phone rang, and he paused, looking at the number before he answered it. "It's the hospital."

"You have to answer it," Mattie said.

"My life is on hold for my sister. Always. I don't want her to ruin this."

"Jeff, you won't ruin anything with me. It's me, Mattie."

Jeff answered his phone, and his lighthearted countenance changed instantly. "Thank you." He hung up and stared at Mattie. "My sister has run away from the hospital. They don't know if she's strong enough to make it without the IVs they had her on." He shook his head, his teeth clenched.

"Well, we have to go look for her."

Jeff sighed. "I know. Can you ever forgive me?"

"There's nothing to forgive. You go ahead. I'll get our food to go and meet you at your grandmother's."

Jeff dropped a twenty-dollar bill on the table. "I'm sorry, Mattie." He then kissed her on the lips. "Hang in there with me, Mattie. This can't go on forever."

But Mattie thought it could, and yet she hardly cared. A little of Jeff was better than none at all. She'd had ten years to come to that conclusion.

Chapter 5

Monday came, and no sign of Jeff's sister was reported. Mattie loaded her paints into the car and headed out for the long, traffic-laden drive to Scottsdale. Most of her supplies were still in the magnificent hacienda where she'd been working. Mrs. Cox, the home's owner, had allowed Mattie to keep things in the pool house so that transport wouldn't be as difficult. But this Monday morning the drive away from Jeff and Kenny, who needed her support, burdened her heart. Her task of finishing an elaborate mural almost embarrassed her while Jeff searched for his sister, tried to care for his nephew, and held down his job.

The drive went unusually fast, as Mattie's mind flittered in and out of conscious driving. It appeared the car knew the way, regardless. Mrs. Cox was directing some furniture movers as Mattie appeared. She parked her car around back, lest anyone see her tacky economy car in the neighborhood. Mrs. Cox met her at the back door.

"Mattie, Darling, you won't believe what's happened."

Try me, Mattie thought sarcastically but smiled instead. "What has happened, Mrs. Cox?"

"Alexa says the ponies on her ceiling scare her. She can't sleep. I've had workmen paint over them, but she still wants the ponies on her wall, so you can get started on that today." Mrs. Cox's thin smile was genuine. The woman had no idea she'd set Mattie's schedule back a week, and Mattie thought she would burst into tears right there. She felt her own lip quiver. A week might cost her the next job or, worse yet, Jeff's extra room for Kenny.

With uncharacteristic boldness Mattie spoke. "Mrs. Cox, I will have to come back to do the ponies again. I have other clients waiting for my services." Mattie flipped open her ragged paper calendar while Mrs. Cox put her hands on her hips.

"This is ridiculous. Your other clients will have to wait. I have you now, and that's the way it works. You finish your job for me first."

Mattie tried quickly to calculate if she could afford to drop the job and take only the advance she'd received. Figures of her car payment floated through her head then her reputation. Would Mrs. Cox tell her friends Mattie was unreliable? Or would her waiting clients be more of a problem?

"Mrs. Cox, I'm sorry, but I was scheduled to finish up today, and my murals are highly sought after during the summer when schedules are easier to manage." Mattie squared her shoulders. "Alexa can wait for me to paint her ponies, or I can give you the names of some other artists I could recommend."

Mrs. Cox inhaled like some kind of zoo animal, with depth

and snarl. "Mattie, I told my husband this house would be done by a certain date. I've given you every allowance—even let you keep the paints in my pool house. Surely you owe me something akin to finishing the job I paid you to do."

Mattie wavered. She hated to let anyone down. Yet the employer had technically only paid for the supplies, not the work. And Mattie had done the work.

Mrs. Cox's phone rang inside the house, and the waif-like woman walked away in her black capris, looking very much like the long limbs of a spider easing across a sparse desert.

"Hello?" Mrs. Cox paused. "Yes, she's here, but she's here to work, Mr. Weatherly. I suggest you find another time to arrange a date. Humph." The click of the phone resonated in Mattie's head, and Mrs. Cox came back to the door. "I'd appreciate it if you would tell your friends this is a private number, and you are working here. I am not your secretary."

Mattie's cheeks heated. "I need to use your phone, Mrs. Cox. I gave that number to my grandmother in case of an emergency only."

"Anything you have to say to Mr. Weatherly can wait until you're off my clock."

Mattie could barely breathe she was so nervous. And angry. Jeff would never interrupt her work for something trivial. "If you won't let me use your phone, Mrs. Cox, I have no choice but to find a payphone. My cell phone doesn't work out here."

"Mattie, my daughter wants her ponies. I hate to be an ogre, but you're leaving me little choice. You were contracted to do a job."

"A job which I did."

"Not to my satisfaction." Mrs. Cox opened a drawer and pulled out her contract. A contract Mattie wrote and felt confident about.

"I have to go." Mattie threw what supplies were hers into the car and rushed toward town to find a payphone. Mrs. Cox screamed something at Mattie while the car left the driveway. Mattie considered herself fortunate she hadn't heard the barb.

She wound around the desert roads and pulled into a mall parking lot. She ran toward the payphone, beads of sweat building quickly. She dialed her calling card into the phone and punched Jeff's cell phone number.

Jeff answered on the first ring. "Hello?"

"Jeff, it's Mattie. You called me?"

A long sigh erupted. "Oh, Mattie, I had to tell someone. My sister called the authorities. She's left custody to me. She's abandoned Kenny. I'll have to go through all the channels to make it final, but I need you here to pray with me. To help me with God's will."

"I don't understand, Jeff. I thought you wanted custody."

"Not this way, Mattie. How do I tell Kenny his mother isn't coming home?" Jeff paused for a moment. "I can't even fathom what this will do to him. He's so much older in his mind than a four year old."

"But he is a four year old, Jeff, and you need to let him rest in his childhood. Is your sister all right?"

"She's okay," Jeff practically spat out. "She met up with some of her biker buddies, in some bar nearby, and took off for

California. Says she wants to be free again and that her new man doesn't want Kenny around."

"Her new man? Jeff, she's been gone two days."

"It's the drugs talking, Mattie. Don't try to make sense of it. I want to be with you, to pray with you, and just have your support. Can you take the day off?"

"I think I'll have a little time, Jeff. Mrs. Cox probably won't want me back."

"I'll pay you whatever she was paying you to paint Kenny's room. Then we're together, and you're not out a job."

"I appreciate the offer, but I couldn't take your money. Especially not in a situation like this. I'm a Christian. I did what I vowed to do for Mrs. Cox, and I tried to please her, but it's over now."

"Meet me at my grandmother's, will you? I'm going over there to tell Kenny now that his mother is gone for awhile."

"I'm praying, Jeff."

Jeff explained everything to Kenny, and with adult awareness the child nodded and complied. The ease at which he took the news only reiterated that Jeff was doing the right thing. He'd come back to Heaven with two goals: to help Kenny grow up and to court the only woman he'd ever loved. Now that he was ready to start a family, not as he'd once planned, but a family just the same, he needed to let Mattie understand his love.

The last thing he wanted was for Mattie to think he needed a mom for Kenny and she would do. He questioned God's timing on his family's chaos and prayed with his whole heart that his sister would get help. Jeff's grandmother prepared hot dogs for their lunch, and it wasn't long before Mattie's car pulled up in the driveway. He walked to her car and opened the door. Mattie's fresh complexion and sage green eyes glistened under the hot Arizona sun. Her freshness was so inviting; she was like the morning dew on a summer peach.

Jeff clutched her in an embrace. "Mattie, thank you for coming."

Mattie talked into Jeff's shoulder, muffling her voice yet bringing him an intimacy with her he'd dreamed of countless nights. "I know you wouldn't have called if it wasn't bad."

He pulled away; his heart was caught in his throat. How could he be so happy and yet so miserable at once?

"It's hard to imagine Joanie will ever turn away from drugs now. If Kenny wasn't enough to make her want to change, what else is there?"

"There's God. And you're underestimating Him. Joan's only been away from Kenny for a weekend. Things could change overnight."

"Let's go grab breakfast. Kenny is at the pool with my grandmother and a group of her friends. They'll be gone until lunch, and we have yet to finish our date."

Mattie looked down at her paint-laden shorts and T-shirt. She brushed her hair from her face, and the motion moved Jeff to his core. "Do you think I'm dressed okay to go out? Should I go home and change first?"

"No!" Jeff said too abruptly. "We have tried this date twice before, and today I'm going to finish it. You would look beautiful in a garbage bag, and we're going out." He grabbed her arm and his keys, and they were soon headed toward town.

Jeff pulled into a small pink shopping center and parked near a natural-type breakfast spot. He mentally thought about the meetings he was missing today and which clients would have to be rearranged. But he needed this. Mattie was one of the main reasons he'd come back to Heaven, and for one day he intended to show her his seriousness.

"Do you like Angel's?" Jeff asked, pointing toward the restaurant where he could already smell the strong cinnamon from the signature tea.

"I love it. Breakfast out is such an indulgence. I can't remember the last time I did it." Mattie licked her upper lip. "Here I thought I'd be spending my day painting a ceiling for a spoiled child, and instead I'm eating breakfast out with an incredibly gorgeous man. Life holds so many wonderful surprises."

The smile on her face appeared angelic, and he was reminded of how Mattie enjoyed the simple pleasures in life. How her freshness and enthusiasm permeated everything she did. The energy within her filled him with a joy he couldn't describe. It made him thank God for the privilege of being beside her. He forgot about work and all the bullet points on his to-do calendar. He sucked in a deep breath and focused on what the Lord had given him today.

"I'm sorry, Jeff. I'm rambling. I suppose things aren't looking so cheery for you."

"On the contrary. For once, things are looking grand."

"What do you do now for fun? Do you still play chess?"

"Not too often. Sometimes I'll find a willing partner at Grandma's social club, but I play rugby on Saturdays. I learned in college, and it just stuck."

"Rugby? Isn't that a little violent?"

Jeff thought about all the nicks and scratches he'd endured. Not to mention the broken wrist in college. "Not all that violent. Active, and it certainly gets my mind off the numbers. I find that with accounting I don't have the mind to enjoy chess as I once did. What about you? What do you do for fun?"

"My job is fun. I get to paint every day, which is pure joy for me. In my spare time I enjoy changing my apartment around quite a bit, depending on which color I'm in the mood for. But mostly I read voraciously. My library card looks like my cousin Callie's credit card. It's worn out."

His eyes focused on her beautiful, full lips as they spoke. How was it he'd never realized how intelligent Mattie was? That she was capable of doing anything—yet she wanted to do something creative like painting? He chastised himself for always thinking he was so brilliant and for seeing Mattie as the beautiful cheerleader, instead of the multifaceted mind and pure heart that she was. What Mattie possessed, Jeff wanted to take hold of for himself. To look at life with the glass half full for a change. He wondered who indeed the smartest kid in school was. He wasn't it, or he wouldn't be living the same life he'd lived for twenty years. He'd be playing more rugby, enjoying more time with Mattie.

"What do you like to read, Mattie?"

"Oh, everything! I love Greek literature, and I love the latest murder mysteries and the biographies on the bestseller lists. For me, reading isn't about a style; it's about grasping as much information as I can and trying to see how other people see the world. Why they don't have Christ in their lives and what types of things stop them."

"It all sounds fascinating. Do you have anything you'd recommend?"

"I couldn't begin to give you one title, but I'm happy to share my personal library with you. That's another hobby, by the way. I've learned to install my own bookcases."

"Mattie, is there anything you don't do?"

"I don't really like to cook. I can—Gram taught me—but it's not my favorite thing in the world. I love to see what other people cook, though." Mattie held up her menu. "Did you see this omelet with Brie in it? Doesn't that sound heavenly?"

"I'm more of a pancake man myself." He winked at her, and the grin she returned poured over his heart like the freshest, thickest maple syrup in his college state of Vermont.

"I'm sure those are wonderful, too." She nodded.

"Thank you for taking the day off for me. You don't know how I needed this."

"I believe I do. You can't do everything for everyone else without refreshing at church and being around friends who support you. It's the way God made us. He wants us in fellowship."

"Why do you make me feel like a lightweight spiritually?"

Her smile faltered, and she shook her head. "I didn't mean to do that, Jeff. I'm no spiritual giant. I'm weak myself—that's how I know these things."

"Mattie Stevens, I never stopped loving you. And I never will."

Mattie dropped her spoon in her tea with a clank. She blinked rapidly but said nothing in return, and Jeff hoped he hadn't ruined their future together by scaring her away. She grasped Jeff's hand but said nothing. She only blinked her wide blue eyes at him until he thought he might steal her away to Las Vegas and get the wedding over with at once. No one would ever touch his heart like this. If only Mattie felt the same way, but her thoughts remained hidden throughout breakfast.

❧

Kenny's angry gait marched out the front door. His arms swung straight out to the side. Without warning he hauled off and punched Mattie in the thigh. "You're the reason my mom left. She didn't like you." Kenny's brows were furrowed in an angry V-shape.

"Kenny!" Jeff was in shock. "Mattie? Are you all right?"

"Yes, I'm all right." She knelt beside Kenny and tried to speak with him at his level, but rage engulfed the little boy, and Jeff had to stop Kenny from hitting Mattie again.

"Kenny! What are you doing? Mattie is my friend, and we don't treat anyone that way."

"She stole my mommy!" The venom with which he said the words flustered Jeff. He didn't know much about parenting, but he knew this was not normal behavior for a four year old. Yet he felt powerless about what to do.

"Mattie did no such thing. Now you apologize to my friend," Jeff finally said.

"No!" Kenny crossed his arms defiantly across his chest.

"Kenny."

"No!"

Mattie shifted uncomfortably, and her wide eyes blinked in obvious confusion. "Jeff, this is going to take some time. Why don't you call me when things calm down?"

Jeff looked to Mattie and then to Kenny. He closed his eyes and sighed before facing the two people he loved. One much too young to understand, and the other not believing his heart.

"No, we're going to settle this. Kenny, this is my girlfriend. I love her, and you will, too, once you get to know her."

"I hate her!" Kenny stamped his foot vehemently.

Mattie put her hand on Jeff's shoulder, and it took all his willpower not to embrace her again. The pain in her eyes forced him back. "Mattie, please don't leave. We have to discuss this. We have to discuss our future."

"Not today we don't. Thank you for breakfast." She placed a kiss on his cheek, near his lips. "Kenny needs you right now."

"Stop talking about me! Don't say my name! I hate you!" Kenny spat out.

If Jeff had said such things as a child, his father would have reminded him painfully not to do so again. But Kenny needed unconditional love right now. "Kenny! That's enough. You are hurting. We know that, but it does not excuse rudeness. Now go in the house and see Great-Grandma for awhile. We'll talk about this later."

Kenny stomped away but turned before reaching the door

and stuck his tongue out toward Mattie.

"Well, that went well." Mattie smiled slightly.

Jeff threw up his hands. "Mattie, I'm sorry. I'm a terrible parent. I don't know why I was thinking I could take this on." He rubbed his forehead to stop the throbbing.

"Jeff, this isn't ideal, but Kenny will adjust. You have to let him know he comes first."

"But he doesn't come first. My wife comes first. That's how I was raised."

Mattie stepped back, her face as pale as the jimsonweed. "I'm not your wife, Jeff. We had a great time, but you obviously have bigger priorities, and I don't want to get in the way of those."

"Mattie, you don't understand. I planned this before Kenny and I were an option. I came home for two reasons, and you were one of them." Jeff hated the desperation he felt, and he could have kicked himself for not being forthright with Mattie. Now he sounded like some hopeless loser in search of anyone for a mate.

"But I wasn't the only one, Jeff. And one of those reasons needs you more than the other." She stood on her tiptoes and kissed his cheek again. "I love you, too, if it's any consolation."

"Consolation? No, it isn't a consolation. Mattie, what can I do? That boy needs me, but there's only one woman for me. I knew that ten years ago."

"I knew it ten years ago as well, but now I'm not so sure. Love shouldn't be this complicated. This much of a game. I loved you, Jeff, and you left town without a word."

"Mattie, I explained all that. Why must we go back to that again and again?"

"Then let me explain something to you. You're a great man, Jeff, but my life was so peaceful until you came. I don't think love should be this much turmoil." Mattie grabbed his hand then climbed into her hatchback. "I have to get back to Scottsdale and apologize to Mrs. Cox."

"Mattie, wait—"

But she closed the door. Jeff saw the tears in her eyes as she backed down the driveway, and he kicked the grass in frustration. He closed his eyes in prayer, asking the Lord to show him the way. He listened to silence for a moment before calling out to Mattie's taillights. "This isn't what you want, Mattie! I'll do whatever it takes this time."

Chapter 6

M attie couldn't see the road through her veil of tears, so she pulled to the side. Staring out at the expanse of Sonoran desert, Mattie wondered if such a barren life lay before her. Would she ever find a man who wanted her? Not to be the mother of an adopted child or selected because of proximity and familiarity, but because someone sought her out to love her truly?

She knew better than to hope. Hope pulled everything you had within you and lifted you up, not to have you drop back in a deep pit of despair. She laughed through her tears. Gram always said she was the dramatic one. Yet her mood couldn't be helped today. Everyone else managed to find love. Callie, Mel, and Chelsea had no problems with Gram's arrangements.

While life rushed at her like a monsoon thunderstorm or a drowning flash flood, Mattie watched idly as her loved ones gripped all life had to offer. They were the desert flowers on the levee, the spot of rain in the midst of drought, while she waited for a small refreshing drop.

She could turn the car around, she reasoned. She could tell Jeff she loved him solely and that she didn't want to think about a future without him. But what kind of Christian stole the only parent a child would have? Kenny's behavior told Mattie how much he needed security. To know Kenny was first would haunt Mattie like the night when her prom came and went. Second to chess. Second to Kenny. Always second to something.

Mattie had no business messing with that arrangement. Kenny needed Jeff. Mattie did fine on her own, and she guessed that's how God wanted it. She wiped the tears from her eyes and headed to Gram's.

Gram would know what to do, and if she didn't, Mattie could drown herself in chocolate chip cookies and avoid thinking of the subject. Revert to her childhood and be happy with a tall glass of milk and Tollhouse joy.

Mrs. Cox and her "unfinished" job fell to a distant memory. Mattie wouldn't go groveling for the job she didn't need nor agree to do. God had ordered the day differently, and Mattie tried to find peace in that.

Gram's pink apartment shone brightly in the hot afternoon sun. The apartment looked sparse and abandoned, and Mattie guessed Gram was off to Internet class or the like. She knocked on the door and was surprised when Gram answered, a look of shock covering the weathered face.

"Mattie, what on earth? Why aren't you at work?"

"Mrs. Cox—" Mattie started her explanation but quickly resorted to tears. "Oh, Gram." She clutched her grandmother and felt the older woman's comforting arms around her. A cave of shelter underneath a late summer storm.

"What's the matter, Sweetie? Is it something with Jeff?"

Mattie sniffled and nodded her head through her violent inhaling of jagged, little breaths. "I'm never going to get married. I'm an old maid!" Mattie wailed. "I won't even be a bridesmaid anymore, because everyone I know is married."

Gram pulled away and smiled. She shook her head, "Mattie, Mattie. Come and sit in the kitchen. I'll get you some cookies."

"I know what you're thinking. I'm the dramatic one."

"You should have gone to Hollywood." Gram lifted her eyebrows and led Mattie to the kitchen. "Now tell your Gram what could be so bad. Is Jeff marrying someone else?"

"Worse. He has custody of Kenny now. His sister ran off to California and left that poor boy with no one but Jeff and his grandmother. What kind of Christian would I be if I stood in the way of that? The boy needs a home."

"Mattie, did Jeff say he didn't want to pursue a relationship with you because of Kenny?"

"Well, no, but—"

"Mattie, aren't most parents married?"

"Yes, but this situation is different. Kenny hates me. He told me so himself." Mattie crossed her arms.

"And how old is this child?"

"He's four." Mattie sat up straighter, to make her argument more effective. Gram had that way of making something so real to Mattie seem ridiculous. "But you don't understand, Gram. Jeff came back to Heaven to care for Kenny. Kenny's the priority. I'll never be a priority. I'll always come third.

After God and after Kenny."

"Honey, Jeff is not willing to sacrifice everything for the boy. Besides, the boy will need a mother. Have you thought of that?"

"A mother he likes, maybe. But not me."

Gram set a glass of milk on the table. "I'm going to tell you this once. It may sound harsh, but I think you need to hear it, Princess. You, unlike the rest of us, are a princess. You've always had people bow down before your beauty. You've had whatever you wanted to be disposed of as you felt led. But Jeff's the one thing you've wanted that you couldn't control. Go ahead—tell me it's not true. I dare you."

Mattie pondered the thought for awhile, unwilling to admit it might be true.

"You're afraid if you admit how deeply you love Jeff, and if he doesn't love you back in the same way, you'll be made a fool of. Am I right?"

Mattie's jaw twitched. How she hated that her grandmother saw right through her. How she hated that it was truly pride that held her back from Jeff. Not her sacrificial love for a child. That's what she wanted it to be, but it wasn't that. She was afraid of coming in second.

"You lost him once to pride, Mattie. Will you let it happen again?"

Mattie steeled herself, pushing away the plate of cookies her grandmother had set down. "How can you say that, Gram? Jeff left me all those years ago. I didn't control anything."

"You know, you've been telling that story so long that you actually believe it, don't you?"

"It can hardly be disputed. I'm still in Heaven, aren't I? I went to junior college here. I've made my living locally, painting rich people's houses. I didn't go off to some fancy school and grow away from this place."

Gram sat on the couch and smirked.

"No, no, Gram. You are not right about this. Jeff did leave me, and he'll do it again."

"Jeff didn't leave you, Mattie. You never gave that boy an inch. If he wasn't at your beck and call, like the night of the prom, you decided he wasn't worthy. This woe-is-me stuff might work on some of your friends, or even your cousins, but I know better. I know that man's heart, Mattie, and I know yours. Now swallow your pride and go tell that man how you really feel. The boy will get over it, and he will love you as his mother."

Mattie shook her head. "No, I don't think so. He's had an earful from his real mother. She probably told him what to think of me."

"You're a smart girl, Mattie. You'll figure it out. He's four. I have no doubt that you're brighter than he is. You probably have more up your sleeve to win his heart. Now quit being a spoiled brat and go find Jeff. He needs your support, not your games."

"Gram!"

"You won't get any sympathy from me, Mattie. You've been single long enough so that I know it's your choice to remain that way. You rarely accept dates, and if you do, you've never accepted a second date that I know of. I've lived a long time, and I'm no fool. If I'd played this many games with your grandpa, he'd have married someone else. And that's the truth. Now the only thing you have to lose is that pride of yours. Go tell Mr. Weatherly how you feel before he decides you're too high maintenance." Gram shoved a cookie into her mouth.

Visions of Mrs. Cox floated through Mattie's mind. The desperately flawed, rich woman who never had enough, who thought the sun rose and set against the red rocks for her alone. Was that how Mattie appeared to her cousins? Was she waiting for someone who didn't exist to ride off into the pink romantic sunset? The possibility tore Mattie's heart to shreds. Jeff deserved better. All the people in Mattie's life deserved better.

"Thank you, Gram. It's been an enlightening afternoon. I don't like it, but I suppose I have it coming."

"I love you, Sweetie, and I'm praying for you. Now go."

Mattie grabbed a cookie and started for the door. "You have a funny way of showing love, Gram. But all I can say is I'm happy you like me, or I don't think I could take what you've said."

❧

Jeff cleared the lunch dishes from the table and set Kenny in front of a TV cartoon for an afternoon break. Jeff had a major presentation for a client due, and yet his mind was full of racing, more pressing thoughts. Where was Mattie? Would he see her again? Or had his profession of love scared her away for good? How did he let Kenny know the boy was loved, without giving up everything he'd worked so hard for? Without giving up Mattie? He felt so powerless, and it drove him crazy. With work he just took what he wanted: promotions, clients—it all came easy to him. But Mattie was another story. She confounded him like nothing else.

His grandmother came up behind him at the sink and stroked his back.

"Kenny will adjust. He's adjusted to far worse."

"I scared Mattie off for good this time."

"I don't think so, Honey. Mattie's a good girl. Give her some time, and she'll realize this may be the life God planned for her."

"What if it isn't?"

"It has to be hard for someone to accept an instant family. You'll find the right girl to share your life if it's not Mattie. Kenny can't take over every part of you, Jeff. Don't let him. He's a hurting little boy, and if I had the vigor, I'd take him myself. But I don't. He's blessed to have you and that you chose a different path from his mother."

"I'll need to find a day care center for him."

Grandma nodded. "He's been in day care for some time now. It might be a little out of your way, but I think it's best to keep him in familiar surroundings. It might not be the best situation, but being born into an illegitimate family, with a drug-addict mother, has its consequences, unfortunately."

"I wanted to provide the best for him," Jeff said. "I wanted Mattie to be his mother. I wanted to give him a little brother or sister."

"Did you ask the Lord about any of that? Or Mattie for that matter?"

The doorbell rang, interrupting a conversation Jeff didn't want to have anyway. He dried his dishpan hands and lamented how his life had become distinctly not his own.

He opened the door to Mattie's wide blue eyes. He watched her swallow then search for the right words. He couldn't hide his own smile.

"You—"

"No, I'm going to say what I came to say, Jeff." Mattie's chin locked, and she looked the epitome of seriousness, but Jeff had to say something.

"I was just going to tell you that you have cookie crumbs on your face. Have you been to your Gram's?" He brushed the crumbs from her lip and kept his hand there to feel the current between them. She closed her eyes and kissed his fingers as softly as a pink cloud in the magnificent Arizona sky.

She giggled and brushed self-consciously at her face. The sweeping tendrils that surrounded her face moved easily from around her chin to behind her neck. Jeff took in the sight as though he'd never seen it before.

"How about another date, Mattie? Just you and me out on the town like normal people."

"Normal people? What are those?"

"Maybe I assumed too much, and maybe you don't want to be part of my very messed-up life. But if you do—if you're willing—I'll make it worth your while."

"But Kenny—"

"Kenny is a child, and we're not talking about him. This is about you and me. We deserve the chance, Mattie. I'll be

327

everything I can to Kenny, but I've saved the best for you, if you're willing."

Mattie's cheeks were flushed. "I—" she stammered. "I would be first?"

"Yes, you'll be first. Come to dinner with me and let me prove it. I have so many things I want to tell you. Go home and put on your best dress. You and I are going to be the talk of the restaurant."

Mattie didn't speak, but her wide eyes did so for her.

"Can you do that for me?" Jeff asked, unsure if he'd been understood.

Mattie nodded. "Yes, I'll be ready by—"

"Six. I'll keep Kenny up all day, and my grandmother can put him down at seven. That's only one hour, and they can watch a video tonight. I'll run him ragged on the soccer field after his quiet time."

"Jeff, really?"

"I want nothing more than to court you as I intended to court you, Mattie Stevens. You deserve nothing less. You've had a whole lot less." He bent down and placed a light kiss on her nose. "See you at six, at your house."

She nodded then turned on one toe and skipped to her car. Jeff's heart followed at a rapid pace.

Chapter 7

Mattie's shower felt cleansing and more refreshing than normal. She emerged from the steamy stall ready for anything. The emotional strain of the day had been far more stifling than the Arizona summer heat.

In a single day Mattie had managed to lose a job, lose a boyfriend, and get a four year old to hate her with the venom of a heat-seeking rattlesnake. Now, as if all the bad events had simply evaporated, she dressed for the man she loved. She had a new determination not to play childish games, but to speak her heart and take the consequences, whatever they might be. With a light step she slid into some strappy heels she'd been saving for the next wedding. Which, undoubtedly, would be someone else's.

Mattie dried her hair with a brush and a hair dryer, which was a rarity in dry Arizona. Usually before she could get the dryer out, her hair hung limp and set in its ways. With a complete lack of humidity her full dark hair barely made it past ten minutes of being wet. She patted a little powder on her face and a dab of blush and applied a sheer lip gloss. She smiled to herself in the mirror feeling that tonight she and Jeff could overcome anything.

Mattie went to the closet and looked for something to wear to match her great new sandals. Being a casual person and most of her clothing being strewn with dried paint of various colors, Mattie looked in her church clothes for something appropriate. She decided on a gray linen sheath that brought out the blue of her eyes and added a Navajo silver bangle bracelet with touches of turquoise. She spent the final minutes straightening up the living room and fluffing her pillows. When the doorbell rang, Mattie was ripe with anticipation, and she was not disappointed.

Jeff's appearance at her door made her stomach flip like those early days in high school. He wore a pair of khaki linen pants and a white dress shirt, and he looked as casual as he looked good.

He shook his head, letting his gaze fall to the ground and land on her new shoes. "You look incredible, Mattie."

"I was about to say the same thing to you."

"I like the shoes." He raised and lowered his eyebrows.

Mattie smiled to herself, lifting one foot off the ground. "I'm glad I finally had a place to wear them."

"We've established we look good." Jeff laughed. "Now we need a place to go that's worthy of our dressing up."

"I agree." Mattie playfully stuck her chin toward the sky. She sighed. "But what place is worthy of such glamour? Does Heaven have such a place?"

"Of course. Les Saisons. We'll see what the country-club set enjoys."

"Les Saisons? Do you know—I've never been."

"Then you've obviously never been courted properly here. It's a good thing I came home. These men are oafs here in Heaven." Jeff feigned disgust. "It's a travesty, I tell you. Such beauty wasting away."

"It is a good thing you came home, Jeff. The women of Heaven don't know what they've been missing."

Jeff shook his head. "Oh, this deal isn't good for anyone. There's only one woman who can redeem such a courting coupon." Jeff winked, and Mattie's stomach tumbled in her exhilaration.

Mattie closed the door behind them, and Jeff took her hand. He opened the door of his Cherokee and waited for her to be seated before shutting it behind her. An inner grin spread throughout Mattie's frame. She was with Jeff Weatherly, and things felt right. Troubles with Kenny and Joan seemed to slip away. Tonight was theirs alone, and she would do everything in her power to forget all the outside people who threatened to take away the only man she ever loved. She would enjoy what she had of him, however long it lasted.

Jeff drove slowly to the restaurant, as if he were trying to take in every moment. He looked over to her often, smiling as though he knew some secret. The restaurant was tucked away on a long drive near one of Heaven's most prestigious golf clubs. Everything reeked of money. From the bright splash of green against the taupe color of the desert to the expensive foreign cars in the parking lot, this was where Heaven's richest came to play. Mattie suddenly panicked, thinking about the college girls Jeff had probably dated in college. Would they know how to act in such a place?

Mattie fretted she might use the wrong fork or, worse, appear to be the Arizona native she was. She pressed her lips together before getting the courage to ask about the restaurant. "Will I be dressed okay?"

Jeff pulled the vehicle into a slot and put his hand over hers. "I'm sorry, Mattie. Does this place make you feel uncomfortable? I can cancel the reservation, and we can go somewhere else." He turned off the car and looked straight at her. "Where would you like to go?"

Mattie rubbed the back of her neck. "Jeff, I'm not like those college girls you've dated. I don't know about French food or the difference between grape juice and an expensive bottle of wine."

Jeff laughed. "Mattie, I don't drink. Nothing's changed there. I brought you out here to impress you, and all I've done is make you a nervous wreck. Look at you—you're shaking."

Mattie slouched down in the seat. "Oh, no, there's Mrs. Cox! What is she doing way out here?"

"Who's Mrs. Cox?"

"She's the woman I painted the ponies for. They scared her daughter, and so she had a painter cover everything on the ceiling, and now she wants me to do the walls again."

"Well, I'm not going to cover for you if you're scaring small children." Jeff winked. "Seriously, Mattie, I'd take you anywhere you wanted to go, but you need to stop separating yourself from the wealthy. God didn't give you a spirit of fear."

"Oh, sure—quote Scripture at me. Make me feel guilty for not wanting to indulge in an expensive meal."

"We're going in," Jeff said with authority, as if they were talking about fighting some sort of battle. Mattie could almost hear the marching music. Jeff came around and opened her door and held out his hand. She forced herself to remember this was Jeff, and he was the same person she'd always known. Even with his fancy education and advanced degrees.

Once they entered the restaurant, she heard the quiet tinkling of silverware and hushed conversation. It was almost like entering a cathedral. The maitre d' gave them a quiet corner table with a view of the extensive golf links and called Jeff "Dr. Weatherly."

Mattie laughed at the table. "Did you tell him you were a doctor for a better table?"

"I am a doctor, Mattie. I have my doctorate in economics. I just don't use the title very often."

Mattie felt faint. Jeff was nothing as she remembered. Everything in his life was complicated and beyond her, and she felt like a country bumpkin beside him. She fanned herself with the leather menu and took a quick sip of water. She got caught up in the lemon, which had a tiny net wrapped around it to keep the seeds from falling in the water.

"I think we should go," Mattie said.

"Mattie." Jeff's low tone was that of a stern parent. "You belong here. You belong anywhere you want to be. I brought you here to try the lobster bisque, which I know you will love.

I'm not asking you to live this way. I like Mexican food, too, but this night is special. Let me make it special for us."

Mrs. Cox suddenly appeared at the side of their table. "Mattie, is that you?"

"Yes, Mrs. Cox. How are you?"

"I'm so glad you're here. I want my husband to talk some sense into you. There are no other artists. I'm sure you know that, which is the reason for your attitude, but I want you to finish that room. You don't make your murals kitschy or something that will be out of style in a year. We want that for our home. Something classic."

"Very well, Mrs. Cox. I'll check my calendar on Monday and get back to you. We'll work something out."

Mrs. Cox exhaled audibly. "Wonderful. I'm sorry for the way I treated you, Mattie. I was worried what my husband would say about more workmen in the house. He so likes his privacy." Mrs. Cox said "pri-vi-cee," and Mattie had to contemplate what she meant for a moment.

"That's understandable, Mrs. Cox. Privacy is a very important state. Now if you'll excuse us, this is my date, Dr. Weatherly, and I'm on his clock now." Mattie suppressed a grin as the woman walked away, and she noticed that Jeff shook his head ever so slightly.

Jeff leaned in toward her, and she could feel the warmth of his breath. "You are incorrigible."

Mattie giggled and covered her lips with her fingers. "I didn't think that doctor bit would come in so handy so quickly. This is fun."

"So I guess it doesn't make you uncomfortable anymore."

"Gracious, no, Dr. Weatherly. I'm quite enjoying it." Mattie stuck her chin toward the sky. "I'm seeing a doctor."

"Mattie Stevens, you are trouble, and the worst of it is, you know it. And enjoy it. Do you want me to order for you?"

"Nothing weird. I want to know everything I'm eating. No snails or anything like that." The tension in her shoulders eased, and she relaxed against the high-back chair. She might actually start to enjoy this good life.

"I'll find you the French equivalent of the chicken enchilada. Deal?"

"Deal."

The courses for dinner kept coming, and Mattie thought she'd explode until she saw dessert. Then she had a whole new outlook on hunger. Scanning the tray the waiter brought, she had a terrible time deciding.

"What is this?" she asked, pointing to one.

"Crème Caramel," the waiter said.

Mattie leaned into Jeff and whispered, "It looks just like flan."

"That's basically what it is. That's how I knew you'd like it. I didn't think you'd like the soufflé as much, and it cost twice as much."

Mattie thinned her eyes. "Ever the economist."

Jeff leaned in on his elbow and watched her eat the luscious dessert. "You are so beautiful, Mattie. I can't believe I'm sitting here with you now."

She lost all interest in dessert. The sweetness of Jeff's words was far superior to anything with calories in it. She placed the fork on the plate and took his hand across the table. "I feel the same, Jeff. That I'm so fortunate to be here, that I waited so long for this moment."

"Do you remember in the Bible when the servant is sent out to find a wife for Isaac—and the man prays that the woman for his master will bring water? And Rebekah is there?"

"Yes." Mattie nodded.

"I prayed that, if I came back and you were still available, I would take it as a sign from God." Jeff knelt on the floor beside her and took both of her hands. Two violinists came behind him and quietly played romantic music on their stringed instruments. Jeff took a small blue velvet case from his pocket, and Mattie's fingers flew to her mouth.

She shook her head, unable to believe what was happening.

"Mattie Stevens, you make the world turn for me. You make me excited to be back in Heaven. You make me remember all I lost when I left this town. You are the woman God created for me. I know it in my heart." Jeff opened the little box, and a sparkling diamond the size of a small marble glistened toward her. "Will you do me the honor of becoming my wife?"

Chapter 8

Mattie looked at the ring then into Jeff's aqua-blue eyes. Her first thought was how she wanted her future children to have those eyes, but then she thought of the ring and its enormous size. She would be a wealthy wife. She would have a four year old right away. Everything in her life would change for Jeff Weatherly. Yet her mouth betrayed all these objections.

"Yes, Jeff. Yes, I will marry you."

A spattering of applause followed, and she looked around to see the patrons smiling at them. He lifted her chin and kissed her lightly. "When?"

She looked self-consciously at the violinists and wondered if she heard right over their romantic squealing. "When?"

"When."

"I guess when the church will marry us." *Let your yes be yes.* Those words haunted her at the moment. Was she ready to make such a big commitment? Such a change in her life? Yes, she loved Jeff, but Kenny still despised her. Mattie knew nothing of parenting, and trading in her paintbrush for baking cookies scared her feverishly.

Jeff took her arm and led her from the restaurant. Once in the car she felt herself exhale. *Oh, Lord, help me. What am I doing? Is it enough to love this man?* Although she'd been in love with Jeff since she was sixteen, how much of that was real? And how much was the imaginary hero she'd created for herself in her mind? She'd known he had his doctorate for less than two hours. What else didn't she know? She needed to pray.

"Jeff, I am so flattered. I am so incredibly happy and the idea of being your wife sends shivers down my spine—"

"But?"

Mattie took a deep breath. "But this is all happening so fast. I'm worried we don't know the new Mattie and Jeff well enough yet."

Jeff nodded, pursing his lips together in obvious thought. "I completely understand. But, Mattie, one question."

"Yes?"

"Have you ever known me to do anything lightly? Anything by the seat of my pants?"

"Only play in a certain chess match that changed your plans for our senior prom." Immediately she wished she could take her accusatory words back.

"I prayed long and hard about that night, Mattie. And I've prayed even harder about this. I bought this ring before I came home to Arizona. I knew in my heart we were meant to be together, and when I found out you were still free, I knew God thought so too."

His certainty scared her. Mattie couldn't remember being certain about anything except salvation. Even now she wondered if she should have become more educated. Would her painting business have been more successful if she were a better manager? These thoughts and doubts plagued Mattie. She tried to focus, to think what else might come along that was better than this offer. An offer from the man she loved. That old saying haunted her: *Marry in haste, repent at leisure.*

"May I remind you, Mattie—you said yes."

"I did, didn't I?"

Jeff laughed. "Relax, Mattie. I'm teasing. This ring belongs to you. If you don't feel you're ready to wear it yet, I'll keep it for you until such a time comes." Jeff reached for the ring, and Mattie felt a surge of anger.

"Don't you touch that ring!" She raked her hands through her hair. "Oh, Jeff, I'm so sorry. I don't know what I'm thinking. You must think I'm absolutely crazy. I'm just so taken off guard, so surprised. Everything is too good, too right. Something has to be wrong."

Jeff leaned in and kissed her forehead. "Why does something have to be wrong because you're happy?"

"What if I'm a terrible mother to Kenny?"

"What if I'm a terrible father?"

Mattie shook her head. "That's ridiculous. You're wonderful at anything you choose to do."

Jeff's eyebrows went up. "As are you, Mattie. Now is this a yes or a very slow no?"

For the first time since leaving the restaurant, Mattie looked into his eyes. The pale light of the evening pink sky provided a soft light, and Mattie knew. In those eyes was a soul she loved more than anything on earth. Nothing had changed about Jeff. Only their circumstances.

"I can do all things through Christ who strengthens me."

"Pardon me?"

"Do not be anxious for anything, but by prayer and petition, with thanksgiving, present your requests to God."

Jeff's eyebrows furrowed. "Is the Scripture for me or for you?"

"It's for both of us. Come on." Mattie opened the door and slipped out of the Cherokee. Jeff met her at the back, and she walked alongside him to a perfectly groomed piece of grass on the golf course. The Arizona sky lit up in a million sparkling lights, and Mattie reflected on the greatness of God. She wondered if she would ever be this happy again. All her joy culminated in this one moment in time. The creation of God called to her from the stars. The realization of the love she had sought for so many years stood beside her, beckoning her, and she would not be the only cousin unmarried. Was it possible?

Jeff and Mattie prayed together until they didn't have enough light to see. In the desert without the moon shining, the darkness surrounded them. Mattie laughed out loud as she and Jeff tried to find their way to the Cherokee by Braille. She felt perfectly at ease now. Ready to take on the world. And a certain four year old. Her heart was light and her whole being never happier.

Once inside the vehicle, Mattie breathed in Jeff's delicious scent. He smelled masculine and attractive. And dangerous.

Being married was obviously the only safe course of action.

"I'm ready to go home now, Dr. Weatherly. And when you pick me up the next time, I shall be sporting this rather gaudy rock to show all my friends I am to be married." She fluttered her hand in the air, but it was far too dark to see her movements.

"Mattie, if you don't like the ring, we can get something simpler."

She shook her head vigorously. "Bite your tongue. It's grown on me. We'll get you a simple one to make me feel better—how's that?" Mattie enjoyed teasing her straight-laced love almost as much as she loved looking into his eyes.

"Is tomorrow okay to get the supplies for Kenny's room?" Jeff asked, abruptly changing the conversation.

"Absolutely. I have a portfolio of ideas I'll drop off before work tomorrow. He can dream about the perfect mural all day. Maybe that will get him excited about shopping with us."

"Work is going to be harried for me in the next couple of days. I'm afraid I've let some things go to care for Kenny lately. I also need to make sure I approve of his preschool. If it's not okay, it's better to pull him out now."

All the severity of their relationship rushed into Mattie with the vengeance of a hungry coyote. Jeff seemed to sense in her quietness that something was bothering her.

"I'm sorry. This is our night, and I'm rambling about parental duties. I guess if you haven't figured it out by now, I'm not very romantic."

Mattie found his lips in the dark. "Then I can't imagine what romantic is. I've been whirlwind-romanced, and I get to marry my Prince Charming. All I'm missing is the glass slipper."

"Well, those expensive sandals you bought should make a nice substitute."

"Jeff, you made a joke!"

"Come on—let's get somewhere into the light. I miss looking into your beautiful face." Jeff opened the sunroof, and a shadow of light danced across his jaw. "There's the woman I fell in love with. Stars or no stars, I want to see my beauty in the light."

Mattie practically danced on air when she arrived home. Once inside, she studied the ring again and again, wondering how she'd ever thought it was too big. It seemed perfect now.

Thank You, Jesus.

She fell into a dreamy sleep with her jeweled hand resting on her heart.

❧

The next morning Mattie made a special trip to see Kenny before he started back to preschool. She brought her portfolio and a big smile, hoping the little boy would forget his last reaction toward her. As she knocked at Jeff's grandmother's door, hope filled her.

"Hi, Helen. Did Jeff tell you I would be stopping by before I went to work?"

Helen nearly squeezed Mattie with an embrace. "Did my grandson tell me about my future granddaughter-in-law coming by, you say?"

After returning the warm greeting, Mattie felt as though she'd stepped into a new family. A family she would love as much as her own.

"Did you see the ring?" Mattie lifted her ring finger, wishing she'd taken the time to buff her nails or use nail polish. Something worthy of the ring that now graced her usually paint-covered hand.

Helen winked. "I saw it when Jeff announced his first date with you, Mattie. I've never known my grandson to set his mind toward something he didn't follow through on. With him and his prayers I don't think you ever stood a chance." Helen backed away from the door and allowed Mattie to step over the threshold. Kenny sat watching a train video but was wholly interested in Mattie's entrance.

"Hi, Kenny."

Kenny sent her a glowering glance then turned his head away without speaking.

"Uncle Jeff told me you liked trains so I brought you some of my paintings. We're going to paint your new room with trains."

"No, thanks." Kenny sunk his elbows into the carpet and turned back toward the television.

Helen stepped forward and turned off the set. "That's enough, young man. You apologize to Miss Stevens."

"Oh, please, Helen—I want him to call me Mattie."

"Apologize to Mattie, Kenny, or there'll be no macaroni and cheese for lunch. You'll eat a liver sandwich."

Kenny's eyes widened. He apparently wasn't sure if he believed his grandmother or not. But clearly he wasn't willing to risk it. "Sorry," he answered, but the curl of his lip and defiant tone told Mattie the apology was in word only.

Mattie knelt down on the carpet and opened her oversized book. Her children's fantasy creations quickly captured Kenny's attention. "Is that Thomas?"

Mattie nodded. "It is."

"I like James the best. James is the red engine."

She turned the page, and Kenny's eyes grew round. But they quickly reverted to normal size. "I don't want nothin'."

"Your uncle and I are going to take you to pick out the paint tonight. You just need to choose one of these pictures."

"No! I don't want any dumb picture. My mom hates you." Kenny's eyes thinned to slivers, with a look so angry that Mattie feared what lurked inside the child. She quickly banished such thoughts, knowing this little boy needed her. Whether he knew it or not.

"Kenny, your mom knew me a long time ago. We didn't get along so well then, but I'll tell you what: I'm going to marry your uncle Jeff, and I want to love you because he loves you. And because Jesus loves you. I don't care if you love me. That's not your job, Honey." Mattie resisted squeezing the little boy's shoulders affectionately.

"My mom's coming home, and she still won't like you."

"But your uncle Jeff likes me. Can't you try to put up with me because he likes me?"

"No!" Kenny crossed his pudgy arms, and Mattie knew it was going to take time. Nothing else would help the situation. She would start James the red engine tonight and be there for Kenny. She would pray and look to God for comfort. She said her good-byes and focused on all that was right in her world.

Now it was time to tell Gram she was batting one thousand in the matchmaking department. Gram took the news with all the grace of a professional quarterback, whooping and hollering and talking about prayer's outcome like Mattie didn't have a thing to do with Jeff's affections. Mattie smiled to herself. All was right with the world for the time being.

Epilogue

Six months passed as if they were mere seconds. Of course, Gram still took all the accolades for scoring a perfect ten for her four granddaughters. Gram welcomed everyone at the church doors as though she herself were marrying today. If Mattie had any doubts left, they had quickly passed with her family's happiness. Jeff was an admired man, and it was impossible not to feel everything for him that everyone around her felt. She was fortunate to be marrying such a kind-hearted, successful, intelligent man, and she never wanted to forget it.

As she stared down the church aisle at Jeff's tall build, with his gentle hands upon Kenny's shoulder, she knew there would never be another for her. There never had been. Mattie almost turned to see if Jeff was looking toward her. Her heart was swelled with joy like a ripe, red strawberry.

Callie, Cassie, and Mel looked elegant in their bridesmaids' gowns, and Mattie closed her eyes for a moment. She wanted to capture everything inside her mind and never forget this moment when love and family collided into one precious mold.

She reached the end of the aisle, and Jeff took her hand. Together they faced the preacher. She promised to follow Jeff anywhere, to be his helpmate, come what may.

Jeff pulled out a letter, and Mattie's heartbeat became rapid as he cleared his throat to speak.

"I thought I might be too nervous to speak, so I wrote some things down. For those of you who don't know our history, Mattie and I met in our high school youth group and fell in love. We might have married right out of school were it not for a very important chess match."

The congregation laughed, and Jeff cleared his throat again.

"If you're not familiar with this woman, all I can say is that it is a privilege to know her. All through my college career, both undergraduate and post-graduate, she never left my mind. I knew someday I would return for her as my bride. My mind never contemplated anyone else. I only prayed that she would still be here for me when I returned. In my heart I knew God meant for us to be together, though, and that prayer was answered. We've had an interesting voyage. I almost dated her cousin Melissa, hoping to spur some interest and announce that I was back in Heaven."

Mattie felt her cheeks flame red, and the congregation gave a spattering of applause.

"Besides being incredibly beautiful, Mattie has a heart wholly for God. She has readily agreed to help me parent Kenny until Joan returns, which for those of you who have been praying should be soon. Joan met a wonderful biker, who led her back to the God of her youth. She has been in rehabilitation for three months now, and we will soon have to part with Kenny."

Jeff rubbed Kenny's hair lovingly.

Mattie recalled all the miracles God had performed in their lives in the last six months. Joan's phone call had been a desert bloom. Once Kenny heard from his mother that it was okay to love Mattie, the little boy's allegiance was no longer divided. Raindrops of joy fell into their lives one by one.

Jeff continued. "So thank you to all of you who are here to celebrate the happiest day of my life. I have a feeling it only gets better from here." He folded the paper and slipped it into his pocket.

"You may kiss the bride," the preacher said.

Jeff kissed her for the first time as her husband, and Mattie thought she might burst from emotion. Jeff had come home again, and they would live in Heaven together.

KRISTIN BILLERBECK

Kristin lives in northern California with her husband, an engineering director, and their four young children. A marketing director by profession, Kristin now stays home to be with her children and writes for enjoyment.

A Letter to Our Readers

Dear Readers:

In order that we might better contribute to your reading enjoyment, we would appreciate you taking a few minutes to respond to the following questions. When completed, please return to the following: Fiction Editor, Barbour Publishing, Inc., P.O. Box 719, Uhrichsville, OH 44683.

1. Did you enjoy reading *Blind Dates?*
    - ❑ Very much—I would like to see more books like this.
    - ❑ Moderately—I would have enjoyed it more if _____

    _____

    _____

2. What influenced your decision to purchase this book?
    (Check those that apply.)
    - ❑ Cover   ❑ Back cover copy   ❑ Title   ❑ Price
    - ❑ Friends   ❑ Publicity   ❑ Other

3. Which story was your favorite?
    - ❑ *The Perfect Match*   ❑ *Mix and Match*
    - ❑ *A Match Made in Heaven*   ❑ *Mattie Meets Her Match*

4. Please check your age range:
    - ❑ Under 18   ❑ 18–24   ❑ 25–34
    - ❑ 35–45   ❑ 46–55   ❑ Over 55

5. How many hours per week do you read? _____

Name _____

Occupation _____

Address _____

City _____ State _____ Zip _____

IF YOU
LIVED HERE
YOU'D BE
HOME BY NOW

IF YOU

LIVED HERE

YOU'D BE

HOME BY NOW

Why We Traded the
Commuting Life for a Little
House on the Prairie

CHRISTOPHER INGRAHAM

HARPER

NEW YORK ◦ LONDON ◦ TORONTO ◦ SYDNEY

HARPER

Portions of chapter 1 have previously appeared in a different form in the *Washington Post* story "I Called This Place 'America's Worst Place to Live.' Then I Went There."

Portions of chapter 5 have previously appeared in a different form in the *Washington Post* story "I Ordered a Box of Crickets from the Internet and It Went About as Well as You'd Expect."

Portions of chapter 8 have previously appeared in a different form in the *Washington Post* story "Why These Rural, White, Gun-Owning Guys Didn't Vote for Trump."

Portions of chapter 3, chapter 5, and the epilogue have previously appeared in a different form in the *Washington Post* story "What Life Is Really Like in 'America's Worst Place to Live.'"

FIRST HARPER PAPERBACKS EDITION PUBLISHED 2020.

Illustration by Vector Bang/Shutterstock, Inc.

Library of Congress Cataloging-in-Publication Data has been applied for.

ISBN 978-0-06-286148-1 (pbk.)

20 21 22 23 24   LSC   10 9 8 7 6 5 4 3 2 1

To Briana

IF YOU

LIVED HERE

YOU'D BE

HOME BY NOW

I t's cold. Not *really* cold, mind you—none of that minus-twenty-or-forty business we'll get later in the season. But the mercury's somewhere just south of zero, the winds are whipping like mad up and down the frozen river, and the twins are getting bored.

"Daddy, when can we go?" Charles asks. A certain falling inflection on the "Dad-dy" suggests he's about five minutes away from losing it completely, melting down right here on the snow. He's in his jacket, snow pants, heavy boots, mittens, neck warmer drawn up above his nose, one-size-fits-all Northern Grain hat drooping over his five-year-old head, just the way he likes it. But we've been out here too long, cold's creeping in between the layers, wind's starting to bite.

"Just a few minutes, kiddo, we're next," I tell him. I gesture over to the small playground where his twin, Jack, is gleefully whizzing down a metal slide, landing with a hard thud on the ice every single time but not minding it at all. "Why don't you go play with your brother for a few more minutes?"

"I don't want to," he says, same inflection. Despite being twins, Jack and Charles are about as different as two brothers can be. Among many other things, Jack doesn't mind the cold at all; he'll run around outside for hours until he's soaked through from the snow on the outside of his jacket and the sweat within, big clouds of hot, happy exhaled kid breath following him wherever he goes. He's a furnace. Charles, meanwhile, is hypersensitive to the cold. He's taken to insisting on having his snow pants on for even the shortest excursion outdoors, even if it's just a quick hop from the heated house to the heated car and back. He hates the feel of cold pants on his legs.

"Well then, go over there with Mom and William," I say. My wife's helping the one-year-old, our Minnesota baby, chuck fifteen-pound frozen turkeys at an assortment of short PVC pipes standing on their ends. "Turkey bowling," they call it up here. Yet another way the natives stare down the relentless winters with whimsy and good cheer. William's mostly given up on trying to manhandle the frozen birds and is basically just flinging himself down the ice alley toward the pipes. His overstuffed winter gear gives him roughly the same proportions as a bowling ball, so it's not a bad idea.

"I don't *wan*na," Charles says. He's about to go code red and I've exhausted all my other options so it's time to go nuclear: I push him down into the snow.

He's too shocked to say anything at first but I can see the rage and the laughter duking it out across his face. "*Dad*dy," he says, trying to get back up, but I knock him down again. Got 'em—he's laughing now. "DADD—" but I give him another shove before he can get it out and he's rolling around in the snow giggling. Jack hears the commotion, comes tearing over to where we are, and jumps on my back. It's on.

The three of us tumble through the snow, down the slight slope to where the deep stuff is by the river shore, among the frozen cattails still standing from the fall. I briefly wonder if one of us is going to break through some thin ice to a layer of mud or worse below but I realize that's stupid—the temperature hasn't been above freezing in months, it's barely even been above zero. The river's been frozen solid for a month at least, probably longer than that.

Soon Briana drops William on the pile and then we're all there, tumbling around in the frigid snow, the kids whooping and hollering and not even caring when one of them lands face-first in it. Suddenly Jack sits bolt upright.

"Do you hear it?" he says. We all stop and sit still. The sounds of distant baying and yipping grow louder and suddenly there they are—a team of eight lean, muscular dogs hitched to a pair of canvas sleds. It's finally our turn to run the river.

Back in the summer of 2015 I had no idea that I'd just stumbled across the dataset that would change my life, uproot me and my family from our cozy but constrained suburban D.C. life, and plop us down 1,400 miles away at the edge of the vast, open prairie. A place where it snows eight months out of the year, where winter starts in October and doesn't end until May. A place where taking the kids out on a weekend dogsledding excursion is just one of those things people do.

The dataset in question was an obscure late-1990s project of the U.S. Department of Agriculture, intended to quantify every single county in America on the physical characteristics that "enhance the location as a place to live." It assigned a score to counties based on physical characteristics—hills, valleys, bodies of water, nice weather—that most people would agree make a place pleasant to live in.

As a data reporter for the *Washington Post*, I thought I'd seen it all: numbers that explain everything from the economy to waffles to the zombie apocalypse. But here was something different—natural beauty, quantified. And with impeccable federal credentials.

Even better, the project ranked the counties according to where they fell on the scale. Which of America's more than three thousand counties are the "ugliest," according to the federal government? And which the most scenic? And where, reader, does your *own* county fall into the mix?

The story practically wrote itself, a perfect diversion for D.C.'s August recess doldrums. I mapped the numbers out, wrote a few hundred words to accompany them, slapped a headline on it all ("Every County in America, Ranked by Scenery and Climate"), and called it a day.

Like countless other pieces of data-driven ephemera I've written, I forgot about it almost as soon as my editor hit "publish" the following Monday.

Funny thing about ranking places—for every city or town or county that's at the top of some list, there has to be one all the way down at the bottom. As a country we're obsessed with superlatives—we want to raise our families in the best places, visit the most famous landmarks, climb the highest mountains, and swim the clearest, bluest seas.

But what about all those other places that don't make the cut?

This is a story about one of those forgotten places—an obscure corner of the heartland that, from the vantage point of an Excel sheet on a coastal desktop, appeared to have nothing going for it. No distinguishing features whatsoever, save a last-place finish in a county beauty pageant run by federal statisticians in the late 1990s.

Red Lake County (pop. 4,055) in northwestern Minnesota is a place so lacking in superlatives that proclaiming itself "the only landlocked county in the United States that is surrounded by just two neighboring counties" is the closest thing to a boast that you'll find on the county's website.

As it turns out, Red Lake County doesn't have any actual lakes. It doesn't have any hills. The summers are hot, and the winters are brutally cold. You crunch all those numbers together on a spreadsheet, and it may not be a surprise that the place came in dead last.

I tossed the county website's border trivia into the story along with a joke about Red Lake County being "the absolute worst place to live in America," and didn't think twice about it.

But now "the absolute worst place to live in America" is the place I and my family call home. This book is the story of how we got here, what we found when we arrived, and everything we've experienced since then. How our lives changed when we moved from one of the nation's wealthiest suburbs (median household income: $110,000) to a working-class farming community (median income: $50,000) hundreds of miles from anywhere.

It's a story about an education in the ways of small-town life. It's about the people whom I've come to call friends and neighbors, who've taught us how to fry walleye, make corn shocks, and press apple cider by hand—and who also have gently mocked our big-city "eccentricities" like goat cheese and eggplant parmesan.

But it's also bigger than that. It's a tale about two Americas—the coastal centers of power and money, like D.C., and the thousands of towns and villages in between them who feel like they've been left out of the national conversation. As the 2016 election came to a close it became clear that the gulf between those Americas is larger than it's ever been—but is it really?

It's about a journey to the other side of what social scientists call the urban-rural happiness gradient—surveys consistently show that city dwellers are the least satisfied members of society, while those who live in the countryside and small towns are the happiest.

This book is written specifically for people, like me, who are feeling increasingly stretched thin by the frenetic pace and ever-escalating cost of the big city and suburban lifestyle. People like me commuting fifteen hours a week and rarely seeing their kids because of the vast distance between where jobs are good and where housing is affordable.

People who have driven through long-forgotten rural areas on the way from one big city to another and wondered, "Who actually lives here?" People who have fantasized about throwing their big city jobs away, moving out to the middle of nowhere, and living a simpler life. People who've always wanted to raise their kids in a small town like the one they grew up in, but couldn't figure out a way to make it work.

Data from the Pew Research Center shows that more than half of Americans—54 percent—say they'd prefer to live in a small town or rural area. But more than 80 percent of us live in the cities. That's a huge disconnect—up to a third of all Americans, living in the cities but dreaming of the country.

On that icy January afternoon the mushers who were running the event helped Briana and all three kids into the front sled. The guy who was guiding us, a grizzled old former sled dog racer, climbed in the back sled.

"Wait, where am I going to go?" I asked.

"You stand on the footboards back there," he said, gesturing to the runners protruding from the sled's rear. "Hold on tight, do what I tell you, and don't fall off."

"Do you think that's wise?" I tried to ask, but by then he had given a high-pitched whistle and the dogs were off, baying with the electric excitement of animals doing the one thing in life that they were born to do.

The dogs pulled us away from shore and onto the icy expanse of the river, which meanders 193 miles from Minnesota's massive Red Lake to the Red River of the North, along the North Dakota border. Our short journey that day looped us around just a few miles of that distance, under the bridges of the town of Thief River Falls and into the open country beyond.

Once the dogs reached cruising speed they became silent, our motion along the river a frictionless glide, the only sounds the whisper of sled runners on the ice punctuated occasionally by an excited outburst from the kids in the front sled.

There used to be sled dog races all over the northern part of the country, the musher said. But not anymore. Winters were getting warmer; the sport was retreating north. Places that still got enough cold and snow to put a team of dogs out on the ice? Those places were special.

I reflected, for a moment, on the long path that had brought us here.

CHAPTER 1

What was it that stopped the train that day? "Signal problems"? Wet leaves? A body on the tracks?

The specifics didn't matter then and they sure don't matter now. All that mattered, back on that damp August morning in the summer of 2015, was that the train was running late, again. Which meant I'd be an hour, maybe two, maybe three late to work, again. Which meant I'd be staying late and not getting home until well after the kids had gone to bed. Again.

I was well into my second year writing for the *Washington Post*, a dream job by any measure. With a beat that amounted to "data, writ large" I had wide latitude in selecting topics that interested me. Bear attacks, for instance. The geography of jorts. Boats that can be parked inside other, larger boats.

My professional life, in short, was grand, except for one teeny, tiny problem. The *Washington Post* is based in Washington, D.C. My wife, Briana, and I, along with our two-year-old twins, Jack and Charles, lived just outside of Baltimore. Between our home and the *Post* newsroom lay 90 to 120 minutes of commute by car, train, subway, and foot. On a good day.

That damp August morning? Not shaping up to

be a good day. When the train finally arrived we all grumbled on. I did my best to avoid even glancing at my fellow commuters—I was never much of a people person, and chatting it up with a chipper stranger on a train, before coffee, seemed like the absolute worst way to spend that time. Some mornings I absentmindedly scrolled through my phone, searching social media for grist for the day's stories. Others I slept. Most of all, I tried not to think of how much of my life I was spending there, on the tracks, in cramped quarters surrounded by strangers.

That morning the train limped down the tracks toward D.C. much slower than usual. Eventually the train stopped, for good, about halfway to D.C. at the Bowie State University platform. There was a slight drizzle. The conductor came over the loudspeaker to inform us that the train was unable to go any further and that they had no additional information at this time.

I decided to bail, hopping off the train and calling an Uber. If I ever wanted to see my family, or my job, again, the best bet appeared to be to cut my losses, head back to Baltimore, and salvage whatever was left of the workday at home. Between the surge pricing and the distances involved, the ride cost a hundred dollars. Finally, four hours after the start of my commute, I pulled my car back into the parking space at my house. Right back where I had started.

⸻

I'm far from the only person to live like this. According to census data, roughly four million American workers, representing about 3 percent of the total sixteen-and-over workforce, have one-way commutes of ninety minutes or more. It's probably easiest for me to explain why I did. because my wife and I couldn't afford to do anything else, at least not if we were going to have our own place. According to Zillow, the median home value in Washington, D.C., is now somewhere north of half a million dollars, which was well out of the realm of affordability for Briana, then a government worker, and me.

Neither one of us came from money. I was born and raised in the village of Oneonta, an upstate New York college town of about 13,000 people situated in a kind of geographic no-man's-land between the Catskills and the Adirondacks. The region was hilly but not mountainous; populated but not populous. To the extent the

Total annual time spent commuting

Average American worker

9.3
full calendar days

Me, in 2015

31.3
full calendar days

Source: US Census Bureau

town had anything like a civic identity it was based on its adjacency to Cooperstown, home of the Baseball Hall of Fame.

My upbringing was solidly middle class for the region. My dad was a veterinarian, not a particularly glamorous career but one that provided enough money to pay the bills—or would have, had his taste for expensive status-signaling gadgets like watches, computers, and cars not put the family tens of thousands of dollars in credit card and second-mortgage debt.

My mom, a vet tech by trade, was the more pragmatic of the two. When my dad wrecked the household finances with fountain pen purchases, she did her best to restore balance by keeping the household running on generic store-brand food and thrift shop clothing. The contrast between the two provided no shortage of amusement for my high school friends, who couldn't understand why my dad was driving around town flashing his Rolex while his family ate Grand Union-brand cereal for breakfast.

My parents, in short, had a decent income but no wealth to speak of when I was growing up. They divorced my senior year in high school, a mostly amicable affair because there were no assets to fight over. After graduating from high school I made it to Cornell University in part due to my good grades, and in part due to a legacy admissions preference stemming from my dad having gone there. I ended up taking on thousands of dollars in student loan debt by the time I graduated— bills I'm still paying off today, nearly twenty years later.

Bills that, for the entirety of my twenties and thirties, set the parameters for what was financially possible in life, and what wasn't.

Briana and I weren't really keen on renting a place in the city, even before we had kids. We had a dog and a couple of cats. We wanted a bit of yard, maybe someplace to put a grill. We didn't want to be crammed in on top of millions of other people.

So we looked farther afield. Even outside of the cities, however, the economics of home ownership were daunting. In the Baltimore suburbs, which we eventually settled on, a typical detached single-family home goes for somewhere around the same price as a cramped D.C. condo. In 2010, when we were looking, this seemed insane to us: where were people getting the money for these houses? Was everyone in Baltimore an investment banker?

In the end we settled on a 952-square-foot row house on a lot totaling .0359 acres. At the time it was perfect: built of stone in the early 1800s in the mill town of Oella, originally it served as millworkers' quarters. The village was charming and historic (most houses, including our own, didn't receive indoor plumbing until the 1980s) and abutted a state park where the dog could roam.

More important than any of this, however, was the price: $245,000, a relative bargain on account of its old age. Paying a quarter of a million dollars for 952 square feet felt obscene; it was obscene. But by Baltimore/D.C. standards it was a bargain, and in 2010 it was what we could afford.

All that 952 feet of living space was spread across three stories, so we spent a lot of time hiking up and down stairs. We shared walls with neighbors on either side but they were quiet most of the time. Stone walls make for surprisingly poor insulators, so in the winters we heated the place with a pellet stove. In the spring, if you opened a window and listened real hard, you could hear the murmur of the Patapsco River in the valley below.

For a young professional couple with a handful of pets, it was perfect. Then we had the twins.

When we found out we were pregnant—several years after moving into our tiny Oella home—we thought about trying to move to a bigger place. But it was well out of the question. We had nowhere near enough money to make the numbers work.

So we decided to do the best we could with our millworkers' quarters—after all, we reasoned, back in the early 1800s a family would have packed twelve kids into the place. Surely we could find room for two.

And it did work, for a while. While the twins were still babies and mostly immobile. The finished attic became their nursery, with just enough room for two cribs, two dressers, and a rocking chair.

The living room downstairs, meanwhile, could accommodate a double pack-'n'-play for nap times, which along with a love seat for two adults and a wood chair put it at just about maximum capacity. Yes, the pellet stove was in there, but we'd worry about how to block that off once the twins figured out how to move.

But as the twins grew and became mobile it quickly

became apparent that 952 feet wasn't going to cut it any more. As they approached the year marker it felt as if the house was stuffed to the breaking point with baby paraphernalia. They were trying to crawl and walk, but didn't have a lot of space to figure things out. One afternoon, Charles, trying to master crawling in the tight confines of the living room, instead ended up backing himself fully under the couch. Toys, pillows, stuffed animals covered every horizontal surface in the residence. We let the twins crawl around in the dining room for more space, but we had to keep a constant eye out lest one of them squeeze himself through the cat door and tumble down the basement steps.

We needed a bigger place, but we were priced out of the market for a larger home that could accommodate our growing family. We were making decent money, and probably could have convinced a lender to approve a loan of a half million dollars or more if we were ever able to scrounge up a down payment to match. But between child-care costs and the burden of tens of thousands of dollars in student loans, our monthly budget already felt like it was pushed to the breaking point. Taking out more home debt and doubling the size of our monthly mortgage seemed reckless.

Given the demands of our professional lives, time was in short supply as well. My fifteen-hour-a-week commute meant that I barely saw the twins at all during the workweek. I was out the door well before they woke up. If I was lucky I'd see them for maybe forty-five minutes in the evening before it was time to put them to bed.

This time wasn't typically quality time, either. It was the end of the day; the twins were tired and cranky because they were two, and that's how two-year-olds are in the evening. Briana was tired and cranky from working a full day at the Social Security Administration and then coming home to deal with the twins by herself for several hours until I made it back. I was tired and cranky from working and being on the train all day.

None of us were at our best between the hours of 6 and 7 p.m. on those weeknights. But that was all the time we had with each other.

The weekends, which we used primarily to recover from the travails of the prior workweek, were not much better. There's a nearly unlimited number of things to do with kids in the Baltimore-D.C. area on a given weekend—take them to the aquarium, or the museums, or the Eastern Shore.

Problem was, of course, that doing just about anything still entailed a lengthy fight with the region's heavy traffic while the twins grew ever more agitated in the backseat. Most activities cost money, which was already in short supply. And the twins had the attention spans of your typical two-year-olds, which meant we'd spend an hour driving somewhere only to have them fuss and fret and complain of boredom and hunger within fifteen minutes of arriving.

So while we were surrounded by the riches the D.C. region had to offer, we typically lacked the time and the energy to enjoy them.

After seven years of living in the D.C. area my health

was bad enough, but the arrival of the twins pushed things over the edge. Shortly after their birth I was beset by a feeling of hopelessness that I now recognize as depression. It had been there most of my adult life, I realized, not terribly severe but always hovering around the margins, waiting to swoop in at inopportune times.

Things had gradually gotten worse during our time in D.C. This, again, isn't a surprise. studies have consistently shown that life in major metropolitan areas is associated with higher rates of mental illness, relative to people who live out in the country.

There's the crime, the pollution, and the paradoxical sense of isolation you experience when surrounded by millions of unsmiling strangers. Where we lived, in a suburb of Baltimore, there was a greater sense of community than in your typical anonymous city. But we were still smack in the heart of a major metropolitan area where it's easy to get lost in an uncaring crowd.

Studies have also consistently shown a link between population density and happiness: the fewer people around you, the more satisfied you are. A study on well-being in Canada found, for instance, that the average population density in the country's 20 percent most miserable communities was more than eight times greater than in the happiest 20 percent of communities.

Surveys in the United States, meanwhile, find that people who live in rural areas are happier than those who live in the suburbs, and suburbanites are happier than city dwellers. Some evolutionary psychologists have proposed a sort of "paleo-happiness" theory to explain this. The human brain, they reason, evolved for life on the African savanna, where our primal ancestors hail from. In that environment you'd find a population density of less than one person per square kilometer. In modern-day Manhattan, by contrast, you've got a population density greater than 27,000 people per square kilometer. Take a brain evolved for the former environment and drop it into the latter and you can see how certain problems might arise.

I'm not sure I completely buy this theory, but it certainly speaks to me on a purely experiential level. The strains of new parenthood, particularly with two children, brought the marginal feelings of dread front and center. I have the twins to thank for being the crisis that finally pushed me to seek help for my depression and treat it with medication. While not a cure-all by any means, the antidepressants I started shortly after their birth helped me keep things in perspective and function like a person unburdened with an irrational sense of dread.

Then there was the blood pressure. Through a stroke of bad genetic luck it's predisposed toward being high—my father had his first stroke at age fifty-six, and doctors had noted with alarm that my numbers were what they called "pre-hypertensive" in my early twenties, in what was otherwise my peak physical fitness.

Years of stressful work, long commutes, and bad eating didn't improve things, and by the time the twins were born my systolic pressure was pushing 150. Time to add another prescription to the regimen.

To cope with all the stress, I was also drinking—a lot. Ten to fifteen drinks per week, maybe? That put me somewhere in the top 20 percent of Americans by alcohol intake. Federal survey data show that binge drinking and heavy alcohol use are more prevalent in urban areas than in rural ones, with evidence of a gradient of use running from the least- to most-populated areas.

In the end, it seems that city life is slowly driving many of us mad. That was the case, at least, for me. Urban life is hazardous to your personal safety, your physical health, and your mental health. Why do we do it? In a word: jobs.

We move to cities that wear us down because that's where the jobs are. Happiness, health, safety—nice things to have, but you need to have a roof over your head before you can even start worrying about them. Historically, city residents have tended to be "well compensated for their joylessness," as one team of economists put it. "The desires for happiness and life satisfaction do not uniquely drive human ambitions," they rather dryly conclude. "Humans are quite understandably willing to sacrifice both happiness and life satisfaction if the price is right."

For many years, in America's cities, the price has been right. But particularly in recent decades the annual return on urban and suburban living has been declining. Rising housing costs and longer commutes have taken big bites out of disposable incomes and the time people have to enjoy them. Wages, meanwhile, have been largely flat for many workers, even those with the best-paying urban jobs.

There's a lot of good things to say about life in a functioning modern metropolis. Economies of scale, access to new people and technologies and ideas—historically the economic case for urbanization has been rooted in ideas like these.

But at what point does present-day urban dysfunction outweigh those economic gains, and even make the return on urbanization negative? What good is it to have a large pool of talented workers if they're all commuting ten hours or more a week? How many mental health days does it take for a modern office worker to achieve equilibrium with the stresses of the modern office?

It had been easier for me to ignore the toll of the commuting lifestyle before the kids were born. The body adapts. If a ninety-minute commute is what it takes to put a roof over your head, then that's what it takes. I would put a good face on it, talk about all the reading I could get done, or all the goofing around on the internet I could do via my phone.

But there's one big piece of evidence that cities aren't all they're cracked up to be: in 2014 the Pew Research Center surveyed Americans on the following question: "If you could live anywhere in the United States that you wanted to, would you prefer a city, a suburban area, a small town or a rural area?"

You might expect that most people answered "city" or "suburbs"—after all, that's where 80 percent of us live. But in fact, given their druthers, more than half of Americans—54 percent, to be exact—say they'd prefer to live in a small town or rural area. Just 24 percent said the city was ideal, and only 21 percent said they'd want to live in a suburb.

The implication is that a considerable chunk of the U.S. population—potentially as much as 30 percent—is stuck in the cities and suburbs and dreaming of escape to the country.

In the summer of 2015 I was one of them.

D.C.'s one redeeming late summer feature is that many of its people are out of town. Congress is on recess, and much of the nation's bureaucratic apparatus—the lobbyists, think tankers, and news media—along with it.

Journalists stuck in D.C. newsrooms in August are often kicking around light, offbeat story ideas that wouldn't see the light of day at other times of year, when there's actual news to write about. This particular context—the lack of real news and the greater tolerance of editors for general dicking around—is important for understanding everything that follows.

Bear in mind, too, that in 2015 the country hadn't yet gone mad over the Trump campaign and eventual presidency; the man was still largely seen as a sideshow, a novelty candidate along the lines of Vermin Supreme, the perennial oddball candidate from Vermont who wears a boot on his head.

What this meant is that readers still had plenty of appetite for quirky, out-of-left-field stories that would take off like social fire on Facebook and Twitter. I just so happened to excel at this sort of story.

In the midst of those August doldrums I happened to see a news release about a Baylor University study finding that people who live in more "beautiful landscapes" are less religious. Apparently it's tough to spend the morning in church when the beach or the mountains call. As a data reporter, however, I was immediately drawn to the independent variable in this scenery-versus-religion equation—how the heck did these guys measure and quantify natural beauty?

As it turns out, a group of data nerds at the U.S. Department of Agriculture did just that in the late 1990s, creating what they called a "natural amenities scale." It all started when the USDA's statisticians were searching for a better understanding of what was driving population change—and more specifically, population decline—in rural areas.

Economic concerns—jobs, again—were a big part of this. But the researchers knew there was another factor at play: the weather. Between 1950 and 2000, for instance, there's a striking correlation between January temperatures and overall population growth in a given city or metropolitan area.

The warmer a place's winters are, in other words, the more people seem to be drawn there. The USDA's researchers reasoned that temperature wasn't the only such amenity. People like interesting landscapes, for instance—craggy peaks and rolling valleys. They like to have water nearby for swimming and boating.

These are the things, in short, that regional tourism boards put in their brochures, or that newcomers call back home to brag about after they arrive. In the end, the researchers arrived at a set of six different measures:

1. Average January temperature (warmer is better)

2. Average January days of sunshine (more is better)

3. Temperate summer, measured as the difference between average temperatures in January and July (a smaller gap is better)

4. Average July humidity (lower is better, for fairly obvious reasons)

5. Topographic variation—hills, valleys, and mountains (more are better)

6. Finally, water area—coastlines and lakes (more are better)

"Natural aspects of attractiveness," as the USDA puts it. They're physical characteristics, products of the landscape and the planetary environment. They're immutable, unchangeable, invulnerable to the machinations of mankind. "Natural amenities pertain to the physical rather than the social or economic environment," the USDA writes. "We can measure the basic ingredients, not how these ingredients have been shaped by nature and man."

The USDA's researchers took all of these measures from existing federal datasets, mashed them together in a statistical blender, and voilà—the natural amenities index was born.

Here's the great thing: there are 3,108 counties in the contiguous United States, according to the Census Bureau. In creating the natural amenities index, the USDA statisticians went ahead and ranked every single one of them according to where they fell on the scale (sadly, Alaska and Hawaii didn't make the cut, in part due to a lack of comparable climatological data for those states).

It was an official federal ranking, in other words, of the lower forty-eight's most beautiful and ugliest places to live.

I pitched the idea of a map based on the index—"a government ranking of the best and worst counties to live in," as I characterized it—to my editors. They gave the thumbs-up, and the rest is the history you're about to read.

The coasts, as it turns out, look pretty good on the natural amenities index, as does much of the mountain west. Ventura County, California, came in at number one on the list—not surprising given the shore, the hills, and the temperate climate. In fact, every single one of the ten highest-ranked counties is located in California.

The county that came in dead last on the list, meanwhile, was a little place I'd never heard of called Red Lake County, Minnesota, which appeared to be far up in the northwest corner of the state.

I had never set foot in Minnesota in my life. So I googled, naturally, which led me to a generic-looking midwestern county government website containing, among other things, a "community calendar" for August that was completely blank.

"Fun fact," the website proudly proclaimed, "it is the only landlocked county in the United States that is surrounded by just two neighboring counties."

Fun!

According to Google, Red Lake County was so far north that in order to get to Fargo from there you'd have to drive two hours south. It was tucked so far away in the middle of nowhere that it was twenty miles from the nearest McDonald's, forty miles from the closest Starbucks, and three hundred miles away from the nearest Whole Foods.

Wikipedia wasn't much help, either. It noted that the county seat was the town of Red Lake Falls, population 1,427. "The last significant historic event in Red Lake Falls occurred on August 27, 1927," Wikipedia's editors noted, "when the famous aviator Charles Lindbergh and his wife landed at the nearby airport during a barnstorming trip through the Upper Midwest and were taken on automobile rides to Huot and Crookston."

Lindbergh, the only famous person to visit the town in the past century, evidently left just as soon as he arrived.

I wanted to add some local color to the story but there simply wasn't much to work with, at least not from my vantage point of a D.C. newsroom. It looked to me like one of those sleepy flyover places that dot the middle of the country, just barely holding on as migration and urbanization slowly whittle its population down to zero.

So I wrote this:

> The absolute worst place to live in America is (drumroll please) . . . Red Lake County, Minn. (claim to fame: "It is the only landlocked county in the United States that is surrounded by just two neighboring counties," according to the county Web site).

And that was it! My first encounter with Red Lake County amounted to just forty-two mildly snarky words, tossed off on a slow Friday afternoon.

The story went up at 9:27 a.m. on Monday morning. By 9:32, the hate mail started rolling in.

It started, as so many unpleasant things do, on Twitter: "As someone who grew up in the heart of 'ugly country' on this map, I hereby declare this map garbage," a Minnesotan named Matt Privratsky wrote.

By midmorning, people who lived in and around Red Lake County started sending me photographs of golden wheat fields, meandering rivers, and deep blue prairie skies. "This is what the 'worst place in America to live in' looks like in late summer," one of them said.

The photographs eventually morphed into a hashtag campaign, #ShowMeYourUglyCounties, inviting Minnesotans to showcase the state's natural beauty and refute claims of a lack of amenities. Many of the responses contained a variant of the word "uffda," an all purpose Minnesota-ism roughly synonymous with "good grief!"

To be honest, I felt pretty good watching this all unfold from my desk in D.C. People were clicking, reading, and sharing the article, which is just about all most of us in the media asked of our audiences in that era.

One striking thing, however, is that the volume of feedback wasn't accompanied by much vitriol. I write about all sorts of controversial topics, like guns and politics, where even mundane observations can incite frothing rage. There was none of it, though, in the response to the natural amenities story. To the extent that I knew anything about Minnesotans it was that they had a tendency toward humility and politeness, an impression I had gleaned solely from hearing Garrison Keillor on NPR growing up. The weird thing was that, in my first interaction with Minnesotans as a class, they were valiantly living up to their stereotypes.

The other thing: they didn't let up. The social media campaign escalated throughout the day, to the extent that regional news outlets decided to get in on the action.

"Red Lake County was minding its own business," Minneapolis alternative newspaper *City Pages* wrote. "Then out of the blue prairie skies some East Coast media type with a hogwash government index calls the swath of northwest Minnesota 'the absolute worst place to live in America.'"

That reporter called up county commissioner Charles Simpson to ask what he thought of the fracas. "What they've got to say, it's bullshit," he said.

The *Star Tribune* subsequently asked Simpson what he thought of me, personally, for their own story. "He can kiss my butt," Simpson said.

By this time the story had received wide enough traction that then-senator Al Franken weighed in. "You're totally right @washingtonpost—Red Lake County has no natural beauty," he wrote in a sarcastic Twitter post accompanied by a bucolic photo of the county's Old Crossing Treaty Park. Tagging my employer's account in that tweet was a nice touch, ensuring that our social media team were aware of the abuse Minnesotans were facing in my careless hands.

I want to pause for a minute here to point out something interesting. If you go back to the original map, you'll see that it's not just northwest Minnesota—there are a lot of places in the United States that don't look good on the USDA's index. The North Dakota side of the Red River Valley fared just as poorly, as did a wide swath of the rust belt region running down through Iowa, Illinois, and up through Ohio.

I didn't hear a single word of complaint from any of these states, though. Not even one. No indignant Iowans. No outraged North Dakotans. I did, however, receive an email from a resident of Nebraska. He had noticed that his region of the state didn't look good on the map, and had considered lodging a complaint. But the more he thought about it, he told me, the more he felt he agreed with the ranking. "I guess Omaha really is kind of a dump," he said.

I must have written dozens of similar pieces to this in

the course of a career—find a dataset, map it out, call out the highs and lows, and call it a day. But I had never received a torrent of feedback from a low-ranking locality like I did from Minnesotans that August.

In fact, there's a phrase among statisticians: "Thank God for Mississippi." The idea is that in just about any state-level ranking of a given quantity—whether it be economic, demographic, cultural, social, or anything else—Mississippi usually ends up at the very bottom of the list. If you're from, say, Alabama, that's something to be thankful for.

I've done an awful lot of stories where Mississippi ends up at the bottom of some ranking or another. And again, I don't believe I've ever heard a single word of complaint from a Mississippi resident. Minnesotans were a different breed entirely.

In a lighthearted attempt at amends-making, I rounded up a bunch of the best responses to the original article and published them in a follow-up piece several days later titled "Thick Coats, Thin Skins: Why Minnesotans Were Outraged by a Recent *Washington Post* Report."

For the piece I asked one of the original instigators, Matt Privratsky, what his deal was. "Minnesotans are known for being very humble and even reserved," he said, "but as this reaction shows we're also very proud of our state—especially when in competition with those around us."

If Red Lake County wasn't the ugliest place in the nation, what was? "I wouldn't be doing my job as a born and bred Minnesotan if I didn't tell people to avoid Wisconsin," Privratsky wrote.

Later in the week I got an email with the subject line "An invitation to come visit Red Lake County." It was from a guy named Jason Brumwell. His family, he wrote, owned a river tubing business based in the town of Red Lake Falls. "I would like to cordially and officially invite you to come and check out our little county which has now been dubbed, 'The Worst County in the United States,'" he said. Citing the online criticism that had been going on, he said that "I would also like to reassure you that you would be given plenty of good natured 'ribbing' but would be greeted with open arms and a lot of people showing you why they feel our county is far from the worst."

Hmmm.

The first thing I did after reading the email several times over in search of obvious signs of mental instability was to google Brumwell and his business, Voyageur's View. Everything seemed to be on the up-and-up. The Francophile spelling was an interesting touch—a nod, as it turned out, to the French explorers who played a major role in settling the region in the 1600s and 1700s.

I have to admit that at this point I was plenty curious to see what the place was actually like—to get the view from the ground, rather than from a spreadsheet. I had never been to Minnesota; in fact I'd never really even spent any time in the Midwest.

When Briana got home that evening I told her about the email and asked her what she thought. I should point out that even under the best circumstances my job was a source of anxiety for her, given the torrents of vitriol I'd often stir up in the comments section of my stories and on social media.

"So, a guy out there wants me to come and visit," I told her.

Her eyes grew wide. "Oh my God, they're going to kill you aren't they," she said.

"Come on, no," I said. "You saw how polite everyone was. This guy seems really nice; there's like seven exclamation points in his email."

"So they're gonna what, tar and feather you instead? It's a trap. Don't do it."

It took some convincing but I finally got Briana on board with the idea. My editors were easier to convince. In fact, they were suspiciously enthusiastic about the idea. "D.C. Reporter Gets Tarred, Feathered by Indignant Minnesotans" would be a nice story to end the summer with.

At any rate, a few days later I was on a plane headed to the North Star State. It was time to experience Red Lake County firsthand.

Getting there, it turned out, was a bit of a challenge. Red Lake Falls is so far out of the way that the closest "major" airport (with just two gates) is in Grand Forks, North Dakota—an hour away and across the state line. As I flew in for my visit, the view out the airplane window was a rigid grid, straight roads stretching out to the horizon interrupted only by other straight roads running perpendicularly. Everything was flat, square. It certainly looked like it could be America's worst place to live.

I did some reading before I left to find out what kind of place I'd be parachuting into. By most economic metrics, the county seemed to be doing okay. The unemployment rate that July was 4.6 percent, well below the national average. The median household income was $48,000—less than half the typical income in the Washington suburbs.

The median home value, on the other hand, was just $89,000, or one-fifth the typical home price where I was living. That works out to a home price to income ratio of about two-to-one—a hell of a lot more favorable than D.C.'s eight-to-one ratio.

The county was home to just a hair over four thousand people, 95 percent of whom were white. The median age of 42.1 was about five years greater than the U.S. average. Overall the county's population density was ten people per square mile—approximately 99 percent less dense than Baltimore County, Maryland.

The big business in the county was farming—more than three hundred farms, according to the U.S. Census of Agriculture. In terms of landscape it was 80 percent farmland, 10 percent forest, and 7 percent grassland. Just 1.6 percent of the land area was devoted to towns and residences. It was home to approximately twice as many cows as people.

A picture was starting to emerge in my head of a place older, whiter, sparser and struggling—I imagined it not wholly unlike the hardscrabble farming communities that surrounded the town of Oneonta, New York, where I had grown up. People in the "big city" of Oneonta (pop. 13,000) looked down on these other communities, and I had been no different. We thought of them as hicks.

Secretly, though, I had always been fascinated by these places. In high school I dated a number of girls— Briana was one of them—from these strange, small towns. I was struck above all by a sense of familiarity among the people who lived there. The kids, for instance, seemed to move around these towns as if the entire place belonged to them. They would enter stores and have long conversations with the people behind the counter, or hang out at the schools long after the closing bells, striding confidently along the halls like they had the keys to the place.

It wasn't like that in Oneonta. Boundaries between places you were and weren't supposed to be were strictly policed. People were more anonymous and you didn't know everyone. The town was full of strangers, which is a key difference between a place with 13,000 people and one with 1,300. Social science literature talks a lot about third places, like coffee shops and libraries, that serve as community focal points. Places not home, and not work or school, where people can gather and feel like they belong. In the small communities outside Oneonta it seemed to me that the entire towns were third places for many of the people who lived there. In Oneonta, by contrast, it felt like there weren't any. More often than not, kids who were bored after school would end up at the local Wal-Mart with a group of friends, seeing what kind of trouble they could get into.

Jason Brumwell was extremely enthusiastic about the visit. Ahead of my arrival he sent me an email detailing the plans he was making—lining up people to talk about why they stay; even in "mid winter when it's 40 below zero we have six hours of sunlight . . . there are so many people who want to show you so many things that I'll try and narrow it down so you can take in the best of the best and we'll cover more when you inevitably want to come back again!" I was skeptical, to say the least.

He closed his missive by offering to put me up at his house and warning me to prepare for "a huge helping of Minnesota nice!" The email contained nineteen sentences, twelve of which ended in an exclamation point.

Jason told me to meet him at the county courthouse in Red Lake Falls once I arrived. "Some of the community actually wanted to greet you," he explained. I rented a car from the rental desk at the airport, which was near a large, possibly military-grade lawn mower on display from a local retailer. A scale model of a drone hung from the ceiling, an evident nod to the University of North Dakota's aviation program.

I drove through the city of Grand Forks, crossed the Red River marking the border between North Dakota and Minnesota, and hit the upper midwestern prairie roads for the first time. At Jason's suggestion I took the "back way," a county highway traversing the forty miles of nothing between East Grand Forks and Red Lake Falls.

What struck me first wasn't the flatness or the emptiness or the complete lack of people or cars anywhere within my field of view—it was the sky. Unencumbered by hills and valleys, the sky seemed impossibly vast to my east coast eyes that afternoon, a clear blue dome dotted by plump, poofy clouds straight out of a children's book. The horizon was truly infinite, the sense of scale and space and openness almost humbling.

Agricultural fields vectored off in every direction. The road I was on shot eastward indefinitely, crossed every mile by dirt roads running north and south, bearing well-ordered names: 170th Street, 160th Street, and so on. It was vast but tidy.

At one point I pulled my car over to the side of the road to take pictures and ended up standing there for a few minutes, luxuriating in the silence. The only sounds were the occasional bird chirp rising above the rustle of the wind through cornstalks.

As I approached Red Lake Falls some unexpected variation presented itself—after twenty-two miles of straight-arrow eastward driving, the first turn. As I got even closer to town the road veered south, and then dipped down a small valley toward what a sign proclaimed to be the Red Lake River, the county's namesake.

Crossing the river I saw the sign for Jason Brumwell's business, Voyageur's View Camping and Tubing, overlooking a wide swath of mowed grass leading to a collection of red-roofed wood buildings.

Passing the campground the road broadened as I entered the town of Red Lake Falls proper, demarcated by a large wooden sign that proclaimed "Welcome to Red Lake Falls" over a background that suggested mountains and lakes, rather incongruously given the flat agricultural landscape. A large, handcarved wooden loon was propped up against one of the sign legs.

I drove past tidy homes with trim, tightly cropped lawns, the domestic counterpart to the orderly fields outside town. There was what appeared to be a bar, T&J's, on one side of the road, standing next to an evidently vacant building that resembled nothing so much as an old bank.

Turning onto the town's main drag, the first order of business was crossing a large sloped bridge over another river, the Clearwater. Looking down the riverway I saw a series of large chalky cliffs rising fifty feet or so above the water. They offered just the slightest hint of the stark, arid landscape of the Dakotas, a reminder that the region stands at the border between the forests of the east and the more dramatic landscapes of the west.

I found the courthouse—not difficult, given that it was the largest building in town—parked the car, and didn't even manage to get the door all the way open before I was surprised by a microphone in my face. It was a member of the local media, asking me what I was doing and how I liked the place so far and what my plans were for the next few days. I did my best to answer his questions before an older gentleman pulled me aside. I noticed he was wearing a Voyageur's View shirt.

"Are you Jason?" I asked.

"No, I'm his dad, Dick," he said. "Jason's over there," he added, gesturing toward the courthouse. At this point I was able to take in the scene for the first time.

There weren't just a "handful" of people waiting to meet me, as Jason had suggested—there were dozens. There were camera crews, four or five of them. I heard music—there was a color guard from the local high school in full uniform, arrayed along the courthouse steps and striking up a patriotic tune.

Dick led me over to a guy about my age with a thick layer of facial scruff and a Minnesota Twins hat, sipping from an energy drink. This must be Jason. I noticed then that the air was thick with yellowjackets, and that a number of them kept trying to crawl into the drink can. He was swatting them away absentmindedly.

We greeted each other, then Jason took a swig from his can and made an odd face. "Oh, I think I just swallowed one," he said nonchalantly. There was a certain odd forwardness to the "oh" that made him sound like an extra from *Fargo*, the Coen Brothers movie.

We stood there in awkward silence for a few minutes to watch the band play its number. I was quite literally dumbstruck, slowly grappling with the full realization that at this point I was less reporting a story than becoming one myself. I quietly fretted over whether I'd get in trouble with my editors for creating a stir.

Jason led me inside the courthouse. Given the amount of media interest, the locals thought it best I sit down with the reporters for an impromptu press conference before getting on with the day's business.

I knew they'd probably be expecting a snooty east coaster, so I tried to answer their questions with some humility and gee-whizzedness to play against type. I told them about the nice emails I had received from Minnesota people, the response from politicians, and my wife's misgivings. I tried to frame the whole thing as a useful refresher on the limitations of viewing the world through a spreadsheet—limitations that would be obvious to a normal person, but easy for someone in my position to lose track of.

After that I chatted with the town's mayor, Kevin Harmoning, and city administrator Kathleen Schmitz. I asked them about the biggest challenges facing the town, hoping for something juicy—crime? Meth? Crippling poverty?

No, it was "just making ends meet," Harmoning said, referring to keeping the town running, the bills paid, and the lights on. During the recession, they had actually been forced to turn some of the streetlights off to keep everything else running, Schmitz said. But all in all, the downturn's effects hadn't been as harsh here as elsewhere. Many of the farms outside of town that form the economic backbone of the county weren't affected much at all. "People still needed to eat," Schmitz said.

It reminded me of what a social studies teacher had told me way back in high school, back in upstate New York. The class had been talking about economics, of booms and recessions, and how neither one of those things ever seemed to affect the small towns the way they did the cities. "We don't get the highs and we don't get the lows," he had said. "But we always do pretty much okay." I had thought at the time that there was some comfort in that. After eight years of living in the D.C. area, hearing similar thoughts delivered in a county courthouse 1,400 miles away gave me a pang of homesickness.

From the courthouse, Brumwell and his dad loaded me and a gaggle of reporters and local luminaries onto roofless red tour bus—one of the fleet they used to ferry tubers to the river launch—and took us to a dairy farm outside of town owned by brothers Carl and Joe Schindler. They milk about 120 cows 12 at a time the old-fashioned way, with a simple pump system installed in their dairy barn.

Unbeknownst to my hosts, I had had some experience with dairy farms growing up. My dad, the large animal veterinarian, saw a lot of dairy cows. For several summers in my childhood in upstate New York I would ride around on farm calls with him in lieu of day care or any other more structured and costly activity. I had come to know and love the sensory overload of a working dairy farm—the hot, earthy pungency of the manure, the lowing of the cows, the odd combination of astringency and liquid warmth in the dairy parlor.

It had been ages since I had pet a cow, though, and I couldn't wait to do it again. I bounded off the bus as soon as we stopped and made my way over to the calf pens. A newborn calf suckled my thumb as the brothers told me about life on the farm. The earthy smells of a dairy

operation—manure and hay and sawdust and dirt—
hung thick in the air.

Carl asked if I wanted to check out the inside of the
barn and yes, of course I did. We walked around back
and into it, chatting a bit more as the huge industrial
fans did their best to move the hot midwestern August
air around. A member of one of the camera crews tried
to follow us in for some footage but ended up retching
near the entry of the barn, overcome by the smell.

"I'm really impressed you're in here, actually," Carl
said. I told him about my dairy experiences growing up.
"Smells great to me," I said. "Smells like home."

Carl's story was similar to what I'd heard at city
hall. Yes, life was challenging. A lot of the dairy farms
had closed up shop years ago, victims of the relentless
trend toward bigger and more high-tech operations
that was happening all over the agricultural industry.
Red Lake County wasn't immune to any of this. In the
1950s, for instance, there were close to one thousand
active farms in the county, according to USDA data.
But by 2012 the number had fallen by more than half,
and their average acreage had roughly doubled. Fewer
farms means fewer families: the population of the
county fell from 6,805 people in 1950 to just a hair over
4,000 people in 2012.

But Carl and his brother were still here, and despite
their small size they were doing okay. Five years, ten
years down the line? Who could tell. But for now the
numbers added up.

I found myself thinking of Jack and Charles as we

toured the property, petting calves and feeding hay to the lumbering heifers. Wouldn't it be great for them to grow up in a place where they could have this kind of experience? There was a petting zoo fairly close to home in Maryland that we had visited several times. The disinterested animals did their best to avoid the crowds of kids always running around the place; they'd seek out the shady corners of their enclosures to escape the sweltering Maryland summer sun. My own kids would quickly tire of competing with others for the attention of a stray goat and would be clamoring for snacks and other diversions within fifteen minutes of arrival.

After the farm, the next activity was a chance to reckon with the reality of the Red Lake County landscape via a kayak ride down the Red Lake River. I was prepared to be underwhelmed. On the bus ride over to the kayak launch, I learned that there were no lakes in Red Lake County—the name derived from the Red Lake River, which in turn was named after its source, the Red Lake, a massive body of fresh water about fifty miles east of the county.

"What about the falls?" I asked.

"What falls?" Jason said.

"Red Lake Falls?"

"Oh, there aren't any falls in Red Lake Falls."

"So there's neither a lake, nor falls, in the town of Red Lake Falls?"

"Nope," he said.

Still, you can't complain about an afternoon kayak

trip on work time. We got to the launch and Jason shoved me off onto the river in the company of four locals.

Our boats glided silently under an old railroad trestle. The tracks above had been converted to a paved trail some years back, my companions told me. As we rounded the river bend we came to the brick shell of a power station that used to sit on the river. Someone mentioned it would be a perfect place to convert to a riverside dining establishment, and it was hard to disagree.

The river wasn't particularly large, maybe just ten kayak widths across. In the Northeast any river of this size tends to be shallow and rocky, but this one was tranquil, carving deep meanders through the landscape as it went. Dusty cliffs rose up on one side and then the other, pocked with holes where swallows nested. It felt like a western river but on miniature scale.

At one point one of my companions, a woman named Melissa Benoit, surreptitiously pulled out her phone and played the dueling-banjos theme from *Deliverance*. Melissa was a Red Lake Falls gal roughly my age; she'd moved around the country a bit after high school and ended up settling down back here, where friends and family were. She knew I'd probably been expecting a bunch of toothless rednecks and figured she'd have some fun at my expense. And indeed, to my surprise there was nothing about the place that suggested redneckery. The homes visible from the riverside were well kept, tidy. The rural areas of upstate New York where I grew up had a different feel to them—houses were often ramshackle, lawns over-grown with chunks of old cars or faded playground equipment strewn about. There was none of that here. The word that kept popping into my head was "tidy." The area conveyed a sense of quiet, working-class normalcy.

Two of our other companions were a ten-year-old boy named Jayce, a student at the local elementary school, and his grandfather. Like many kids in the area Jayce was wild about hockey. Because the region was so sparsely populated, teams, even elementary school ones, would sometimes travel two, three, even four hours for the sake of a hockey match.

Jayce also gave me a sense of how the locals viewed themselves vis-à-vis Minneapolis, the state's largest city, some five hours to the south. Jayce said he'd been there with his family and didn't care much for it.

"Why?" I asked.

"There's cars everywhere," he said. "And the people are crazy-looking!"

I found that people up here spoke of Minneapolis the same way upstate New Yorkers talk about New York City—a far-off urban hellscape populated by millions of strange people who manage to draw a disproportionate share of attention and state resources. This was odd for me, since as a lifelong east coaster I'd always imagined Minneapolis as a sort of charming little hobbit village, full of farmer's markets and artisanal craft stores.

Our tour ended at a place known to locals as the Point, where the Red Lake meets the Clearwater at a park in town. I hitched a ride back to my rental car with Jason, and then stopped by my motel room to check in and get a shower before dinner, which was evidently to be open to the public, at T&J's.

My lodgings were at the Chateau Motel & Liquor Store, which is exactly what it sounds like: a regular roadside motel with a liquor store attached to it. Everything a weary traveler needs. As I fired off a few texts to Briana, letting her know I was safe and untarred, I noticed I had literally dozens of Facebook notifications. I opened the app to find that they were nearly all friend requests from Minnesotans I had met earlier in the day. Minnesota Nice, indeed.

The folks at T&J's were outgoing and eager to talk about what made their community so special. Al Buse, for instance, was Red Lake Falls' oldest resident at 101— "like everyone's grandpa," Jason told me. He was the grandson of one of the town's original founders. He still lived alone, in a house on Main Street that was a veritable history museum—photographs and memorabilia of the town's history, and, naturally, an arsenal of firearms stored in the basement.

Al, it seemed, was the living, breathing avatar of the sense of civic pride and duty that made the town of Red Lake Falls tick. In the summers when the weather was nice, every morning he would load his tools in the back of his bright yellow golf cart and make his way through town, fixing things that need fixing, watering plants, generally doing whatever he could to keep the town, well, tidy.

For dessert, the restaurant served a cake built as a map of the county by baking prodigy Matt Weiss, a local high school student. I helped myself to the Red Lake Falls portion of the cake.

"See all these other little towns?" Jason said, pointing to places on the cake labeled Brooks, Oklee, and Plummer. "That's where we're going tomorrow."

Jason had procured a tour bus from his friend Jesse, the guy who owned T&J's. They had decked it out for the occasion, with a sign reading "America's Worst Tour" splayed above the windshield. He had also invited a number of luminaries from the county's four major towns to accompany us.

We visited a wheat farm in Brooks (pop. 139), where fourth-generation farmer Alex Yaggie, twenty-seven, showed me the cockpit of one of his forty foot combines and let me drive it around an empty lot as much as I dared. We stopped at an asparagus farm outside Red Lake Falls, the first of its kind in the region, and sampled from a fiercely flavorful jar of pickled asparagus.

We stopped for lunch—fried cheese curds and a "Minnesota burger"—at T.J.'s Tavern in the town of Oklee (pop. 418). U.S. representative Collin Peterson, a Minnesota Democrat, swung by and sang an ode to ugliness on the bar's main stage. Ugly women in particular, something he probably wouldn't have done in our current post-#MeToo era.

We stopped at the Plummer Area Sportsmen's Club, where county commissioner Chuck Simpson—the gruff fellow who'd given such spicy quotes to Minneapolis media about my original story—showed me around the shooting range.

By the end of the day I was worn out from all the glad-handing. It was a good kind of worn out, though. Over and over, the folks I spoke with told me it was that sense of community that kept them here and contributed to that enormous outpouring of civic pride in response to my original article. "There's lots of freedom here," Jason Brumwell told me later that night, at a barbecue at his dad's house. "But everybody's still watching out for each other."

CHAPTER 2

The next day, following my whirlwind tour of Red Lake County, I packed my bags and flew back to Baltimore, to Briana, the twins, and the job. I had plenty to think about on the flight back home.

The trip had been a jarring break in the well-worn routine I'd established for myself in D.C. and Baltimore. It cast the shortcomings of our family's situation in a jarring light. When I told people in Red Lake Falls about the length of my commute, for instance, their jaws dropped. I realized I had built up a protective layer of apathy around myself that allowed me to ignore the steep cost of the big commute, the small house, the disconnect among the crowds, all of it. After all, it was simply something that everyone did, on some level or another, out in D.C.

And yet, Red Lake County—and other places like it— were filled with people whose lives were radically different. They had space. Yards. Breathing room. Small communities where people knew and looked after one another. The very existence of Red Lake County and the people who lived there was a direct challenge to the way of life we had slid into in the city. It undermined the inevitability of modern urban life.

Like many people on the coasts, I had a foggy notion

that places like Red Lake County were out there. We all knew about the rural-urban divide in the United States. But I had previously thought of rural places as fundamentally other, strange lands where unfamiliar people held tight to ancient customs and beliefs. Even though I grew up in upstate New York, after a decade in D.C. a rural midwestern farming community seemed about as remote and foreign to me as an Amish enclave, or an Amazonian tribe that hadn't yet made contact with modern society.

But the most earth-shattering revelation of my trip had been this: the people in Red Lake County were just like the rest of us. They watched the same TV shows, followed the same news, consumed the same popular culture, and cracked the same dumb jokes. I went out there expecting to find a tribe of people who were radically different but instead I was shocked to find out they were just like me. How, then, had I ended up wasting my life in a cramped town house, riding a cramped train, while they got to enjoy the clean prairie air and the wide-open spaces of northwest Minnesota? Why couldn't I be more like them? Where had I gone wrong?

Back at the grind in D.C., my days in Red Lake County took on a positively Norman Rockwellian cast. While there I had relentlessly poked and prodded the people I talked to, puzzled by the optimism, the pride, the sense of belongingness. "Yes, but what about all the bad stuff?" I asked. What about the drugs? The crippling poverty? The squalor and misery of a benighted life in the countryside?

Yet no matter how hard I pushed, I couldn't find any sign of rot beneath the region's bucolic exterior. The people had their trials and headaches, of course. Downtown Red Lake Falls wasn't what it had once been. Affordable health care was a challenge. The sheriff's office had the occasional speeder or shoplifter to deal with.

But while the rural communities I had known as a child seemed to be almost devoured by their challenges, the people in Red Lake Falls were rising up to meet theirs. There the pressures of modern life seemed manageable, in a way that they must have seemed across the entire nation in say, the 1950s and 1960s. I wanted that manageability in my own life. I wanted to take my family to a place where it didn't feel like the trend lines of time and money were always converging, squeezing us into an ever-narrowing sphere of existence. I wanted to turn the trends around, set them outward and away from each other, opening up wide spaces of possibility with room to breathe. I wanted what the people in Red Lake County seemed to have.

I wrote my follow-up story on my visit, closing it with these lines: "When people and places halfway across the country are just a mouse-click away on your computer, it's easy to assume that we live in a nation made small and manageable by technology. But traveling to a place like Red Lake County, hours away from any major metro area, is a reminder that in much of the country, the rhythms of daily life are, still, markedly different than the coastal city grind of long commutes and high-octane jobs.

"For some of us, it takes a place as small as Red Lake County to drive home just how big this country really is."

As I got back into the D.C. grind I found myself unable to shake the memories of the trip. Jammed into a hot, overcrowded Red Line train, I thought of the guy I'd talked to in Plummer who complained about how sometimes getting stuck behind a tractor would add five minutes to his fifteen-minute commute.

Wading through diesel fumes on the streets of D.C., crowded in by the city's squat, blocky buildings, I would have given just about anything for five more minutes on a dirt road out on the prairie, hemmed in by nothing but a warm breeze.

I dreamed about the people I had met, nothing crazy, just about running into them and chatting them up at the store.

My wife noticed a change in my demeanor when I returned. I am not exactly what you'd call a people person. I'm a natural introvert; given the choice between socializing with others or doing something by myself, I'll nearly always choose the latter. There's a reason why I spend most of my reporting time interrogating datasets, rather than people.

The running joke in the Ingraham household is that Briana is a normal, functioning social adult while I am "dead inside." Yet when I came back from Minnesota, Briana noticed that I wouldn't stop talking about how great the people were. Their warmth, their friendliness, their fiercely held determination to make their communities better. Even for an introvert it was striking to see.

I contrasted that with what I had known from the neighborhoods I had lived in. In our early twenties Briana and I spent a particularly miserable year in grad school in Southern California, living in a corporate-managed apartment complex that catered mostly to low-income families. The apartments were crammed in on top of each other and it was impossible to escape the sight, sound, or smell of your neighbors at any hour of the day or night. But nobody talked to one another—everyone kept their heads down, desperate to avoid having to humanize the people you knew only as, say, the source of the music that blared every weeknight at 11 p.m., or the arguments you could hear through your paper-thin walls.

We had lived in Vermont for a couple years shortly thereafter—our initial goal in relocating there was simply to put as much space between us and Southern California as we could manage. But New Englanders, as we discovered, are not known for their openness to outsiders. We were able to find nonsqualid rental accommodations and managed to make a couple of close friends there. But the communities we lived in, outside of Burlington, made zero effort to help residents get to know each other, or to develop a sense of community identity beyond the occasional appeal to NIMBYism whenever someone wanted to install a new windmill or power line.

After Briana got recruited to work for the Social Security Administration, we moved to the Baltimore area and came to like it much more than we thought we would. We settled in the historic district of Ellicott City, a charming collection of shops and restaurants tucked away into brick and stone-crafted buildings. The historic district had something of an identity of its own, but its location in the middle of one of the east coast's largest metropolitan areas tended to dilute that. It was also marred by a busy connecting road that cut right through the middle of the district, essentially shoving the town's civic life to the margins of the roadway.

We made a number of friends when we moved to Oella, many of whom were struggling with the same issues we were—how to raise children in a cramped, pedestrian-hostile space? How to pay bills without burning most of your nonworking hours on interminable trips to D.C.?

That fall Briana and I were coming to the realization that we had to do something about our current situation. It was killing us, in both a metaphoric and also a very literal sense. The problem was that no matter how hard we tried, no matter how far outside the box we started to think, we couldn't make the numbers add up.

We looked into selling our home and renting a place closer to D.C. The problem was there was no way to increase our square footage without drastically raising our monthly housing costs, and even then we'd be stuck on the fringes of some dodgy area like Laurel or Odenton, almost certainly living in cramped, factory-style

quarters like we'd done in California. The only difference now would be even higher rent, and we'd have kids
to manage to boot.

We looked at going in the other direction—what if
we moved waaay out to the fringes, to the very farthest
reaches of where the MARC train traveled? Make peace
with the long commute, embrace it even. Live in say,
Harpers Ferry, West Virginia, and cajole the bosses to
let me work from home two days a week. The problem
was that unless we got way out into the boonies—like six-
hour-a-day commute instead of three—the home prices
were still insane. Even in the easternmost reaches of
West Virginia, a $300,000 single-family home is a rarity.

The truth is that that phrase—single-family home
meant little to me before the kids came along. I had
absorbed and understood all the urban-lefty critiques
of single-family home ownership that are so prevalent
on the coast: high-density living, in condos and apartments and town homes, is better for the environment.
It fosters interpersonal communication, and creates
urban spaces better suited for humans than for cars.

But I had come to suspect that much of the urbanist
critique of single-family home ownership was really
a critique of *suburban* single-family homeownership.
My time in Southern California had certainly illus-
trated the limits of the "planned community." Despite
the "master plan" governing Irvine and much of Orange County, the area was still a riotously unpleasant
place to live. The landscape was shredded into pieces by
heavily trafficked roadways, a necessity due to zoning

regulations mandating that the places where people worked, gathered, played, and shopped be rigidly separated from the places where they lived.

The suburbs' pitch, in theory, is that they offer the best of both possible worlds: reasonable proximity to urban centers with all their options for work and play, with a little bit of space to stretch out in and call your own. In reality, I began to suspect, many suburbs were just offering the worst: high-density, high-traffic neighborhoods rivaling the most congested urban areas, wedded to rural notions of car ownership and resource consumption.

After the kids arrived I wanted that single-family home. I wanted the yard, the space, the lack of neighbors sharing walls. But I didn't want the suburban version. I didn't want Southern California, or Columbia, Maryland. I didn't want a city, or a suburb. I wanted a town. A village. Hell, a house in the country miles away from anything, I didn't care. Whatever its faults, the town I grew up in, Oneonta, New York, was like this. We lived in a medium-sized house on a main road at the west end of town. There was an auto body shop on one side of us and a Dunkin' Donuts on another. Just down the block and off the main road lay the quiet residential neighborhood where most of my friends lived growing up. We had free rein of the place pretty much as soon as we were old enough to pedal a bike. We played hide-and-seek in the cemetery, built forts in the adjacent woods, biked to the nearby Ames to buy candy, and terrorized the servers at our local Ponderosa. It was a childhood that was completely unremarkable, except for the fact that anything like it now appeared to be unobtainable anywhere within one hundred miles of a typical city.

I wanted that kind of childhood for my own kids, which is another way of saying that I wanted them to have that kind of childhood for myself. I wanted to live in a place where the economic, physical, legal, and cultural conditions all came together to make it possible: affordable homes. Reasonable commutes. Neighborhood spaces where you could walk, play, explore, get lost, maybe even get into a bit of trouble. Adults not accustomed to calling the cops every time they saw a kid unattended. Enough people to look out for one another, but not so many that crime was an issue.

As I was working through these issues, Briana was getting burnt out at work. She spent day after day in meetings and on conference calls, talking around in circles with career bureaucrats who seemed to be checking off time until they collected their pension. She wanted to make things better, but the federal bureaucracy didn't make it easy.

She'd get home exhausted at the end of the day and hear about all the wonderful things Jack and Charles had done with Heather, the nanny. Jack took his first steps. Charles said his first words. They went to the park, to the aquarium, to McDonald's. Milestone after milestone passed by, hours and days of priceless early childhood bonding outsourced to a third party while we labored to keep a roof over our heads, memories left unmade while Briana sat in conference rooms and drafted emails.

Early childhood is another realm where Americans have grown accustomed to going against their own best wishes in the name of paying the bills. In 2016 the Pew Research Center reported that about 60 percent of Americans said children were typically better off with a parent at home. This belief cut across political as well as gender divides, with majorities of nearly every demographic group holding it. Yet in close to half of two-parent households, both parents work full-time.

The actual research into the question of whether kids are better or worse off when both parents work is mostly a wash. To the extent that any effects are observed, they appear to stem from far more fundamental questions: if life at home is safe and stable and generally free from economic woes, the kids are probably going to be all right.

But the research has less to say on the nonquantifiable aspects of early child-rearing: how do you assign a value to the hugs missed, the boo-boos unkissed, the songs unsung, and the experiences unshared? Most of us don't become parents in order to celebrate the outcomes tracked by economists and developmental psychologists: the endgame of parenthood isn't a 90th percentile PSAT score or an above-average place in the national earnings distribution.

Rather we do it for more primal, fundamental reasons: biological necessity. The thrill of creating a new life. The human experience in all its agony and glory. Perhaps above all, love.

Yet those are the very things we deprive ourselves of when we outsource child-rearing to a third party.

Briana and I were both feeling that loss acutely. What if, instead of moving, one of us quit work to be home with the kids? What if we reclaimed that full experience of parenthood? To actually be there to watch our sons grow up?

Yet again, the math didn't add up. Our salaries were similar at the time, which meant that regardless of who left work, our income would be halved. Yes, the childcare expenses would disappear, too, but it wouldn't make up for the forgone income. Between the mortgage, student loans, and various credit card debts incurred in the first expensive years of the boys' lives, one income in the D.C. area was simply out of the question.

We were back at square one.

It was October, and by this point the answer was practically staring us in the face, although we didn't realize it yet. And we wouldn't, until one long weekend when my mom and stepdad flew in from Tampa to visit their grandsons.

The boys were in bed and the four adults were unwinding in our tiny living room, glasses of wine in hand. Seating-wise that room accommodated little beyond a two-person love seat—my mom was sitting on a footstool, and I was squatting on the floor.

Briana and I were talking through all these issues—the boys, the house, the jobs, the commutes, and how we couldn't find a way out of any of it. In the end, my mom was the first one to come right out and say it: "Well, what if you moved to that nice little Minnesota town Chris visited over the summer?"

We all laughed.

"No, really," she said.

The room went quiet.

For me, in that moment, suddenly all the pieces fell in place. One of us would work from home. The other would take a break to be with the kids, which we could afford given the low cost of living. We could get a bigger, cheaper home. There would be no more commute.

"I don't know," I said, suddenly. "Maybe this idea is—"

"Ridiculous," Bri said suddenly. "Who moves to northwest Minnesota?"

"No, wait," I said. "Let's talk about this."

"We're gonna, what?" she asked. "Buy a house in the ugliest county in America?"

"I mean . . . it's not like we have a lot of other options at the moment."

"Mm-hmm. And how cold does it get there in the winter?"

"Uh . . ."

This had the potential to be a problem. I don't mind the cold but Briana is notoriously pro-heat and cold-averse. A big part of the reason that Red Lake County, the place, became Red Lake County, America's worst place, was its bone-chilling winter cold. I prevaricated.

"Maybe it gets like, a *little* bit colder than upstate New York," I admitted.

"Forget about the stupid cold!" my mom said, coming

to my rescue. "Buy some sweaters, for Christ's sake, who cares. Think about the time you'd have with the boys! Think about raising them among all those nice people you said you met there."

"It's true," I said. "I hate most people, but those were some of the best people I've ever met. You'd love them, Bri."

Bri raised an eyebrow. I realized this could be a fruitful line of persuasion.

"Now, wait a minute, just how cold are we talking?" my stepdad interjected. Goddammit, Jeff, I thought.

"Cold winters, warm hearts," I said, sounding like an idiot.

"How are we going to work out there in the middle of nowhere?" Bri asked.

"I can work remotely," I said, not sure if I actually could. "It's the perfect place—the *Post* will want a correspondent in Real America for the election year. And you won't have to work at all!"

"I'm not sure if I want to not have to work at all," she said.

She had started building her career when we lived in Vermont, first as a disability adjudicator with the state's Social Security office (we both applied for the job shortly after moving; she was the one who got it). From there she was recruited to the home office in D.C. and worked her way up to the front office, where all the big policy decisions were made. Despite everything she hated about it, by 2015 her career was a big part of her identity. She liked making more money than either of her parents did. She liked having an identity independent of her husband, her kids, or the rest of her family. The job was a pain in the ass, yes, but it was also independence, financial security, a seat at the world's table.

Now she was supposed to throw all that away and what, move to a tiny midwestern farming community, sight unseen?

We didn't make any decisions that night. But over the next few days, as we intermittently talked it over, the plan—if there was going to be any plan—gradually came into focus. It would obviously make the most sense for me to work and her to stay home. My job traveled—99 percent of it was done via phone and internet, which meant I could do it from anywhere. Hers did not—it required lots of meetings, lots of face-to-face time, access to government terminals that existed only within the physical confines of a specific building.

Beyond that it was clear that I simply liked my job a whole lot more than she did, at the moment at least. So if we went out there, I would work.

We grappled with what that would mean for a typical workday. Well, she'd be home with the kids and I'd be there, too, ideally sequestered away in something like a home office. But I'd be there to help get the kids up. To help with meals. To take over when work was done and she'd had about as much of them as she could reasonably handle.

We tried to run a more thorough accounting of the numbers. We figured that relative to our current baseline, each month we'd be able to save . . .

- $3,000 in nanny wages
- $1,000 in reduced mortgage/rental costs
- $250 in train and metro fares
- $100 in gas
- $150 in workday meal costs

All told it added up to about $4,500 a month, which, while it didn't exactly account for the loss of all of Briana's after-tax income, sure made up a big chunk of it.

Plus, we'd be gaining time: fifty hours a week for her, and fifteen for me. We assumed that each of those hours had a dollar value equal to our respective hourly wages. When you added those up and factored in the decreased expenditures we came out way ahead in the ledger.

Eventually we talked ourselves into the view that it would be fiscally irresponsible of us to *not* move to Red Lake County.

In the end what it boiled down to for Bri was that she needed a break from her current job, and she didn't want to miss out on any more of the twins' childhood. Whether this was a long-term thing, whether she was abandoning her working mother identity to become a stay-at-home mom, whether this amounted to a betrayal or renunciation of all she had worked so hard for in high school and college? She didn't know. She would figure it out. What she did know was that this was what she needed *right now*, what felt right for her and for her sons.

I assured her, over and over, that she'd love the people in Red Lake Falls, that it was a totally different kind of community than the hardscrabble upstate New York towns we'd grown up in.

"Tell me about this Jason Brumwell guy then," she said. She saw a photo of him that had run in the story of my visit, all scruffy beard, dark glasses, and baseball cap. She wasn't impressed.

"He looks like . . ." she trailed off uncomfortably.

"A redneck?" I asked.

"A redneck."

"He's not a redneck."

"Honestly he looks a little scary."

"He's neither scary nor a redneck, and definitely not a scary redneck. He's a nice, sweet, thoughtful, educated guy. And everyone there is just like him."

"So they're all scary rednecks?"

It was a tough sell. The cold was another factor. I had to promise a lot—flannel sheets, warm mittens, a well-insulated house with a fireplace, if possible. "Remember, there's no such thing as bad weather!" I admonished glibly. "Only bad outerwear."

I knew, finally, that Briana was on board one day when I opened a package that had arrived in the mail and found two sets of Minnetonka slippers inside, one for each of the twins. "So wait, we're doing this? It's officially happening?" I asked.

"Yes, let's do it," she said. "But first go talk to your boss."

That, of course, was the remaining piece of the puzzle. All I had to do was convince *Post* brass that I should be able to stop showing up to work physically and instead live and file stories from a virtually unheard-of farming community 1,400 miles away from the action in the nation's capital. Easy!

In reality, it wasn't as crazy as it sounds. Newsrooms, perhaps more so than most other organizations, are ideally situated for remote work. At any given time the *Post* had perhaps dozens of correspondents filing stories from far-flung corners of the world and country. Some were traveling, some were based permanently in newsmaking regions like Silicon Valley and the Koreas, and some others had simply negotiated remote work arrangements upon hiring in order to stay in their current cities, chief among them New York. Telework, in other words, was already part of the fabric of the organization, and the *Post* already had the infrastructure—online meeting software, remote log-in capabilities, and the like—to handle it.

I was particularly fortunate in that my beat, such as it was, wasn't tied to any one exact place. If you're a Hill reporter, for instance, a big part of your job is wandering the halls of the Capitol and getting in-person quotes from policy makers. Being physically there is part of your job description.

My beat, on the other hand, was data. And in this day and age, data lives primarily on the internet, so that's where I spent most of my own time. Instead of roaming the halls of Congress, I spent my days digging through federal and academic websites looking for statistical diamonds in the rough—that's how I ended up with the ugly-counties story in the first place.

So in the middle of October I nervously scrawled some notes on a piece of paper and made the pitch to my editor: we'd move to Red Lake County in the following spring. I'd keep writing as I always did, via a home office that included a landline and high-speed internet access. Hell, I could even write periodic longer, data-driven feature-y pieces of interest to a national audience on life in rural America. I could come back to D.C. as needed.

We'd set a time period of a year, at which point we'd reassess: Were we desperate to come back to civilization? Was my work remaining consistent (or, ideally, improving)? Would we want to stay another year or move back?

And of course, we'd have an escape valve: if there was a sense that, God forbid, my work was getting worse as a result of being out of the office, I'd be willing to take any steps necessary to fix the situation—including uprooting everyone and heading back to D.C. for good, if needed.

My editor, Zach, was quiet throughout my whole spiel and when I was finally done he said, "Okay, sure, why don't you put together a memo and we'll run it up the flagpole and see what happens." There was neither pushback nor encouragement; the man reacted no differently than he would have if I'd asked for something completely routine, like an afternoon off for a dentist appointment.

But I wrote the memo and sent it to Zach, who sent it to his editor, who sent it to *his* editor, in a chain of editors reaching all the way up to executive editor Marty Baron, whose generally gruff no-bullshit demeanor can be summed up by the fact that the same actor who played

Marty in *Spotlight,* the 2015 Oscar winner about the *Boston Globe*'s efforts to uncover child abuse in the Catholic Church, also played Sabretooth in 2009's *X-Men Origins: Wolverine.*

"So basically Sabretooth decides whether we go to Minnesota?" Bri asked, when I mentioned how the proposal was being received at work.

"That's correct, yes."

A month later the official word came in—we were going to Minnesota.

Suddenly it was real. We sat down with the boys, then two and a half, to discuss what was happening.

"We're going to live in Minnesota," we said.

"Minnsota," they said. They had no idea what it meant, but the word soon became a universal totem of anticipation in the house, encompassing all our hopes, dreams, anxieties, our struggle for a better life. Minnesota.

One thing I figured I should do was let Jason and the other folks I'd met know we were coming. I didn't know exactly how to do this, though. "Hey, I called your community a shithole and then turned it into a circus for three days, and now I'm moving my entire family there!" What if it was an imposition? What if they were simply like, "What the hell is this guy on about?"

Eventually I shot Jason an email describing our plans. "I hope this doesn't seem too weird!" I wrote. "But the truth is I've thought about the place and everyone I met there a lot since my visit, and I think it would be a great place to live and raise the boys for a year or two.

And we're ready for a change—we've lived in plenty of places on the coasts, but never in the Midwest."

Then I waited for a response.

And waited.

And waited.

Five days later I still hadn't received a reply back. Jason had always been quick to reply in our correspondence leading up to and immediately following my visit, so I naturally assumed this was an ill omen. He had talked it over with some folks in town and was trying to figure out a way to tell me that no, maybe it might not be best for us to come out there. Or maybe it seemed like a completely weird, bizarre stalker thing to do. As Briana had wondered earlier, who the hell actually moves to northwest Minnesota?

Fortunately he put an end to my suffering later that evening with a characteristically chipper reply. "Wow Chris, this is unbelievable!" he wrote. He suggested we come out to visit and look at rentals and homes immediately. "We'd absolutely love to have you and whenever you plan your visit, plan on staying with us! I'll get some listings for area homes for you as soon as I can too!!!!" His exclamation points were reassuring.

Finding homes, as it turned out, was proving to be a challenge. We scoured realtor.com but there were never more than a small handful of places available in the area. Still, what we saw was promising: a five-bedroom house in Oklee for $45,000. A farmhouse with acreage for $100,000. With a D.C. salary, even on one income northwest Minnesota was our oyster.

Population density

Baltimore County, MD

Red Lake County, MN

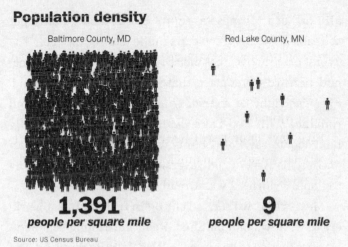

1,391
people per square mile

9
people per square mile

Source: US Census Bureau

Online, at least, there were no rentals to speak of. The closest Craigslist was for Grand Forks, North Dakota, and it listed zero rental houses for anywhere in or near Red Lake County. The papers, like the *Red Lake Falls Gazette* and the *Oklee Herald*, didn't have websites. It was looking increasingly like we'd actually have to buy something.

But as the months went on, even the promising listings started showing cracks. The $45,000 house in Oklee? A "fixer-upper" needing work. Same for the farmstead, on an even larger scale. Could we maybe camp in the barn while we fixed up the house? We were starting to find out why nobody ever moved to northwest Minnesota—it was impossible to find a place to live.

I started getting desperate, searching listings farther afield: Polk County, Pennington County, Duluth. It was all northern Minnesota, right? But Briana quickly put the kibosh on this. "You can't make a big stink about the 'worst place to live' in America and then move to the second- or third-worst place; that would be stupid," she said. She was right, of course. And capping my whirlwind romance with Red Lake County by moving my family next door to, say, Polk County would probably whip up an entirely new set of controversies. Best not to stir up any regional rivalries; I was already on thin ice.

Meanwhile, we started cluing in friends and coworkers to what we had planned. Reaction among other colleagues tended to be mixed, with a definite dividing line by age. Older coworkers, particularly ones with small kids, would come up to me and tell me how great an idea it sounded. "Wow, that's so cool!" is something I heard over and over again. "God I would love to get out of D.C." Clearly we weren't the only ones struggling with work-life questions.

Twenty-something coworkers, meanwhile, were curious but slightly horrified. "Do they even have internet out there?" a number of them asked. Yes, I explained. "What do people even . . . do out there?" Well, I said, I'm going to find out.

Briana faced a similarly divided reaction among her coworkers, particularly among the women. Some questioned whether she'd be okay walking away from a promising career that she was finally beginning to get established in. But others said yes, it'll be amazing for the kids and you can always come back to the career later when you're ready. Hearing that sentiment, particularly from some of the older women in the office, helped reinforce the idea that this didn't have to be a permanent change—she could come back. This was particularly true of jobs in the federal government, which has rules in place making it easier for people who've stepped away for a few years to return to work at their previous level of pay and responsibility, provided that a job is available.

My mom was ecstatic, a reaction driven primarily by her safety concerns. She fretted endlessly about the possibility of one of the twins tumbling down one of the three sets of steep stairs that linked our current living space together. The sidewalks around our place were dodgy and abruptly ended in odd locations, which combined with narrow twisting roadways meant that a grandson getting struck by a car was always in the back of her mind.

Briana's family was supportive, but a little more guarded in their response. Her parents, having lived the military lifestyle of frequent moves that took them far from family, understood that this kind of thing can happen in the course of a person's career. But a number of them asked, "If you're going to do that, why don't you just move back to New York to be closer with us?" We had, in fact, briefly considered this. But putting a few thousand miles between ourselves and upstate New York was a feature, not a bug, of our new plan. Our New York families were complicated, and all things considered it would be nice to have some distance between us and them.

As winter turned into spring I wrote to Jason and told him we'd like to take him up on his offer to stay if it was still open—it would be just Briana and me for a long weekend. We'd fly in to Minneapolis, rent a car, and drive up the state to Red Lake Falls. Bri would get to see some of the countryside that way, which she insisted on—keep in mind she had agreed to this whole adventure sight unseen, on the basis of my recommendation alone.

I mentioned we'd been having difficulty finding places, and Jason and his dad, Dick, got to work right away. They set us up with a Realtor friend of theirs and started asking around town to see who was privately selling a home, or would be considering doing so in the future. Dick and the Realtor, Loren, managed to rustle up a list of eleven properties to look at. Most of them had no internet footprint whatsoever—they were all but invisible to anyone looking for housing online. As we came to realize, private sales—direct transactions between a buyer and seller, unmediated by any Realtor or other professional—were a lot more common out there than in Baltimore.

On March 10 we arrived in Minneapolis and began our trek up the Minnesota countryside. Much of the Minnesota landscape, particularly in the eastern half of the state, resembles upstate New York—dense maple and pine forests covering rolling hills, dotted with small towns and lakes. Along the way we stopped at Lake Itasca State Park, where the mighty Mississippi River starts its journey from its source, just a tiny trickle a child can jump across.

We pulled over at a scenic overlook and turned off the car. The silence was profound, almost deafening. We hadn't heard anything like it in months, years maybe, so accustomed were we to the background din of a dense urban environment. After several minutes of adjustment our ears became attuned to a whole new soundscape, the subtle rhythms of nature that usually get buried beneath humanity's hue and cry—a rustle of leaves, a creak of ice on the lakeshore, an unseen animal skittering beneath the snowline.

The silence was a relief, and helped put our minds at ease about what we were getting ourselves into. Surely nothing but good could come of taking our children out of the clamor and bustle of the city to a quieter, slower place—one where they would have the space and silence to think, to develop an interior life, to learn to listen to and appreciate life's quieter, subtler rhythms.

Briana told me later that that moment at Itasca was a turning point in her decision that moving to Red Lake Falls was the right thing to do. "The silence . . . it filled me up," she said. "It was peace. I wanted our family to have that kind of peace."

We continued north and west, following the thinning forests to the plains. We got to Jason's house that evening, a little later than we thought we would. Dick came stomping down the driveway to meet us. "Well where in the hell have these east coasters been, who told us they'd be here at seven?" he thundered. Briana was mortified. Dick laughed a hearty laugh. "Welcome to Red Lake County," he said, offering her a big bear hug. "Nothing to worry about, you can't be any worse than that husband of yours."

We went in for a meal Jason cooked while Dick laid out the itinerary for our whirlwind real estate tour, which stretched out from one end of the county to another. "We've had people beating the bushes all over the place looking for somewhere for you to stay," he said. "You remember Chuck Simpson?" Commissioner Kiss-My-Butt. "He's been out there working harder than everyone; even he's excited you're coming to stay."

The next day started early. Most of the places we were scheduled to look at were for sale, not rent, but they were well under our price limit of $150,000. Dick and Jason drew what appeared to be a big distinction between places that were "in town" and those that were "in the country." Briana and I thought this was hilarious, since as far as we were concerned everything from here to Grand Forks was "the country."

But we soon understood that when folks in northwest Minnesota say "in the country," they mean it. One of the stops on our itinerary was a tidy little place on the edge of the county. To get there we drove through the fields of the western county on the paved roads, then turned off on a dirt road. No problem, we had lived on a dirt road for a period of time in Vermont. We could handle this.

After bumping down the road for a few miles we hitched a right onto an even smaller and more rustic dirt road. It appeared to be somebody's driveway but no, Jason assured me, it was a road. "I got the bus stuck at the turnaround up here a few years ago picking up the kids who live out here," he said.

After several bumpy miles we at last arrived at the property, a low-slung modular home on six acres. Aside from the house, a barn, and a shed there were no other buildings to be seen anywhere, in any direction. The nearest neighbor was miles away.

We toured the property and talked to the owners, Shari Rolf-Baird and her husband. "Yeah, it's pretty peaceful out here," Shari said. "Lotta space for the kids to run around; there's the whole barn for them to explore and build forts in." I could just picture it: Jack and Charles running about in the country, no cars, no strangers, no hassles. It was beautiful.

"Of course, you gotta keep an eye out for the wolves and the bears," Shari added nonchalantly.

"I'm sorry, what?" said Briana.

"We keep the rifle by the door for the wildlife, especially the bear. He's around so much we've got a name for him; we call him Brutus. Haven't had any problems with him yet but you never know."

After the tour we got back in Jason's car.

"No," Briana said before I had even opened my mouth.

"Come on," I said. "We can teach the kids about, like, wildlife safety."

"Absolutely not."

"But there's nobody around for mi—"

"That's exactly what I'm afraid of!" she said. "You think I want to be cooped up all alone in that house with you all winter? Me taking care of the twins and you trying to write and doing some kind of weird *Shining* thing? No."

"Okay, fair enough."

So that was "the country." We kept looking, visiting homes within the limits of the towns of Brooks and Red Lake Falls. We stopped for lunch in the middle of the day at Carol's Cozy, the only bar-restaurant in Brooks. When we walked in a bunch of workers from nearby farms were already in there, and it felt like a classic record-scratch, freeze-frame moment—conversation stopped, and all eyes turned to us as we walked in. I saw what I thought were a few familiar faces from my trip the previous summer, but they either didn't recognize me or didn't care to extend a greeting. Forget Minnesota Nice, it was downright Minnesota Nippy in there.

I began to feel a mild panic attack coming on. What the hell were we doing, anyway? Walking into a strange community a thousand miles from anywhere, assuming we could just set down roots and elbow our way into society? People usually move for familiar reasons—a job, a spouse, a family. According to the census, among people who moved five hundred miles or more in a given year, half moved for job-related reasons, a third moved for family, and about 18 percent moved for housing. Just 2.4 percent of long-range movers cited a reason that didn't fall neatly into one of those categories. But our move was 100 percent of our own volition, prompted by little more than a desire to get the hell out of D.C.

It was nearly inevitable that at some point I would write a story that would piss off a bunch of people in the country. Say, about gun control, or about the Republican Party. What would happen then? Would they show up at my door? Leave threatening messages on my phone?

I'd received plenty of angry and unhinged emails during my time at the *Post*, but nothing that ever made me fear for myself or my family. We lived in a large metro area where there was some safety, I felt, in anonymity. I came home from work and I wasn't Chris, the National Reporter, but Chris, the guy from 738 Pleasant Hill.

But that anonymity would be gone in Red Lake County—even if my relationship with the place hadn't been the subject of a media circus, there's no getting lost in the crowd in a small town. That's great for raising kids or feeling like a part of the community, but what happens if you do something that really pisses that community off?

Despite my misgivings, lunch went by uneventfully. At the end of it, in fact, the waitress surprised everyone in the place by bringing us all out a free slice of pie, on the house. Maybe I was overthinking things.

I didn't have high hopes for one of the last places we looked at, a property in Red Lake Falls that the Brumwells referred to as "the purple house." It wasn't much to look at from the outside—it was basically a large, light purple box with a garage attached. Given slightly different trim it would have been easy to mistake for an auto repair shop. But it was on a big lot, even by northern Minnesota standards, somewhere between a half and whole acre as best as I could tell. There were lilacs, lilies, and Concord grapes planted along much of the perimeter, although under the previous owners they hadn't been tended to for years. There was also the shadow of a huge garden near a spacious shed. If nothing else, there was lots of room for the boys to run around.

We went in through the garage and it looked like, well, a garage. No surprises there. I was prepared to write the whole place off until we stepped through the door to the house proper, where we were surprised to see a large, wide-open space with a gently vaulted ceiling. Everything had a fresh coat of paint. John and Sandy Klein, the neighbors who had purchased the place from the prior owners and cleaned it up to sell, assured us it was move-in ready—a big plus, given that we weren't going to have much time for any remodeling with a pair of two-year-olds in tow. Even more surprising, there was a spacious finished basement below, with three bedrooms in addition to the master bedroom on the main floor. One for the twins, one for guests, and one for my home office. Plus, a roomy play area where all the twins' toys and assorted toddler paraphernalia could go.

We tried to play it cool but I could tell by the look in Briana's eye that she was sold already—this was the place. Just thinking of what we'd do with it felt like winning the lottery. It had a staggering two and a half large bathrooms, more than either of us had had in a home in our entire lives. The two main bathrooms each had two sinks—one for each member of the family. I'd never lived in a place with a garage—this one had a double attached to the house. I'd also never lived in a place with more than a patch of a yard—this one practically came with a hayfield. The refrigerator even came with a built-in ice machine, an unthinkable extravagance. That comfortable, well-apportioned life—the one that seemed impossibly far away in D.C.—was now tantalizingly within reach.

We told the Kleins we'd get in touch with them and let them know the next day. But that night, over dinner at Jason's house, we resolved to put an offer in. The Brumwells, of course, got into motion right away to help us make it happen. Dick called on his Realtor friend Loren, who lived about an hour north, in the town of Grygla, to help us draw up the necessary paperwork. We inquired about a commission and Loren said he wouldn't hear of it; the house wasn't officially listed so he couldn't technically do anything with it anyway.

"Tell you what, get me a nice steak dinner after you get settled in town and we'll call it square," he said.

Late in the evening, when we were almost done with the paperwork, things hit a snag. Someone mentioned that there had been rumors of drug activity at the place before the Kleins had bought it.

"What was it?" Loren asked. "Were they manufacturing there?"

We had no idea.

"Because if it's a meth house," he said, "and there's chemicals soaked into the walls or the foundation or something like that, you might not know until six months after you move in and one of your kids starts having a seizure."

Holy shit.

This new information was paralyzing. I had done enough drug policy reporting to know that that assessment seemed extreme, but on the other hand I was no expert. How the hell would we get around this?

"Well, why don't we just give the sheriff a ring?" Jason said.

Briana and I were dumbstruck. "You can just do that?" we asked.

"Well sure, it's ten o'clock, Mitch is probably home right now," Jason said. "I've got his number right here on my phone."

Jason proceeded to give the number a ring and launched right into a chipper conversation, as if calling up the sheriff to inquire about meth houses was something he did every Saturday night.

"Yep. Okay. Thanks, Mitch!" he said, as he hung up. "Yeah no, there was no meth lab there," he told us. "They had some calls about possible drug use on the property, but they never heard anything about manufacturing on premises."

So there you had it. A question that could have derailed a home transaction for weeks in Baltimore County was resolved in Red Lake County with little more than a neighborly five-minute phone call on a Saturday night.

Early the next morning, paperwork in hand, we drove back over to the house to make an offer to the Kleins. John was a farmer and a trucker, gruff and a little intimidating with a horseshoe mustache, while Sandy was chipper and full of sunshine. We stood around the kitchen counter and hashed it out—within about five minutes we were all shaking hands over a deal. Dick and Jason were there, too, and though the topic hadn't even come up, Dick announced he'd put down the five-hundred-dollar honest money deposit. We objected, but we hadn't even thought to bring our checkbook. He had nothing of it. "Just send me a check whenever you get a chance," he said.

So that was it—later that day we were on our way back down to Minneapolis, purchase agreement in hand. We were going to be Minnesota home owners. It was starting to get real.

Over the next couple of months we packed up our life in Baltimore and prepared for the move as the Brumwells oversaw the home inspection and other technicalities in Red Lake Falls.

As May rolled up we finalized our packing and said our good-byes, and on the fourth we closed the door on our old house for the last time. We were going to Minnesota.

Cross-country moves are generally a horrible affair and ours was no exception. I had the easy job, driving the rental truck stuffed with our belongings. Briana followed in our little Honda CRV, stuffed with Jack, Charles, Tiber (our seventy-pound beagle-basset mix), and Ivy (our twelve-year-old cat).

The CRV crew could only tolerate a few hours cooped up in the car before everyone started having meltdowns, so we stretched out the twenty-two-hour drive over five exhausting days. Technically, at this point, we still didn't even have a home to roll up to. We'd be getting in on a Sunday but the closing wasn't scheduled until the following day. But the Kleins told us they'd leave the door open and put the keys on the kitchen counter, letting us move in a day early. Not typically the way a real estate transaction would happen in Baltimore.

Eventually we pulled up to our new home in Red Lake Falls. The boys knew it by then only as the Purple House. We hadn't even gotten the kids out of their car seats before we were enthusiastically greeted by a sweaty, half-naked man. Rob Conwell, his name was, our new neighbor who lived across the street.

He was shirtless and sweaty because he'd been mowing his lawn, he explained. In about five minutes we'd heard half his life story—he was from Oregon, met a Minnesota girl who'd grown up in the area, they ended up moving back here to start a family two decades ago.

He and his wife, Alice, were active in music and theater in the area—did we play any instruments? There was a great little community band the next town over and they were always looking for new players; the conductor was fantastic and rehearsals were on Monday and Wednesday nights at 7 p.m. and—

"That sounds amazing," I cut him off, hopefully less rudely than it felt. "Maybe we can talk it over once we're all moved in?"

Of course, Rob said, of course. Welcome to the neighborhood!

We experienced a lot of this in the coming days and weeks—invitations to *get involved*. The Civic and Commerce Committee needed volunteers. The Northwest Minnesota Arts Council needed board members. The school needed a guest to come read to the kids. Churches needed folks to staff their basement dinners. Rural areas may not have a lot of people but they still needed to get stuff done. In the cities, economies of scale mean either these tasks are professionalized—people get paid to do them—or competition for the most desirable activities, like music and theater groups, is stiff. Here, by contrast, getting involved is easy. If you want to join a band or help with kids or put out fires, just show up. There's plenty of work that needs to get done.

As soon as we got the kids out of their car seats, Jack

tore ass up the garage stairs and into the house. Charlie, however, was transfixed for the moment by the garage. "Dad!" he screamed. "The Purple House has a garage door!"

The first order for the kids in the new place was to run around, opening and shutting all the doors and then flipping all the light switches they could reach. For the first several days you could always tell where in the house Charlie was by the "boi-oi-oi-oi-oing" of the spring door stops he was compelled to flick every time he entered a room.

"There's three bathrooms?" Jack said. *"That's crazy."* Indeed, compared to our old row house, where there was just one bathroom for all four of us, it was downright extravagant.

That first day the Brumwells and the Kleins came over to help us get all our stuff out of the van. Northern Minnesota boys don't fuck around when it comes to lifting and moving heavy things, and with their help we wrapped up the job in just a couple of hours—even though Ryan, Jason's brother, was deathly hungover from a wedding the night before. A few neighbors wandered over to pitch in as well, perhaps more out of curiosity than anything else. One of them, an old guy with a gray ponytail, brought over a six-pack and introduced himself as Larry Eukel.

Larry told us he had actually grown up on the property we now lived on, had swung on a tire swing from the very same oak tree that now overlooked the yard.

"It's a great place to grow up," he said, "and boy is it nice to see a young family in that yard again."

We subsequently came to learn that the property had something of a checkered past in more recent years. Neighbors told us of how, one summer, the electric company had shut off power to the place because the people living there hadn't been paying their electric bill. Well, the Presbyterian church sits right across the alley from the Purple House, and one morning staff arrived to find an extension cord running from one of their external outlets over to the garage. A handwritten note said it was connected to the freezer and could they please not unplug it? In the spirit of charity, they didn't. There were mean dogs in the yard, neighbors said. At one point somebody had parked an RV on the lot and appeared to be living out of it. Just a lot of weird stuff going on, and in a quiet, tiny midwestern neighborhood like this one, weird is bad.

The house is in an area of town known as the Hollow, a little quarter circle of the Clearwater River floodplain that's protected to the south and east by the modest hill leading up to the main level of the county. It bears the distinction of being the coldest neighborhood in town. One winter several years back, the Kleins told us, the water main under the street froze up and they were left without water until spring. The town told them to run a hose from a neighbor's house and they'd prorate both the bills. What else could they do? You can't unfreeze a northern Minnesota water main in February. I was glad Briana didn't learn about this until well after we had moved. And sure enough, our second winter here it

happened again. The Kleins' water went dry, and they
again had to run a hose to the other neighbor's place.
Our water appeared to be fine but the folks at city hall
instructed us to keep a tap running at all times, until
the spring thaws came. They told us they'd just bill us
our usual amount on our water bill so we didn't have to
pay extra for the privilege of helping the town keep its
infrastructure working.

Red Lake Falls feels like the kind of town your
grandparents lived in, and I mean that in the best possible way. The town's 1,400 residents keep tidy homes on
tidy lawns with sprawling vegetable gardens out back.
To an adult living here for the first time, it feels like the
kind of place you remember visiting during summers
in childhood, where memories are built on lazy after-
noons spent on broad, sunny lawns while the adults relax on a screened-in porch, cocktails in hand.

The town is home to a weekly newspaper, the *Red
Lake Falls Gazette,* which publishes mostly high school
sports news. In the summer when things get slow a new
lawn gnome in someone's yard is enough to merit a front
page spread. While it's nice to see a small-town print
newspaper alive, nobody would mistake the paper for
a bastion of hard-hitting journalism. The contents are
mostly taken up by photos of goings-on at the schools in
town. Coverage of genuine local events, like city council
meetings and the like, is virtually nonexistent. There
was no coverage of local political races in 2016 and 2018,
even though a dazzling array of candidates were on the
ballot for everything from school board seats to county

water commissioners. At one point the paper ran what appeared to be a story about a local college professor who gave his students a clever lesson illustrating the dangers of socialism. The story was fake, and had been cut-and-pasted from an email forward.

The town has two gas stations that double as social hubs—in the mornings different crews of cantankerous old-timers shuffle off to their favorite tables to discuss the day's news. There are two bars serving nearly identical foods and drinks at opposite ends of town, the kinds of laid-back midwestern places where little kids can be found running around in the back until late at night when their parents finally go home.

There's an independent grocery store, Brent's, that offers roughly the same variety of goods as the Grand Union in Oneonta, New York, did thirty years ago. Avocadoes are the most exotic produce they stock. For cheeses they have Swiss, cheddar, and something called "farmer's cheese," which is sort of like a milder version of Monterey Jack, if such a thing were possible. Transplants to the area inquiring about delicacies such as "goat cheese" or "cilantro" are met with quizzical stares. The meat section offers Norwegian delicacies like pickled herring in a jar and slabs of lutefisk around the holidays. There are large sections of the store devoted to pickling, canning, and sausage-making, with an underlying assumption that many locals grow or shoot much of their own food. Pet owners can purchase dried cat food at Brent's but not canned—the cats of Red

Lake Falls are evidently expected to do their own for-
aging as well.

There's a town library, which keeps a surprisingly
liberal section of children's books in stock, including
Jacob's New Dress, about a young boy who decides to
wear a dress to school. Some controversy attended the
addition of this book to the library in nearby Thief
River Falls, where it was nearly banned, but parents in
Red Lake Falls either didn't care or didn't notice.

There's a post office, of course, where you never have
to offer your name or ID to pick up your mail because the
employees already know who you are. There's the town
pool, the one that residents fund-raised and built themselves, where Alice, the head lifeguard and our neighbor,
will encourage your children to strap on a life preserver
and take a plunge off the diving board even if they haven't
fully mastered how to swim yet.

The town's four houses of worship encompass its religious diversity: one Catholic, one Presbyterian, and
two flavors of Lutheranism. The pastor at Bethany Lutheran, Gary Graff, made a point to stop by our house,
welcome us to town, and invite us to attend worship
there if we were so inclined. There are two small doctor's offices offering limited standard services like
checkups and X-rays several days a week.

There's a small pharmacy, open nine to five Monday
through Friday, where the staffers inquire about your
ailments with genuine concern, and will gladly tell you
all about theirs if you've got a minute to stop and chat.

There is industry in town—Homark, a manufacturer of modular homes, and Wood Master, a maker of outdoor wood furnaces. A paved trail runs from the golf course at one end of town to the farmland at the other, following the length of the old railroad bed and traversing the Clearwater and Red Lake Rivers via sturdy steel trestle bridges.

Those first few days were a whirlwind of new faces—smiling ones, much to my relief. People from all over town dropped off welcome baskets—baked goods, fresh produce from gardens, a surprising variety of pickled vegetable products. Beth Solheim, an older woman with roots in the town who now lived several hours away, stopped by to drop off a watercolor portrait of Tiber that she had painted, based on a photo she'd seen of him on Facebook.

After a decade in the city it's a shock to move to a place and realize that everybody already knows who you are. People we'd never met would stop us on the street and ask how we were liking it so far, diving into deep personal conversations as if we were familiar friends who'd just had lunch together a few days ago.

One day not long after we moved in we got a call on our new landline phone, which we had to put in since the cell reception was spotty to nonexistent. Briana answered; it was a receptionist at one of the doctor's offices. This was odd because we hadn't been to the doctor's yet.

"Hey, are you guys home?" the receptionist asked, casually.

"Umm, yeah, why?" Bri asked.

"Well, the UPS guy is here and he says he tried to drop off a package at your place but nobody was home, but I told him I was pretty sure you were there today. Do you want me to send him back down there?"

"Uhh, sure, thanks?" Bri replied.

After a while we started to get used to our notoriety. Part of it was due to the publicity that had attended our decision to move, sure. But eventually we realized that this was simply the kind of place where everybody knows everyone—and they even know whether or not you're home.

A few weeks after the move we attended the wedding of Heather Wallace, Jason's sister. The reception and dinner were held at the American Legion on Main Street, which we thought was weird—did we have to be veterans to get in? But no, out here the Legion posts were basically just public bars, where anyone could walk in and grab a drink. Inside, dusty old photographs of previous Legion luminaries with strange Scandinavian names lined the wood-paneled walls. The wedding was closed-bar, but the Legion beer was cheap. For dinner there was an enormous vat of pulled pork, a staple at large gatherings in the area. Jack and Charles mingled with a crowd of kids of all ages at the back of the hall, where the door was propped open and children ran freely in and out well into the wee hours of the warm early summer night.

The sense of community contrasted sharply with what we had previously experienced in places like Vermont and Maryland. One of our neighbors in our old row house, we'll call him James, kept mostly to himself, for instance. He was a strange guy, a little older than me, and didn't work because he was on disability due to an ankle problem, or so he told us.

Since he didn't have a job he was always around, and he could be prickly toward his neighbors. Shortly after we moved into our home there he blew his top because, in mowing our tiny patch of a lawn, we had mowed a little bit over onto his portion of the grassy hillside. Weird guy, in short, and we generally tried to avoid him (bad neighbors connected by a common wall: another drawback of high-density living).

One day early in the summer before the twins were born we noticed that James's car had been parked outside his place for several days but nobody had heard or seen him around. This was strange because we'd usually see him coming or going, or hear him or his TV through the walls, often at late hours of the night. But for several days now, silence.

After a week went by we spoke to some of the other neighbors on our row of six houses. No, they hadn't seen him, either. It was odd, of course, but none of us were what you'd call his friends, and nobody wanted to try to dig deeper and risk getting involved with whatever weirdness he was surely involved with.

As we learned later, James's mother, who lived across town, had been trying to get in touch with him, too. No luck. Roughly two weeks after we had noticed him missing, she came by his house with flowers. It was his birthday.

She knocked on the door; no answer. She tried the handle; it was locked. Windows were locked, too. The house was all sealed up. Not knowing what else to do she called a locksmith and the police. They forced their way in and followed the smell to where his body lay alone in the basement, dead by his own hand. He had killed himself two weeks ago and nobody had any inkling.

We felt a little bit of guilt—was there anything we could have done? But of course, there wasn't. We didn't know the guy, our interactions with him tended to go poorly, and if we were being honest, life became a little easier knowing we wouldn't have to hear him banging on the walls at 3 a.m. or screaming at us because of a lawn-mowing impropriety. James's tale became a macabre story we told acquaintances and friends. Bri was about six months pregnant with twins around this time; one of our close friends remarked that during the two weeks his body lay in the basement, James's ghost had traversed the wall between our units and taken residence within one of the twins. We all laughed. But that's life in a lot of cities—surrounded by humanity, you can still die alone.

Needless to say, when I tell this story to folks in Red Lake Falls they gasp in shock and disbelief.

The thing I remember most from those first few weeks is the collective sense of wonder at having a home—a real, honest-to-goodness single-family home. I had grown up in one of these, after all, so it represented something of my default expectation for what a family should live in. But after a decade on the pricey east coast it had seemed like the expectations of childhood were being trampled by the cold fiscal realities of metro life in the twenty-first century. Out here, though, it was different.

Perhaps our greatest sense of having "made it" as adults came one evening shortly after our move. The kids were in bed and we were watching TV on the couch. At the show's end I got up to go to the bathroom, prompting Briana to leap off the couch and run into the room ahead of me, a trick we often played on each other in Maryland.

"Come on, you've gotta be kidding me," I said. "I really have to go!"

"You realize we have two other bathrooms now, right?" she asked before shutting the door in my face. I was thunderstruck. It was a revelation—no more fighting over the one cramped little commode of our Maryland house. If we both had to take a dump at the same time we could do so, in private and at our own pace, like civilized people. It seemed extravagant. According to the U.S. Census's Survey of Construction, in 2016 just 3.7 percent of new homes were built with one bathroom or less, while about 35 percent had at least three or more. Moving from Maryland to Minnesota vaulted us from the bottom 4 percent of the American toilet distribution almost all the way to the top third.

The house seemed huge to us. After we'd lugged all our belongings in—everything that had our old place bursting at the seams—there was still empty space everywhere. We turned some of the leftover space downstairs into a play area for the twins. In the coming weeks Briana filled it with maps and educational posters, as well as the twins' collection of toys brought from Maryland. It was like having a preschool classroom right in the house. The twins were thrilled to have a space of their own to ransack and make a mess of, as they saw fit, provided they cleaned it up somewhat before bedtime.

The house isn't huge by any stretch of the imagination—maybe 2,000 square feet, roughly 25 percent smaller than the typically newly constructed home, according to census figures—but to us it may as well have been a palace.

We started to understand the profound effect of living space one evening after dinner, when Jack and

Median home listing price

Washington, DC

Red Lake County, MN

$493
per square foot

$53
per square foot

Source: realtor.com

Charles linked arms and announced they were headed off to the playroom together to play. They were typically fractious; they often quarreled and squabbled over toys and attention and countless perceived slights, real and imagined. But after years of constant policing and keeping a watchful eye on their every move, suddenly here, in Red Lake Falls, in a house with space they could truly call their own, for the first time they were ready to go off and be themselves by themselves, with no need for parental intervention. They finally had the space to become themselves without constantly chafing against each other. If tall fences make good neighbors, large playrooms make good siblings.

People with an affinity for dense urban spaces—many who happen to be employed at the universities and media outlets that shape so much of contemporary public opinion—tend to take a dim view of the classic single-family home. They take up too much space. They foster car culture. They're unsustainable from an environmental standpoint. High-density housing—condos and apartments—is far preferable to suburban sprawl, or so they tell us. It's better for *everyone*.

But a lot of the writing on this topic doesn't really grapple with the draw of the single-family home to begin with, the huge place it occupies in the American psyche and culture. For a body of thought that deals with the proper role and uses of physical space in society, it's remarkably blind to the importance of space to individuals. It doesn't wrestle with what it can really mean to a person to not have to share walls and floors with noisy neighbors. It doesn't fully appreciate the difference between living out one's life in a cramped space versus an expansive one. To have ample outdoor space to run, to breathe in, to call your own. The market urbanists in the nation's media centers acknowledge, on some level, that people tend to desire these things. But many of the people who write about the topic don't seem to truly understand these desires themselves. That's a big blind spot, especially considering that so many of these people are responsible for creating the culture consumed by the entire country.

Beyond that, the market urbanists seem to view the choice of living spaces as a binary one: either you're in the cities (high density, good) or the suburbs (low density, bad). Given that roughly 80 percent of the country lives in the cities or their suburbs this is an understandable place to start the discussion, but it overlooks the completely different modes of living available in small towns and rural areas.

Then there was our new lawn. Given the sheer size of it—approaching three-fourths of an acre—it was clear we'd have to get a proper lawn mower to take care of it, something I'd never had to do before—we'd relied on a small human-powered reel mower to deal with our tiny patch of Maryland greenery.

I picked up a proper gas-powered push mower from Wal-Mart that spring and was excited to give it a spin for the first time. But the instruction book said I needed to add some oil to the engine before I fired it up, and damned if I couldn't figure out how to get the oil cap off.

The cap was an odd-looking yellow thing. I twisted it, pulled at it, tugged it this way and that. It didn't budge. I referred to the instructions. I pulled up YouTube videos on my phone. Nothing.

Miraculously, after I'd been puzzling over the mower for about an hour a pickup truck pulled into the driveway. It was Michael Baker, the fire chief in the nearby town of Plummer and an engine mechanic at Arctic Cat in Thief River. He'd been one of the local voices gently chiding me on Twitter after my first story ran, sending me photos of the view of the Red Lake River from his back porch.

"Gonna do some mowin', eh?" he asked.

"Only if I can figure out this oil cap," I said. He walked over, crouched down, and popped the cap off with a flick of his wrist.

"Here you go," he said. I thanked him and finally got to mowing. As of this writing, more than two years after that day, I still haven't changed the oil on that mower. The truth is I still can't figure out how to get that cap off.

At the *Post* I'd penned a number of columns railing against lawns. "Lawns are a soul-crushing timesuck and most of us would be better off without them," I wrote on August 4, 2015, less than two weeks before I saw the words "Red Lake County" for the first time. They soak up water—nine billion gallons *a day* nationwide, according to the U.S. Environmental Protection Agency—they kill native biodiversity, and according to the American Time Use Survey the average American spends more than seventy hours a year on lawn and garden care. What a waste!

I still believe all this on some level. And yet that summer, when I stopped to consider *my own lawn*—my own patch of land, an environment for me to shape and cultivate as I pleased, a place for my children to play, grow, explore, and run free—I couldn't wait to get out there and start mowing for myself. One of the foundational principles of statistics is that what's true at the population level is often not true at the individual level. The average American can expect to live 78.6 years— but that doesn't mean that *you*, the individual reading this book, will live that long. Maybe you'll live to be a hundred. Maybe you'll get hit by a bus tomorrow. Who knows? The point is, things can be true for populations that aren't true at all for individuals. Do I still believe the median American lawn is a waste of space? I do. Would I defend my own to the death, weed whacker in hand? Absolutely. The numbers often make hypocrites of us all.

Lawn care in northern Minnesota is a highly fraught topic, filled with land mines for unsuspecting newcomers. People here trim their grass down to about the length you'd find on a putting green. If your grass is much higher than that you're expected to apologize for it to everyone you meet, especially if someone catches you outside doing something other than mowing it. You're responsible for upkeep of the sidewalk in front of your house, too, which includes keeping weeds from growing in the cracks. One day that summer I was outside with the boys and Rob, the half-naked neighbor, came by. He gestured toward a couple of dandelions springing from a gap in the sidewalk. "Growing a hedge, eh?" he said. He didn't need to say anything else. After the boys were down for a nap I slunk back out to the sidewalk with the weed whacker.

One of the first things we wanted to do after moving in was to start a garden. There was already space on the property set aside for that, a partially fenced-in corner of the yard that had been used as a garden in years past but which was now just a tangle of weeds and long grass.

We spent several weekends cleaning out the light brush and mending the fence all around the garden plot—we'd see regular patrols of deer in the neighborhood in the evenings, and rabbits were everywhere. Plus, Dick Brumwell showed us a picture of a black bear that he'd been watching rummage through his bird feeder that spring. We didn't know what bears do to gardens and didn't want to find out.

Finally, it was time to work the soil. The garden area was too large to till by hand, but the Kleins had a large, gas-powered roto-tiller from the farm they let us borrow. One thing we came to understand was that pretty much everyone up here owns "equipment."

One mild Saturday afternoon I finally took the tiller to the garden. It was satisfying work, guiding the machine along a gridded path, turning dead grass and compacted dirt into rich, fluffy black soil. At one point when I was nearly finished I took a break and turned the tiller off, and that's when I heard the sounds.

They were tiny, almost imperceptible squeaks. Kind of like little birds, but the pitch was a little off. I searched for the source and found it coming from the ground, one of the patches I had just finished tilling. I shoved some dirt aside, and realized with shock and horror that I had roto-tilled a nest full of baby rabbits.

They were tiny, with their eyes barely open. They had been grievously wounded by the blades of the tiller, but unfortunately none of them was quite dead.

Shit.

When I was a kid, about eleven years old, a group of my friends and I came upon a baby bird on a sidewalk that had fallen out of its nest. It had no feathers yet and its eyes weren't open. It was very badly injured and appeared to be gasping for air. We knew we'd have to put it out of its misery, and after a few minutes of hushed discussion it was decided that one of us would ride over its head with our bike tire, which was the most humane option for ending its suffering among the limited tools we had at our disposal. As the son of a veterinarian I was elected to carry out the mercy killing. I rolled my tire forward and there was a quick crunch and then it was over. To this today I have occasional agonizing dreams involving small, delicate creatures past the point of mending and in horrible pain.

The rabbits were the bird all over again. It was obvious that they were beyond repair—taking them to the local veterinarian was out of the question. But I couldn't simply leave them there to suffer in the dirt until they expired. Instead I opted for the humane choice—I walked into the shed and grabbed a metal shovel. I used it to decapitate each of the wounded rabbits as swiftly as I could. The work was excruciating, but mercifully short. I placed the tiny bodies in a bag for the garbage and worked the blood-soaked dirt back into the bed of soil with my boot. Thus was the Ingraham family's Minnesota garden consecrated.

I had kind of a queasy, uneasy feeling afterward, like a nightmare had come to life. But part of me was strangely invigorated. After all, wasn't this part of what we came out here for? To get out of the city and closer to the land, to live a life where the stakes were real and messy, where we'd be exposed to nature's teeth and nails and learn whether we had any of our own?

Granted, killing five baby rabbits with a shovel didn't exactly make me Grizzly Adams. But it made me a little different than the person I'd been back in Maryland. When I told coworkers and friends from the east coast about the rabbits, they recoiled in shock and horror: "Oh, the poor bunnies!" they'd say. When I told folks in Red Lake Falls about the mishap, on the other hand, it barely merited a reaction. "Eh. Gotta do that sometimes," John Klein told me.

Several weeks later another baby rabbit appeared in our garage one morning. It was older than the ones I'd killed in the garden, old enough to be out hopping about on its own but not smart enough to avoid getting stuck in the garage. I saw an opportunity for redemption.

"We talked about getting a pet rabbit when we came out here, right?" I said to Bri, holding forth the baby rabbit in a cardboard box. "Maybe this is a sign. This is how we atone for the dead bunnies in the garden."

"You realize wild rabbits die pretty much immediately when you try to bring them into a house, right?" she said. "They freak out. They literally die of fright. Their hearts basically explode."

"Not this rabbit," I said. "You watch. This rabbit is here for a reason. It has a purpose. This rabbit will live."

It was dead by the next morning. Another tiny corpse wrapped in a grocery bag and set in the trash.

After that we decided the only thing to do was to purchase some proper domesticated rabbits. We picked a pair up at a nearby county fair later that summer. We bought them off a kid who was charging ten bucks apiece, cash, for them. We gave him a twenty and he handed us a box with two rabbits inside. Easy-peasy. The kids christened them Mubba and Bubba, since "mubba" had been Charlie's word for rabbit when he was still learning how to talk.

Among our other animal adventures that first summer was a memorable trip with the kids to Carl Schindler's dairy farm. This was the same place I visited during my reporting trip, where I proved my regular guyness by letting a calf suck on my hand. Now it was the twins' turn.

Carl took us all to the main barn so the boys could feed the cows some hay. He showed us how to pick out the tightly packed leafy bits of the hay that the cows really liked. The boys were a little put off by being surrounded by a herd of thousand-pound beasts with big wet noses and long, rough tongues, but they took to it surprisingly well.

As we petted the cows, I saw out of the corner of my eye the mangy old yellow farm dog from my prior visit trotting up to us. His tail was wagging and his head was high. He had something in his mouth. When he got a little closer I realized it was a dead kitten.

Charles turned and examined the gruesome spectacle. "Kitty sleeping!" he said.

"Ha-ha, yeah, kitty . . . sleeping," I said.

"Oh geez, sorry," Carl said. He shooed the dog out of the barn. "Been a while since he did that," he said nonchalantly.

"Kids, we're not in Baltimore anymore," I said.

"Kitty sleeping," Jack said.

That first summer we spent many of our evenings and days down at Voyageur's View, the Brumwells' campground and tubing business. The place had kind of a perpetual spring break vibe—on the weekends in particular big groups of college-age kids would rent out campgrounds and spend the days drinking on the river and the nights drinking by the fire. Large groups would often come down from Canada—the border was only ninety minutes away. Those groups had a particular reputation for rowdiness. Canadian kids evidently treated Red Lake Falls the same way American kids treated, say, Tijuana—a place to drink and go wild south of the border.

But as many people in town explained, when the Brumwell siblings took over the business from their dad, Dick, they actually cleaned things up a lot—requiring advance reservations to camp and cutting down on after-dark partying, among other things—in an effort to put a more family-friendly face on the business. It seemed that everyone in town under a certain age had worked at the campground as a teen one summer or another, and they all had hair-raising stories to tell—drunken brawls, knife fights, late-night debauchery of all sorts. Ryan and Jason had spent nearly all their childhood summers at the campground and partook in the madness from a young age, drinking and partying with friends and campers starting in their early teens.

Those days were over, however. They had spent enough beer-soaked nights at the campground for many lifetimes and now, as adults taking over the business, they wanted to dial things back. Folks in town generally gave them credit for their efforts, even if there was still work to be done.

One of the twins' favorite things to do at the campground was ride around in the short red bus the Brumwells used to deliver firewood to the various campsites. They'd clamber into the back, where the seats were stripped out and replaced with a wobbly pile of firewood rising up to the ceiling, and then hold on for dear life as Ryan or Jason or whoever tore ass around the property, stopping to drop off wood and shoot the shit with their often drunk clientele.

Briana and I were mortified the first time they did this—is there anything more dangerous than letting a two-year-old bang around on top of an unsecured wood pile in the back of a bus rattling down a bumpy dirt road? But the Brumwells seemed unfazed by it, as if it were something they did every day. Eventually their ease became ours.

The campground was an education for all of us that summer. The boys got to ride around the place on all manner of recreational vehicles the Brumwells had lying about—golf carts and ATVs and beat-up old buses. Going fast, off-road, atop a vehicle powered by a combustion engine was simply part of the fabric of childhood out here. For the boys' third birthdays Briana and I had got them tricycles. I had dreams of teaching them the simple pleasures of being outdoors on a bicycle. But the Brumwells one-upped us by getting them Power Wheels, the little battery-operated vehicles that kids sit on and operate with the push of a button. I was trying to teach them the joys of human-powered transit, but the Brumwells were giving them an education in how kids in rural Minnesota got around.

The nights at the campground tended to go late. One of the most disorienting things we experienced after the move was the length of the late spring and early summer days in northern Minnesota, on account of how far north we were. Red Lake Falls is farther north than the northernmost tip of Maine. It's farther north than Toronto, Montreal, and Quebec City in Canada. In fact, it's farther north than more than half the entire population of Canada, owing to how much of the Canadian population is packed into the southernmost section of the country that dips down into the Great Lakes. Demographically speaking, it's accurate to say that Red Lake Falls is farther north than Canada.

The extreme latitude means that summer days run long. On the solstice the sun doesn't set until 9:30 p.m., a full hour later than in D.C. But the sky remains light far longer than that, owing to the tilt of the planet. True darkness doesn't arrive until well after midnight, and the sky begins to lighten again less than ninety minutes later. D.C., on the other hand, gets more than five hours of total darkness on the summer solstice.

The long evenings mean that the neighborhood kids are often out late on summer nights. The playground at the park down the road didn't really start to get hopping until about eight o'clock at night. One evening one of Melissa Benoit's sons, four-year-old Henry, rang the doorbell to see if Jack and Charles wanted to play. It was quarter after nine.

That playground was something else to get used to. It was made of wood and steel and dated back at least to the time the Brumwell boys were small children, and maybe even earlier. It was huge, towering at least three times the height of the more safety-oriented play structures the twins knew from Maryland. The slides were fast and the modern safety features, like rubberized surfaces and rounded corners, were virtually nonexistent. It was the kind of place where a kid could really break a femur. Naturally, the twins loved it.

One thing we couldn't get over about the neighbor-hood kids was how nice they were. Even the older kids would welcome Jack and Charlie into their games that summer. Without any prompting they'd help the little ones clamber up a difficult playground ladder, or loosen the rules of whatever games they were playing to accommodate the clumsy toddlers.

Briana and I had never seen anything quite like it. When I was a kid, for instance, if a younger child attempted to horn in on whatever game we were playing we'd tell them to fuck off, in exactly those words. Here, however, the kids were kind, warm, welcoming to little strangers. You could tell that they enjoyed it, too—they weren't taking Jack and Charlie under their wings simply because adults expected them to.

One day we saw a group of older kids, maybe twelve or thirteen years old, hanging out by one section of the playground. One of them was holding what appeared to be a packet of cigarettes, and they were all discussing it heatedly. They had clearly found it in the park and were trying to decide what to do with it. In upstate New York in the early 1990s there would have been no question: we'd take those cigarettes off to a secluded corner of the woods and then we'd smoke them.

Imagine my surprise, then, when the kid holding the smokes eventually broke off from the group and walked over to the garbage can near Briana and me and tossed them in. "We found these in the park," the kid said. "And we didn't want the little kids to pick them up so we're throwing them out."

"That . . . is absolutely the correct thing to do?" I said, dumbfounded. Was this some kind of weird trick they were playing? Like some kind of knockout game variant where they were gonna crack me over the head with a rock and then put it up on Snapchat? But no, they tossed the cigarettes away and then went back to whatever it was they had been doing before.

"Did that really just happen?" I asked Briana.

"That really just happened." Rates of teen smoking have fallen by roughly 75 percent since the two of us were in high school, so perhaps we shouldn't have been so surprised.

These Minnesota kids are okay, I thought. We might actually make it here.

CHAPTER 4

The transition from commuting to D.C. to working from home was, so far, everything I could have hoped for. We would get up early with the boys, get them fed and dressed, and then I'd head down to the office, coffee in hand, to fire up Twitter and catch up on whatever fresh horrors the 2016 campaign was dishing up on that particular day.

Things were proving to be more challenging for Briana, however. She had the hardest of our two jobs: managing the children all day long. She would take them on hikes at a local nature preserve or go on a day trip to see the headwaters of the Mississippi on Lake Itasca, ninety minutes away. But whatever the drawbacks of working for the federal government, there was no question that her new bosses, at three years old, were proving much more difficult to manage than her old ones.

Our new life was, in some ways, a double whammy: she was feeling both the acute isolation of being cooped up at home with small children all day, and the loss of the many close friendships she had forged in Maryland. Unlike me, she thrives on human contact. She missed her "tribe"—friends, coworkers, fellow moms—back in Ellicott City.

Briana and I are, strictly speaking, high school sweethearts. We met the summer after my senior and her junior year of high school, interns at a biological research station on Otsego Lake in Cooperstown, New York.

Briana and I sparked a friendship, then a romance, over tubs of seaweed and cultures of fecal bacteria in the lab. I went off to college at Cornell University and a year later she followed. We dated through most of college, with a few breakups thrown in for good measure. And we married not too long afterward, when I was just twenty-four and she twenty-three.

From a big-picture economic standpoint our upbringings hadn't been too different—if the Ingrahams were middle-middle class for upstate New York in the 1990s, the Wilsons were lower-middle. She was one of four children in a very religious military family. In the course of her childhood her dad had been stationed in Pennsylvania, Georgia, Germany, and Arizona, so she had moved around a lot. After her dad retired from the military when she was ten, they moved to the tiny town of Jordanville in upstate New York to be closer to family roots.

Their first night in Jordanville the family stayed in a camper on the property where their new home was being built. It was nearly finished and would be move-in ready in a day or two. That night the family was awoken by the sound of shattering glass. Briana's dad jumped out of the camper and ran toward the house, where he found several young men in the midst of trashing the place—smashing windows, kicking in cabinets and

doors, tearing fixtures off the walls. The men fled to a
pickup truck and drove off. In the course of speaking
with the police and other people in the community they
found out that a rumor had been started that Briana's
mother was black. Somebody had paid a group of yo-
kels twenty bucks to trash the house and send a message that "that's not okay around here." Briana's entire
family is white but it didn't matter. In upstate New York
in 1991, the mere rumor that a black person was coming to town was enough to prod the good old boys into
action. Briana's dad got the plate number of the escape
vehicle and gave it to the police. The police told him that
the truck owner denied he was involved and that there
wasn't anything else they could do about it. The racially
motivated violence would go unpunished and uninves-
tigated. Welcome to New York.

For most of her childhood her family was just barely
holding on to the bottom rung of the middle class. They
were fiercely proud of the fact that they never had to
rely on food stamps, and looked down on those who did
with a ferocity that only people who've barely missed
the cutoff for government assistance will understand.

Briana's mom wanted her to be a nun, but by the time
she was in her teens Briana had gotten other ideas in her
head. She was the only one of her siblings to fully throw
herself into her studies at school, driven in part by her
Catholic-girl fear of letting down the adults in her life.
But even at a young age, she knew she wanted a better
future for herself than what her parents were able to provide. A foundational moment in her childhood happened

at the age of twelve, when she stumbled upon her mom's bank statement and saw that the balance was negative. "How could a family have less than zero?" she asked herself. At that moment the precariousness of her parents' financial situation became apparent to her, and as she tells it she vowed to herself, that day, that she would do whatever it took to ensure that as an adult, there was never a negative balance on her own bank statement.

She excelled at school—she was involved in sports. Art. Singing. Theater. She didn't just join academic clubs, she became the president of them. With that drive came opportunities from completely outside the family orbit—an Outward Bound trip to Maine, environmental camp in the Catskills, a congressional youth leadership summit in D.C., a summer scientific excursion to Puerto Rico. Since her parents couldn't pitch in to cover family costs, Bri saved up the money herself from the jobs she worked after school, and researched and applied for all sorts of scholarships and grant programs to help make the trips a reality.

Those trips had opened her eyes to the possibilities of the world that lay far beyond the borders of Jordanville, and by the age of seventeen she had come to see the small town as a dead end and couldn't wait to go off to a four-year college—the first in her family to do so. We met that summer, when she was headed into her senior year and I was already off to Cornell. In the throes of a summer romance she decided to apply there, too, and unlike myself (the beneficiary of legacy admission preferences, thanks to my dad) she qualified for admission solely on the basis of her own talent and drive. She was one of just a handful of students in her graduating high school class of eighteen kids to attend a four-year school, and it was an Ivy League one at that.

From the minute she set foot in Ithaca, New York, the town of Jordanville represented the past, a place of limited viewpoints and few opportunities. It would always be her childhood home, with all the attendant messiness and complication, but it stood in opposition to the bigger, brighter, more exciting world beyond.

She dove into her studies at Cornell with the same enthusiasm she'd shown in high school, managing a double major, a double minor, and a year abroad in Geneva, Switzerland, some theater and singing for extracurriculars, all while also working constantly at two, sometimes three jobs to support herself (her parents had made it clear from day one that any educational expenses were hers alone to bear).

From Cornell we traveled together to Southern California for an ill-fated year at the University of California, Irvine. I was enrolled in an English PhD program, primarily because I dreaded the idea of entering the workforce and wanted to prolong the lazy academic lifestyle for as long as possible. She was working on a master's in history.

That year I essentially crashed and burned; having lived in bucolic corners of upstate New York my entire life, the suburban madness of Orange County was simply too much to bear. I stopped going to class and spent my days mountain biking, the landscape (or what was

Where Briana and I have lived together

left of it) being the area's one redeeming feature. Briana, having bounced all over the place as a child, was more adaptable. She didn't much care for the place, its materialism, its politics, its utter unaffordability. But she didn't mind it as much as I did, either. It was just another place, after all, like Pennsylvania or Arizona or Germany.

I ended the year with two "did not completes" and an F on my aborted graduate school transcript. Briana, on the other hand, had managed to accelerate her coursework and escape with her master's degree a full year early, despite the additional burden of a thirty-hour-a-week waitressing job to help pay the bills. At the end of the academic year we fled to Vermont, and then several years later Briana's government job brought us to Baltimore, where she went to work for the Social Security Administration.

She excelled at her job, rising up rapidly through the

ranks on the basis of her talent and her enthusiasm for the work. She solved thorny policy problems in the disability arena, helping spearhead an initiative that drastically reduced the waiting times for federal disability assistance for people with the most intractable medical conditions.

There were headaches, of course, but the work provided a deep sense of meaning—she could confidently say that she was helping people, that the world was made a better place by her actions. Plus, the job was the ticket to the solid middle-class security that life at her parents' house had lacked. It had become a big part of who she was.

Now, in Minnesota, that part of her identity had been stripped away. It's a shock to go from days filled with meetings and high-stakes policy decisions to the full-time care of two small children. You start to forget what it's like to be a professional adult. The person that you are slowly gets replaced by the person your kids need you to be. Every parent goes through this on some level, but Briana experienced this transition in its most extreme form.

We talked a lot about it those first few months, after the kids went to bed. Or rather, she did—I'm a crappy conversationalist but a half-decent listener. It wasn't that she regretted the move, exactly, but it was a big change for her in a way that it wasn't for me. I still had a job, coworkers, obligations to the wider world. She no longer had any of those things. I tried to tell her things to put the situation in the best light. Think of all the

time we have now, I'd say. All the things you get to experience with the kids that you missed before. Think of
the incredible privilege we have to be in this situation.

The privilege, of course, was all mine, and she reminded me of that. There's nothing privileged about
chasing three-year-olds around all day. Nothing privileged about being thousands of miles away from your
dearest friends. Nothing privileged about giving up a
career that you worked decades toward.

There were good moments in those first few months,
magical ones even. But there was no doubt she was
in a funk. It was proving more difficult than I'd expected, too. One thing that we, as a society, don't fully
acknowledge is just how difficult, how taxing, how
utterly exhausting and draining it is to care for little children. It is *work*, in the purest, rawest sense of
the word. And in early childhood, a time of screaming and fighting and boundary-pushing and frustration and potty training and neediness, above all the
endless, incessant neediness, the rewards can be few
and far between. I would get off work and go straight
into the living room to relieve Briana from twin duty.
There were many days when I missed that long commute, the hours of peace and quiet on the train. The
twins were just so much.

I began to doubt whether we'd make it here. The
strain it was all putting on her made me nervous.
Maybe she was heading toward a meltdown like the
one I'd had in Southern California, where I couldn't
take it anymore, just had to get out, as far away as pos-

sible. I had made us abandon SoCal, so it would only be proper and fitting for us to leave Minnesota for her sake.

But Briana, as I should have known, is a much stronger person than I am.

We started by putting the kids in day care a day or two a week, with Jason Brumwell's sister, Heather. It felt like a weird thing to do at first—wasn't the whole point of coming out here to get the kids *out* of day care? But Briana needed it, and hell, I needed it, too. The extra time freed her up to respond to one of the probably dozens of volunteer opportunities that people had dangled in front of us since we got here.

She started with the Zehlians, a local chapter of the General Federation of Women's Clubs. It's a service club, and they put her to work doing everything from teaching art history to fourth graders to delivering meals on wheels. Then she joined the board of the Northwest Minnesota Arts Council, a nonprofit funding arts projects in the region. Then a local chorus. Then the University of Minnesota, Crookston Concert Band, which happened to be short on oboe players. At the urging of Dick Brumwell, she rounded up some local business leaders to restart the Red Lake Falls Civic and Commerce Committee.

Soon she was being invited by various civic groups all around the region to deliver talks about our experience moving out here. I had been doing this as well, until the *Post* put the kibosh on it—scrutiny on the media is tighter than ever these days, and my bosses didn't want to give the impression that their reporter was in the pocket of the Northwest Minnesota Soybean Growers' Association.

After one of these events, Briana overheard a pair of women talking in the lobby.

"I saw her husband give a talk about their move, too," one of them said. "Honestly hers was a lot better."

But that remark encapsulates a lot of Briana's experience of moving out here. When we first got here, it irked her somewhat to be known primarily as "that reporter's wife." Now, more often than not, people in the area know *me* as "Briana Ingraham's husband." My identity basically hasn't changed since coming out here—I'm still the *Washington Post* reporter. But she's had to rebuild hers from the ground up: first as a mother, then as a volunteer, and now as a pillar of her community—a phrase I'm able to say, for the first time in my life, without the slightest hint of irony. Because there's a true *community* out here, in a way that there wasn't in upstate New York, or in Vermont, or in Maryland. And a community like this one needs people like Briana—people who thrive on making things better. It's not a difference that you'd necessarily even notice if you were just driving through a place like Red Lake Falls. You have to live here for a while to understand it, have to feel how people like Briana, and the Brumwells, and Al Buse are the lifeblood of a small town.

CHAPTER 5

This is going to sound strange to anyone who hasn't spent much time in the Midwest, but the prairie is a lot like the ocean. It's broad and vast and flat and has a way of making you feel tiny, insignificant, but in a good way. The texture of the landscape is also constantly changing: black soil sprouting tiny shoots in the spring, growing to a green riot in the summer and then turning to shades of gold and brown in the autumn, and then finally, as winter approaches, returning to black as the last remnants of the harvest are plowed back under to await the spring.

In the summer you can sit by a field and watch the wind blow its designs on the tassels of the corn, as mesmerizing as a rolling sea. It's hard to learn to appreciate these things from the window of a car going eighty miles an hour down a highway, which is how most of us experience farm country (if at all). But as our first summer in Red Lake Falls went on we were learning to watch and listen to the land. The boys acquired an odd taste for dried soybeans and the freshly hulled wheat kernels that a friend who worked at the local grain elevator had dropped off in a bucket—"wheat crunchies," they called them. One day in late summer as we drove out of town on some errand or another I pointed out to the boys a lumbering green machine ambling through the fields. "Check out that tractor," I said.

"No, it's a combine," Charles said matter-of-factly.

Exactly one year, to the day, after I had penned the initial story that eventually brought us to Red Lake Falls, I sat in a dunk tank in the parking lot of the American Legion, on Main Street, as part of a fund-raiser for the town pool.

Being in a dunk tank is one of the few occasions a grown-up can hurl invective at elementary school kids in public without fear of censure, and I took full advantage as kids stepped up and lobbed softballs in my direction. But the finest arms of J. A. Hughes Elementary School were out in force that day and they were hungry for revenge—I was dunked into the lukewarm tank, mercilessly, over and over as kids squealed in delight, a fitting vengeance for the journalistic malfeasance I had inflicted upon the unsuspecting town.

Red Lake Falls isn't a wealthy community by any stretch. But when there's a call for help people respond. That day in August, for instance, the town of 1,400 people managed to pull together $70,000 to fund some needed maintenance on the town pool—the equivalent of $52 for every single man, woman, and child in the community.

Service and volunteerism—the forces that keep many rural Minnesota towns afloat—happen to be the same things Briana thrives on. Economists and demographers have a name for this—social capital. "The links, shared values and understandings in society that enable individuals and groups to trust each other and so work together," as the Organisation for Economic Co-operation and Development puts it. Many places in America are suffering from a social capital deficit, most famously outlined by sociologist Robert Putnam in his book *Bowling Alone*. Americans are withdrawing from one another, Putnam's argument goes. Social trust is declining, neighbors are becoming strangers to one another, political divisions are putting up walls between people. Instead of joining a league to bowl with others, we're increasingly just bowling by ourselves—if we get out of our houses and away from our screens at all.

One way sociologists indirectly measure social capital is via census response rates. People who take the time and effort to diligently fill out their census questionnaires every ten years are, the thinking goes, more likely to be civically and socially engaged in their communities. They understand or intuit that an accurate census count is necessary for a representative government to function properly.

As it turns out, the upper Midwest has the nation's highest rates of census response. Red Lake County's response rate of over 86 percent puts it in the top tier of counties nationwide on that measure. By contrast, the median U.S. county's response rate is 81 percent. Some of the lowest rates of response are found in places like Alabama, where in one county fewer than half of residents filled out their census forms in 2010.

You don't even need to trust the spreadsheet on this one: spend a little bit of time in a place like Red Lake

County and it's impossible not to notice that people here are highly invested in their community. See that little park with the gazebo on Main Street? Dick Brumwell built it as a memorial to his late wife, Diane. See that garden on the hill across the street from the county courthouse? That's a project of the local Lion's Club. See that train-shaped light display on the old railroad trestle during the holidays? That's the brainchild of Jim Benoit, who thought people should have something nice to look at when they drive into town.

Social capital is built, in part, on trust. Americans, in general, have grown more wary of their neighbors over the years. Data from the General Social Survey, a long-running survey of American attitudes, show that the share of Americans saying most people can be trusted has fallen from nearly 50 percent in the 1970s to just over 30 percent today. A 2014 YouGov survey found that more than three-quarters of Americans said they keep their doors locked when they are at home.

In Red Lake Falls, on the other hand, I haven't met anyone who locks their doors when they're at home. Many rarely even lock their doors when they're not home. People here trust each other so much that they often leave their cars running with the keys in the ignition when they run into Brent's to pick up some groceries. Neighborhood kids, as I've mentioned, often run about unsupervised well into the evening hours—not a problem when you trust the folks in your neighborhood to keep an eye out for any trouble. And of course there was the time Dick Brumwell wrote us a five-hundred-dollar earnest-money check for the house we eventually bought, despite his having known us for approximately thirty-six hours.

Crime in Red Lake Falls is virtually nonexistent— mostly bad checks and the occasional drunk driver, if the weekly sheriff's report in the *Gazette* is to be believed. The latest county-level federal crime data for Red Lake County, from 2014, show that that year there were 0 murders, 0 rapes, 0 armed robberies, 1 aggravated assault, and 13 reported instances of property crime in the county. That works out to a violent crime rate of about 25 cases per 100,000, or one-fifteenth of the national average.

In 2018 I got summoned to serve on jury duty at the county courthouse. It was essentially a three-month, on-call deal: I had to be ready to show up for any cases that came to trial in a three-month period. To my disappointment, none did.

Trust and social capital are so high in Red Lake County in part because it's so demographically homogeneous. A number of researchers, including Robert Putnam, have noted with some dismay that diversity tends to erode social capital. Americans simply tend to trust people more when those people look like them. Red Lake County, if you'll recall, is 93 percent white. It's one of the whitest counties in the country. The biggest demographic schism is between Catholics and Lutherans.

I've thought a lot about this during our time here. Would the people of Red Lake Falls have been so welcoming if I were, say, a black reporter? And what about me—would I have moved my family halfway across the country if the ugliest county had turned out to be, say, a majority-Hispanic county along the Mexican border?

I wish I could answer an unequivocal yes to both those questions but the truth is I don't know. Social scientists know that all of us are subject to beliefs and attitudes that are motivated by racial attitudes we barely understand or are even aware of. The technical term for this is "implicit bias," which is really just a polite way of saying "racism."

What I can say definitively is that, as a white guy, I see a lot less casual racism tossed around in Red Lake County than I've seen in upstate New York. Not long after the twins were born, for instance, Briana and I visited a bar in the town of Little Falls, New York, near her parents' home. At the end of the night we stopped on our way out and struck up a drunken conversation with an older couple who were standing outside having a smoke. Somehow the topic of kids came up and we mentioned we had twins.

"Oh, good," the man said. "Be sure to raise them white."

"Raise them right?" Briana asked. We thought we had misheard.

"Raise them *white*," he said, poking the air with his cigarette for emphasis.

We didn't need to ask what that meant. "White" was code for "one of us," an upstanding citizen, a full person, a member of the in-group. Nonwhite would be, well, everything else—everything wrong with the world.

Imagine what kind of environment you have to live in—what kind of people you have to surround yourself with, the types of things you have to believe and discuss with them on a regular basis—that telling strangers to raise their kids white is a just a normal utterance that pops out in the course of a casual conversation. How saturated with racist ideology does a community have to be before "raise them white" passes almost for a greeting between strangers on the street?

Briana exploded with rage before I even fully registered the comment. "What the FUCK?" she yelled, stepping up close to them. "Who says that? WHAT THE FUCK IS WRONG WITH YOU?"

I had known her for about fifteen years at this point and had never seen her like this. I had to physically pull her away from the situation, dragging her toward the car as she screamed profanities at the couple. My only thought was avoiding a brawl with drunk racists outside a Little Falls dive bar at 1 a.m. on a Saturday.

That's upstate New York, where a lot of people assume that it's safe to say racist things if you're talking to another white person. You're on the "same team," after all.

In conservative, rural northwest Minnesota, by contrast, I've never observed even the slightest inkling of these things. I don't assume it's some magical realm where racism doesn't exist—Minnesota folks are subject to prejudices just like anyone else. But any racism here isn't the type that openly speaks its name to fellow white strangers on the street.

Research, incidentally, backs this up. In 2015 an economist named Seth Stephens-Davidowitz compiled reams of Google search data on variants of the n-word. He controlled for usage that wasn't as likely to be linked to prejudicial attitudes—for instance, appearances of the word in the context of hip-hop lyrics.

That study found that the highest percentage of racist Google searches occurred along much of the Appalachians, extended well into upstate New York and parts of New England. Certain pockets of the South, unsurprisingly, were also hotbeds of search engine racism.

Nearly every region of the study west of the Mississippi, by contrast, had much lower than average instances of racist Google searches. That includes nearly all of Minnesota, with the exception of the northeastern region of the state.

Again, this doesn't mean that those regions have liberated themselves from racism. It only means that the prejudices at work in those parts of the country aren't the type that you type directly into your Web browser, looking for racist jokes, perhaps, or for like-minded people to subject to a rant.

Jack and Charlie's godparents happen to be black, close friends of ours from Maryland. Kelly, the twins' godmother, worked with Briana at Social Security. "How are you gonna expose those boys to different cultures when you're living all the way up there?" Kelly asked us once.

It was a good question. How do you raise children to

appreciate everything the world has to offer when you live hours from the nearest "real" city? Would we be depriving them of the rich cultural experiences that cities and more diverse areas provide by raising them in Minnesota? Kelly and her husband, Sean, have come out to visit us a couple of times now. They had their concerns, initially. During Kelly's first visit here, for instance, she had been worried about driving while black in northwest Minnesota. She didn't have any issues, fortunately, not then and not during any of the other trips she's taken out here to visit. But as a black motorist visiting an area that's roughly 95 percent white, it's the kind of thing that never really leaves your mind.

After several trips out here, experiencing the place, meeting the Brumwells and some of the other folks in the area, Kelly and Sean feel a little more at ease about their godsons' upbringing. Sean grew up in a tiny little community in Virginia, just a few thousand people. So he understands the draw of the small-town life, even if it's not what he chose for his own kids. But they still do little things to make sure the boys don't lose touch with their Baltimore roots. They made the boys an "essential black music" Amazon playlist, for instance—Prince, Stevie Wonder, Al Green, the classics. For Christmas in 2018 Kelly and Sean got the boys a book called *K Is for Kwanzaa*. I'm reasonably certain they're the only six-year-olds in northern Minnesota who know what a dashiki is.

On the other hand, there is culture of a sort up here— plenty of it, in fact. Norwegian festivals abound in the summer, where you can eat lefse, learn about Scandinavian history, and watch re-creations of famous Viking battles. There's a rich agricultural tradition in the area, memorialized in places like the Tri River Pioneer Museum in Plummer, the Engelstad Pioneer Village in Thief River Falls, and the annual Western Minnesota Steam Threshers' Reunion in the town of Rollag.

Every fall L'Association des Français du Nord, a local nonprofit, hosts a French-Canadian festival in the largely forgotten town of Huot, in eastern Red Lake County. The festival draws French-Canadian musicians and artists, as well as members of the Métis Nation—a primarily Canadian community of mixed Native American and Anglo-French heritage.

There is culture and diversity here, in other words; it's just the type that you have to actively make an effort to seek out and experience. It's not like living in a big diverse city, where you can experience the world simply by walking down the street.

We did, however, find Minnesota culture to be sorely lacking in at least one respect: the food. Minnesotans have forged deep attachments to their culinary traditions over the years, which is unfortunate because Minnesota food is almost universally bad. Minnesotans are particularly fond of "hot dish," which is a folksy midwestern term for what normal people refer to as casserole.

Minnesotans wax rhapsodic about their hot dish, particularly to newcomers. This is puzzling—during my childhood, casserole was typically something my mom made when she was too busy to cook a proper meal.

Casserole was always something to be served with an apology. In my experience there's little to distinguish Minnesota hot dish from casseroles served elsewhere. It typically consists of a mishmash of spare ingredients held together with a glue of cream of mushroom soup.

Minnesotans are particularly fond of "tater tot hot dish," which is basically a casserole in which one of the ingredients is frozen, pre-made tater tots. It tastes about as good as it sounds, although Minnesotans consider it the ne plus ultra of upper midwestern cuisine.

Hot dish is probably held in such high regard in part because Minnesotans have very little in the way of real cuisine to compare it to. The dominant culinary tradition in the state is Norwegian, and if you aren't familiar with Norwegian food it's probably because there's very little reason to eat it outside of Norway. The most famous Norwegian dish in Minnesota is lutefisk, which is freeze-dried cod reconstituted to a gelatinous texture and baked in an oven. It's exactly as appealing as it sounds.

Minnesota's lutefisk tradition is largely kept alive in community suppers held in the basements of Lutheran churches around the holidays. Nobody in Minnesota actually *likes* lutefisk, but they hold on to the tradition partly out of spite (if I had to eat this as a kid, the thinking goes, then I'm going to subject my own kids to it as well), and partly because when it comes to food there simply isn't a whole lot else to cling to.

The counterpart to lutefisk is lefse, which is a bland flatbread whose primary appeal is that it isn't lutefisk.

Lefse is *okay*. It's a perfectly serviceable product for human beings to ingest. If you were a member of an advanced alien civilization raising a large number of humans as pets, you'd probably feed them lefse for the same reason that alfalfa pellets are fed to captive rabbits: it provides adequate nutrition and is not likely to upset anyone's stomach. Lefse is what a food scientist would invent if she were tasked with creating a less exciting alternative to white bread. Lefse is fine.

There's also walleye, of course, a favorite of anglers that Minnesotans rave about despite it being a perfectly unremarkable type of whitefish. Like lefse, walleye benefits from the comparison with lutefisk. Minnesotans love walleye; it's the state fish and the Department of Natural Resources keeps strict quotas on the number that anglers are allowed to catch and keep in a season. Walleye is the lefse of fish: bland and inoffensive, and cherished by Minnesotans simply because it's here.

Minnesotans view intense flavors with suspicion. The driving principle behind Minnesota cuisine is blandness: if in doubt, add water, flour, or mayonnaise. Minnesotans display a quiet sense of pride at taking their coffee black, for instance, but this is only because what passes for coffee here would be charitably described as coffee-flavored water elsewhere.

In 1984 the Minnesota legislature designated an official state beverage: milk.

Minnesota pizza is universally bad. Shortly after we moved we ordered a takeout pizza from one of the local bars and were shocked to discover it was topped, among other things, with cheddar and American cheese. Last summer I was hanging out at the Brumwells' campground when one of the campers brought over a homemade pizza to share with the staff. It was topped, no joke, with sliced grapes. I screamed.

The best pizza in Minnesota is DiGiornio's. The second-best is Domino's. Eating any other pizza is not advised.

On another occasion we went out to try the food at the closest Mexican restaurant, which was twenty miles away, in Crookston. The fare was not noticeably different from what the median Minnesotan might be expected to concoct from an off-brand supermarket Mexican meal kit: the tacos, for instance, were topped with iceberg lettuce and shredded cheddar cheese. Perhaps they got this idea from the very popular "taco in a bag" found in hot trucks here. It's literally a bag of Doritos, with lettuce, tomatoes, and sour cream added on top.

Another product you won't find in northwest Minnesota: any type of sparkling wine drier than grape soda. Ask for "champagne" and you're likely to be served a Moscato that tastes like carbonated corn syrup. Try to order a "Prosecco" and you'll be asked to speak English, please. One benefit of a small town, though, is that you can typically wheedle storekeepers into carrying stuff you want, especially if you buy a lot of it. That's how Bri and I solved our Prosecco problem—once we explained what it was to Mike Swendra, titular owner of Mike's Bottle Shop, he was happy to keep some of it in stock for us. Judging by our monthly alcohol bill, I suspect it was a wise business move.

The sad truth is that northwest Minnesota may be one of the most culinarily impoverished regions of the nation. One thing I expected northwest Minnesota to excel at, given the popularity of hunting here, was venison. I was sorely mistaken. There is no rich tradition of venison steaks or venison rib or venison soups in this part of the country. No, the common thing to do with venison up here is to grind it up, adulterate it with large amounts of ground pork, and turn it into sausage. It's nominally referred to as "venison sausage," but you'd have a hard time distinguishing it from a typical store-bought sausage. This is partly on account of the pork adulteration, and also due to the fact that northwest Minnesota deer feast on soybeans and corn all throughout the autumn. The mild diet removes nearly all trace of gaminess from the meat, which, from the standpoint of the typical Minnesotan's taste buds, is just fine.

Adding to our own particular misery was the fact that we were saddled with two three-year-olds who were picky eaters even under optimal circumstances. Minnesota cuisine is, in fact, perfectly calibrated toward the diet of a three-year-old who refuses to eat anything other than chicken nuggets and french fries. As a result I've given up all hope of my children becoming adventurous eaters. Several weeks ago one of the twins tried a slice of Domino's pizza and complained that it was "too spicy."

Minnesotans are, however, the unacknowledged masters of one culinary realm: pickling. This is in part a reflection of their heritage: in Scandinavian countries, as in Minnesota, the growing season is short and people rely heavily on canning and pickling to make summer's flavors last through the winter.

You can't buy real Minnesota pickled products in stores—the best pickles come directly from neighbors and friends, by the jar and bucket toward the end of summer. Our first summer here, Jim Benoit, a retiree living on the south end of town, stopped by one day with a plastic ice cream tub filled to the brim with pickles from his garden. Inside, cucumber slices soaked in a broth of vinegar, onions, garlic, and what appeared to be entire dill plants. Each bite combined salt, tartness, and crunch in perfect proportion.

We found other ways around the region's food short-comings. Amazon turned out to be a lifesaver—not just for "exotic" food items, like curry paste, but also for staples that we otherwise would have had to drive long distances for: diapers. Wipes. Dog food. Cat litter.

Amazon helped ease the transition from Maryland, where we were no more than twenty minutes from a store selling literally anything we needed, to Red Lake Falls, where the nearest Home Depot's an hour away and specialty retailers are virtually nonexistent. Judging by the questions we got from some Marylanders about our move, a fair amount of city folks' reservations about moving to the country involves difficulties of buying stuff you might currently take for granted, like clothing or toys or housewares. That might have been the case thirty years ago—moving to the country might have entailed a certain type of material deprivation for the well-heeled—but Amazon and the internet in general render those concerns more or less moot.

There were notable exceptions, however. In December 2018, for instance, we decided to add a bearded dragon lizard to the family zoo. Beardies, as they're known, grow to about two feet in length, most of which is tail. One of them can be comfortably housed in a fifty-five-gallon aquarium. Their heads, necks, and the sides of their bodies are covered in rubbery spikes, which give them a misleadingly fierce appearance. They have a reputation for being outgoing and curious, and don't mind being picked up and handled the way many other reptiles do. Ours, whom we named Holly, gets particularly snuggly as she's falling asleep, and will gladly nuzzle against a warm human hand or neck or chest for comfort.

One of the first things we discovered about Holly was that she likes to eat. A lot. And the thing she loved the most when we first got her was crickets. From the get-go, I knew that keeping an ample supply of crickets on hand would require some planning. The closest pet shop, the PetSmart where we purchased her, is an hour away in Grand Forks. Restocking our cricket supply would require a time commitment of at least two hours out and back.

By Christmas Day that year, Holly's cricket supply was running low. I decided to order crickets online, a first for me, in order to save the trip to North Dakota. I bought the crickets from Fluker Farms in Louisiana, one of the more well-established online insect vendors. There are, in fact, hundreds, perhaps thousands of websites that will ship a dazzling array of live insects directly to your home—crickets and mealworms, sure, but also more exotic fare like hornworms, silkworms, black soldier fly larvae (for example, maggots), waxworms, millipedes, roaches. But as a neophyte I opted to keep things simple. 250 crickets, which seemed like a reasonable amount for a lizard who was theoretically capable of gobbling up to fifty of them every day.

I sprang for the next-day shipping to ensure there was no gap in Holly's cricket supply. But the package ended up getting delayed by a fierce blizzard that roared through the northern plains that week, dumping up to a foot of snow and sending temperatures plunging below zero. The cricket box ended up spending an unplanned overnight at a FedEx sorting facility in Grand Forks. I feared they would all be dead on arrival.

On Friday morning I anxiously met the FedEx delivery man at the door. He appeared to be relieved to unburden himself of the six inch-square box emblazoned with the words "Live Insects" and decorated with life-size cricket silhouettes. We exchanged no words. If you're a FedEx driver, you probably try to avoid conversations with the types of people who order boxes full of insects from the internet.

Having never ordered internet crickets before, I naively assumed that I'd open up the box and find the crickets in some sort of sealed bag or plastic bin to facilitate easy transfer to their final storage place in the home. I also assumed that given the near-zero temperatures we were experiencing that morning, any crickets in the box would be groggy and disoriented and easy to manage.

I was wrong on both counts.

I cut open the tape and opened the cardboard flaps and was greeted by dozens of beady little cricket eyes staring eagerly up at me. I had a brief vision of the aliens in the claw machine from *Toy Story* before the crickets started doing what they usually do when they are suddenly exposed to light—hopping maniacally. I quickly closed the flaps before too many escaped.

This was a conundrum. There was no immediate way for me to transfer 250 clearly active and ravenously hungry crickets from the box to the shallow plastic container we were storing them in at home. The only solution would be to grab a spare fish tank we had out in the shed (incidentally, the one we had briefly kept the doomed stray bunny in), which would take a bit of time, requiring a trip outside in the deep snow and chilling cold. Back at my desk, after all, I had a nearly finished story that was due to my editor. Rather than upend my workday for the sake of $11.50 worth of internet crickets, I decided to retape the box and store it in a secure location until I had time to deal with it.

In retrospect, this was a huge mistake.

Given the disruptive possibilities posed by the dog, the cat, and the twins, there was only one place where I thought I could put the cricket box without it getting overturned or split open: the bathroom adjacent to our kitchen. I put the crickets in the cabinet above the toilet and went back to work. For about twenty minutes, everything was quiet.

Just as I was about to file my story, I heard Briana, in the kitchen, utter the following words: "Where are all these goddamn crickets coming from?" I should point out here that I told her offhandedly that I had bought crickets online, but I hadn't told her when they'd arrive and she hadn't been around when FedEx came.

At this point, I reasoned that there was no crisis, that she had probably encountered one or two stray crickets that had hopped out when I initially opened the box. So I decided to keep working.

As I was making final edits to the story, I continued to hear increasingly frantic cricket-related outbursts from the kitchen. Briana later told me that she first realized something was terribly wrong when one of the cats suddenly leaped onto a pumpkin pie that had been warming on the countertop. It was going after an unusually large cricket that was munching the filling.

Eventually the commotion was too much to ignore. I went to the kitchen. Briana whipped around to face me, wild-eyed.

"So uh, remember when I said I ordered some crickets?" I said. "They got here toda—"

"*Yes, I see the crickets are here,*" she said. "*Why are they all over the kitchen?*"

"Huh," I said. "That is weird. Let me check something." I walked over to the bathroom. I opened the door.

There were crickets. Everywhere.

Crickets on the floor. Crickets on the walls. Crickets in the sink. Crickets in the toilet. A clump of at least twelve crickets were attempting to cram themselves underneath the baseboard. A cricket jumped at me from the stack of folded washcloths on the shelf. Two crickets appeared to be chasing each other around the plunger. The crickets in the toilet were propelling themselves around the bowl at an astonishing speed.

For some reason my first instinct was to flush the toilet, as if that would do anything to solve the problem of crickets in all the other places that were *not* the toilet. I shut the door. "Uh, don't come in here!" I yelled. My voice was unnaturally high from trying to force myself to sound nonchalant and cheerful.

Evidently, I had not resealed the box as well as I should have. Later inspection also revealed that in my haste to ascertain the crickets' condition, I had opened the box from the wrong side, despite the presence of large arrows indicating the proper side with an all-caps warning that read,

SEE INSIDE FLAP FOR CARE INSTRUCTIONS!

There was nothing to do now but execute the Spare Fish Tank Protocol on an emergency basis. I threw on my boots, ran out to the shed, and grabbed the spare tank. I brought it back to the bathroom, threw the box inside it, and began scooping up the strays wherever I could find them.

Roughly forty-five minutes later, the bathroom was clear. But in the interim, the earlier escapees had begun migrating elsewhere. There were crickets in the kitchen closet. Crickets in a pile of shoes. Crickets making their way downstairs to the kids' playroom. The cats were in a state of high alert, having what I can only imagine was the greatest day of their lives.

I tried to collect all of them. It was like the world's shittiest game of Pokémon. Well after the initial cleanup concluded, crickets kept turning up in inconvenient locations throughout the day. They were in the playroom and under the couch. At one point I heard Charles shout gleefully from the bathroom, "There's another cricket in the toilet!"

We did, eventually, round up all or nearly all of them, although I imagine there's still a contingent of them lurking in the kitchen closet to this day. Several days afterward, Briana approached me in the kitchen with a grave look on her face.

"The crickets made me realize something about you," she said.

"Uh-oh," I said.

"It's always been crickets in the bathroom with you. Always."

"I . . . don't follow?"

"It's the way you do things. You *try* to do the right thing, but you just . . . don't try enough." She opened a kitchen cupboard, where I had jammed all the Tupperware in a chaotic jumble. "Crickets in the bathroom," she said. She pointed near the door, where I had taken

Beardie ownership, by the bug

Holly's total bug consumption in her first 60 days

500 *crickets*

500 *mealworms*

350 *dubia roaches*

200 *black soldier fly larvae*

50 *superworms*

off my wet snow pants, jacket, and mittens and left them on the floor. "Crickets in the bathroom." She walked me to our bedroom closet, where I had placed a pile of dirty laundry on the door of the laundry chute, but hadn't bothered to actually open the door and toss the clothes all the way down. "Crickets in the bathroom." She walked me back to the living room. "Charles, come here," she said. Charles ambled over.

"Who dressed you today, Charles?" she asked.

"Daddy!"

She turned to me. "What color are his socks?"

I looked. One dark red with astronauts, the other dark blue with dinosaurs. "Well, at least they're both—"

"Crickets in the bathroom," she said.

I didn't expect the bearded dragon to prompt a profound shift in how we understood the dynamics of our marriage, but here we were.

After the great cricket escape, I switched to a live dragon food that was slower-moving, not prone to jumping, incapable of climbing slick surfaces, and not prone to chirping in the middle of the night. In mid-January the FedEx guy brought the first shipment, of many, of these wondrous new bugs. I brought the box in, placed it on the kitchen table, and opened it up.

"Aha!" I said. "See, these come in a plastic container *inside* the box! No risk of escape!"

"What are they?" Briana asked, coming over for a closer look.

"Roaches!" I popped off the top, revealing dozens of brown, scuttling creatures in a pulsating mass.

She looked me dead in the eye, turned around, and walked out of the room without saying a word.

To think that, had we still been back in Maryland, with a Petco right up the road, none of this would have happened.

As of this writing we are still married.

CHAPTER 6

But I'm getting ahead of myself now. Back to that first summer. One of the visitors to our home was a poofy long-haired orange cat. It showed up in the yard one day, got chased up a tree by Tiber, and yowled until I came over to rescue it. It followed me around for the rest of the day, and subsequently started coming over to visit every day.

The cat was extremely friendly and appeared to be fairly healthy, so it was evidently being cared for by someone. But nobody in the neighborhood seemed to know who. Jason Brumwell remarked that it had often sat at the bus stop with the kids in the mornings during the school year. Melissa Benoit said it had gotten itself into their basement one summer and was stuck there for an unknown length of time. When she finally freed it, it stuck around, so Melissa offered the cat some food, which it ate ravenously.

The cat started sleeping at our house: it had to be shooed out of the garage in the evenings, and we'd find it curled up on the rocking chair on the porch first thing in the mornings. We started feeding it. One afternoon when a particularly fierce thunderstorm rolled through town, accompanied by a tornado siren, we made sure to scoop it up from outside and bring it downstairs to the basement to huddle with the children, our pets, and us as we waited for the all-clear. From that day forth it assumed it had the right to enter the house whenever it pleased, and started pawing at the window of my office and yowling whenever it saw me in there.

Whether we liked it or not, the cat appeared to be adopting us as its owners. We called it Orange Cat, because everyone in the neighborhood just referred to it as "the orange cat." Orange Cat was shockingly gregarious, and unlike our skittish gray cat Ivy, who had always been terrified of the twins, Orange Cat would let them pet her and didn't flinch whenever they came trundling over shouting "kitty!" at the top of their lungs. I also hold certain beliefs about orange cats vis-à-vis cats of different colors, stemming from my childhood: we had a fat orange cat named Butterscotch who had a bobtail and was the best cat any boy could hope for. He wasn't shy, he loved to play, he sought out the company of people. While I do not have any hard evidence to back this up, I firmly believe that orange cats possess certain genetic traits that make them cooler and generally more bad-ass than other cats. Nearly every veterinary clinic I've been to, for instance, has a clinic cat that just loafs about the place and generally gives zero fucks about anything: those cats, in my experience, are almost always orange cats. When we lived in Vermont, our neighbors had an enormous orange cat named "Compton" for his general street smarts and devil-may-care attitude. Garfield? Orange cat. Morris, of Nine Lives fame? Orange cat. Captain

Marvel's Goose? Orange cat. Winston Churchill had an orange cat, named Jock, he loved so much that after his death, his family insisted that an orange cat be kept at Chartwell, his estate, in perpetuity.

We developed an understanding with our own Orange Cat: we would provide her food and shelter in the garage, as needed, and in return she would make herself available for pets and chin scritches to all members of the Ingraham household. She happened to be a ferocious hunter, and as a deal sweetener she took to leaving decapitated bats and choice mouse organs for us on the porch.

Everything was fine up until the day I got a text message from Heather Wallace, one of Jason's sisters: "Trouble on Facebook, you better take a look."

Indeed there was. Heather had attached a screen shot of a neighbor's Facebook status, someone I realized I still hadn't met. "Love it the new people that wrote a bad review on red lake falls moved next door to me," the guy wrote. "Today he come into my yard and steels [*sic*] my plums off my tree wow and I have never meet [*sic*] him some balls."

Wait, what?

"Not to mention feeds and houses our cat, that she no longer comes home," a woman, who appeared to be his wife, wrote in reply.

"Go tell him to quit feeding her," a friend of theirs offered.

"I'm going over there tomorrow," the woman said, rather ominously from where I was sitting.

Hoo boy. This was it, I thought. Finally. The good

people of Red Lake Falls were ready to peel back the veneer of Minnesota Nice. Shit was about to get real. You expect a certain amount of gossip in a small town—the fact that everybody knows everybody else's business is one of rural life's challenges and charms. I was ready for it. But accusations of plum theft? That was something else entirely.

The couple in question, I soon learned, lived across the back alley from us, next door to the Presbyterian church. We hadn't met them because the husband, Danny, worked on gas and oil pipelines and had been off in the Dakotas for most of the summer. His wife, Missy, and their two small kids had been with them. But they had left their cat in the care of Larry, our older neighbor across the street, for the summer, and Larry had let it freely wander the neighborhood. Now they were back in town and their cat didn't want to come home.

The allegation about the plum tree was a mystery, to say the least. I had never been over to their house. The only thing I could think was that I had spent some time in the alley trimming back some of the overgrown brush from our lawn—maybe someone had seen me there and through the game of small-town telephone, "trimming brush in the alley" had transformed into "stealing plums from the neighbors"?

Later that day I told Bri about the Facebook posts and watched all the color drain from her face. She had warned me, intermittently, that the cat probably belonged to somebody else and they'd be pissed off once it stopped coming home because we were feeding it. I had pooh-poohed these concerns—if it was somebody else's cat then what the hell was it doing in our yard all day for weeks on end?

But her fears had proven justified and now we had a mess to clean up. I was prepared to let the people come over so we could tell them to go take a shit in their hats, and if their cat was so important to them they shouldn't have left it alone in the neighborhood all summer. Briana, more diplomatically minded, insisted instead on a proactive peace offering. It was late summer and she was in a baking mood, so she said she would bake them an apple pie and I would bring it over to their house and make amends. We ran the plan by Jason Brumwell to make sure it didn't violate any unspoken small-town Minnesota norms regarding neighborliness.

"Why don't you bake them a plum pie instead?" he suggested.

"This isn't funny!" Briana yelled at him.

The next day, fresh pie in hand, I embarked on the long walk from our house to Missy and Danny's. I took Jack with me based on the purely cynical calculation that a small child would help humanize the evil out-of-town reporter and that they'd be less likely to start any serious shit in his presence.

We went to the front door and I knocked. It was answered by a petite woman with long red hair.

"So uh, I'm your new neighbor and I heard that—" I began, but I didn't get a chance to finish my opening spiel.

"Yeah, look," she said. "We left the cat with Larry over the summer, okay? And he wasn't supposed to let her outside, but we found out he kept leaving her outside, and now we're back home and she won't even come see us, I guess because you've been feeding her."

"Yeah, sorry I had no idea who she belonged to!" I said. "When she started showing up we asked around but nobody seemed to know. I guess we should have asked Larry. But anyway we're sorry, we weren't trying to like, steal your cat, I promise! Briana feels really bad and she baked you a pie." I offered the pie.

"Look, kids!" Jack said. Missy's two daughters, about Jack and Charlie's age, peered out from behind her.

"Thank you," Missy said. "Could you just . . . stop feeding her?"

"Yes, of course. What's her name, by the way? She's a great cat."

"Her name's Honey."

"Honey!" one of the girls squealed.

"That's a good name for an orange cat," I said. "Maybe some time if you want, the girls could come over and play in the yard with Jack and Charlie? They love making friends in the neighborhood."

"Yeah, sure," Missy said.

And that was it. Briana's face was pressed up against our kitchen window as Jack and I walked back. "How did it go?" she asked.

"Well. Not great? But not bad, either," I said. "I told her if her kids ever wanted to come play with Jack and Charlie they were welcome to."

"Great, now they're gonna think we're trying to steal their kids, too."

That was the end, for the time being, of the Great Orange Cat Debacle of 2016. We learned our charm offensive had worked several months later when for Christmas, Missy, out of the blue, gave us four tickets to a performance of the *Nutcracker* in Grand Forks. This was surprising to me: based on our experiences in other places where we'd lived I'd assumed that Danny and Missy were now our sworn enemies and would continue to be so until we either moved away or died. When things go south with neighbors it's often impossible to put them on the right footing again. But Danny and Missy have since become good friends. Their girls come over to play with our boys in the summers, and vice versa. And in the end, oddly enough, we ended up adopting the orange cat after all. In 2017 Danny was off to West Virginia for work on the pipeline, and Missy and the girls went with him. They were gone for much of the year and Larry was put in charge of the cat again. Eventually he told them he couldn't take it anymore—it was too much of a hassle to run over to their place every day and deal with the damn cat. So they agreed to let him see if anyone else was interested, and of course when we found out, we volunteered immediately. Now the orange cat—Honey—lives with us but still spends plenty of time with Missy, Danny, and the girls when they're in town.

Other challenges began to present themselves as our Minnesota honeymoon wound down. Finding after-hours medical care out here is not so easy. The closest urgent care facility is the hospital in Grand Forks, an

Distance to nearest E.R. or urgent care (actual routes, drawn to scale)

Our home in Ellicott City, MD   Our home in Red Lake Falls, MN

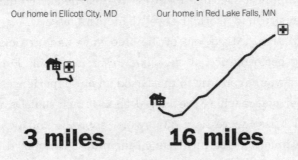

3 miles   **16 miles**

hour away, although we found that "urgent care" typ-ically means just getting checked into the emergency room. One day in the fall Jack began complaining of pain when he peed. Back in Baltimore this would have been a standard urgent care call—drive out to the place around the corner, get a quick exam, and most likely be prescribed some antibiotics. Instead Briana had to take him to the emergency room in Thief River Falls, where they did the exact same procedure but we had to pay a lot more for it out of pocket due to how our health insurance is set up.

But we really didn't appreciate the medical chal-lenges of living in a rural area until the next summer, when Jack and Charles were getting screened to enroll in preschool at the elementary school in town. We were excited to learn that the county offers universal one-day-a-week preschool. Part of the enrollment process was a standard hearing and vision screen. Charles, who had always been oddly sensitive about his ears, took great offense at having headphones placed over them and couldn't complete the screening. No worries, the staff told us, just see if you can get it done at your pediatrician's office before school starts.

The boys loved the pediatrician we had lined up for them, a Dr. Sreedharan in Thief River Falls. Charles had no problem completing the screening there but afterward Dr. S., as he told people to call him, took Briana aside.

"Has Charles ever been screened for autism?" he asked.

Dr. S. laid out the potential markers. Charles rarely made eye contact with unfamiliar people. He occasionally engaged in nontypical behaviors, like walking around the perimeter of large objects, like tables, while intently staring at them out of the corner of his eye. His cognitive abilities were quite literally off the charts—he had all his numbers memorized before the age of two. On the flip side, his expressive communication abilities were a different story. He was harder to understand, and had a much more difficult time articulating his needs, often causing him to erupt in frustration.

In the backs of our minds, we admitted to ourselves later, we had always wondered about this. Charles had lagged behind Jack on most of the big developmental milestones, like crawling and walking. Potty-training Jack had been a cinch, but Charles had been fiercely resistant to it. We knew that because they had been born six weeks prematurely they were at greater risk for autism and any number of other health problems.

Dr. Sreedharan explained that he wasn't a specialist and couldn't offer a definitive diagnosis, but it would be good to take Charles someplace where they could. There was no such facility in Thief River Falls. Ditto for Grand Forks, an hour away. The closest place was in Fargo, two hours to the south. When we called to set up an appointment, we found that they were booked out for months.

Those months, through the fall and winter of 2017, were a period of profound unease and uncertainty. If Charles was autistic, what sorts of services—speech therapy, physical therapy, and the like—would he need to live to his fullest potential, and would northwest Minnesota be able to provide them? It's one thing to move to the middle of nowhere with a healthy, self-sufficient family whose chief needs could be fulfilled by the occasional Amazon order. But how would a child with special needs fare out here? Would we be depriving him of the care he required by not living in a place like D.C. or Baltimore, where there were world-class medical facilities?

The evaluation in Fargo was less than ideal: he's not on the spectrum, they said, he's just a genius. Their "autism evaluation," as it turned out, was based largely on a written questionnaire we filled out. That wouldn't cut it as far as the school was concerned: they—and we!— wanted a rigorous clinical evaluation, which is what we thought we were going in for. The results, or lack thereof, from Fargo left us grappling with what to do next. Was there even a clinic within a thousand miles of the place that was used to dealing with kids like Charlie? Was he doomed to get written off as a "bad kid" in school just because teachers and doctors out here didn't have much experience with kids like him?

We needed another opinion. We turned to what we knew: Johns Hopkins in Baltimore.

At the Kennedy Krieger Institute's Center for Autism and Related Disorders (CARD), Charles underwent an additional two days of evaluations. He was, in fact, on the spectrum. But, as far as the doctors were concerned he'd be best off in a regular classroom with an individualized instructional plan. And he'd benefit greatly from regular speech, physical, and occupational therapy sessions to help him catch up on the skills that other kids just took for granted. The important thing at this point in his life, they stressed, was small classrooms with regular routines and familiar faces. We wanted to know if we should move back to Baltimore. Sure, they said, we could find a Maryland public school for him, but class sizes would be larger. We might be able to find a private school in Maryland that would take him on, but it would not come cheap. If we had found a great small school where he could get the assistance he needed in Minnesota, then perhaps, they suggested, we should stick with that rather than spend so much time trying to find the equivalent for Charles in Maryland.

In the years since the diagnosis, ferrying him back and forth to all those appointments—and dealing with the bills associated with them—has proven to be one of the great challenges of living here. The Pew Research Center recently reported that for the typical suburban and urban residents, the closest hospital is about a ten-minute drive away. The average rural hospital, on the other hand, is about seventeen minutes away from the average rural resident. Our nearest hospital was twenty minutes, in Thief River, but it doesn't provide any of the specialist services Charlie needs. So we've patched together a plan of care based on what's available, and what we can reach in a reasonable drive. One specialist is in Grand Forks. Another is in Crookston. One comes to the clinic in Red Lake Falls, but only periodically. Since I'm the one working, Briana bears the brunt of the ferrying duties. It's exhausting, no doubt. But then we ask ourselves: would it be any easier in Baltimore? There would probably be more options for service. But with both of us needing to work there, whoever was driving the Charlie bus would end up burning through sick time at a prodigious rate. Yes, the clinics would probably be closer. But once you factor in the traffic congestion for late afternoon appointments. the travel time would probably be similar. A ten-mile trip in suburban Maryland can easily take longer than a forty-five-mile trip in northwest Minnesota.

Once we had a diagnosis, the other big anxiety was how the community would respond. The Brumwells were the first people we told. Somehow, it was like they knew exactly what to say. Kristin Weiss, Ryan's fiancée, said simply "Oh. Well, that's his super power!" Jason quipped that he took after his father. All of them said, emphatically, that Charlie was Charlie and that this didn't change anything. It was exactly what we needed to hear.

The other wild card was the school. Would the teachers treat him differently? Was a tiny school like J. A. Hughes Elementary (typical grade size: twenty kids) be equipped to work with a kid like Charlie? Would they try to redirect him to a special ed program? We let the school know about the diagnosis, in kind of a casual "FYI" kind of manner since we didn't know what the typical protocol was. To our surprise the teachers and administrators immediately sprang into action. They bumped him up to two days a week of full-time preschool, in order to help him develop the social skills he was lacking. They worked with a special educator to put in place some in-classroom interventions, like a cool-down corner where he could take a break when he got overstimulated. They quickly performed their own evaluation, to ensure he met Minnesota state guidelines for requiring educational assistance.

Within a couple of weeks of learning about the diagnosis, the school put together a meeting between us, the principal, the pre-K teacher, a school psychologist, a special ed teacher, and a speech pathologist. They agreed that he should be in a regular classroom, on an individualized educational plan and with para-educator assistance when needed. They were extremely supportive, and to my relief and embarrassment they didn't seem to think of Charlie as a burden, or a drain on school resources. He was just a kid with a certain set of needs.

By all appearances he is currently thriving at J. A. Hughes Elementary in the town of Red Lake Falls. His kindergarten classroom is small—fifteen kids—and filled with friendly, familiar faces. As luck would have it, his kindergarten teacher, Hannah Seeger, had formerly taught special education. It is difficult to think of a more ideal environment, anywhere in the country, for a child with his specific needs than the place he is at right now. The small scale of the school drastically reduces the risk of things going south during the unstructured moments, like recess or the bus ride, that kids on the autism spectrum often have trouble with in a typical public school setting. Jason Brumwell drives the bus that picks him up for school in the morning, and Ryan drives the bus that takes him home. In larger public schools, in particular—like the ones we left behind in Maryland—kids like Charlie can easily get lost in the crowd. A special need can become a special burden, and overworked, underpaid educators can be forgiven if they don't have time to comfort a five-year-old having a meltdown because somebody else is using the crayon he wanted. Westchester Elementary, the school the boys would have attended had we stayed in Maryland, has about six hundred students. J. A. Hughes has less than a third as many. It's the kind of place where at the end of the school day, every single day, Principal Chris Bjerklie stands by the door to greet and high-five every single kid who walks out. If he can't make it, school secretary Julie Buse does it instead. In the wintertime they make sure every kid is properly attired—boots, snow pants, hat, mittens—before heading outside to face the cold.

Even with the smaller school, Charles still has his challenges, of course. He and Jack joined 4-H in kindergarten, for instance. Briana volunteers with the program, in part to keep an eye on Charlie and in part because she just enjoys helping out. One day a month they board a different bus than usual in the afternoon, which takes them to the community center in town where 4-H is held. I had some reservations about letting five-year-olds navigate an unfamiliar bus situation by themselves, but for the first few months everything went without a hitch. But then, one day in February, everything went wrong.

Jack was out sick from school that day, so the brothers wouldn't be able to look after each other the way they usually did. We found out later that Mrs. Seeger, Charlie's kindergarten teacher, was also out. So was Ryan, the usual bus driver. And on top of it all, the 4-H bus did something different that day: rather than take the 4-H kids directly to the community center it made a number of stops beforehand.

Charlie's usual support structure—brother, teacher, bus driver—wasn't in place to help him deal with the double whammy of both riding a different bus and dealing with a different route than usual on that different bus. When the bus pulled up to the community center to let the 4-H kids out, Briana realized with horror that Charlie wasn't there.

She called me. Had he gotten on his usual bus instead? No, that bus had already come and gone and he wasn't on it.

She talked to the other 4-H kids. Had Charlie been on the bus? Yes, they said. He had gotten off at an earlier stop, the one down the road. She flew out the door and ran down the road.

The temperature that day was right around zero—not too cold by northern Minnesota standards, but cold enough that a kid wandering around outside could be in some serious danger before long.

Fortunately, Charlie's snow pants are bright, Day-Glo orange—his favorite color. That was the first thing she saw, his bright orange snow pants walking down the road between two older kids. She ran up to them, breathless.

They had gotten off at the same bus stop Charlie had and he had just started walking with them, the kids said. They took him to their place and their dad, with some alarm, told them to walk him over to the county social services office, which was at the courthouse right down the road. That's what they had been doing when Bri found them.

Charles didn't seem particularly fazed by the incident, but with his expressive communication being what it was, we had a hard time figuring out his side of the story. He believed that he had gotten off the bus *after* the 4-H stop, rather than before. He saw the red brick Catholic church outside the bus and mistook it for the red brick community center. He tried to go into the church but the door was locked. He went along with the other kids because he didn't know what else to do.

It didn't end anywhere near as badly as it could have—just google "autistic child missing" for a sense of the worst-case scenarios. But it badly rattled us, and it rattled the folks at the school, too. His teacher called us. The principal called us. Jason and Ryan called us when they heard what happened. An administrator called us. Another administrator who lived in our neighborhood showed up at our door to apologize and broke down in tears.

It's hard to work out the counterfactual of how this would have played out in Baltimore schools. Would they have had five-year-olds navigating unfamiliar bus routes to begin with? Would Charlie even have been able to enroll in a regular kindergarten class with extracurricular activities? Had he gotten lost in a much larger, much stranger neighborhood, would the consequences have been much worse? Would administrators have even had time to care?

Impossible to say, in the end. What we do know is that everyone at J. A. Hughes took the incident seriously and have put in place different protocols for bus boarding to ensure something like this doesn't happen again. And when they say it won't happen again, Briana and I believe them. We can't protect a kid like Charlie from the world forever. But in a place like Red Lake Falls, he has the freedom to face a world where the scale is smaller, the faces are friendlier, and the consequences for screwups are less severe.

On the other hand, there's no question that a big school in Maryland has more to offer a bright kid than a small one in rural Minnesota. At J. A. Hughes the gym doubles as a cafeteria, and the library is used as the auditorium. There is no full-time librarian. The school shares a band teacher with the high school. Phys ed classes are mysteriously referred to as "phy ed." Sitting here it's easy to imagine all manner of wondrous, world-expanding extracurriculars that my kids are missing out on because they attend a tiny school in the middle of nowhere.

This, in fact, was one of Briana's primary concerns about moving out here. She had attended a tiny K–12 school in upstate New York—eighteen kids in her graduating class! The education she received there was substandard, at best. She was one of just four kids who went on to a four-year degree. Most of the kids simply planned to work on their parents' farms after graduation, or worse, they didn't have a plan at all. The school was poor and had little money to attract decent teachers, much less make them stick around for more than a year. Staff turnover was high. Bri had five different English teachers her senior year in high school. Most of that year was spent watching movies with various subs rather than reading real books. They didn't have Advanced Placement tests. They didn't even offer *calculus*. Briana recalls that her twelfth-grade physics teacher spent much of the class time wrestling and horsing around with the guys in her class. At the end of this year, this teacher handed another student, one of the boys who hadn't bothered to hand in any work, her lab folder. The teacher told the boy to copy what he needed from Briana's folder in order to fill out his missing work, so he wouldn't fail. Bri didn't know about any of this until after graduation.

But these drawbacks only instilled in her a desire to

rise above them all. She took advantage of every extra curricular she could get her hands on. Some of the better teachers—and there were a few—keyed her in to life-changing experiences like Outward Bound, which made her realize the world had a lot more to offer than what Owen D. Young Central School let on. She graduated valedictorian and got accepted into Cornell. She remains pissed off, to this day, that her high school math level was so below the level other incoming freshmen received that she had to take remedial classes in her first year of college, mostly because her school didn't have enough student interest in what was considered "advanced" math.

Her principal, in fact, had made a point of telling her, during her senior year, to "get off your high horse" regarding her class ranking. Owen D. Young Central School was tiny, he said. She was just a big fish in a small pond. Compared to the other kids across New York State? She was nothing.

Nevertheless, she persisted. She made it to college, and she made it out. And she—and I—want our kids to succeed *because* of what their K–12 education offers, not in spite of it. In all honesty we don't know if the schools in Red Lake Falls can make that happen. They don't offer calculus, either. Or trigonometry. They have a robotics club, but no school paper. For the time being we're pinning our hopes on two factors.

The first is that parental involvement can pick up a lot of educational slack. A kid's success in school is largely dependent on his innate curiosity and his willingness to learn new things. That's something we can help our kids develop; it just means we'll have to take on more of the work of their education ourselves. Jack, now six, wants to play the violin, for example. There's nobody at his school who can teach him that, which means we'll have to ferry him off to lessons in Thief River or Crookston.

Looking forward, the bigger point we discovered is that high school students in the state of Minnesota are allowed to take college courses, for college credit, at a local postsecondary institution for no charge through the state's Postsecondary Enrollment Options program. If we're still here by the time Jack and Charles get into high school, and they find that the courses there aren't challenging enough, we can simply ship them off to classes at the University of Minnesota in Crookston for their junior and senior years. Our neighbors Rob and Alice told us that their son Alex took advantage of this program, and they couldn't speak highly enough of it. In addition to advanced coursework he was able to get involved in the school's music and theater programs, eventually parlaying that experience into admission to the music program at Oberlin College, one of the best music departments in the country. No such program existed in New York State when Briana was watching her physics teacher tackle her classmates in lab.

For the time being, we're at a place where we know the elementary education being offered to the boys is ideal, particularly for Charles. And we know that beyond elementary school there are more challenging instructional opportunities available to the boys, should they need it. For the moment, that's enough.

Honestly, it's a relief to not have to game out the educational arms race that so many parents grapple with on the east coast: placing your toddler in the right day care, so they can get admitted to the right pre-K program, so they can go to the right private elementary school, followed by the right prep school. It's exhausting to even contemplate the triangulation necessary to put a kid through school in that kind of environment.

When there's just one school, those concerns are largely rendered moot. As a country we've become so fixated on "choice" in our educational systems that we've forgotten how freeing it can be when you don't have to choose.

Shortly after we moved, incidentally, the Annie E. Casey Foundation published its annual rankings of the best places to grow up in America. The rankings were drawn from various official data sources, concerning things like education quality, poverty and hunger, family structure, test scores, rates of grade repetition, you name it. Minnesota came out at the absolute top of the list. "Where the children are all above average," indeed.

As summer trundled into fall our first year in Minnesota, we were feeling good about things. We had made peace with the neighbors. We were figuring out the schools, the doctors, and where to buy food. Our cupboards were stocked with applesauce made with apples from our tree in our yard, and jam made with chokecherries from another. The boys were three, somewhere between toddlers and little boys, and they were becoming easier to manage. We lived in a house that, for the first time, felt truly like home. There was space to stretch out in and fresh air to breathe. Work was going well—my output hadn't imploded since leaving the D.C. newsroom. It was refreshing to be able to log off at the end of the workday, to step away from the social media madness of the news cycle and into a home life that was more grounded, more solid, in many ways more real.

It felt like we were getting everything we had hoped for when we first moved. Yet somehow, it felt like something was missing. We couldn't quite put our finger on it. The feeling didn't express itself as a lack, or a shortcoming, necessarily, but rather as a space for something more. Space that had never even been imaginable back in Maryland.

Briana blames me for suggesting what came next, and I blame her. Regardless, whichever one of us gave voice to it first didn't face much opposition from the other: "What if we tried for a girl?"

Throughout the twins' infancy we had made dark jokes about having another kid, usually during the most trying moments. One memorable day in Maryland, for instance, both twins had been sick, the drain hose to the washing machine had come undone, flooding the basement, and the dog had eaten something he shouldn't have and was alternately puking and shitting all over the house. "At least we don't have triplets!" we would say at times like those.

But we had never seriously entertained the thought of another kid in Maryland. We were barely getting by with just two of them. We, evidently, were not alone.

The U.S. fertility rate has been on a long, steady decline, from nearly ninety births per woman age fifteen to forty-four in 1970 to about sixty in 2017. A lot of that decline is due to things worth applauding: expanded access to abortion and contraceptive services, and greater autonomy for women and men to decide whether and how to have kids.

But economic pressures are playing a role in this, too. Middle-class wages have stagnated. Housing has become staggeringly expensive, particularly in coastal urban areas. Day-care and educational costs are skyrocketing. And among the world's wealthy nations, the United States remains a stubborn outlier when it comes to policies like paid parental work leave (the United States doesn't mandate any) and universal child care (ditto). In many states, day care is now more expensive than a college education.

Those competing pressures have made it more difficult than ever to have kids, and Americans aren't exactly happy about it. Data from the U.S. Centers for Disease Control and Prevention (CDC) and the General Social Survey show, for instance, that the gap between how many children women say they want to have (2.7 on average) and how many they'll actually have (1.8, on average) is the highest it's been in forty years.

If you want to be strictly utilitarian about it, you might say that policy makers have pursued such an aggressive probusiness agenda over the past forty years that they've overlooked the question of whether parents will be able to afford to continue producing the customers who will buy stuff from those businesses in the future. To be more blunt, as a country we've pursued economic policies that are good for corporations and their shareholders, but lousy for their employees and their families.

We weren't interested in producing another future Wal-Mart customer, of course. But we suddenly found ourselves in a place where we had the time, the money, the space, the community support, and the love to bring another life into the world. Given my own anti-kid past, I'm not the kind of person to go around insisting that people who don't want kids will someday change their minds, or that people who already have kids secretly want more. But our own experience does make me wonder how many other couples might not realize that, given the right circumstances, there could be space for more children, more love, in their own lives?

The big thing we were worried about was the possibility of another set of twins—or worse. Parents who have twins once are more likely to have twins if they get pregnant again. At Johns Hopkins, where the twins were born, Briana's doctor told a story one day about a couple who had twins—two boys—and then decided to try for a girl. They ended up getting pregnant with triplets, and subsequently found out that all three would be boys. The parents left the office sobbing that day.

We decided to go for it, though. Briana was pregnant within two months of going off birth control. We were greatly relieved to discover that this time there would be just one baby. Our Minnesota child was on the way.

It's 9 a.m. on a crisp northern Minnesota fall morning. I'm standing in the driveway of a Red Lake County farmhouse, decked out head to toe in hand-me-down blaze orange from the Brumwell brothers. There's a dead deer hanging from the raised bucket of a tractor in front of me. It isn't mine. Two or three guys with knives circle around it, slicing downward through gut and tendon to remove the hide.

They eventually give it a mighty tug, stripping it clear of the back and rear haunches until it remains attached only at the shanks. One final heave and the hide drops to the ground with a plop. The carcass steams in the morning sun. The farmer's dog looks up briefly from the severed foreleg it's been chewing on, and then gets back to business.

"Now that's Minnesota deer season," Dick Brumwell, who's been overseeing the whole operation, announces with a grin.

It was the opening of deer season in 2016, November 5, three days before the election. We'd been out since well before dawn, part of the local hunting party that the Brumwells have been a part of for decades. I'd shivered alone in the indigo predawn hours, listening to the birds wake up around me. I didn't see a single sign of a deer myself, which was just as well—after the group reconvened at the house in midmorning I realized that I'd forgotten to even load the rifle the Brumwells loaned me.

My own dad loved guns. He was a champion skeet shooter as a kid, and went target shooting all his life. But as a veterinarian he preferred healing animals to shooting them. As a result, while I'd shot the occasional handgun in the course of my life, I'd never been deer hunting before, much less fired a gun at an animal. The Brumwells were determined to change that.

Hunting's on the wane across America. Since 1980 the national population has grown by one hundred million, while the number of people hunting each year has slowly dwindled. Urbanization has taken its toll.

But the hunt is still huge in northwest Minnesota. Statewide nearly half a million people go hunting each year, five times as many as back in Maryland. Even if you didn't hunt it would be impossible to miss deer season up here. Once the season opens it's hard to drive a block in town without seeing a deer carcass hanging from a tree, waiting to be butchered.

Dick Brumwell and his buddy Russ Coenen, a retired high school science teacher, had been hunting the same patch of Russ's land religiously, every single year since the 1970s. As soon as Dick's kids were old enough to get a hunting license they started going out with him. As a born-again Minnesotan the Brumwells were adamant that I experience the hunt for myself. For starters that meant getting my own license. Because I'd never had one in Minnesota before, I had to take an online hunting safety course intended for teenage hunters. I had to sit through several hours of videos full of idiotic safety tips, like "do not point the gun at yourself," and then take a test afterward. Ryan and Jason thought it was hilarious. I demonstrated my on-paper hunting prowess by scoring a 92.

Now that I was qualified to haul a rifle through the woods, the next step was target practice. The brothers planned a special treat: one afternoon in late October, Ryan picked up several pounds of Tannerite from a hunting supply store in Thief River. Tannerite's an explosive that only ignites when it gets hit with a fast-moving gun round. You can pour it, shake it, throw it around, no problems. But when you shoot it, it explodes. You can find YouTube videos of guys (yes, almost always guys) stuffing old cars and appliances full of Tannerite and then nearly getting beheaded by a flying door or wheel.

We were going to stuff it into pumpkins.

"Does that really sound like a smart idea to you?" Briana asked as I geared up to join the brothers down at the campground.

"No," I said, "but I kind of have to do this. It's part of my Minnesota education."

"It's fucking stupid is what it is," she said. "Did you see the video of the guy who blew his leg off with a lawn mower full of this stuff?"

"Yeah," I said. "It's just pumpkins, though. Worst that'll happen is I get hit with a flying stem."

"Right through your eyeball and it would serve you right," she said.

In all honesty it was kind of amazing to me that you can just walk into a store and buy the stuff by the bucketload, with no special permits needed, no placement on a government watch list. But I went down to the campground, where the Brumwell boys had already laid out a veritable arsenal—handguns, long guns, everything in between.

"Pour this into that pumpkin over there," Ryan said. He handed me a bottle of Tannerite, thousands of tiny white pellets, like mini mothballs.

"Why aren't you doing it?"

"I don't feel like losing a hand today."

"It won't explode unless you shoot it, right?"

"Sure."

I filled the pumpkin up to the top. Once I'd placed it on the ground, the Brumwells handed me a rifle. "This is the one I used when I was a kid," Ryan said. "Should be just right for you." They showed me where the safety was, showed me how to load it, sat me down at a picnic table, then told me to point it at the pumpkin and pull the trigger.

"You sure this is legal?" I said. "I mean there's houses right over there."

"We're just outside town limits; anything goes out here," Jason said. "Pull that trigger, find out what freedom feels like."

I inhaled. Exhaled slightly. Held. I pulled the trigger.

The sound was cataclysmic. My understanding of gunfire acoustics is drawn primarily from video games, where small guns go "pew-pew" and big ones go "BOOM-BOOM." I was expecting a pew but the rifle BOOMed. Almost instantaneously there was a second, even louder report as the pumpkin exploded in a cloud of yellow smoke. Chunks of orange meat rained down, seeds flying everywhere with pumpkin gobs attached.

The Brumwells hooted and hollered. I hooted and hollered with them.

"Gotta tell you—I thought there was no way you'd hit it on the first shot," Ryan said.

"Yeah, well, I did score a ninety-two on that test," I said. "Hope you're not mad when I bring home a bigger buck than you."

The season started off inauspiciously, however. My alarm didn't go off on the day of, which meant Ryan had to bang on our door for ten minutes at five o'clock in the morning to wake me up, and then wait around another fifteen minutes while I rushed through the house gathering my gear for the day. That subsequently made us late to meet Jason and Dick at Jason's house, and the three of them chewed me out up one side and down another all the way on the drive out to Russ's property.

Once at Russ's, the brothers and I hopped on a four-wheeler and took a bumpy ten-minute ride through the pitch darkness, across fields and through oak woods to the stand they had decided to post me at. I didn't find out until later that it was by far the worst stand out of the dozen or so on Russ's property, being located near a dirt road and far away from any of the well-trod deer paths.

The brothers dropped me off at the stand, armed with their old rifle and a five-round magazine, bristling with cartridges that looked large enough to take down a small aircraft. Jason sent me off with a thermos of coffee, black.

And with that the brothers tore off to their respective stands.

Before I go any further I should probably clarify what "deer stand" means in Minnesota. Where I'm from, in upstate New York, a deer stand is basically a couple of planks nailed to a tree at a haphazard angle, most likely constructed under the influence of alcohol. Six people died of hunting mishaps in New York State during the 2017 deer season. Just one involved a gun. The rest involved tumbles from tree stands.

A deer stand in northwest Minnesota, by contrast, is more properly understood as a small dwelling. Nearly all the stands on Coenen's property that year, for instance, were free-standing structures. I helped the Brumwells set up a new stand there prior to the start of the season. It towered above the ground on a base of four-by-four pressure-treated timber posts. It had four square walls and a sloped roof, precision-engineered by Dick back at the workshop at the campground. From each wall, a sliding Plexiglas bus window provided a commanding view of the surrounding terrain. The interiors of the walls were covered with foam insulation board, to keep the chill out, while the exterior was clad in vinyl siding. Two large northern Minnesota men could sit comfortably in the cabin side by side. The flooring extended several feet beyond one of the walls to provide a sort of patio.

But the Brumwells' stands were downright spartan

compared to some of the other options locals spring for. There are companies that sell luxurious molded plastic or fiberglass structures with upward of eight sides to ensure an optimal shooting angle no matter which way the deer approach from. They resemble nothing more than World War II pillboxes on stilts. Russ himself had one of these, erected at the top of a hill with sight lanes cut through the forest at every angle for maximum visibility.

As the new man in the group I was afforded none of these luxuries, although my stand was still a palace by upstate New York standards. It was at least a decade old and accessed via a rickety hatch in the floor. When I stationed myself within it, perched on a folding chair, each of the four walls was just inches from my body. It was insulated with scraps of foamboard presumably left over from more lavish projects, but most of them were falling off the walls, gnawed for years by whatever rodents I heard skittering about the structure as I settled myself in for the morning. The windows were aluminum-framed rejects from one of the campground buses and most of them appeared to be wedged shut. I managed to open one just a crack, producing a screeching sound that was certain to scare off any mammals within a three-hundred-yard radius. Due to the cramped quarters I had difficulty finding an angle to lean my rifle that didn't end up pointing the muzzle toward my face. The Brumwells had lent me a portable propane heater, which, they assured me, was safe to use in close quarters and presented no danger of asphyxiation by carbon monoxide. I was nervous about using it, but even with the unseasonable warmth that day—it was about 30 degrees—eventually the chill became so intense that I had little choice. Orange waves of sublimating propane radiated across the surface of the heater. I was terrified to move, lest I accidentally catch a bit of cloth on it and send the entire structure up in flames.

Still, after some time I began to relax, watching the inky black sky turn purple and eventually a deep navy blue. Around the time the birds began to wake, the silence started to be punctuated by distant rifle shots, rich and booming, like fireworks heard from a distance. The hunt was on.

Judging by the thunderous reports coming in it sounded as if hunters were picking off deer in every direction. But as the sky continued to lighten I still hadn't seen a single one. I fidgeted in my seat, craning my neck toward all four windows. Not so much as a squirrel rustling in the underbrush. Suddenly I heard an unidentifiable noise. It sounded like something big. I froze, felt my muscles tense, reached for my rifle. I held it close and continued to listen. There it was again! It was a moo. *A fucking moo.* The cows at the nearby farm were waking up. I sank back into my seat.

By this point I had to take a leak something fierce. Figured I may as well make my way down to ground level and stretch my legs. Problem: it was so cramped in the stand that I couldn't figure out how to open the hatch beneath me, which took up almost the entire floor, without somehow wedging myself between the walls and dangling above it, Spider-Man style. After spending twenty minutes repeatedly shifting myself, the heater, the chair, and the gun around in the stand, like one of those awful sliding tile puzzles with only one free space, I gave up on trying to climb down and instead decided I'd straddle the hatch, wedge it open as best I could, and simply take a whizz through it. That way, I reasoned, I wouldn't have to deal with repeating the whole process in reverse once I was done.

I finished up, closed the hatch, and just managed to get myself settled again when I heard the four-wheeler rumbling down the trail. Jason and Ryan were coming to pick me up. After a good deal of fumbling I managed to worm my way down through the hatch. As I descended toward the ground I was puzzled to find that the ladder rungs were wet. Then I realized that I had peed on them.

Jason and Ryan regaled me with tales of the giant bucks they'd seen but decided not to fire on.

"Saw about thirty doe and an eight-pointer but he looked scrawny," Jason said.

"Little six-pointer came by and rubbed his antlers on the base of my stand," Ryan said. "No point in wasting my tag on him."

"I didn't see shit," I said.

"That's because you slept in too late," Jason said.

We went back to the farmhouse, where Russ and the rest of the crew were dismembering the deer one of them had shot. For Russ, the hunt wasn't so much about bagging deer as it was about making venison sausage. He had an enormous smoker set up in his barn. As the deer came in he and an old friend would process the meat, running it through a massive grinder alongside a generous portion of pork and some spices. They'd run the mixture through casing, tie it off, and hang it in the smoker for hours. While he waited for the deer to come in, Russ fretted with the smoker, ensuring that the moist wood chips at the bottom were putting off just the optimal amount of smoke at the precise temperature. When the season's sausage making was done he would vacuum-pack them and distribute them to members of the party and stockpile mountains of the stuff for himself.

Dick loves the hunt. He remarked several times that day that "hunting would be a lot more fun if it weren't for the damn deer." He loves the hunt, just not necessarily the gory bits involving the shooting and the cleaning and whatnot. But he likes being outdoors, alone in a stand, just him and his thoughts and the wild prairie around him.

People living in cities pay thousands of dollars to psychiatrists, spiritual healers, and meditation gurus to learn how to cleanse their minds and achieve just a few moments of inner peace. Dick does it every year for a week in November for no more than the cost of a Minnesota deer license. If he happens to bag a deer, well, that's just something to piss and moan about to his buddies at the end of the day.

"All right," Russ announced after about an hour of BS'ing with the group in the barn, "time to walk the woods."

"What are we doing now?" I whispered to Jason as everyone trudged out of the barn and toward the fleet of ATVs and farm vehicles idling nearby. Nobody had bothered briefing me on what a full day of deer hunting actually looked like.

"We're walking," Jason said, "through the woods. Is there something about that that's confusing?"

"So like, just walking through the woods looking for deer? Like, all of us?"

"This is *deer* hunting you signed up for, so yes."

"And so like what, if we see a deer we shoot it?"

"Yes, that's what the goddamn gun is for or haven't you been paying attention? Did they not cover this in your junior hunter's certification class?"

The vehicles reconvened atop a slight rise, where Russ had a big tract of open field bordered by a shallow wood. All of us lined up at the edge of the wood, spaced twenty or so yards apart. As I walked over I let the muzzle end of my rifle dip too low for Dick's liking. "Point that goddamn thing somewhere else!" he snapped.

"It's not loaded!" I protested.

"Every gun's loaded," he snapped. Fair enough.

"So when they say 'go,'" Jason explained, "we all walk forward through the woods. Stay parallel with the guys on either side of you. Don't get too far ahead or behind, or you'll get shot if a deer jumps out in front of you."

I adjusted my orange cap so it was sticking up as high as possible. "That seems dange—"

"GO!" someone yelled. Everyone crashed forward directly through the underbrush. There were no trails;

we waded through thickets of scrub and felled trees. "Hey, deer!" people yelled, hoping to scare up some game. "Ho, deer!"

I was falling behind, stumbling through the brush, unable to find my footing. Branches snapped at my face, vines grabbed at my boots. I looked up and couldn't see anyone to either side but it seemed the rustling of leaves and crackling of branches were everywhere. A gunshot rang out somewhere ahead of me.

"Shit!" I yelled.

I heard Ryan a few yards ahead. "Get up here, Ingraham." I careened forward and suddenly I was out in the open again, blinking in the cold morning sun.

"Jesse saw a deer running along the tree line on the opposite side of the field," Jason explained. "Took a shot but no luck. If you had kept up you would have known this."

"I'd be happy never doing that again," I said.

"Good, we've got about five more woods to walk today."

And we did. As the sun reached higher and the air got hotter our motley caravan crisscrossed Russ's land, hitting every major tract of woods on it. We trundled down into little valleys carved by streams and hiked across recently tilled fields through clumps of rich black dirt as big as your boot. At one point the group split up: one contingent would walk through a chunk of woods, and the rest of us would take up posts outside it, ready to fire on any deer they rustled up. "If you shoot, shoot north," Dick said. "Don't need anybody shooting at me today."

"Where do you want me to post?" I asked.

"You're gonna need to post on the eastern edge of the field, by the neighbor lady's house."

"The one who doesn't like hunting?"

"Yep."

Russ had evidently had some sort of hunting-related altercation with the neighbor some years earlier, and as a result they weren't on the best of terms. To reach my assigned spot, I would basically have to walk half the perimeter of her property, in full view of her house the entire time.

I made my walk with my head held high and my rifle leaning responsibly across the shoulder, just an upstanding young hunter doing his part to control the deer population and certainly *not* looking to aggravate any nonhunters by dint of my presence or behavior. As I walked by the section of fence closest to the neighbor's house a door opened, and I saw a woman standing in the doorway, arms folded. I gave a big wave and smiled my best smile, trying to appear as nonthreatening as a strange man with a long gun can appear. She shook her head and went back in the house. I finally reached my post. I saw that the other guys had already flushed out their woods and hadn't found anything. Everyone was already heading on to the next section. I turned around and walked all the way back the way I came.

Regrouping back at the barn, the party enjoyed a late lunch of ground venison chili cooked by Russ's wife, Inez. I know I've spent a considerable number of pages of this book complaining about Minnesota food but this chili was *phenomenal*. Easily among the best I've ever had. One reason? The chili's chief ingredients—the tomatoes, onions, carrots, and peppers from Inez's garden, and the deer from Russ's woods—had all been harvested directly from the very land we were sitting on.

After lunch it was time to hit the stands again to catch the evening movement of the deer. Since a few guys had already gotten their bucks there was some shuffling of stands going on, with the net result that I got to sit in a different stand that was less of a piece of shit than the one I'd had in the morning. The stand overlooked a food plot of soybeans, which the Brumwells assured me would be Grand Central for deer once the sun started sinking. The stand was a little bigger so I could maneuver around in it more easily, and the windows actually worked so I could crack them open and practice poking the barrel of my rifle out of them in quick succession. I looked at birds through my scope and practiced loading and unloading the chamber of the rifle, and attaching and detaching the five-round magazine. Still, no deer showed up. I considered trying to vaporize a sparrow to practice my aim but decided against it, realizing that the Brumwell brothers would hear the shot and give me hell for wasting their ammunition on a bird. So I continued waiting, until darkness, when their four-wheeler pulled up to bring me home. Still no deer.

"Well," Jason said as we got back into his car. "Same time tomorrow?"

I thought about this. That night the clocks would turn back, meaning that Ryan would need to show up at my house at 4 a.m., which meant that I'd need to be up by at least three thirty to avoid another late start.

There was no way I'd be able to do it and I told them as much. Way too goddamn early, I said, to sit shivering in a box and wait for some hypothetical deer to show up. They howled and gave me hell all the way home. The only thing worse than being late for the hunting party, apparently, was deciding to bow out of it the next day. I stood firm. I wasn't about to leave Briana home with the twins for another full day, I said. I'd wait until the following weekend. I'd come out for one afternoon. I'd sit in the stand in the evening but no way in hell would I be doing another round of woods walking. I stood firm. If I didn't get a deer then, well, it wasn't meant to be.

Fine, they said. Get out of here. We're gonna bag the biggest goddamn bucks anyone's ever seen tomorrow and you'll hear all about it.

Thus ended my first day of deer hunting.

That year, 2016, was a mild autumn in northwest Minnesota. The colors changed, a chill crept up the river valleys, and the tempo of life sped up a little for the harvest. Trucks barreled down dirt roads carrying hauls of wheat, corn, and soybeans. Combines and tractors worked the fields at all hours of the day and night, lights shining and engines rumbling under the clear moon.

But autumn is fleeting here, too. In 2017 there was a thick blanket of snow on the ground by Halloween, and the landscape wasn't completely clear of snow again until the following May. In 2018 we got our first snow in late September, less than one week after the last official day of summer.

That first fall I realized, with some chagrin, that I'd have to deal with leaf maintenance and removal in a much more serious way than I'd ever had to before. We've got a number of huge oak trees on our property and in September they dump prodigious amounts of brown leafy biomass on the grass below. I did some research and found out that in some cases you could simply mulch up the leaves with your lawn mower and leave them there until spring.

Perfect, I thought. I'll just run the mower across the lawn a couple of times in the fall and that'll be it. No raking, no bagging, no hauling off to the dump. Christopher Ingraham's momma didn't raise no fool.

In early October, when about half the oak leaves had fallen, I took the mower out and made a pass through the leaves. In my mind's eye, the leaves would disintegrate into brown specks that settled on the dirt around the blades of grass, creating a nutrient-rich mulch that would nurture them the following spring. But when I looked back at the path of destruction behind me, I realized that my lawn was now simply covered in ragged chunks of leaf material rather than whole leaves. In another couple of weeks the leaves would bury the property completely, and if I left them there the grass would be dead come spring.

This was discouraging.

So I sat and thought. Well, I reasoned, the chief hassle of removing leaves is the bagging. Perhaps I can skip that step by simply raking all the leaves toward the garden and piling them up in there. They'll decay by spring, leaving behind a nutrient-rich mulch that would nurture the garden the following year.

The next weekend I got out my rake and began the laborious work of gathering all the leaf litter toward the garden on the edge of the property. Our neighbor John, who owns approximately six thousand pieces of heavy equipment, each tailored to any specific task that might need to be done at home or on the farm, was happily trucking around his lawn on his ride-on mower with an oversize vacuum attachment that hoovered up the leaves and deposited them into three pre-bagged bins on the back.

Hah, I thought to myself as I heaved piles of leaves over the garden fence. No need for *me* to spend hundreds of dollars on a lawn mower accessory I'll use once a year.

John drove the mower over by where I was working.

"Whatcha doin' there?" he asked.

"Well," I said, "I'm gonna put all the leaves in the garden and let them decompose over winter, and then use them as mulch in the spring."

John narrowed his eyes and slowly shook his head. "Nope," he said. "Those leaves ain't gonna break down."

"Sure they will," I said.

"You know how cold it gets here in the winter? You think anything's gonna break down when it's below zero for three months straight? You'd have better luck sticking them in your freezer."

I hadn't considered this. The truth of what he was saying became obvious to me immediately. But half the leaves were in the garden already. I couldn't stop now.

"Well. We'll see I guess!" I said, not wanting to admit the fatal flaw in my brilliant plan.

"You sure?" he said. "You can borrow my mower when I'm done if you want. Pull up all the leaves nice and easy."

"Nope," I said. It was a matter of pride now. You could bury me in those goddamn leaves before I'd accept anyone's help with them. "No, I'll be good. Thanks, though."

Next spring the leaves were still there. We didn't end up planting a garden that year, so the pile overwintered another year. And guess what? They were still there in 2018, too. That fall I officially gave up and hired a professional lawn service to do the mowing. The guy came out to do an estimate.

"You want me to haul away that pile of leaves in the garden there?" he asked.

I still couldn't admit defeat. "No," I said. "I like them there."

Briana called him back the next day. "Will you please take away the pile of leaves in the garden?" she asked. "We'll pay you whatever it takes. Yes, I know what my husband said. You need to understand he has a problem and he needs somebody to do this for him. Yes, thank you."

The next day, the leaves were finally gone.

John also gave me a crash course in the fundamentals

of the sugar beet harvest that year. You may think, as I did, that you have some idea of what a sugar beet is, but take it from me: you have absolutely no clue. A sugar beet resembles one of the dinky purple beets you grow in your garden the same way that a Sherman tank resembles a Honda Civic. The median sugar beet is the size of a large child's head and perfectly white. They're typically a foot long and weigh anywhere from three to five pounds. You know those weird white vegetables that Mario yanks out of the ground in *Super Mario Bros. 2*, the ones that are half the size he is? That's the most accurate depiction of a sugar beet ever produced by popular culture.

In the eighteenth century the sugar beet's predecessors were fed to cattle before somebody realized the beets contained sucrose, the same stuff that makes sugarcane sweet. A few centuries of selective breeding produced those fat, sweet monsters that farmers plant today. At roughly 20 percent pure sugar, a single beet can yield up to a pound or so of refined sugar.

You probably think that most of the table sugar you consume at home and in restaurants comes from sugarcane. You're wrong. Between 55 and 60 percent of it actually comes from sugar beets, according to the U.S. Department of Agriculture. You think that most of the stuff you sprinkle into your coffee comes from tropical plantations, but most of it is grown in the mainland United States, in places like the Red River valley on the border between North Dakota and Minnesota.

About thirteen thousand years ago, an area of North America roughly the size of the Black Sea was covered by a glacial lake called Lake Agassiz. For thousands of years, the lake's animal inhabitants ate, pooped, and died in its waters, depositing a thick layer of organic material along its bottom. When the glaciers receded the lake drained, fairly rapidly, leaving all that material behind as beautiful black soil and raising global sea levels anywhere from two to nine feet in the process. As a result the Red River valley's farmland is some of the most productive in the entire world, despite the short growing season of the northern climate.

In addition to your staples like corn, wheat, and soybeans, the soft soil makes for ideal beet-growing conditions. When October comes the beets are ready for harvest, and every last person in the area knows it on account of the hundreds of semi-trucks laden with tons of beets that go barreling down the country roads at this time of year.

In 2016 John took me out on the harvest one afternoon. We met at the grain elevator in the town of Euclid, northwest of Red Lake County on U.S. Route 75. John's job was to pick up the freshly harvested beets from the field and haul them several miles away to one of the holding stations operated by American Crystal Sugar. There the beets would be weighed and then piled and left to sit out in the cold until the big processing stations in East Grand Forks and Crookston were ready to take them.

I assumed that there would be some sort of large piece of beet-holding equipment along the side of the road that John would drive up to, and it would dump the load of beets in his trailer. Instead he wheeled the semi, trailer and all, directly into the field and pulled up alongside the massive treaded beet harvester that was waiting. When the harvester started up, John had to drive through the dirt alongside it, maintaining a constant distance and pace so the beets tumbling off the machine's conveyer dropped into the trailer. He also had to keep an eye on his mirror to make sure the beets weren't piling too high in any one part of the trailer. If they were, he had to speed up or slow down as necessary to ensure they were being distributed evenly.

If you're wondering how an eighteen-wheeler laden with twenty tons of beets drives through a soft field without getting stuck, the answer is it doesn't. Things usually start to get dodgy near the end of a pass through the field, when the truck and the harvester have to turn around. The truck is almost bound to lose traction, so what happens is he gets a tow from a guy in an enormous tractor outfitted with treads. The tractor has a tow hitch on the back and the truck has a matching bar on the front for just this purpose. The tractor backs into the truck with a thud, the hitch grabs the bar, and the trucker gets a quick 180 degree tow so he can start the process all over again. Once the trailer is full the trucker drives off the field and the next truck waiting in line takes its turn.

The trucks end up absolutely covered in dirt, and deposit enormous amounts of the stuff on the roadways during this season. Locals like to bitch about the beet dirt but none of them really mean it; lots of dirt means a good harvest and money in the pockets of the farmers, the truck drivers, the processing plant workers, and all their families.

Once we had a load full of beets, John drove us out to the receiving station. There he stopped to get his truck weighed and the weight recorded, and to tease the girl behind the weigh station window about this thing and that thing. Once that was done he'd pull up alongside an enormous conveyor belt. The different components of the belt would swing into place at the dump end of the trailer, and John would lift the trailer and dump all the beets out the back. We'd watch them roll up the conveyor belts, and at the top get flung out onto the massive beet mountains that eventually end up covering the entire receiving station grounds. Once the load was empty he'd go do it again, dozens of times a day, until the field was fully harvested or he needed to take a break. Pitching in with the harvest for a few days is a good way for a guy with a truck to make an extra thousand bucks or so before the winter finally sets in.

Another sign that autumn is in full swing is the presence of corn shocks in people's front yards, particularly out in the country. Dick Brumwell taught us the term for the bundles of standing cornstalks tied near the top with twine, usually accompanied by some decorative gourds and straw bales.

"Corn shocks," he said.

"Corn *stalks*?" we asked.

"Corn *shocks*. What in the hell's the matter with you

east coasters anyway?" Dick couldn't bear the thought of us spending our first fall in Minnesota without a proper shock gracing our yard. So he brought us out to his expansive garden down by the river, where some of his corn plants grew ten or twelve feet high.

"All right, chop off some of these and drag 'em over to your car. I'll go get you some pumpkins."

Bri and I set about hacking at the thick stalks with knives and pruning shears while Jack and Charles chased each other through the rows. We eventually ended up with a pile that looked like it would fill our CRV to the brim, just barely leaving enough room for the boys. Dick came back over.

"All right, that's a good bundle," he said. "Now go get three more of those."

We protested, but he told us to shut the hell up since we didn't know what we were doing, and that he'd bring anything that didn't fit in the car over to our place on his Prowler.

In the end we stood all the stalks up in our yard and tied them together near the top. The final shock was generally the shape of a tall triangle with a bunch of tassels springing out of the top. It was kind of like a fall version of a Christmas tree. Dick, we later learned, was particularly fond of corn shocks because it was a project that he and his late wife, Diane, had always done with their children around this time of year. We were glad he could show us how to carry on the tradition.

We were surprised to find most people pulled their shocks down shortly after Halloween.

"That's stupid," I said. "They should stay up until at least Thanksgiving, add a bit of cheer to November."

"They probably take them down because they freeze in place and then you're stuck with them until the spring," Bri said. "You should go take ours down while we still can."

"Like hell I will," I said. "Look how seasonal and goddamn festive that is. I'll take it down after Thanksgiving, when we put the Christmas stuff up."

"Don't you think these Minnesotans might understand this a little better than you, seeing as how this is our first fall here?"

"These people don't even know how to cook venison," I said. "They don't have a monopoly on all things autumnal. We're gonna teach them a few things, you watch."

The next weekend it snowed and the temperatures plunged well below freezing, not to return again until spring. The corn shock was rooted in place, as were the straw bales and gourds, which were now also solid as a rock. The arrangement remained there all winter, mocking me as the snow piled around it.

"What do you think is decaying faster," Bri asked in January, "the pumpkins in the front yard or the pile of leaves in the garden?"

I said nothing.

With a beet harvest and a proper corn shock under my belt there remained one item on my Minnesota bucket list before fall was out: I still wanted to bag my first deer. In the week following my disastrous first foray into the field, Ryan had swung by one evening, grinning from ear to ear, with a ten-point buck strapped to a trailer behind his car.

"See?" he said. "This is what you miss out on when you don't show up to hunt."

"Show me proof you didn't just hit it with your car."

"Go fuck yourself, Ingraham." He drove off.

Jason got himself a deer, too, an even bigger buck, a twelve-pointer in fact. I told them I wanted to go one more time, set myself up in a stand on Russ's property some afternoon. The next weekend was the last weekend of the season so it would have to be then. That Saturday the Brumwells again drove me out to Russ's property. Dick was already there; he'd bagged a deer earlier in the week but kept going out to the stands just because he enjoyed it so much. As we readied ourselves for my final attempt he told a tale about some deer he had watched out in one of the fields that morning.

"Well, there's this group of doe grazing in the field," he says, "and along comes this young buck, little guy, maybe six points, looked like he had a tine missing on one of his antlers. Well, he comes over to the does all puffed out but they want nothing to do with him, they keep running off and you can tell he's getting agitated. Well, finally this great big older buck, this experienced old man, walks slowly over to him and nods his head at him, like he's calming the young guy down. Telling him to take it easy, he's still young, he's got lots of time, no need to be in a hurry and rush things. Well, what do you know, eventually the two of them go walking off together, just quietly out of the field side by side. It was the neatest goddamn thing, I tell ya."

Once again we load up the Prowler. This time they give me a prime location—Jason's new stand that I'd help put together earlier in the season, the one with the porch overlooking the corn plot.

"If you can't find a deer here, Ingraham, I don't know what to tell you," Ryan says.

I climb up the ladder, get comfy in the seat, luxuriate in the space. I slide the windows open and shut just for the hell of it; they're quiet as a whisper. I check my rifle; there's a round in the chamber and the magazine's attached. I've got six shots if I need them.

The sun goes down and there's nothing moving in the corn except for a few birds. I'm about to write the whole thing off, convinced that these sonofabitching Brumwells have probably been spraying my stands with deer repellant before I get there as a joke, when suddenly I see them: a whole herd of deer making their way into the feed plot.

I look them over from my tower: doe, doe, doe, all doe. They have no idea I'm here. It's silent, you can hear their footsteps, the rustling of the cornstalks as they pass. They're in no hurry, ambling casually about the corn. Some of the deer on the edge of the group look up from time to time with a wary eye but there's no sense of hurry about them. Hunting season is almost over; the deer that are still here have nearly guaranteed themselves another trip around the sun.

I see a slightly larger deer emerge from the edge of

the woods and my heartbeat quickens a bit. It's a buck for sure, six points at least. I could give it a shot, or take my chances and see if something bigger comes by. I could just let it go, after all. As a general rule I try not to hurt animals. If there's a spider in the house I try to scoop it up and put it outside. I come from a family of animal healers. Shooting one is against my nature. I could be like Dick, relax and watch the deer mingle, see what they have to show me.

Fuck it, though: I didn't move to Minnesota to be a passive spectator. Murdering a deer goes somewhat against my morals but it's something I need to experience, if nothing else than to be able to lay claim to some of that delicious ground venison. I decide to go for it.

Slowly I rest the barrel of the rifle on the window frame, sliding it out just enough to make it comfortable to fire from my spot. A couple of the doe look up toward the cabin of the stand but don't act as if anything's amiss. I center the crosshairs on the buck, just behind the shoulder blades. I inhale. Exhale slightly. Hold. I pull the trigger.

Safety's on.

Shit.

I flip the safety off. I inhale. Exhale slightly. Hold. I pull the trigger.

It feels like the cabin explodes. The muzzle flash is blinding in the near-darkness and the walls of the cabin capture the deafening sound waves almost in their entirety, sending them ricocheting back toward my brain. For a few seconds I can't see anything. At the edge of my hearing, beyond the high-pitched ringing, I hear a commotion out in the feed plot and then silence.

I step out onto the porch to survey the scene. It doesn't look like there's anything out there at first, but then I see movement, see the buck struggling on the ground right where I'd shot at it. It's still alive.

Well, shit.

In truth, I wasn't prepared for this. I had thought through everything up until the exact moment I pulled the trigger. I had assumed at that point that I would either hit the deer and kill it, or miss it and have it run off. I had envisioned the outcome as binary: hit or miss, alive or dead. I wasn't prepared for wounded and suffering.

I climbed down from the stand carrying the gun with me and walked over to where the deer was, about one hundred yards away. It was flailing about on the ground. I couldn't see a wound anywhere but it appeared that its hind legs weren't working. The only humane thing, at that point, was to put it out of its misery. There was a knot in my stomach. It didn't feel right—my instinct on seeing pretty much any animal, wild or domesticated, is to squat down on my haunches and make "here, kitty kitty" sounds. To reach out a hand and see if it wants to be pet. To ruffle its fur, see how soft it is. Instead, I had to end this deer's life. Destroy it.

I stand a safe distance away and put the scope up to my eye. I inhale. Exhale slightly. Hold. I pull the trigger.

Safety's on.

Shit.

I flip the safety off. I inhale. Exhale slightly. Hold. I pull the trigger.

There's another boom, less deafening for being out in the open this time. The deer looks at me for a moment, almost as if it's disappointed. Then it resumes its flailing unabated.

I realized immediately what the problem was: for some dumb reason, I had aimed with the scope even though I wasn't more than ten yards away. The scope was calibrated for a distance of two hundred yards. The round had probably sailed above the poor creature by a foot at least.

God damn it.

I pull back the bolt and put another round in the chamber. I lift the rifle up again, sighting down the line of the barrel this time, just kind of eyeballing it. I inhale. Exhale slightly. Hold. Safety's already off. I pull the trigger.

There's a sucking sound from a new hole in the deer's chest and then it is still. The animal's suffering, and mine, are finally over.

I flip the safety back on and rest the rifle on the ground. I sigh deeply. I feel deeply unsettled and weird. There's a nearly full moon rising above the clearing. The deer's blood, pooling around its body, shines black. I'm exhausted. I feel bad, honestly. Queasy. Like I've just done something horrible and irrevocable. It was something I'd wanted to experience, to even prove to the Brumwells that I could do it. But now that I had done it, I wished I hadn't.

Soon I hear the sound of the Prowler and see its lights as it comes down the trail toward the feed plot. I wave my flashlight and hail them over. Ryan gets out.

"Jesus Christ, Ingraham, was that three shots I heard? How many deer did you shoot?"

"Just the one," I say.

"Christ, I would have given you two magazines if I had known your aim was gonna be that shitty."

Ryan calls Jason and his dad. "You'll want to get over here quick," he says. "Ingraham's about to gut his first deer. I think he's gonna puke."

"How many goddamn deer did he shoot?" I hear Dick say on the other end of the line.

It's a relief to be at the butt end of the Brumwells' abuse again. The intensity of the moment I first pulled the trigger had narrowed my frame of reference down to just myself and the deer, the only two players in a life-and-death drama acted out on a stage of black dirt at the end of the world. The Brumwells yanked me back to the real world. I kept my ambivalence about the killing to myself. It was easier to just go along with the joshing, let my tragedy dissolve into farce.

Dick and Jason rolled up with Kristin, Ryan's fiancée, along for the ride.

"That's gotta be the smallest buck I've ever seen," Jason said. "What is it, a two-pointer?"

"It's six," I said defensively.

"More like five," Dick said. "Look, it's missing a tine on that one antler. It's that same sonofabitchin' young buck I saw earlier."

"The one that was too small to shoot?" Ryan asked.

"I guess he didn't heed that old-timer's advice after all."

The first thing they did was a traditional trophy shot, with me kneeling behind the corpse holding the head up by the antlers. In the pictures it looks comically small.

Then they handed me some rubber gloves and a large knife.

"So what am I supposed to do?" I asked.

"Put on those gloves and we'll show you."

Gutting a deer is not for the faint of heart. I am fully confident I would have puked if it hadn't been for all the summers I had spent as a child at my dad's veterinary practice, watching spays and neuters and seeing all manner of animal viscera sprayed across an operating room.

"So you grab 'em by the balls," Dick said. "And you start your cut between the balls and the asshole there,

Size of bucks shot

Ryan Brumwell   Jason Brumwell   Me

11 pts.   **12 pts.**   **5.5 pts.**

and then you just kind of just tug the balls all the way up to the ribs, cutting as needed along the way."

So that's what I did. The Brumwells hooted and hollered and expressed some dismay that I neither barfed nor was forced to turn away. After the cut was done I plunged my hands into the open cavity and began pulling the steaming entrails out. They were warm and squishy against the gloves, an almost soothing sensation in that chilly evening hour. Once it was properly hollowed out we strapped the deer to the back of the Prowler, conveyed it back to the car and trailer at Russ's farm, and drove it back into town.

A light layer of snow started falling to mark our return to Red Lake Falls. My first hunt was over, and winter was coming.

As summer turned to fall in 2016 the nation became increasingly consumed with the presidential election, which was at that point lumbering toward its conclusion. The most striking thing about politics in northwest Minnesota that autumn was that there simply wasn't a whole lot of it.

In October 2016 in Red Lake Falls, for instance, you'd be hard-pressed to find a single yard sign for either Hillary Clinton or Donald Trump. There were a smattering of signs for various local offices—school board members and county commissioners and the like. Several yards, in fact, proudly displayed signs for multiple candidates competing for the same office—Minnesota Nice on the campaign trail. But the national election was nearly invisible from the roadside.

That's not to say that the locals are above partisanship. Dan Benoit, Melissa's husband, was a die-hard Trump supporter. In the run-up to the election he'd amble over to discuss the "fake polls" and rib me for my faith in the numbers. "I can't believe that garbage those pollsters are putting out," he'd say. I'd try to lecture him on survey methodology and likely voter models. I told him there was no chance in hell Trump could win the general election. He wasn't having it.

"We'll see," he said.

Melissa, on the other hand, was a Clinton voter. "I can't stand that he likes Trump," she would tell us. "But a couple years ago we had a big fight over politics and we decided to stop talking about it, and it's been great ever since." No point in ruining a marriage over stuff happening 1,400 miles away in D.C.

Broadly speaking, northwest Minnesota is today a deeply conservative area, but it wasn't always this way. The 2000 election marked the first time Red Lake County voters supported a Republican presidential candidate going back to at least 1960. They voted for Bush again in 2004, but flipped for Barack Obama by 6 percentage points in 2008. In 2012 Mitt Romney barely eked out a victory. Overall, Democratic candidates had never polled lower than 40 percent going back to, again, at least 1960.

Moreover, state-level Democratic candidates tended to perform strongly in Red Lake County. In 2012, for instance, Democratic senator Amy Klobuchar trounced her Republican challenger by 40 percentage points in the county. Representative Collin Peterson did her one better, beating his opponent by more than 50 percentage points in the county that year. Peterson's Seventh Congressional District spans most of the western half of the state. It's deeply conservative, but Peterson, one of the last of the Blue Dog Democrats, has held on here since the 1990s. In 2018 a Georgetown University study rated him the most bipartisan legislator in the House, due to his propensity to get along with Republicans.

He's also one of the few Democratic lawmakers still receiving money from the National Rifle Association.

Overall in 2012, Democrats on the ballot in Red Lake County won every partisan contest, with the notable exception of the presidential race. But then 2016 happened.

On election day Briana went to the local consignment shop to purchase a white pantsuit. We brought the twins to Red Lake Falls' sole voting location, the basement of the town hall, to introduce them to the concept of civic duty. The scene was right out of a Getty Images slideshow on voting in the heartland—wood-paneled walls, tables draped with bunting, red-white-and-blue drapes over rickety old booths where we filled out paper ballots.

The precinct volunteers were cheery and polite. There was a different sign-in table for each of the city's three wards. We had no idea which ward we belonged to but it didn't matter, as the volunteers recognized us by sight and shuffled us efficiently to the proper table. When everyone knows everyone else by sight and name there's not a whole lot of concern over voter ID. Once we had voted we went back home to watch the returns roll in. By the end of the evening we were just as shocked as everyone else.

I wish I could say that I had known what was coming, that my immersive experience in "real America" had revealed insights that the Beltway elite were blind to. But that's a load of bollocks, as any honest observer of the election in any corner of the country would tell you.

The truth is nobody had any idea. I lived in the heart of Trump country for six months prior to the election and had no idea that the election would unfold the way it did. There were rigid partisans in either camp, of course, who would have shouted their certainty of victory regardless of what any of the polls had said. The partisans on the Trump side have been gleefully I-told-you-so'ing for the past three years, but had just eighty thousand people in Wisconsin, Michigan, and Pennsylvania voted differently, Hillary Clinton would have won and her fiercest defenders would be doing the same today.

Judged solely by the yardstick of prior presidential elections, Trump's victory in Red Lake County was a stunner. Hillary Clinton won the support of fewer than 30 percent of voters, an unprecedented margin of Democratic defeat in more than a half century of presidential contests. This was a sharp contrast from say, Washington, D.C., where Clinton won over 90 percent of the vote. The down-ballot results offer some insight into what voters here were thinking: they weren't supporting Trump as much as they were opposing Clinton. Democratic representative Peterson, for instance, bested his Republican challenger by close to 25 points. In the race for retiring state senator LeRoy Stumpf's seat, Republican Mark Johnson edged out Democrat Kip Fontaine by fewer than 2 percentage points. Clinton's poor performance relative to down-ballot candidates was unprecedented for a Democratic candidate.

There were signs that Red Lake County wasn't terribly enthusiastic about either of the major-party presidential candidates. You can see this in the fact that in 2016 about two hundred fewer people cast a vote for either the Republican or Democratic candidate relative to 2012. In 2012 about 3 percent of the county's total presidential votes had gone to a third party or write-in candidate. In 2016 that share was 11 percent. Libertarian Gary Johnson more than quadrupled his vote total in Red Lake County, from 24 votes in 2012 to an even 100 in 2016. Ten Red Lake County voters—one-half of 1 percent of the electorate—opted to vote for the no-name candidates on the "Legal Marijuana Now" ticket instead of Trump or Clinton.

Still, as the sun rose on November 9 it was clear that we were officially living in Trump country. Like every media outlet in the country, the *Washington Post* was scrambling to figure out what the hell had happened. Dispatches from Trump country were suddenly in high demand. I volunteered to go talk to some of the geezers at Eagle Square one morning to get their take on the news—if there's any place to find a Trump voter, I reasoned, it would be a Red Lake Falls gas station at nine in the morning.

Imagine my surprise, then, when I found that the grizzled crew of retired teachers, farmers, and laborers at Eagle Square that morning were mostly loyal Democrats who had voted for Clinton. They had had no idea that a Trump surge was in the works, either. And like so many other people in the country, they were wondering how their friends and neighbors with deep ties to Minnesota's Democratic-Farmer-Labor Party—the state arm of the national Democratic Party—ended up pulling the lever for Trump.

"I was shocked by the election," said Jim Benoit, a retiree and veteran who has lived in Red Lake Falls nearly his whole life. His voice carries a raspy lilt that comes from a decades-long cigarette habit cultivated on the northern Minnesota prairie. I knew Jim from all the times he had stopped by our house to say hi to the boys or drop off pickles and walleye recipes. But until that day, I had no idea what his politics were. "I say hold on to your shorts," he said, "because we're in for a ride. And not a good ride—I'm really scared to death."

Ed Dahle, who retired some years ago after decades of teaching music at the Red Lake Falls High School, said he wasn't impressed by Trump's obviously farcical promise to build a wall and make Mexico pay for it. He had taken to telling anyone who asked that he planned to build a wall around his house to keep Trump supporters out.

"It's hard for me to vote Republican when I was raised by a grandfather that was solid Democrat," he said. "And he told me every time he had a chance, 'Don't ever vote Republican because the Democrats help the farmers.'" It's in the name of the party, after all.

Allen Bertilrud stopped by to shoot the shit. Bertilrud had just been elected mayor in a race that exemplified northwest Minnesotans' distaste for the political process in general. His predecessor, Kevin Harmoning, had decided earlier in the term that he was done being mayor and was ready to step down. Harmoning in the time I had known him had always seemed slightly embarrassed to be the mayor, as if politics were a disreputable pursuit that good people should try to avoid getting wrapped up in.

The thing was, nobody else wanted to be mayor, either. The good people of Red Lake Falls evidently resembled the founding fathers, in that they viewed electioneering and politicking as a base pursuit. The very act of seeking a political office disqualified a person from being elected to it. The candidate filing deadline came and went with nobody submitting their name for the ballot. In a town of 1,400 people, not a single one wanted to be mayor. As the election approached in the fall, Dick Brumwell ultimately took it upon himself to play the role of kingmaker and organize a write-in campaign via phone. Allen was his choice for mayor, on the basis that they'd spoken a few times and Dick considered him "a pretty levelheaded guy," which is the nicest thing I've ever heard him say about anyone, including his own children.

That day Dick was, in fact, helping Jason fix a garage door at his house. Dick, incidentally, is also a lifelong Democrat. He voted for Obama twice. But he said a vote for Clinton was off the table—just never liked her. He vacillated on whether he could pull the lever for Trump. He was going to vote for "Johnson or that McMullin guy" instead of Trump but in the end a phone call with his Trump-supporting sister convinced him to vote for the reality TV star. He decided to go for it on the basis that Trump would shake things up a bit and that's what the country needed, and after all what's the worst that could happen? "I think America is so gosh-darn tired of the status quo politicians, lifetime politicians, it's time to get somebody who isn't associated with the government, who has new ideas," he said.

Less than a month later, Dick was regretting his decision. "Shouldn't have let my damn sister talk me into it," he said. It was clear, even at that early date, that the man wasn't going to grow into the office the way presidents typically do. Trump was still going to be Trump. Several years later his brand of politics—the bullying, the boasting, the schoolyard insults—rubs a lot of people the wrong way in a state that defines itself by its niceness.

Still, there's evidence that Dick's a local outlier in his Trump regret. In the 2018 elections, for instance, the partisan breakdown of the state and U.S. house elections in the county was exactly the same—there was no sign, in other words, that unhappiness with Trump was translating into discontent with down-ballot Republicans.

The aftermath of the election prompted a new wave of analysis of the working-class voters who pushed Trump over the finish line. There's a temptation to treat these white rural voters as a monolith. The sense often seems to be that they're fundamentally different than their urban counterparts—on culture, on politics, and across so many other social vectors—and similar to each other.

Statistically, of course, there is some truth to this.

There is a commonality out here. Nearly everyone is white. Most folks own guns. Many have a tie to the agricultural economy.

But it's easy to overstate these commonalities. What was starting to become apparent by the 2016 election was that folks in this community—and probably many others like it across the United States—defy easy stereotypes. Yes, Red Lake County turned out overwhelmingly for Trump. But there are plenty of Clinton voters here, too. For me, nothing hammered this point home quite like selecting a group of guys for an interview based on my preconceived notions of what a Trump voter looked like, only to find out that most of them voted Democrat.

Our usual red state/blue state framework does a poor job of capturing the nuance in the country's political landscape. If you're just looking at a state-level map, it's easy to come away with the impression that everybody in certain places votes one way, and everybody in other places votes another. But even in the deepest, reddest states in the country there are millions of people who vote Democrat, and conversely millions of Republicans in places like California. If this is true at the state level, it's even more so at the level of counties, cities, and towns. If you drill down to precinct-level vote returns, for instance, you realize that even in the heart of Trump country there are thousands of pockets of places where voters chose Hillary Clinton. Those voters usually live in the small cities and towns that dot the nation by the thousands.

Take West Virginia, the reddest state in the nation in 2016. Even there, islands of liberalism dot the landscape. Charleston? Blue. Harpers Ferry? Blue. Huntington? Blue. Red Lake County was, of course, dark red. But even here, Clinton managed to pull off a win in one precinct just outside the town of Red Lake Falls. She bested Trump by more than 2-to-1 in that precinct, a mirror image of the county results as a whole. Granted, just twenty-three people voted in that precinct.

Shortly before the 2018 election I spoke with Brent Lindstrom, the Democratic-Farmer-Laborer candidate to unseat Republican Deb Kiel in Minnesota House District 1b. Lindstrom was a union guy from East Grand Forks, a veteran, and a first-time candidate for state office. He expressed dismay at the state of progressive politics in northwest Minnesota, the apparent lack of energy and coordination in Red Lake County in particular. The county didn't even have its own DFL party meetings, Lindstrom pointed out—instead, progressives in Red Lake Falls and elsewhere were encouraged to organize via Polk County.

Lindstrom ultimately went on to lose to Kiel by close to 30 points, nearly the exact same margin his predecessor had managed two years ago. A simple truth about politics here and everywhere else is that a lot of it simply comes down to what letter comes after the candidate's name on the ballot—is it a *D* or an *R*? Political scientists increasingly find that when voters make decisions on candidates, partisanship comes first, and policy concerns come after. This is good for political parties, and it's good for media organizations that treat politics as a spectator sport. But it's not necessarily great for voters.

Progressive politics is very much alive even in the heart of Trump country, in its own quiet way. It's deeply outnumbered, but it remains vibrant. I recently met with some Red Lake County progressives at the farm of one Virgil Benoit, the uncle, as it turns out, of my staunch Republican neighbor Dan. Virgil's family farmed the rich Red Lake County soil for the better part of a century but have since mostly dispersed. Virgil remains behind on what's left of the farmstead. He recently retired as a professor of French at the University of North Dakota in Grand Forks, and is the guy who puts together the annual French-Canadian festival in the long-forgotten Red Lake County hamlet of Huot.

Virgil and his wife, Sherry, were hosting a French dinner at the farmstead. Sherry teaches English at UND, including classes on literary theory. A guy named Dan Juhl and his wife, Mary, were there, too. Dan is a wind energy pioneer, one of the first people in the country to get into the business of wind in a major way back in the 1980s. He grew up in Red Lake Falls, went to high school here, and after living and working all around the country throughout his career he came back to the town and makes his home here. Another UND professor, Sharon Carson, was there, as was a reporter from the CNBC based in Winnipeg, Pierre Verriere, who had met Virgil initially through reporting on our move to the area, and subsequently on the history of French and Native American culture in the region. Pierre was originally from France and had come to North America owing in part to an obsession with American culture as a teen. He was there with his girlfriend, Daniella, a native of Honduras who had emigrated to Winnipeg.

I mention all these names and professions simply to underscore that these are the kinds of people who also make their homes on the northern plains, far from the coastal centers of culture and power. Their voices and experiences are no less authentic or important than those of the blue-collar diner attendees who play center stage in so much of American media's characterization of the heartland. When's the last time you read a national media profile of these voters?

Politics is also experienced in a quieter, more personal way up here—that may be one reason yard signs for national candidates are so hard to find. Ideological disagreements tend to be hashed out in conversations between close friends, rather than shouting matches between strangers. Decisions and judgments about politics are subtler and less polarized than the election's results might make it seem.

At Eagle Square, Bertilrud and Dahle were arguing over the severity of future threats the country might face.

"We're nineteen trillion dollars in the hole," Bertilrud said. "If interest rates go to five percent, we can't even pay our interest."

"I don't give a hang about that," said Dahle.

"Remember your great-grandchildren? They're going to have to pay for this."

Dahle wasn't buying it. "They're not even going to be alive if we don't get this global warming done and get rid of the damn coal. They aren't going to be alive if they can't breathe!"

But at the end, the political talk was just talk and little more.

"We're friends," Dahle said. "Politics is one thing. You disagree, and then you go on with your life. You can't hate people forever."

Discussion soon turned to what Bertilrud intended to do, as the new mayor, about the plague of squirrels in Dahle's backyard.

Unfortunately, if you've been following the news since the 2016 election, you know that most major media outlets' coverage of rural areas hasn't exactly improved. There's been a never ending stream of Trump-voters-in-a-diner stories, which stopped being useful or illuminating right around the time the final vote tallies were certified. There's also been the rise of an entire cottage industry of partisan journalists who view themselves as Trump-whisperers, sending dispatches from Pennsylvania gas stations where wise rural voters whisper gnomic truths about politics that media elites aren't prepared to hear. Many folks in the media have reacted to their previous indifference to rural voters by bending over backward in the opposite direction, choosing now to perceive flyover country voters as keepers of a secret oracular wisdom that is something to be sought out, unlocked, and delivered back to the coastal public with wonderment.

This characterization of Trump country strikes me as offensive to everyone involved. It turns rural voters into a white working-class version of the magical Negro—patient, wise, close to the earth, existing solely to help the heroes of the coastal upper class on their journey toward enlightenment. It reifies the falsehood that rural Americans are somehow more real, more true, more authentic than the millions who call cities home.

Bad media coverage of rural areas didn't start in 2016. As University of Minnesota sociologist Ben Winchester pointed out to me, the prevailing narrative of "dying rural areas" is shaped in large part by how media outlets cover these areas. In your typical rural America story, a newspaper from a large city sends a reporter to a small town for a day. He arrives at a diner or a gas station in the middle of the week, in the middle of a regular workday. The only people there at those times are retirees, because everyone else is at their job or taking care of their kids or otherwise busy doing whatever they do to make the world and their part of it a better place. The gas station geezers, on the other hand, do what geezers everywhere do: they complain about how the world's going to hell in a handbasket, and talk about how much better things were fifty years ago. Their voices are the ones that end up in the story, simply because they're the ones available to talk in a small town at 10 a.m. on a Tuesday. Everyone else is busy.

So the prevailing rural narrative in the national media becomes one of loss and decline, Winchester says. There is of course some truth to this—census data, for instance, show a relentless trend of migration from the countryside to the cities for at least one hundred years. But Winchester's done some research that adds nuance to this picture. He's found that the rural populations of certain demographic groups—particularly people between the age of thirty and forty-nine—are actually *growing*. They tend to be relatively well educated and highly skilled. They have kids. They're searching for safety, decent schools, a slower pace of life, and above all, an affordable cost of living. Sound like anyone you've read about?

In Minnesota at least, according to Winchester's research, rural populations aren't declining—they're actually growing, albeit at a slower pace than big cities like Duluth and Minneapolis. Sure, the eighteen- to twenty-five-year-olds move out of smaller communities—they pretty much have to if they want to go to college and get a decent start on a career. But by the time they start thinking about kids of their own, many are ready to move back. And many ultimately do.

"We need to write a new narrative about our rural communities, not the story of decline that we've been told since the 1950s," Winchester said at a joint talk he and I gave together in northwest Minnesota not long after we moved to Red Lake Falls.

If there is one thing—one sole, solitary piece of information—that I can convey to you about rural America it's this: rural America is not a nation apart. The people here are just as complex and fallible as people anywhere else. They consume the same media, cheer for the same sports teams, fight over the same political issues, and have the same hopes and dreams for their kids.

I regret to inform you that after more than three years living here I have never been on the receiving end of an earth-shattering knowledge bomb while pumping gas at the Red Lake Falls Cenex. People here are just like people anywhere. Like any part of the country, northwest Minnesota is home to certain quirks and oddities, the cultural textures that make geography such a powerful determinant of how people live their lives. But the same is true of any place: Manhattan, Atlanta, or Kansas City. Coastal reporters who parachute into small towns on election nights have a tendency to mistake local quirks for cultural divides.

Those of us who work with data for a living are forced, as a matter of necessity, to draw arbitrary lines through groups of people: these people are rural, for instance, and those are urban. These ones are middle-class, and those are wealthy. These hail from the Midwest, and those from the mid-Atlantic. It's important to remember that these lines are largely made up. They exist to help us understand and make sense of a large, complicated, messy country. But our cultural baskets aren't God-given; they didn't form of necessity from the formation of the universe like the laws of say, mathematics or physics. They were created by humans, for humans, well after humans came along. Like humans ourselves, our cultural dividing lines are malleable, fallible, prone to error.

None of this is to say that real divisions don't exist.

People who explain American society for a living tend to discount the power of race and class, in particular, in part because they're difficult to talk about. Race and class reflect fundamental differences between people that are mostly (class) or completely (race) out of their control. It's easier to focus on the superficial things that people do voluntarily, like choosing a political candidate. When you discuss Americans in terms of political preferences, for instance, you're placing them all on a level playing field where differences depend primarily upon individual choices: abortion or pro-life, more guns or less, higher taxes or lower. This appeals to our egalitarian tendencies: all people are created equal, so all differences between people are matters of choice.

Moving to Minnesota was much easier than expected for my family and I realize now, three years after the fact, that this was largely because there really *aren't* many fundamental differences between us and most of the people who live here. We share a common skin color. We share a middle-class background. We are financially comfortable, generally speaking, but we have to work hard to stay that way. I am just as subject to the whims of modern capitalist society as the people who've lived in Red Lake Falls for all their lives. Our comfort is precarious: at any minute the rug could be swept out from under us, in my case by the tumultuous economics of the media industry, in their case by the ups and downs of commodity markets and trade winds blowing halfway around the world.

Rural Minnesota politics are pragmatic above all

else. Displays of partisan affect are discouraged—along with the lack of yard signs you see very few political bumper stickers around here, for instance. This marks a sharp contrast between Red Lake County and pretty much everywhere else I've lived, where people tend to wear their politics on their sleeves and take glee in the frankly bizarre notion that their beliefs "offend" the opposing side.

The rate of gun ownership, as Allen Bertilrud suggested, is nearly twice as high in Minnesota as it is in Maryland. Around here it seems pretty much everyone has at least one, for things like hunting or target shooting or protection from bears. But good luck finding a pro-gun bumper sticker on a car in Red Lake Falls: northwest Minnesotans evidently don't feel the need to go around shouting about their gun ownership. In Maryland and upstate New York, by contrast, pro-gun messages were everywhere: NRA stickers on cars, Smith & Wesson decals in windows, messages about "cold, dead hands" printed on yard signs. It's fairly easy to find homes flying a "Don't Tread on Me" flag emblazoned with the silhouette of an AR-style rifle and the words "Come and Get It" or something similar.

Guns, in other words, are a tool here, a means to an end, whereas in many other places in the country they are an identity, a bold statement of who a person is and what they believe in. Minnesotans' levelheadedness with respect to firearms means the state has one of the lowest gun death rates in the nation, according to the CDC.

In the current political environment, no town, however bucolic, can escape controversy. On election day in 2018 a scandal erupted at the polling place in city hall. New curtains had been put on the voting booths for the first time in however many years. The old red, white, and blue striped drapes had been replaced by solid reds and solid blues. Worse, the booths appeared to be segregated by color: the four blue booths were on the left side of the room, while the four reds were on the right. Word got around and soon Facebook was abuzz with the news.

"Why the symbolic divisiveness at a polling place?" our neighbor Alice Conwell asked. "The person who told me this wondered why they weren't mixed up and had to pause to question which one to be seen going into. They did not like it. I think I will vote standing outside a booth."

Other residents agreed. "It felt awkward," one of our other neighbors, Kate Mulvey, said. "If they are going to do that there should be a green one too. It was just weird."

Emboldened, Alice vowed to do something about it. She reported later in the day that she'd made a "dramatic" entrance to the polling place, doing a double take at the booths and registering a polite complaint with the polling workers. Shortly after she departed one of them messaged Alice to inform her that the curtains had been changed to alternate, red-blue-red-blue. Balance was restored, and Minnesota Nice was once again the order of the day.

Two thousand eighteen was an important election

year for another reason: Briana won a seat on the Red Lake Falls City Council. On primary day, August 14, Mayor Allen Bertilrud called her up and said there was a seat opening up on the council, nobody had filed to run for it, and would she please, please, pretty please consider it since today was the last day for a candidate to register? Briana is nothing if not civic-minded and she couldn't turn down a request to serve the town that had treated us so well. So she filed, paying the two-dollar registration fee to the city clerk. She ran unopposed.

She had made quite a name for herself in the past few years by volunteering with the town's Civic and Commerce Committee. By this point in our Minnesota stay she was more likely than I was to be recognized on the street. Given her pleasant disposition and her talent for getting shit done, she was much better liked in town than I was, too. The first person to put a "Briana Ingraham for City Council" sign in their yard was our neighbor Missy—the orange cat's mom. Briana didn't even have any signs made up yet, in fact. Missy had just gone ahead and made her own.

I let my bosses at the *Post* know of Briana's candidacy for conflict of interest reasons. They informed me that in no circumstances would I be able to put up a sign in the yard, that I should limit my tweeting about the campaign to perhaps a congratulatory message after the fact *at most*, and that I would be barred from writing any stories involving the town of Red Lake Falls in the event she won election. Such is the state of journalism in the age of Trump.

Victory wasn't a sure thing, however, given the locals' predilection toward write-in activism. Perhaps there was a secret whisper network in town working under the radar to install somebody else in the seat.

When election day finally came, we took the boys down to the polling place. "Mom's running for city council," we explained to them. Jack's lower lip started to get wobbly. "Well when is she coming back?" he asked, voice quivering. We explained to him that it didn't actually mean she was running away.

The result came in the next day. Briana had won 491 votes, 98.99 percent of the ballots cast, a margin that would have made Saddam Hussein proud. She let people on Facebook know and the response was overwhelming. She was deeply troubled, however, by the five write-in votes for somebody else. Who would do this? Why? Did they not like her? She made me pull up the precinct-level results to see if they were clustered in any particular ward. They weren't.

"We'll find out who they are," I said. "Now you have at your disposal the full destructive power of the Red Lake Falls City Council. We'll use it to crush your enemies. We'll raze their homes to the ground and salt the earth behind us. Your victory will be absolute."

She looked at me gravely. "Absolutely not," she said. And that was the end of it.

She was sworn in on January 2, 2019. She carried with her a handkerchief that had belonged to her great-grandmother, Johanna Loretta Bach, born in New York State in 1904. Before women's suffrage. Briana's middle

Christopher Ingraham

Percent of votes won in Red Lake Falls

Hillary Clinton
2016 presidential election

Briana Ingraham
2018 city council election

30.17%

98.99%

Source: Minnesota Secretary of State

name, Johanna, comes from her great-grandmother. Briana had held on to the handkerchief since 1993, when Great-Grandma Bach had passed away. Briana is the first woman in her family to be elected to public office. We explained all this to the boys and they seemed to understand it, on some level. That handkerchief bridged a gap of five generations in the city council room that cold January night, a tangible connection between three little boys in Minnesota and an ancestor born more than a century before they were, halfway across the country.

CHAPTER 9

By December I had what I felt was a solid northern Minnesota rind on me. I felt more rugged than I had six months ago when we arrived. I was growing out my stubble. My wardrobe had been purged of most of the button-downs, slim-fit slacks, and other appurtenances of the D.C. nine-to-five, replaced with a harlequin selection of fleece tops and hoodies bearing the names of assorted local establishments from the past and present—DiMaggio's Sports Bar, Big Swen's, Northern Grain, Minnesota Barley. Most of these had been scavenged in used condition at Wright's, the town consignment shop–slash–department store. My hair was typically unkempt, and working from home meant there was little reason to shower more frequently than once every other day. A visitor to town could have easily mistaken me for someone who'd lived there all his life.

Here's the thing you need to understand about winter in northern Minnesota: it's the real deal, the main event. I can't emphasize this enough: northern Minnesota winters do not fuck around. The season is well underway months before the official start of Northern Hemisphere winter in December. If you define it as the period between the first and last snows of the season, it's not uncommon for it to last from September through May. Most

people who've lived here long enough have a story to tell
of snow in June. Across the entire state of Minnesota,
July is the only month without a measurable snowfall in
the historic record.

That broad swath of time—well over half the year
even in the mildest years—means that winter has
plenty of time to settle in and make itself comfortable
before December even arrives. The temperature drops
below 30 degrees in November and, looking at the region's climatic averages, doesn't rise above it again until
the following March. In the darkest months of the year
Red Lake County truly earns its last-place spot on the
USDA's natural amenities index.

Yet people carry on here with their day-to-day lives—
and don't bat an eye at celebrating huge life events,
like weddings, in the dead of winter. That first December we were invited by the Kleins to their oldest son's
wedding. It was on New Year's Eve. The ceremony was
scheduled for 4:30. We arrived at the Lutheran church
at 4:25 and barely managed to take our seats before the

Number of days the temperature did not rise above 0 degrees

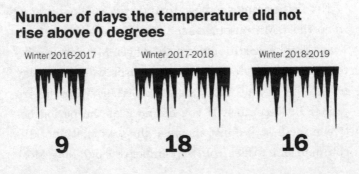

Winter 2016-2017   Winter 2017-2018   Winter 2018-2019

9   18   16

bride started marching down the aisle. Note to self: on Lutheran Standard Time, 4:30 means 4:30 on the dot. If you're on time, you're late.

The reception was held at the VFW in East Grand Forks, which meant a frigid drive across open country in near-blizzard conditions. The temperature that day was somewhere just south of zero. Somewhere between Red Lake Falls and East Grand Forks we saw several cars pulled over to the side of the road, gathered around a pickup truck that appeared to have veered off and ended up in a field. As we drew closer to offer help, we noticed the people were wearing gowns and heels in the blowing cold. It was the wedding party. We pulled up slowly and rolled down our window. "You guys need help?" we asked. "Oh no, we're good," said the maid of honor with a smile. "Go on ahead! We'll see you at the reception." At the reception we learned that the stranded car belonged to the bride's father. He was fine, was already seated waiting for things to get going, in fact. Somebody would get a tractor and drag the truck out tomorrow, maybe Monday, he said. No need to ruin a celebration over a minor inconvenience like that.

The average January low in Red Lake County is 4 below zero, more than 30 degrees colder than D.C. Below-zero double digits are so common as to be unremarkable. Twenty below happens frequently. The mercury's hit 30 below multiple times in every winter we've been here. People from Minnesota don't actually understand how cold this is. Asking a Minnesotan to describe how cold it gets in January is like asking a fish to describe how wet water is. When I tell a Minnesotan I'm from upstate New York, they automatically assume the winters there are similar. But where I grew up temperatures rarely dipped below zero. In northern Minnesota, however, they can linger there for weeks at a time. In upstate New York, you get big snowfalls but the constant seesawing around freezing means that the snow typically melts completely away before the next storm rolls through. You may remember the epic lake effect snow bands that hit the town of Erie, Pennsylvania, in December 2017, dumping upward of six feet of powder in the span of a few days. According to NOAA satellite records nearly all of it had melted away less than a month later. In northern Minnesota, on the other hand, snow and ice that fall don't go anywhere—they just keep piling up. October's snow sticks around until April. Bigger towns like Thief River Falls have to have entire city lots set aside solely for dumping snow in the winter as a matter of necessity. They simply have to cart it off shortly after it falls—if they don't it'll keep piling up and eventually overwhelm the roads. By January the back lot of the Legion in Red Lake Falls is a serious contender for highest point in the county, owing to the mountain of snow that gets dumped there. Minnesotans kind of assume that life is like this everywhere north of the Mason-Dixon Line.

It's hard to describe what 40 below is like to somebody who's never felt it. In all honesty you don't truly understand a northern Minnesota winter until you've been through several of them. Our first winter there

I would tell people back in Maryland that once it gets below zero it doesn't really matter what temperature it is—it all just hurts the same. With a couple of winters under my belt I know that this is not true, that there are infinite gradations of cold, and of pain, as you travel deeper below the zero-degree Rubicon.

Down to about 20 below, things are not so bad, honestly. You don't want to dawdle on your way out to the car, for instance, but as long as you don't spend too much time fumbling with your keys at the door you can usually do the things you need to do without the cold causing too much of a bite.

If it's above minus 20 it's not uncommon to see people out and about running errands wearing not so much as a coat. I once saw a dude—it's always dudes, by the way—in a T-shirt and shorts in the parking lot of the Grand Forks Target when it was 15 below. If you're just running from a warm house to a warm car to a warm store, it doesn't make much sense to spend twenty minutes getting all your outdoor gear on, particularly if you have one or more kids to deal with.

But this all changes once you start going below minus 20. Beyond this point the cold no longer really registers as cold—it's simply experienced as pain. It burns at first, and then after a few minutes it turns into a dull ache. After a few moments, things simply go numb.

In the winter of 2018–19 we experienced several days of minus-40 temperatures, the deep, dark place on the thermometer where the Celsius and Fahrenheit scales converge. We don't actually know, for sure, exactly how cold it got at our house that January. The mercury thermometer on our porch bottomed out at 30 below; when the temperatures plunged below that it shattered. We also had a digital weather station out in the yard, which we found only went down to 40 below. For several hours in the mornings of those coldest days the station simply registered a flat line at minus 40, while the true air temperature plunged even farther below that, to depths unknown and unseen. On one of those days Thief River Falls registered the coldest windchill in the nation, falling somewhere below 70 below.

When it gets that cold the snow underfoot *sounds* different if you happen to be walking around outside—the scrunch of a boot on the snow is higher pitched, crunchier, crisper. For much of that stretch of January there was a 100-degree temperature differential between the air in our house and the air outside. Sometimes our doors would get frozen shut. Sometimes they'd get frozen open, jammed by an outcropping of ice. The house could creak and groan in the middle of the night.

In the midst of all this cold something unprecedented happened: Red Lake Falls schools canceled classes for two days in a row and made the announcement ahead of time. Jason Brumwell, who's lived here all his life, couldn't remember anything like it happening before. Snow days here are so rare that the district doesn't even budget for them, like they do in most schools on the east coast. In Red Lake Falls, every snow day has to be made up later in the year.

"Red Lake Falls is usually the last one to close, and if

they close down you know it's bad," my dental hygienist told me in the course of a cleaning that January in Thief River Falls. "Never seen anything like it."

According to the old-timers in town, that winter also brought the most snow anyone had seen since the legendary winter of 1996 and 1997, when the heavy snowmelt in the spring caused the Red River to flood the cities of Grand Forks and East Grand Forks, sending muddy water three miles inland from the river and causing hundreds of millions of dollars in damages. By February the town was running out of places to put it— snowbanks six feet tall lined most of Main Street, and most of the town's front yards were buried under mountains of snow displaced from driveways. At the Purple House we had a twenty-four-inch base layer of snow for most of the winter, with drifts adding several feet more in places.

One morning as we were getting the kids ready for school I noticed some sunlight shining through the kitchen windows, which was odd because the sun itself was still hidden behind the neighboring houses at that time of year. I went outside and realized the light was coming from an incredibly bright sundog, an optical phenomenon that looks like a false crescent sun appearing on either side of the real thing. The sundog was bright enough that it was casting a warm glow into the house even though the sun itself was still concealed. Driving outside I saw that it wasn't just sundogs: there was a whole array of pillars, arcs, halos, tangents, and rings accompanying the sun that morning. These strange optical phenomena happen when the light hits ice crystals in the air at a certain angle. They're usually associated with the poles, but we're far enough north that we sometimes get dazzling displays of them if the conditions are just right. "Shove *that* in your natural amenities index, USDA," I said to myself.

After two weeks of 20 below, or 40-below lows, a negative 5 feels downright mild. For those of you in milder climates, think of it this way: the difference between 32 degrees above zero and 20 degrees below it is bigger than the difference between 32 and 80. Think of how different those two latter temperatures feel to your skin and you'll understand how much colder than freezing minus 20 really is. Then try to imagine minus 30, or minus 40.

It's fun seeing how your pets cope with this kind of cold. Like humans, different individual animals have different cold tolerance thresholds. We have three cats, two of which regularly go outside. One of them refuses to go out if it's anywhere below zero. The other—admittedly the dumber of the two—will continue to go out down to about 10 below. At least they have it better than the dog, who has to go out to relieve himself no matter what the temperature is. Starting when the temperatures hit the teens above zero somebody needs to be on hand to keep an eye on him because he'll try to take a dump on the deck in order to minimize the amount of time he has to spend outside.

Our Minnesota rabbits, on the other hand, didn't seem to mind the cold that much. The first summer we had them outside we noticed that one of them started digging maniacally at the ground as soon as nighttime temperatures got below about 50 degrees. He kept at it for all of the late summer and fall. One day Briana came in from outside with a concerned expression on her face. "The rabbits are gone," she said. I went out and looked. They weren't in the hutch, and they weren't on the ground outside it, either. Then I noticed the yawning pit that one of them had been digging underneath the hutch. I got a flashlight, stuck my face as close to the hole as I could get it, and tried to locate the bottom. As far as I could tell there wasn't any. I was about to yell back to the house when one of them popped his head around a corner, glaring at the light. They had been smart enough to construct a massive underground burrow of quite literally unfathomable depth before the cold set in.

On the really cold winter mornings the rabbits would be sequestered in their burrow, only emerging when the sun wheeled around the house to shine on their hutch. They happily foraged for their food beneath the snow, and simply took to eating the snow to satisfy their need for water. We would offer them warm water in dishes but they refused. They were happy with the cold.

Unfortunately only one of the rabbits made it all the way through the winter, but not due to the cold. One day in March I didn't latch the top of the enclosure shut as well as I should have. At some point the next morning I looked out the window to see a large animal curled up inside. I ran over to find it was a stray dog. On the ground in front of him lay the body of the white rabbit, its head missing. The brown rabbit, Bubba, sat close by under the hutch looking displeased. I wrangled the dog out of the enclosure, stuck it in our garage, and called the sheriff's office to come pick it up. Thus our cursed luck with rabbits continued into 2018.

Northern Minnesotans take a surprisingly lackadaisical attitude toward clearing the roads of snow. In Maryland, for instance, the slightest chance of flurries was met with the full force of the state's plow fleet, which would be out dumping salt and spraying treatment on the roads hours before the first flakes fell. It wasn't uncommon for the salt to be piled up higher than the snow for any particular storm. Not that that did much to prevent accidents—Maryland drivers are by far the worst I've ever encountered anywhere in the nation. Two classic Maryland driver moves include trying to inch from the right turn to the left turn lane at a stop light, regardless of how many lanes are in between, and missing your highway exit, pulling over to the shoulder, and backing up all the way to your turnoff and into oncoming traffic. Maryland drivers were especially bad during the winter. At a busy Baltimore intersection if you simply roll down your window and whisper the word "snow" every car around you will spontaneously burst into flames.

Not in Minnesota. For starters only the main arteries—the state and U.S. routes—ever seem to get completely cleared down to the pavement during the winter. The country roads and the surface roads in town do get plowed, but the plows always leave a generous layer of packed ice and snow behind. Over time this layer accumulates. On account of the frigid cold it never melts, so it never gets slippery. It's surprisingly safe to drive on at typical town speeds.

If you drive around a residential neighborhood in northern Minnesota in the winter you'll notice a lot of cars with extension cords running from somewhere under the hood back to the house. Those are for the engine block heaters Minnesotans use to ensure their cars will start in the morning after a night of 20-below temperatures.

Residential snow removal is an entirely different story. Rule of thumb: if it has wheels on it, in the winter it'll have a plow attached. I've seen plows stuck on pickup trucks, of course. SUVs. Compact cars. ATVs. A golf cart. Every home owner has a different preferred method of snow removal. People who hire professional removal companies to clear their driveways are regarded with gentle pity. The sight of a hired plow guy in a person's driveway is viewed as a sign that that person is in ill health or is otherwise having trouble managing their own affairs, a signal to neighbors to bring over an extra hot dish to help them make it through the rough patch. Since our driveway is rather long we hired a plow guy for that first winter. We couldn't understand why, shortly after, so many people started showing up at the door with food.

The home of our neighbors Rob and Alice sits atop a fiercely sloped hill across the street from us. Over the course of their years there they have developed the most exacting snow removal protocol I've ever witnessed.

Christopher Ingraham

You can tell right away that they're pros: when working outside in the winter they wear the type of full-body snowsuits that I had previously associated with Antarctic exploration. At the first sign of snow one of them is out on the driveway. They don't use a regular shovel, oh no. They have one of those giant snow pushers with the white blade, basically a human-powered snowplow on a stick. They meticulously push the snow off the driveway, working from the top down. They push the snow all the way to the edge of the driveway, onto where the grass would be, so that the pavement is completely unobstructed. When they get to road level they push a wide berm of snow away from the mouth of the driveway on either side so that the town plow doesn't plow much any of it back up when it goes by. If there's a big snowstorm they'll be out there at it multiple times in one day. The driveway is always immaculate immediately after the snow stops falling.

Residential sidewalk snow removal is a bewildering social game clad like an onion in layers of passive aggression. Similar to hiring a plow guy, letting a neighbor shovel your walk is a sign that either you have abdicated your responsibilities as a home owner, or that someone in your household has died. However, you can't just go charging out to shovel first thing in the morning: if you do you can feel the eyes of your neighbors burning holes through your parka as they peer disapprovingly out their windows. "What the hell's the new guy doing shoveling at seven o'clock in the morning?" you can feel them muttering to each other. "He think he's better than the rest of us?" Ideally everyone in a neighborhood would step out of their door to shovel at precisely the same time, thus avoiding any embarrassing misunderstandings. But it rarely works out that way. As a Minneapolis resident put it to me on Twitter one day: "First winter after buying our house, my neighbor would be out shoveling *my* sidewalk at the start of storms before hardly any snow had fallen. So I had to start going out earlier and earlier to beat him to it and now I do his walk at 5am."

There are unspoken, deeply held norms regarding how people are expected to make small talk about the winter. At the start of that first winter, as temperatures dipped down into the teens, I was eager to demonstrate that I was tough and the cold didn't bother me. "You know it's not as cold as I expected," I'd say to people at the store. I'd get raised eyebrows and looks of disgust. "Uffda, it's freezing out there," they'd say. "Unseasonable. Colder than it should be." They'd wrap their coats tight and hurry away. To a Minnesotan, there's no better way to prove you're a soft-headed idiot than to offer an inaccurate subjective assessment of the weather.

What I came to learn was that it's expected and even encouraged to piss and moan about the temperature in November and December, when the cold first starts to creep in. But when the holidays are over and midwinter's deep freeze sets in, there is only one acceptable thing to say about the weather, no matter how cold it gets: "It's not so bad out there." You hear this all the time in January during the long stretches of below-zero weather.

"Car wouldn't start but it's not so bad out there."

"Front door froze shut but it's not so bad out there."

"Well, the water main froze in the Hollow again. Kind of a surprise since it's not so bad out there."

Older Minnesotans are particularly aggressive in their deployment of "not so bad out there." I believe this is because Minnesota families know that when grandpa starts to complain about the January cold, it's a cry for help, a sign he's no longer able to care for himself, time to put him in a home.

The thing you have to understand about "it's not so bad out there" is that once you say it often enough you start to believe it. In that respect you can think of it as a survival mechanism: it normalizes the unfathomable, endless bitter cold, shrinks it down to something manageable, turns it into a linguistic nicety along the lines of a "you betcha" or an "oh yah." You have to do this because what's the alternative? The alternative is what Jeremy Renner's character says about 20-below temperatures in the movie *Wind River*: "You breathe that cold air deep in your lungs . . . it'll freeze 'em. Lungs fill up with blood, you start coughing it up." Every winter day in northern Minnesota people are presented with a choice: they can let the cold air burst their lungs, or they can tell themselves it's not so bad out and go about their business. They choose the latter.

Minnesotans survive the cold, dark, endless winters partly on the basis of this stubborn force of will. But another factor is that they simply keep themselves busy. There are an awful lot of snowmobiles out here, for instance, which makes sense since the Arctic Cat plant is just twenty miles away in Thief River Falls. The frigid climate means that northern Minnesota is one of the few places in the United States where you're guaranteed to be able to snowmobile all winter long once it starts snowing. Snowmobile clubs maintain a huge network of trails on public and private land up here, running down roadsides and through fields and woods. In the winter you frequently see snowmobiles parked outside the bar or the grocery store—people use them to run errands and get around just as they would a car. Minnesotans have the highest number of registered snowmobiles in any state. In any given year a dozen or so Minnesota snowmobilers end up falling through lake ice or crashing into a tree or otherwise killing themselves, but it's a point of state pride that the snowmobile fatality rate here is lower than in neighboring rival Wisconsin. We managed to get the twins out snowmobiling the first winter, at the Brumwells' campground. Charles loved it—he made the Brumwells' nephew Preston drive him on endless loops around the property until his cheeks started getting frostbitten and we had to drag him inside.

The other major winter activity is youth hockey. When a northern Minnesotan finds out you've got young sons his first question is "They play hockey?" If you answer no, the inevitable follow-up comes: "So when are you gonna put some skates on those boys?" Hockey around here is kind of like a cult. For parents and kids involved it consumes the entire winter, and

for the really serious ones, much of the spring and summer, too. Because there aren't a lot of people in these
parts, teams have to travel long distances to find someone to play against. That means hockey tournaments
are often all-weekend affairs once you factor in driving
time. "Affair" is an apt term as well—while the hockey
kids are generally well-behaved on these trips, rumor
has it that the parental chaperones get into all sorts of
trouble—boozing, fighting, late-night flings in roadside
hotel rooms. The winters are long, the hockey season is
relentless, and sometimes you just need a release.

I consider ourselves fortunate that the Brumwells,
our closest friends here, are not a hockey family. Growing up, the boys played basketball, which most folks here
consider a second-tier winter sport. That put a chip on
their shoulder with respect to all things hockey related,
and they've subsequently informed us that if any of our
boys play hockey we'll be disowned as friends. This
suits Briana and me just fine—the kids already make
life hectic enough without having to factor in midwinter excursions to Warroad, Hibbing, and other far-flung
corners of the state on their behalf. The hockey parents
say it's not all bad, though—one of the dads told us that
the long hours in the car opened the door toward long
talks with his sons that simply wouldn't have happened
otherwise. Now that those sons are in college he says he
wouldn't trade those drives for anything in the world.

There's also plenty of hockey to enjoy purely as a spectator sport. There's an ice rink in town, of course, where
the local teams practice and play their home matches. It

has a reputation among parents in the region as being the coldest rink in northwest Minnesota, a point of quiet pride among the locals. We've taken our boys there to watch the neighbor kids, Marley and Henry, play some of their home matches. Once you're there you realize the point isn't really to watch hockey—it's an excuse to get out of the house, to socialize, to shoot the shit and catch up with friends and neighbors. There's no coffee shop in town, but in the winter the hockey rink becomes the "third place," between home and work, for many of the residents of Red Lake Falls.

We amused ourselves in other ways that first winter. I love the snow, which made winters back east an emotional roller-coaster ride of anticipation and loss: the snow would come, and then it would melt away. As a child I understood the tale of Frosty the Snowman as a profound tragedy: his promise to "be back again someday" did nothing to alleviate the pain of his loss, the horror of watching a fragile, magical friend melt into a misshapen puddle of slush.

But in northern Minnesota, Frosty never melts.

We played outside with the boys when it wasn't prohibitively cold, building snowmen and snow forts and teaching them how not to get their boots and mittens filled with the stuff. Igloo making became an unexpected pastime. Our second winter here I ordered four dozen plastic shoe boxes from Wal-Mart at a buck apiece. I filled them up with snow and set them outside to freeze. After a day or so they would turn to ice. The boys and I stacked them together, mixing water from the house with snow to form slush to use as a kind of mortar to hold the structure together. Several hundred blocks later we had an igloo made of ice large enough for the whole family to sit in. We ran Christmas lights along the interior to light it up at night, and built a small ice block table to have picnics in it during the day. The work, and the sense of accomplishment it brought, kept us sane through the darkest part of winter.

I came to understand the cold itself as a natural amenity. Northern Minnesota is one of the few places in the United States that you can freeze a block of ice in November and have it stay that way until at least March. That's something rare and special, particularly at a time of global warming when winters are generally spoken of in the context of loss and recession. We owed it to ourselves to embrace that cold, to learn from it, to experience what it had to offer.

We had to deal with the darkness, too. Jason often said that it wasn't the cold that got you in the winter so much, it was the dark. On the winter solstice the sun is only up for a hair over eight hours. That's sixteen hours of darkness, every day. Even at noon the sun hangs low in the sky casting long, cold shadows. But you learn to make the best of it. The low-angle sun provides a gentle, paradoxically warm cast to the winter landscape here. On some clear mornings the entire landscape sparkles, practically crackling with light.

The dark isn't all bad, either. Seeing the northern lights undulate through the sky is an experience you never forget, and up here, particularly in the winters, it's almost a common phenomenon. The sparse population means that there's hardly any light pollution. You can lie on your back and look up at a sky twinkling with thousands of stars you've never seen before. You can make out the structure of the Milky Way and even view some deep-space objects, like galaxies and nebulae, with the naked eye. Viewing the night sky is like looking out not just across space, but across time as well. The Andromeda Galaxy, for instance, is 2.5 million light-years away—the light we see from it was emitted long before the first modern humans walked on Earth. You can actually see it without a telescope from Red Lake County—it's the largest, most distant object viewable with unaided human eyes. Seeing that galaxy for the first time, understanding what it is, understanding what has to transpire for the photons emitted by its stars to travel across space and time and strike your eyes at precisely that moment, is a profoundly moving experience. Out here the full moon can seem almost blinding, and even the darkest new moon nights are filled with starlight.

Dark skies: another unacknowledged natural amenity.

Still, a certain amount of cabin fever is inevitable out here. Nobody wants to send their three-year-olds outside to play in temperatures that could make their lungs explode, starlit skies or not. For weeks at a time it felt like we were stuck—crammed into the house with no place to go and nothing to do. Surprisingly, indoor amusements for children are difficult to come by up here. The McDonald's in Thief River Falls, with its indoor play place, became our default excursion for when we absolutely had to get the kids out of the house. We'd pay for it later though, as more often than not the kids would bring home a nasty bug they caught deep in the dark, swampy recesses of the fiberglass play tunnels.

We tried to embrace the Danish concept of *hygge*, making the house as tidy and cozy and inviting as possible while the winter roared outside. We failed. Briana was pregnant all winter and grouchy. There's nothing hygge about morning sickness, or about a three-year-old screaming at the top of his lungs because he dumped milk on himself for the third time that day. The animals grew restless, too. In November we adopted an orange barn kitten from John's farm that we had named Ella. By January the cat was so tired of being cooped up in the house that he—we later found out he was in fact a boy—had taken to launching sneak attacks on the back of the twins' heads as they sat on the couch watching *Paw Patrol*.

Ice fishing is another big winter pastime. The ice on the lakes and rivers up here grows to prodigious thickness—four, five, six feet or more. Thick enough to drive a convoy of trucks across. The prime ice fishing destination is Lake of the Woods, which sits at the northernmost point of the state—on U.S. maps it's that little promontory of Minnesota that pops up above the rest of the 49th parallel border with Canada. After the deer hunt Jason and Ryan were determined that ice fishing was the other great northern outdoor pursuit that I needed to experience. So along with Dick and Justin

Carriere, a former New Yorker who'd cooked up a memorable walleye fry on my first visit out here, we booked a cabin on the lake in February 2017 at Arnesen's Rocky Point Resort.

As before, my upstate New York expectations of ice fishing didn't prepare me for the reality of northern Minnesota practice. I had actually been a couple of times as a kid, with friends of the family. Back then we drove out to a frozen lake, and the dad brought a giant ice auger and drilled a couple of holes by hand, and we sat around on the ice, exposed to the elements, freezing our asses off and waiting for a nibble that never came.

I told this story to the crew on the way out to Arnesen's and they scoffed at me. "Barbaric," Jason said. "That's not ice fishing." Once we got to the resort I understood why. Parked at the edge of the frozen lake was a fleet of rugged treaded vehicles. Their cabins were all shapes and sizes—parts of buses and F-350s, trucks, golf carts, scrap metal, all of it haphazardly thrown together with little thought to consistency beyond a general postapocalyptic vibe. Once we were properly registered at the front desk, a guide led us out to the cabin of one of these vehicles and drove us out about nine miles onto the ice, where he promised the best walleye were to be found. There were markers driven into the ice as we went out, roughly delineating the paths of the ice roads that crisscross the frozen surface all winter.

Our destination was an ice house literally at the edge of the American frontier. The scene was otherworldly—

gray sky and ice fused together to form a landscape more barren and undifferentiated than the landscape photos sent back by Martian probes. There was a stark, minimalist beauty to it, along with a sense of wonder that we humans could plant a flag on this inhospitable terrain and make it our own. Inside the ice house, six holes had already been drilled through the four or so feet of ice, casting the interior in a greenish light, the faint memory of sunlight filtered down through ice and back up through dark water. A small gas heater kept the house warm, and as our guide rumbled off in his ice tank we put our packs down, cracked open a few beers, and set to preparing our poles.

The Brumwells had brought strange electronic devices called Vexilars that looked like props from a 1960s-era *Star Trek* episode. The way they worked was by dropping an attached probe through the ice holes and into the water. After lowering the probe to the desired depth and fiddling with the knobs some, a circular array of lights lit up in yellows and red, which indicated the positions of nearby fish. Or so the Brumwells claimed.

I've spent the better part of my career visualizing information in various ways, from simple charts to more complex abstractions of multidimensional data. But no matter how hard I tried I could not make heads or tails of what the Vexilar device was supposed to be telling me.

"See that yellow and red?" Jason would say. "That means there's a fish right about . . . there." He dropped his line and gave it a wiggle. Nothing happened.

"There, huh?" I said.

"Well, it's a little touchy," he said. He fiddled with the knobs, which caused a completely different pattern of lights to emerge. "Ah there it is." He jiggled the line again. Nothing.

"You guys are fucking with me, right?" I said. "This is like some spare bus gauge that you had sitting around at the campground?" They cussed me out up and down and told me to fetch them more beer while they aimlessly twiddled their knobs.

As it happened we were due to have a TV crew accompany us that day. Steve Hartman from CBS News and his longtime cameraman Bob were in the area to do an *On the Road* segment on my move to Minnesota, and they wanted some footage from the ice-fishing trip to see how I was faring in the rugged environment.

When they arrived they got Jason and me set up in an icehouse next to each other and had us shoot the bull over our respective holes, like something out of *Grumpy Old Men*. We were going through my initial story and first trip out here when I felt a tug on my line. Excitedly I started reeling it in.

"Is that . . . is that a fish?"

"I think so!" I said. "First catch of the trip if I'm not mistaken." Jason shook his head in shame.

It was indeed a walleye, long enough to keep at just over a foot. More important, it was a rebuke to Jason for all the master fisherman shit-talking he had been spewing on the way out to the resort.

"Look at me," I said. "I'm the fisherman now. Your Minnesotan Vexilar witchcraft is nothing compared to my superior upstate New York technique." Even better, it was all captured on film. I went on to catch the next fish, and then the one after that. By the time Steve and Bob had wrapped up their segment the score was Me, 3; everyone else, zero. Of course I didn't catch a single other fish for the rest of the day, and everyone else started getting bites all over the place.

This trip, and the CBS interview, happened at a not particularly great time during that first winter. Everyone else in the household was sick that February. For Jack and Charles, in particular, it had been one raging illness after another since Christmas. We were getting tired and worn out—Briana particularly, since she was at that point five months pregnant with the as-yet-unnamed Minnesota baby. Briana had let me go on that trip on one condition: that I made clear to the CBS guys, in no uncertain terms, that they were not to stop by the house without me present. Bri could barely talk, she hadn't showered in days, the kids had snot coming out of every orifice, it was a nightmare. "The film crew can talk to you and that's it," she said. No problem.

Steve and Bob left the lake before I did that day. They said they were going to meander back to town, catch some landscape shots along the way. I gave them my cell number and told them to give me a ring if they wanted to do an at-home interview that evening. At the end of the day as Ryan and I pulled into the driveway I saw their rental car sitting there. "Oh no," I said.

I ran inside, flung the door open. I heard commotion downstairs, the kids chattering excitedly. I headed down. Briana, Steve, Bob, Jack, and Charles were all in the playroom. The boys were busy pulling every single one of their toys out of storage and showing them to their new friends. "Look!" Charles screamed when he saw me. "Bob's here!"

"There you are," Briana said, with an icy smile that would have struck me dead had I had the courage to gaze directly at it. "Here I am!" I said. "I see you've met Steve and Bob."

"If you've got everything under control, finally I'm going to go change out of my pajamas and do my hair," she said.

The rest of their visit passed uneventfully. We had told our story a thousand times by then, knew when to jump in and complete each other's sentences when describing key events.

"You know, you came at kind of a bad time of the year," I told them. "Winter's wrapping up, the snow's turning brown, everything's ugly as hell, and we've all been sick for months."

"That's why we wanted to come now," Steve said.

I tried to sell them on everything we saw in the place, on the people, on the stark beauty of the landscape even in the midst of the cold. But they weren't buying it.

"I dunno," Bob said. "If I could live anywhere in the United States, I sure as hell wouldn't pick here."

I wish I could show Bob the midwinter evening our second winter here, when a ceremony was held at the gazebo by the frozen river for the inaugural lighting up of a decorative train sculpture that residents had organized to place across the railroad bridge, visible when people first drive into town. Briana and I took the kids since it was right around the corner from home, but we weren't expecting much. It was hockey season so lots of folks were likely to be away, and it was freezing to boot. But when we got to the gazebo we were surprised to see hundreds of people—drinking hot cider under the gazebo itself, huddled around a blazing fire outside it, gathered in clumps throughout the trees along the length of the frozen river.

It was something out of Currier & Ives, a throwback to a time when people gathered close during the winters for warmth and companionship, a time before TVs and electricity and computers in everyone's pockets. It was the type of gathering you'd never see in a place like Baltimore—can you imagine an organized event that let a bunch of kids run loose in subzero temperatures, at night, along the bank of a frozen river with ice of an unknown thickness?

There was a true fellowship that night, a true sense of community, something that Briana and I have not experienced anywhere else in the country where we've lived. When the train lit up everyone clapped and cheered. The people of Red Lake Falls brought light to the darkness and warmth to the cold. We were home.

CHAPTER 10

Sometime around February in northern Minnesota you'll usually get a stretch of a few days where the sun is out, the temperature doesn't dip below zero, and you notice there's still a bit of light left in the sky at 6 p.m. If you'd asked me back in 2015 if a five-day stretch of single-digit temperatures could ever feel like spring I would have said you were crazy. But as you come around winter's final turn in northern Minnesota, weather like that makes you want to put on your shorts and go catch some rays.

On the first calendar day of spring in 2017 in Red Lake Falls the temperature topped off at about 20 degrees. There were still several inches of snow on the ground, but the mercury was rising. Months' worth of compacted snow and ice on our road were finally starting to break up and in some places you could even see the pavement. A thick layer of ice still lay on the Clearwater River as of March 31, but on April 1 it was as if it had shattered all at once, miles of it. All day long, chunks of ice, some of them as big as cars, floated down the Clearwater toward the junction with the Red Lake River, and onward to the Red River of the North in Grand Forks.

One thing we were unprepared for that first spring

was the dog shit. We had gotten behind on picking up after the dog for much of the winter, in part because on really cold days the turds would freeze in place almost immediately, making them impossible to remove with anything short of a pickaxe.

"What are we gonna do about the poop?" Briana kept asking all winter.

"It's fine," I would say. "No point busting our humps to pick it up if it'll just get covered in snow in another couple days."

"And what will happen in the spring?" she said.

"It'll, uh, it'll dissolve maybe? And then it'll be all gone, and we won't have to lift a finger. It's not about working *hard*, you see. It's about working *smart*."

"Mm-hmm."

The turds dissolved, all right. But they didn't exactly disappear. When the snow began to melt, turds previously separated by strata of snowfall, like fossils in limestone, were suddenly revealed, joined back together during the cold nights, disintegrated by the warm sun the next day to form a soupy brown porridge that turned into a fetid swamp covering the entire front lawn. The mailman started delivering packages to the garage door rather than wade through the filth. Briana was mortified.

"I don't know what else I'm supposed to do," I said. "Maybe next year I'll go out there with a jackhammer in February?" The swamp eventually dissipated, but three years later the mailman still has not returned to the front door. We didn't figure out a system for dealing with the poop until the winter of 2018 and 2019. Every few days I'd head out to the yard with a suite of tools: a potato hook, which is kind of like a small pitchfork with curved tines; a pooper scooper consisting of a turd rake and a turd basket on a stick; and a plastic bag. First I'd go through and pick at the turds with the potato hook, freeing them from their icy prison. Then I'd make a second pass with the scooper to pick them up. Finally it would all go into the plastic bag, which would go into the garbage. When I was out there hacking away with the potato hook it felt like nothing more than literal turd farming, which, in a sense, it was. But come springtime we were spared the fragrant soupy mess of prior years.

By mid-April in 2017 we were ready for spring, real spring, even through there was still snow covering most of the ground. The warmer weather brought preparations for our own little Minnesotan—the baby would be a boy, we found out, and he was due to arrive in mid-June. We decided he'd be named William Jeffrey Sean Ingraham—Jeffrey for my stepdad down in Tampa, and Sean after his godfather in Baltimore.

The twins had been born at Johns Hopkins in Baltimore, one of the finest hospitals in the world. Because they'd been so early—six weeks—they spent a lot of time in the neonatal intensive care unit, hooked up to the machines that kept them alive via various tubes, cables, and electrical leads.

Charles, first out of the gate, was impossibly scrawny at 3 pounds, 12 ounces. He was gaunt, a little wizened old man, a miniature Benjamin Button baby. When we

were finally able to hold him he felt so tiny and fragile that my stepfather remarked it was like holding a
squirrel.

Jack, meanwhile, was a full two pounds heavier
than his brother for reasons the doctors were never
fully able to figure out. He was swollen with fluid when
he came out and resembled nothing more than a tiny
purple version of my own father. It was strange to look
at him.

The twin pregnancy had been a harrowing affair.
Keeping two tiny humans alive in your belly is a complicated process, and there had been issues with early
labor and alarming bouts of contractions that we'd had
to drop everything and run to the hospital to deal with
all throughout the summer of 2013. By the time they
finally came into the world via an early labor that was
irreversible, we had steeled ourselves for the reality
that they would arrive well before their due date and
that their first few weeks in the world would be highly
fraught.

William's pregnancy, by contrast, was completely by
the book. There was just one of him, after all. It was a
hassle, as all pregnancies are, but he hit his prenatal
milestones right on schedule without the slightest sign
of complication. In contrast to the twins, William's
pregnancy felt easy. Relaxed. We didn't fret too much
over preparations since we knew we had plenty of time,
that there was essentially no risk of a preterm birth. By
April we hadn't even visited the delivery ward at the
hospital in Crookston where William would be born.

There was no need, no rush. I joked with friends back home that the "hospital" was probably just a workshop in some guy's barn.

Then, without warning, Briana's water broke on April 28. Six weeks early. Just like the twins.

It had been an unremarkable Friday. I was in the office wrapping up the day's stories and pitching ideas for the next week to my editor. Briana burst through the door looking stricken. There was a towel between her legs.

"I'm pretty sure my water just broke," she said, with panic in her voice.

"What? Are you sure?" It was an idiotic question.

"One hundred percent sure," she said.

I felt the bottom drop out of my gut. Memories of our previous ordeal in neonatal intensive care came crashing back—our babies with tubes protruding out of them at every angle, nighttime vigils in front of machines flashing numbers that held the keys to whether they would live or die. Tiny, impossibly fragile creatures not meant for this world, with paper-thin skin you could see their heartbeats through. When they were born we didn't even get to hold them for days. They were pushed out and then wheeled out of the delivery room in a flash. The circumstances of their premature birth were fraught, and the delivery staff at Hopkins were so hard-assed about keeping babies alive that there was no time for niceties like holding the babies, putting their hands in ours, offering them some comfort, however small, in the cold, bright, terrifying world they were cast out into.

I still remember, with crystal clarity, the sound of every single alarm in that NICU. There was one for a heart rate too high, and a separate one for too low. There was an alarm when the nutrient broth delivered to the babies by nasogastric feeding tube was empty. There was one for Jack's ventilator. One for the CPAP he was on afterward. One when the dissolved oxygen was too low. One when the incubator temperature was too high. One when a lead fell off. Then there was the big one, the alarm that resonated across the entire ward, when somebody's impossibly fragile little baby went code blue. The staff would immediately drop everything and rush in the alarm's direction. Sometimes it would be a false alarm and they'd all walk away relieved and smiling. Sometimes it was the real deal and they'd walk away stone-faced and grim. The best thing I can say about Jack and Charlie's NICU stay was that the big alarm never rang for them.

We lived like this for weeks. You could tell exactly what kind of day you'd have in the NICU the moment you walked in just by looking at the nurses' faces. Sometimes Jack and Charlie had a good night. Some numbers on some machine had moved in the right direction. Maybe Jack was breathing well and they were able to step down his oxygen. Maybe Charlie's heart rate had risen just a little bit. On days like that the nurses would relax the rules a bit; you could hold the babies for a while, change their diapers, let them squirm around next to each other in a crib. Then there were the bad days, when the numbers had gone the opposite direction. They'd had to put Jack back on the CPAP. They'd tried to feed Charlie orally but he choked. Then the rules were strict, the road to discharge foggy and uncertain. Sometimes one of them would have a good night while the other regressed, and those were the most confusing days of all.

There is only one question on any parent's mind during a child's NICU stay: when can my baby come home? But the doctors and nurses there don't think like that. They're fixated on the moment, on the vital signs, on the numbers flashing on the screen. It's not clear to me whether the staff at Hopkins were specifically trained not to offer any long-term prognoses to anxious parents, or whether, due to intense, highly specialized training and a laser focus on the here and now, they were simply no longer capable of thinking about time in linear terms. As a result you, the parent, become incapable of thinking that way, too. You become tethered to the moment. Time disappears. The NICU stall where your baby is becomes your whole world. Lights on a screen, the soft whoosh of a ventilator, tiny cries heard off in the distance. Afterward, if you're one of the fortunate parents who gets to bring their baby home, you can no longer tell whether your NICU time was measured in hours or days or months. There's a black void in your memory that you stay far away from because you know, beyond doubt, that it encompasses the absolute worst days of your life.

Four years after Jack and Charlie's NICU stay ended I was standing in the office with Briana asking her what we were supposed to do now. We both struggled not to panic. The kids were running around upstairs, unaware anything was amiss. We hadn't packed an overnight bag. We'd barely discussed what we'd do with Jack and Charles when it was time to deliver, although at one point Ryan Brumwell and his girlfriend, Kristin, told us they'd be happy to take the boys on short notice when the time came.

So we called Ryan. No answer. Kristin. No answer. We tried Jason. No answer. Curse these Minnesotans and their perpetual industriousness! We called Dick. He answered. We told him what was happening. "I'll be right there," he said. Less than five minutes later, he was.

When he saw the looks on our faces he immediately understood the gravity of the situation. We tried to give him a crash course in everything the twins could conceivably need that evening. "Shut the fuck up and don't worry about it!" he said. "Just go!"

"What's the matter with Momma?" Jack asked as he saw us preparing to leave.

"Momma's sick, we have to go to the doctor," I told him. "Be good for Mr. Dick and listen to what he tells you." He and Charles fidgeted anxiously in the doorway. They could tell something was terribly wrong.

We raced down the county highways toward Crookston, past fields covered with a fresh coat of snow from the night before. Briana was breathing hard, straining. The contractions were very close. I tried to keep up a steady patter of reassurances for both of us—we've been through this before, there's only one this time, he'll be bigger, he'll be healthier.

"I can't do this again," she said.

"Yes, we can," I said. "We have to."

In truth I felt the same way she did. When we'd found out we were having just one baby this time, the first words out of my mouth were "Well, no matter what else happens we won't have to go to that goddamned NICU again." Now we were headed toward a NICU at the edge of some cornfield in the middle of nowhere, our support network consisting of near-strangers and people we had known for less than a year. I floored it. If nothing else I was determined to not have to deliver William myself in a Honda Civic on the side of a rural road.

It was all a mistake, I kept thinking to myself. The decision to move here, the decision to have a baby, everything that had happened since that first dumb story. I should have just left things as they were, moved on to other stories, continued living the D.C. life the way I had been. I'd be in the newsroom now, surrounded by colleagues, probably preparing for some TV or radio hit. Our lives would be smaller, circumscribed by the commute and the costs and everything that made us want to leave in the first place. But God damn it, at least we wouldn't be about to bring a strange new baby into the world six weeks prematurely in a frigid field in the ugliest county in America.

We made it to the hospital. I found a wheelchair and wheeled Briana in the main entrance. We had no idea where to go. There was a kindly old woman sitting at a volunteer station. We ran over there.

"Labor and delivery?" I asked.

"Well . . . let me see," she said, slowly rifling through a stack of papers on the table. "Hmm. Okay. All right. Now then. Could I get you to sign this pa—"

"WE'RE ABOUT TO HAVE A PREMATURE FUCKING BABY WHERE IS LABOR AND DELIVERY??"

Some of the staff overheard the outburst and quickly shuffled us off in the proper direction. They got us set up in a room and strapped the fetal heart rate monitor across Bri's belly. Two pieces of good news: we weren't going to deliver him in a field, and his heart rate was strong. Doctors and nurses came in, asked batteries of questions, checked monitors, and went out. Eventually several came in at once.

"Your baby is very early," a doctor said.

"Yes, we know."

"We don't have the facilities to handle a baby that premature here," he said. "You'll have to go to Grand Forks."

Bri and I looked at each other.

"We have an ambulance ready with a team to accompany you," the doctor said. "If need be they'll be able to deliver the baby on the way."

"Only had to do that once so far, in seventeen years!" a chipper voice volunteered from the back of the crowd, the ambulance driver.

They loaded Bri on a stretcher with various machines and monitors in tow. They told me to follow in the car, and to not bother trying to keep up. "We'll be going fast and don't need any accidents," the driver said. Fine with me. I walked back to the car. I got in. I drove. As I crossed the bridge over the Red River of the North thirty minutes later, it struck me that we'd be having a North Dakota baby, not a Minnesota baby. It seemed so strange, and foreign. A child of the West, a frontier baby. To my knowledge no Ingraham had ever been born anywhere west of Niagara Falls. What the hell were we doing out here?

I got to the hospital in Grand Forks and found Briana in an upstairs delivery room. It was quiet and the lights were dim, almost peaceful. Back at Hopkins the twins had been born under harsh lights in an operating room with about two dozen people present, separate teams for each of the babies and one for mom in case things really went south. Here in North Dakota things were more laid-back, partly a simple function of there being only one baby. They gave Bri an epidural and kept an eye on her dilation. Jason texted asking if we needed anything. I sent him a list of things I had forgotten—my meds, a wallet, a phone charger.

About two hours after the contractions first started William was ready to be born. Like his brothers, he wasn't one to dilly-dally. A couple of doctors and nurses came in, Bri pushed once, and suddenly there he was: purple and wriggling, hollering his strange, raspy yowl. His vitals were good. His APGAR score was good. Miraculously, Bri got to hold him to her chest and sing to him for a few moments before they wheeled him away.

The NICU in Grand Forks was completely different

than the one in Johns Hopkins. The Hopkins NICU was home to rows upon rows of stalls, each of those home to a tiny person in an incubator. There were dozens of babies there. In my mind's eye it's vast. The memory of it reminds me of the scene in the *Matrix* where we see the massive facility housing the gel-filled holding cells where the robots harvest energy from twitching humans. The Grand Forks NICU was a single room, smaller than an elementary school class. There were one or two other babies in there but it was quiet. There was hardly any sound of alarms.

When we first went to see him, a few hours after his birth, William was sleeping peacefully on his back in a tight cozy swaddle, a blue and white cap keeping his head warm. His hair was dark like mine but he had a face like Briana's. He weighed a tad above five pounds, heavier than Charles had been but lighter than Jack. He arrived at almost the exact same gestational day of his pregnancy as his brothers had. Briana is nothing if not consistent.

I was rather snobbishly prepared to look down my nose at the NICU doctors—what deficiencies in their training had caused them to be out here in the sticks, in Grand Forks, rather than at a world-class facility like Hopkins? But of course this was stupid of me. The doctors were incredibly knowledgeable. When I offhandedly mentioned some protocol I had observed there that had been different than what they'd done at Hopkins with the twins, one of the doctors told me that new research had come out in the intervening years concluding that the protocol they were now using at Grand Forks was superior. This put me at ease: if these docs were up on the NICU research published since 2013 it was clear they knew what the hell they were doing.

More to the point, they were warmer toward us than the Hopkins doctors had been, almost more human. With just a few babies to manage they had time to talk to us, to answer our questions, to give us a clear sense of how William was doing and what we should expect in the days to come. He was a champ, as it turned out, mastering breathing within a few hours and getting a solid grasp on the breastfeeding stuff within days. The doctors kept warning us that he would probably crash, that NICU babies always do this, that after two or three days of progress something would go to hell and we'd be back at square one. Miraculously, it never happened. While the twins had spent six weeks at the hospital, William was on his way back to Red Lake Falls in less than five days. Our North Dakota baby was coming back east, coming home.

The temperatures warmed dramatically during those five days. There was still snow on the ground when we drove to the hospital in Crookston in a panic. Five days later it was 75 and sunny. The flowers were coming up. It was finally spring.

William's infancy was an odd paradox. On the one hand, it was infinitely easier to deal with just one baby at a time rather than two. On the other, having two toddlers to manage on top of the baby, with one of them on the autism spectrum, presented its own set of challenges.

But the greatest difference between William and the twins was time—time we simply hadn't had back in Baltimore. As an employee of the federal government Briana had a fairly generous paid-leave policy to draw on and she ended up taking about four months off following the birth of the twins, half paid, half unpaid. Four months is a lot, relative to the U.S. average. Nearly one-third of employed new moms don't take any maternity leave at all, according to federal statistics. The national average is just ten weeks. Among moms who do take time off, fully one-third are not paid for any portion of their time. The United States is the only country in the developed world, and one of the few in the entire world, that fails to mandate paid leave time for new moms.

Even though we knew we were fortunate, four months still felt like hardly enough time to spend with

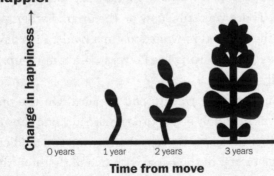

Moving to greener places makes people happier

Change in happiness →

0 years   1 year   2 years   3 years

Time from move

Source: Alcock et al., 2014

two tiny babies who had spent the first weeks of their life tethered to machines in an intensive care unit. But with William we didn't have to make that trade-off. Bri could be here, with him, giving him the direct parental care that he—and all babies—truly need. With William we've been able to experience and share his full childhood—the big milestones like walking and talking, of course, but thousands of little ones, too. His joy at seeing one of the cats jump off a table. His wonderment at a truck driving down the street. The touch of his tiny hand on one of our cheeks. The sweet smell of his round little head as he nuzzles into one of our shoulders to drift off to sleep. We felt, and still feel, incredibly fortunate to be able to have these everyday moments. We wish that we lived in a world where we didn't have to feel privileged to be able to have those moments together.

EPILOGUE

At the outset of our trip it wasn't clear how long it would all last. I had pitched my editors on a year, maybe two, who knows. Thankfully, they hadn't set any preconditions regarding my return. But the longer we've lived here, the more it seems clear that yes, we'll actually be staying here for good. Or at least for the foreseeable future.

As I write these words the twins are in kindergarten. I can hear Briana and William laughing outside, in the snow, from my office window. Every minute we're able to spend together here, as a family, is a reminder of the time we'd be forced to be apart if we were back in the city. With each passing day that old life becomes more unimaginable.

When people and places halfway across the country are just a mouse click away on your computer, it's easy to assume that we live in a nation made small and manageable by technology. But living in a place like Red Lake County, hours away from any major metro area, is a reminder that in much of the country, the rhythms of daily life are still markedly different than the coastal city grind of long commutes and high-octane jobs.

As somebody whose job is to write about "data" writ large, I'm a big believer in its power—better living through quantification. But my relocation to Red Lake Falls has been a humbling reminder of the limitations of numbers. It has opened my eyes to all the things that get lost when you abstract people, places, and points in time down to a single number on a computer screen.

The government's natural-amenities index captures the flatness of midwestern farm country quite well, for instance. But it misses out on so much about that landscape: the sound of the breeze rustling the grain or the way the wheat catches the light at different times of day, the dry-sweet smell of a field full of sunflowers.

Yes, that natural amenities index accurately captured the flatness. The summer heat. The bitter winter cold. But it doesn't tell you how a family can keep itself warm through the coldest of winters by building igloos and sledding down the town hill. Or how the vast winter night's sky shines with the light of thousands of stars that people who live in cities will never know. It doesn't tell you about the warmth put off by a big roaring fire in a town park at the darkest time of the year, how the light dances on the faces of the people gathered around.

Briana and I have lived together all over the country, including in New York, California, Vermont, and Maryland. But we've never lived in any place quite like this.

Most important, the data do not capture how moving to a place like this can be a life-altering experience for kids—for our twins, now six, who've now spent more birthdays in Minnesota than they did in Maryland. Or for little William, now two—a soul as dear to me as anyone I've ever known. There would have been no William had we stayed in Maryland. This whole new dimension of our lives, of familial love, would have remained shut off from us had we stayed there. Worse, we would never even have known what we were missing.

Here there is space for families to play, grow, expand. Space that doesn't exist where life is circumscribed by commutes and high costs and the presence of thousands, of millions of other people. If you keep a fish in a small crowded tank it will grow up stunted and tiny, never attaining its true natural size. Part of me believes that people are the same way, that we need space, room to explore and grow, a certain distance from our neighbors.

In that respect, at least, the Midwest has quite literally broadened our horizons.

One of the big dangers of our glorious, new, quantified world is the emergence of a type of numeric stereotyping—of insights hardened into dogma by the weight of a thousand datasets.

We "know," for instance, that Mississippi is poor, that New York City is expensive, that Chicago is violent, and that Red Lake County is ugly. These things are, of course, true in the aggregate sense, or in comparison with other places.

But each of these numbers and rankings masks infinite nuance behind their finite limits. They overlook the thriving communities in Mississippi, the inspiring stories of tenacity and triumph in Manhattan, and the people quietly working to make Chicago's streets safer.

And they can't, of course, capture the quiet peace of

A year in Red Lake Falls, by the numbers

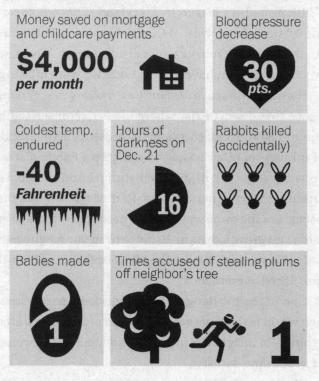

Money saved on mortgage
and childcare payments

$4,000
per month

Blood pressure
decrease

30
pts.

Coldest temp.
endured

-40
Fahrenheit

Hours of
darkness on
Dec. 21

16

Rabbits killed
(accidentally)

Babies made

1

Times accused of stealing plums
off neighbor's tree

1

an evening spent by the bluffs of the Red Lake River,
watching your sons giggle as they toss sticks in the current while dragonflies dance overhead.

I've said it before and I'll say it one more time: it takes
a place as small as Red Lake County to drive home just
how big this country really is.

ACKNOWLEDGMENTS

This book would not have been possible without tho contributions of the following people;

USDA economist David McGranahan, who in 1999 compiled the Natural Amenities Index, quietly planting the seeds of data that would upend my life sixteen years later;

Zach Goldfarb, who as my editor at the Washington Post in the summer of 2015 was surprisingly amenable to nearly every wild story idea I threw at him;

The anonymous individuals behind the Indignant Minnesotan Twitter account, who fanned the initial flames of polite outrage in response to my original story on Red Lake County;

Every indignant Minnesotan who wrote to me in defense of the beauty of their state in the summer of 2015, of whom there are far too many to mention individually;

Every indifferent North Dakotan who did not write to me in the summer of 2015 despite their state's poor showing on the Natural Amenities Index, which served as a tacit confirmation that Minnesota really is someplace special;

Jason Brumwell, whose cordial invitation convinced me to actually visit the place I had trash-talked in the pages of a national newspaper, and who's done so much since then to make me feel at home here;

Dick Brumwell, who's worked so hard to ensure I experience everything Minnesota has to offer, from corn shocks to ice fishing;

The rest of the Brumwell clan, including Ryan, Kristin, Steph, Joe, Heather, and Wade, who have truly become our Minnesota family;

My mom, whose spirit of adventure spurred us to move here to begin with;

My dad, who inspired me to become a writer;

My agent, Rafe Sagalyn, who shepherded this book from idea to proposal to first draft;

My editor, Sara Nelson, who shaped my messy manuscript into a coherent narrative;

The publishing team at HarperCollins, including Jane Beirn, who's done so much to get the word out; Mary Gaule, who's patiently guided me through the publishing process; Hannah Bishop, for her invaluable logistical work; and Christine Choe for her social media expertise;

Editors and managers at the Washington Post, who were shockingly receptive when I pitched them on moving out of D. C. and into the middle of nowhere;

Missy and Danny Maurstad, who showed us the true meaning of Minnesota kindness;

Jim Benoit, for his always-entertaining bullshitting;

Larry Eukel, for welcoming us to the neighborhood and rescuing our idiot cat that one time;

Acknowledgments

John and Sandy Klein, for helping make our dream of a Minnesota home a reality;

Rob and Alice Conwell, for introducing us to the northwest Minnesota arts scene;

Jack, Charles, and William, who inspired Briana and me to seek a better life to begin with;

And Briana, for being my steadfast partner throughout this long, ridiculous, beautiful adventure.

BIBLIOGRAPHY

Prologue

Berry, Brian J. L., and Adam Okulicz-Kozaryn. "An Urban-Rural Happiness Gradient." *Urban Geography* 32, no. 6 (2011): 871–83.

Pew Research Center. "Political Polarization in the American Public." June 2014. Accessed March 4, 2019. https://www.pewresearch.org/wp content/uploads/sites/4/2014/06/6-12-2014-Political-Polarization -Release.pdf.

United States Census Bureau. "New Census Data Show Differences Between Urban and Rural Populations." December 8, 2016. Accessed March 4, 2019. https://www.census.gov/newsroom/press -releases/2016/cb16-210.html.

———. "QuickFacts: Red Lake County, Minnesota." Accessed March 4, 2019. https://www.census.gov/quickfacts/rodlakcoounty minnesota.

United States Department of Agriculture. "Natural Amenities Scale." Last modified February 26, 2018. https://www.ers.usda.gov /data-products/natural amenities-scale/.

Chapter 1

Cook, Philip J. *Paying the Tab*. Princeton, NJ: Princeton University Press, 2007.

Ferguson, Todd W. and Jeffrey A. Tamburello. "The Natural Environment as a Spiritual Resource: A Theory of Regional Variation in Religious Adherence." *Sociology of Religion* 76, no. 3 (2015): 295–324.

Glaeser, Edward L., Joshua D. Gottlieb, and Oren Ziv. "Unhappy Cities." National Bureau of Economic Research, 2014. https://www .nber.org/papers/w20291.

Glaeser, Edward L., and Kristina Tobio. "The Rise of the Sunbelt." Taubman Center Policy Brief, May 2007. https://www.hks .harvard.edu/sites/default/files/centers/taubman/files/sunbelt .pdf.

Bibliography

Helliwell, John F., Hugh Shiplett, and Christopher P. Barrington-Leigh. "How Happy Are Your Neighbours? Variation in Life Satisfaction among 1200 Canadian Neighbourhoods and Communities." National Bureau of Economic Research, May 2018. https://www.nber.org/papers/w24592.

Kanazawa, S., and N. P. Li. "Country Roads, Take Me Home . . . To My Friends: How Intelligence, Population Density, and Friendship Affect Modern Happiness." *British Journal of Psychology* 107, no. 4 (2016): 675–97.

Kwon, Diana. "Does City Life Pose a Risk to Mental Health?" *Scientific American,* May 20, 2016. https://www.scientificamerican.com/article/does-city-life-pose-a-risk-to-mental-health/.

McKinney, Matt. "Minnesotans Seeing Red over Washington Post List of Desirable Counties to Live In." *Minneapolis Star-Tribune,* August 20, 2015. http://www.startribune.com/washington-post-reporter-says-minnesota-is-ugly-minnesotans-politely-beg-to-differ/322350791/.

Rietmulder, Michael. "Minnesota's Red Lake County Named America's Worst Place to Live." *City Pages,* August 19, 2015. http://www.citypages.com/news/minnesotas-red-lake-county-named-americas-worst-place-to-live-7577959.

United States Census Bureau. "American Community Survey." Accessed March 4, 2019. https://www.census.gov/programs-surveys/acs.

———. "QuickFacts: Oneonta City, New York." Accessed March 4, 2019. https://www.census.gov/quickfacts/fact/table/oneontacitynewyork/PST045217.

United States Department of Agriculture. "Census of Agriculture." Accessed March 4, 2019. https://www.nass.usda.gov/AgCensus/.

Chapter 2

Graf, Nikki. "Most Americans Say Children Are Better Off with a Parent at Home." Pew Research Center, October 10, 2016. http://www.pewresearch.org/fact-tank/2016/10/10/most-americans-say-children-are-better-off-with-a-parent-at-home/.

Ihrke, David. "Reason for Moving: 2012 to 2013." United States Census Bureau, Last modified June 2014. https://www.census.gov/prod/2014pubs/p20-574.pdf.

Lucas-Thompson, Rachel G., Wendy A. Goldberg, and JoAnn Prause. "Maternal Work Early in the Lives of Children and Its Distal Associations with Achievement and Behavior Problems: A Meta-Analysis." *Psychological Bulletin* 136, no. 6 (2010): 915–42.

Chapter 3

Ford, Carmel. "Number of Bathrooms in New Homes." NAHB Eye on Housing, December 7, 2017. http://eyeonhousing.org/2017/12/number-of-bathrooms-in-new-homes/.

Ingraham, Christopher. "Lawns Are a Soul-Crushing Timesuck and Most of Us Would Be Better Off Without Them." *Washington Post*, August 4, 2015. https://www.washingtonpost.com/news/wonk/wp/2015/08/04/lawns-are-a-soul-crushing-timesuck-and-most-of-us-would-be-better-off-without-them.

United States Department of Health and Human Services. "Adolescents and Tobacco: Trends." Last modified September 23, 2016. https://www.hhs.gov/ash/oah/adolescent-development/substance-use/drugs/tobacco/trends/index.html.

Chapter 5

Harvard University. "Project Implicit." Accessed March 4, 2019. https://implicit.harvard.edu/implicit/takeatest.html.

ICPSR. "Uniform Crime Reporting Program Data: County-Level Detailed Arrest and Offense Data, United States, 2014." September 12, 2017. https://www.icpsr.umich.edu/icpsrweb/ICPSR/studies/36399.

Ingraham, Christopher. "It's Not Just Rand Paul's Street: Americans Are a Lot Less Neighborly than They Used to Be." *Washington Post*, November 7, 2017. https://www.washingtonpost.com/news/wonk/wp/2017/11/07/its-not-just-rand-pauls-street-americans-are-a-lot-less-neighborly-than-they-used-to-be.

———. "The Most Racist Places in America, According to Google." *Washington Post*, April 28, 2015. https://www.washingtonpost.com/news/wonk/wp/2015/04/28/the-most-racist-places-in-america-according-to-google/.

Moore, Peter. "Obama Isn't the Only One Who Doesn't Lock the Door." YouGov, September 30, 2014. https://today.yougov.com/topics/lifestyle/articles-reports/2014/09/30/obama-isnt-only-one-who-doesnt-lock-doors.

Opportunity Insights. "The Opportunity Atlas." Accessed March 4, 2019. https://www.opportunityatlas.org/.

Chapter 6

Belluz, Julia. "The Historically Low Birthrate, Explained in 3 Charts." Vox.com, May 22, 2018. https://www.vox.com/science-and-health/2018/5/22/17376536/fertility-rate-united-states-births-women.

Ingraham, Christopher. "The Absolute Best Place to Grow Up in America." *Washington Post*, June 24, 2016. https://www.washington

post.com/news/wonk/wp/2016/06/24/the-absolute-best-place-to
-grow-up-in-america.

———. "Start Saving Now: Day Care Costs More than College in 31
States." *Washington Post,* April 9, 2014. https://www.washington
post.com/news/wonk/wp/2014/04/09/start-saving-now-day-care
-costs-more-than-college-in-31-states/.

Lam, Onyi, Brian Broderick, and Skye Toor. "How Far Americans
Live from the Closest Hospital Differs by Community Type." Pew
Research Center, December 12, 2018. http://www.pewresearch.org
/fact-tank/2018/12/12/how-far-americans-live-from-the-closest
-hospital-differs-by-community-type/.

Mackin, Amy. "How My Autistic Son Got Lost in the Public School
System." *Atlantic,* January 3, 2013. https://www.theatlantic.com
/national/archive/2013/01/how-my-autistic-son-got-lost-in-the
-public-school-system/266782/.

National Trust. "Jock VI of Chartwell." Accessed March 4, 2019.
https://www.nationaltrust.org.uk/chartwell/features/jock-vi-of
-chartwell.

Stone, Lyman. "American Women Are Having Fewer Children
than They'd Like." *New York Times,* February 13, 2018. https://www
.nytimes.com/2018/02/13/upshot/american-fertility-is-falling
-short-of-what-women-want.html.

Chapter 7

Harveson, Robert M. "History of Sugarbeets." Accessed March 4,
2019. https://cropwatch.unl.edu/history-sugarbeets.

Kilgannon, Corey. "For Hunters in the Woods, a Quiet Killer: Tree
Stands." *New York Times,* December 22, 2017. https://www.nytimes
.com/2017/12/22/nyregion/for-hunters-in-the-woods-a-quiet-killer
-tree-stands.html.

Li, Yong-Xiang, Torbjorn Tornqvist, Johanna M. Nevitt, and
Barry Kohl. "Synchronizing a Sea-Level Jump, Final Lake Agassiz
Drainage, and Abrupt Cooling 8200 Years Ago." *Earth and Planetary
Science Letters* 315–16 (2012): 41–50.

United States Department of Agriculture. "U.S. Sugar Production."
Accessed March 4, 2019. https://www.ers.usda.gov/topics/crops
/sugar-sweeteners/background/.

United States Fish & Wildlife Service. "National Survey—
Overview." Last modified May 2, 2018. https://wsfrprograms.fws
.gov/subpages/nationalsurvey/national_survey.htm.

Bibliography

Chapter 8

Bloch, Matthew, Larry Buchanan, Josh Katz, and Kevin Quealy. "An Extremely Detailed Map of the 2016 Election." *New York Times,* July 25, 2018. https://www.nytimes.com/interactive/2018/upshot/election-2016-voting-precinct-maps.html#8.22/39.225/-78.231.

Bump, Philip. "Donald Trump Will Be President Thanks to 80,000 People in Three States." *Washington Post.* December 1, 2016. https://www.washingtonpost.com/news/the-fix/wp/2016/12/01/donald-trump-will-be-president-thanks-to-80000-people-in-three-states/.

Centers for Disease Control and Prevention. "Firearm Mortality by State." Accessed March 4, 2019. https://www.cdc.gov/nchs/pressroom/sosmap/firearm_mortality/firearm.htm.

Kalesan, B., M. D. Villarreal, K. M. Keyes, et al. "Gun Ownership and Social Gun Culture." *Injury Prevention* 22, no. 3 (2016): 216–20.

McCourt School of Public Policy. "The Lugar Center, McCourt Unveil 2017 Bipartisan Index." Accessed March 4, 2019. https://mccourt.georgetown.edu/bipartisan-index.

Minnesota Secretary of State. "Election Results." Accessed March 4, 2019. https://www.sos.state.mn.us/elections-voting/election-results/.

Winchester, Ben. "A Rural Brain Gain Migration." University of Minnesota Extension. Accessed March 4, 2019. https://extension.umn.edu/economic-development/rural-brain-gain-migration.

Chapter 9

Pete Boulay. "The Mysterious July 4th Snows of Minnesota." Minnesota Climatology Working Group. Accessed March 4, 2019. http://climateapps.dnr.state.mn.us/doc/journal/july_snow.htm.

National Oceanic and Atmospheric Administration. "National Snow Analyses." Accessed March 4, 2019. https://www.nohrsc.noaa.gov/nsa/.

Rao, Maya. "For Snowmobilers, 2014 Was a Deadly Year." *Minneapolis Star-Tribune,* January 6, 2015. http://www.startribune.com/for-snowmobilers-2014-was-a-deadly-year/287426421/.

Tweet by @mberkowski, December 28, 2018, https://twitter.com/mberkowski/status/1078632108208386048.

Bibliography

Chapter 10

Health Resources and Services Administration. "Maternity Leave." Accessed March 4, 2019. https://mchb.hrsa.gov/whusa11 /hstat/hsrmh/downloads/pdf/233ml.pdf.

Misra, Joya. "The US Is Stingier with Child Care and Maternity Leave than the Rest of the World." The Conversation, April 19, 2018. https://theconversation.com/the-us-is-stingier-with-child-care -and-maternity-leave-than-the-rest-of-the-world-94770.

ABOUT THE AUTHOR

CHRISTOPHER INGRAHAM writes about all things data, with a particular interest in wealth, income, and inequality. He previously worked at the Brookings Institution and the Pew Research Center.